PRAISE FOR
# The Witches of Willow Cove

"A delightfully spooky page-turner . . . Roberts spins an engrossing tale of magic, mystery, and friendship."

**—Kirkus Reviews (starred review)**

"This well-written middle grade book walks the fine line of being effectively spooky without being too scary."

**—School Library Journal (starred review)**

"This atmospheric debut is a nail-biting story of local history, sinister magic, and what it means to be a true friend. With narrow escapes, rising tension, and secrets aplenty, good luck trying to put this one down!"

**—Diane Magras, *The Mad Wolf's Daughter* (*The New York Times* Editors' Choice / ALSC Notable Children's Book)**

"A teenaged coven with ties to the Salem Witch Trials, age old secrets, and powerful magic . . . This is a wild, rollicking adventure whose pace never lets up!"

**—Adriana Mather, *How to Hang a Witch* and *Killing November***

"Atmospheric, just-spooky-enough, and magical, this story celebrates true friendship and standing up for what's right."

**—*A Mighty Girl*, Best Books of 2020**

PRAISE FOR
# The Curse of Willow Cove

"Full of mystery and magic… upper middle grade readers are sure to find a character they relate to and will be hungry for more stories out of Willow Cove.

Roberts is a masterful storyteller—his books belong on school and library shelves everywhere. I loved it!"

**—Lora Senf, Bram Stoker Award-winning author of *The Clackity***

"…an engaging return (or introduction) to Willow Cove; working just as well as a standalone as it does a sequel. Roberts does an exceptional job world-building and integrating New England history into his lore, and the characters are all easy to identify with and root for. I can't wait to continue with this universe that has so many possible paths to explore. Add this to your spooky reading list, you won't regret it!"

**—Darcy Marks, author of *Grounded for All Eternity* and *The Afterlife of the Party***

"Filled with spooky moments and truths about friendships and break ups, this is the perfect story for anyone who loves a good mystery full of creepy adventures."

**—Ally Malinenko, Bram Stoker Award-nominated author of *Ghost Girl* and *This Appearing House***

# The Curse
## of
# Willow Cove

Josh Roberts

Owl Hollow Press

Owl Hollow Press, Springville, UT 84663



The Curse of Willow Cove




Library of Congress Cataloging-in-Publication Data
The Curse of Willow Cove / J. Roberts. — First edition.

Summary: Abby Shepherd and her coven of teenage witches must confront an undead terror that threatens the safety of their friends, families, and maybe even the entire world.

ISBN 978-1-958109-71-7  (hardcover)
ISBN 978-1-958109-70-0 (paperback)
ISBN 978-1-958109-72-4 (e-book)

## Author's Note

This is the second novel in *The Witches of Willow Cove* series. You don't need to have read the first one to enjoy this story, but you might find the experience richer and more rewarding if you have.

Whether you're returning to Willow Cove or discovering it for the first time, I hope you'll enjoy yourself. It's a perfectly nice town… at least until the sun goes down.

*To Dr. MaryKay Mahoney—professor, mentor, and friend.*
*This book would not exist*
*without your relentless encouragement.*
*Thank you.*

# PROLOGUE

Something was bothering the chickens. The anxious trilling from the coop was too loud for Lucinda to ignore, even with her bedroom window closed tight and the howling winter wind rattling the glass. She clicked on her bedside light and rubbed her eyes—it was pitch black outside. She *really* did not want to go out there. The hens were her responsibility, though, and if a weasel managed to get into the chicken coop, her dad would have her doing extra chores for months to make up for it.

She threw off her covers and dropped her feet to the cold floor. The window rattled again in the breeze, louder this time. The squawks and clucks of the chickens grew more insistent. With a sigh, she pulled an oversized sweatshirt over her pajamas and padded barefoot down the hallway. She hated this old house. She hated being the weird farm girl with the old-fashioned name who always smelled vaguely of dairy cows and horse manure. Most of all she hated feeling like the only girl in Willow Cove who hadn't been invited to the middle school dance last night. If she could leave it all behind and start over somewhere else, any-where else, she wouldn't hesitate for even a minute.

Still, the chickens *were* her responsibility.

Downstairs, she sank her feet into her mother's winter boots, clicked on the flashlight her parents kept by the door, and slipped outside into the late January chill. The wind hit her as soon as she crossed the threshold. She dropped the flashlight and swore under her breath as it vanished into a powdery snowdrift. Fumbling around for it, she registered something unusual in the distance. Dim red lights were flickering on and off from the top of the hill on the other side of the salt marsh, the one with all the ghost stories and the creepy name she hated so much.

"Whispering Hill," she breathed, hesitant and low. That's what her best friend Margery Chen called it. All her friends reveled in the rumors that you could hear angry ghosts wailing to be let free from the top of Whispering Hill. Lucinda had always dreaded living so close to it. Who *wouldn't* be a little scared of the crumbling old insane asylum at the top, abandoned but not exactly empty if you believed the stories? She also knew you weren't supposed to call it an insane asylum anymore, but everyone still did—usually right before they'd tell her they wouldn't want to live as close to it as she did.

And now there were weird red lights coming from it!

Probably it was nothing, she told herself. Probably the chickens were just spooked by the wind, nothing more. Definitely nothing to do with those distant lights. Flashlight in hand again, she marched toward the chicken coop, shivering as she walked. The sooner she made sure the hens were okay, the sooner she could be back in her room, in her bed, warm and safe and far away from those strange lights.

But as her boots swished along the snowy path, the lights suddenly grew brighter and… louder? Was that thunder she was hearing? No, probably just some stupid boys sneaking up to Whispering Hill and lighting off fireworks in the middle of a snowstorm, because that was exactly the kind of thing most of the boys in Willow Cove would consider fun. A prank, just some stupid prank.

Drawing closer to the coop, Lucinda pulled up short. The chickens' clucking was becoming even more fretful. She waved her flashlight at their weathered enclosure. Inside, the hens flapped and scratched at their wood shavings like something was actually wrong. The coop door was still latched tight, but there was a jagged tear in the plastic wrap around the enclosure meant to help protect them from the wind and snow. She leaned closer. The chicken wire had been shredded like paper, too. But by what?

Lucinda did a quick count. One hen was missing. Shuddering, she pushed a heavy bucket against the torn chicken wire—that should keep the remaining hens from wandering out—and waved her flashlight beam around the yard. There were footprints in the snow. Footprints leading from the chicken coop to the horse barn. Footprints that definitely did not belong to her.

*Creak.*

Lucinda stood stock still.

Was that the barn door?

She leveled her flashlight toward the front of the barn just as something quick and dark flew through the night, a moving shadow beyond the reach of her light. Her breath caught in her throat. There was someone else out here with her.

Or something.

"Just go back to bed," Lucinda whispered to herself. Instead she took an uncertain step toward the barn, then another as a muffled thumping noise rose above the sounds of the chickens, a nervous stomping of hooves on loose shavings. The horses. "Snowball? Delilah?" she called to her two favorites. A low whine came in answer.

As Lucinda neared the barn, she saw it—a sliver of darkness between the sliding door and the wall. Had her dad left it open by accident? The wind clawed at her sweatshirt as she approached. Sliding the heavy door wide enough to glide through, she felt around for the light switch and flipped it on. "It's all right, Lucy's here," she soothed before pulling up short. The two stalls were side by side, but only Snowball stood snuffling at her over the top of his stall door. The other stall was empty.

"Delilah!"

With her free hand, Lucinda slid Delilah's stall door open, tears already welling in her eyes. But Delilah was there after all, her chin on the ground and all four legs folded beneath her speckled brown body. Her chest rose and fell with slow and steady breaths.

Sleeping.

She was only sleeping.

Relieved, Lucinda crouched in the straw to brush her hand along Delilah's velvety muzzle. Even as the horse nickered contentedly, Lucinda blinked, then sniffed. Something in the stall smelled… wrong. An ammonia scent mingled with the earthy smells of hay and feed and manure. Was it a gas leak? A sick animal?

Lucinda pointed the flashlight into the shadowy areas where the light bulb didn't reach. Nothing. She stood and took a backward step, and as she moved, something thick and hard bumped the back of her boots. She swiveled, then gasped. A *woman* was crouched on her hands and knees in the corner of the stall. A wild mane of raven black hair draped down over her shoulders, so thick and long it covered her body like a cloak. And judging by the movement of her head and neck, the woman was… eating.

"Hello?" Lucinda's voice trembled. "Are you okay? Can I— can I help you?"

The woman's head shot up. Slowly she turned, and then Lucinda screamed. The missing hen drooped limply between the woman's hands. Blood dripped down the sides of her mouth. Lucinda stumbled backward out of the stall, tripping and falling to the ground on something leathery and soft. Delilah's tack. "Don't come near me!" Lucinda yelled as her fingers searched for something, *anything,* on the wall behind her. Even a hoof pick would be better than nothing. "I—I have a—a weapon!"

The woman's eyes bore into her. They were big and wide and red, hypnotic even, and for a moment or two Lucinda found it difficult to move or even think clearly. Those eyes seemed to be evaluating her, *reading* her. Then a wolfish smile stretched across the woman's face. "Lucccciiiiinda, don't lie to me," she said in a terrifying hiss-purr that made the hairs on Lucinda's neck rise.

For the second time in as many minutes, Lucinda gasped. How did the woman know her name? One of the horses whinnied. Lucinda willed herself back to her feet, to leave the barn and run—sprint!—back to her bedroom. But now the woman's eyes were glowing, spinning, and Lucinda was mesmerized. Paralyzed.

"Who—who are you?" she finally managed. "What are you doing here?"

"I was trapped, but now I am free." The woman's accent was strange and thick, difficult to understand. As she moved toward Lucinda, her limbs stretched like shadows, long and angular and unsteady. Her dark hair framed a face as lovely as it was terrifying. A hint of a smile revealed itself around her bloodied lips. "I will only grow stronger now, Lucinda. You will help me grow stronger."

"I… I will help you," Lucinda repeated, still paralyzed, still mesmerized.

"You will find me sustenance. You will be my eyes and ears in this new world."

"I will be your eyes… your ears…"

"You will be the first in a new circle of blood, Lucinda, one that is equal to the young witches of Willow Cove." The woman's smile grew wider, a slash of white in the shadows. "And then at last I will have my revenge."

# Part One

# The House at the End of the Lane

*Nine months later*

Abby Shepherd jerked awake as the minivan rattled to a stop. Her friend and adopted sister, Amethyst Jones, drooped against her in the back row, head tilted and mouth open in an exaggerated snore. In the front seat, Abby's mother tapped the steering wheel, smiling tightly as she craned her neck toward the two girls.

"Only got lost twice," Mrs. Shepherd said. "Here we are at last!"

Abby elbowed Amethyst until her friend opened her eyes to the world. It was a cool Saturday afternoon—the last day of October, and Abby's fourteenth birthday. Outside, thick fog shrouded the minivan, but around the edges Abby could just make out the suggestion of a meadow and a hill, and beyond that a tumbledown farmhouse with overgrown shrubs and shuttered windows. A gnarled apple tree came into focus just outside the van as Abby wiped condensation from the window.

"But *where* are we?" Abby asked, brushing red hair from her face and fumbling for her glasses. "We've been driving for hours,

Mom." They were supposed to go apple picking for Abby's birthday, but her mother had promised they'd be home in time to meet up with Abby's best friend, Robby O'Reilly, and his girlfriend, Becca Ruiz, at the Halloween fair in Willow Cove. The dashboard clock said it was already late afternoon, so they didn't have a lot of time to waste here. Wherever *here* was.

Finally finding her glasses, Abby pushed them on. Things didn't look much better when she blinked through the van window for a closer look. A second car, much nicer than theirs, was parked a short distance away. The top of a wooden signpost poked above its hood, but Abby couldn't make out any of the words on the sign from where she sat. And anyway, her mother was already opening the driver's side door and scooting out of her seat.

"Come see for yourself," Mrs. Shepherd called back to them.

When Abby and Amethyst joined her outside the car, Abby said, "This doesn't look like an apple orchard."

Her mother plucked a wormy apple from a low branch and offered it to Abby, looking suddenly very much like a wicked witch who'd stepped out of some old fairy tale. "See, apples," she said with what seemed like forced cheeriness. "Try one."

"Hard pass, Mom."

Amethyst was staring intently beyond the second car. She squinted, pursing her lips. "Abby, the sign says—"

"*There* you are!" came a high, piercing voice from the direction of the meadow. Tall brown grass swayed as a sharply dressed middle-aged woman emerged through the fog, her arms outstretched. She hugged Abby's mother, then turned to the girls. "You must be the daughters."

"The very confused daughters. Who are you?"

"Abby, don't be rude." Mrs. Shepherd frowned at her. "This is Ms. Delacroix, our—"

"Call me Poppy!" the woman chirped, flashing a set of supernaturally white teeth. "Poppy Delacroix. It's so nice to *finally* meet you girls. Your mother has told me *everything* about you. Abigail, you are in for a *wonderful* birthday surprise…"

"Mom…?" Abby said, trying to catch her mother's gaze.

Mrs. Shepherd's forced smile grew even more strained. Abby turned to Amethyst, whose large brown eyes were trained on something opposite her. "Read the sign," Amethyst said through gritted teeth.

Abby peered over the hood of the second car, wrinkling her nose as the letters came into focus. "'FOR SALE,'" she read aloud, her voice rising an octave in question. "What's for sale? And what's… 'SALE PENDING'? Oh, no, Mom, you *didn't*—"

"I did! Happy birthday, sweetheart. I bought us a new home!"

Abby stared at her mother, wide-eyed, her mouth hanging open. "We can't move," she finally managed in a low, stunned whisper. Everything she cared about was back in Willow Cove. Her school. Her friends. Her boyfriend, Zeus Madison.

*Ex-boyfriend*, a small voice whispered in the back of her mind.

*Whatever*, she told the voice.

Shaking her head, Abby said, "Mom, we *can't*."

"We've talked about this, sweetheart. We need a bigger house. I thought you and Amethyst already agreed—"

"But this one is in the middle of nowhere!"

Mrs. Shepherd's smile faltered. Her shoulders sank, and suddenly she looked as weary as Abby had ever seen her. "It's what we can afford. I think you girls will like it if you just give it a chance. Come take a look."

"It will be absolutely *perfect* for you!" Poppy sang, turning on her heel and marching toward a winding stone staircase up the hillside.

"But what about our friends?" Abby asked. "What about Robby?"

"Robby can visit us any time. Every weekend if you want. We'll have plenty of extra bedrooms." The wind picked up as they followed Poppy to the top of the hill, thinning the mist enough to reveal a sagging Victorian farmhouse with faded blue paint and a chipped slate roof. Squat, scraggly trees pushed up against a wrap-around porch, twining the low railings like vines, nearly blocking the way as Mrs. Shepherd and Poppy climbed the front steps. A barren tree branch poked through one of the first-floor windows, nudging a faded shutter that clung to the side of the house by a single rusty hinge.

Chewing a wad of gum, Amethyst blew a bubble the same purple as her hair and let it pop. "It's clearly haunted. Your mom bought a haunted house. Do you think she paid extra because to-day's Halloween?"

"No, because this isn't really happening." Abby wrapped her arms around herself. "It's a dream. I'm dreaming. We're still in the minivan and you're snoring and drooling on my shoulder and any minute now I'm going to wake up and—"

"I don't snore."

"You absolutely do."

"Well, this is absolutely happening, too," Amethyst said with a dismayed shake of her head. "Unfortunately."

Abby sighed as she and Amethyst joined the adults at the front door. While Poppy fumbled for the keys, Mrs. Shepherd put one arm around Abby and the other around Amethyst, turning them to look back the way they'd come. The sky was a gray sheet, the cars and meadow below barely visible through the fog.

"I know it's a fixer-upper," her mother said, "but it has good bones."

"More like skeletons," Amethyst muttered.

"We need more space now that there's three of us, and look at this yard. We can finally get a dog. You'd both love a dog, wouldn't you?"

The desperation in her mother's voice made Abby's heart hurt, and she felt her anger soften into something dimmer, something more like a dull ache. She removed her glasses and wiped a damp eye. "Of course we'd love a dog."

Mrs. Shepherd squeezed her shoulder.

The porch creaked beneath their weight, and the whole house seemed to sway. Amethyst cast a skeptical eye in Mrs. Shepherd's direction. "You know, I just realized what this house reminds me of. Abby, don't you think it looks like—"

"Oh!" In the doorway, Poppy dropped her keys with a loud clatter. "Sorry, *sorry*!" she trilled, scooping the keyring back up and trying the door again.

"Mom, seriously," Abby said, "did you… is it… official yet?"

"It'll take a little while for all the paperwork to go through, and we still have to sell our old house. But then yes, it will be official. I hoped you'd be happy. Both of you."

"Oh, Mom."

"You'll like it here. I know you will. You'll be safer, too."

Abby's whole body deflated as all at once she understood what this was really about, why they were really moving. Her mother was worried about their safety in Willow Cove because a girl had gone missing not long ago, and because the same thing had happened about a year earlier. But what Mrs. Shepherd didn't know—what she couldn't know, because Abby had never found a way to tell her—was that the last thing she needed to worry about was her daughters' safety. Abby and Amethyst were witches, and powerful ones at that.

Last year, a few adults, including their mentor Tina, had gone missing when a witch calling herself Miss Winters had involved Abby and her friends in a plot to resurrect her long-dead sisters. That threat was long since over, though, and they could protect themselves now—themselves and everyone around them.

"You don't have to worry about us," Abby told her, though she could already tell from the set of her mother's jaw that it was a losing argument.

"Of course I do. In fact, it's my job," Mrs. Shepherd added when Amethyst looked as if she might argue the point. "I know you girls think you're invincible. That missing girl probably thought she was, too. What was her name, the one who lived on the farm?"

"Lucinda," Abby said sullenly. "Lucinda Walker."

"Lucinda Walker, that's right. The poor girl."

Abby was pretty sure her mother remembered Lucinda's name perfectly well. It was all over the television news. No, her mom just wanted Abby to stop and think about the fact that someone in her eighth grade class had gone missing. Mrs. Shepherd waved a hand vaguely in the direction of Poppy Delacroix and the front door and said, "It's my responsibility to look after you even when that means making hard decisions. *Especially* when it means that." Her brow furrowed, and she turned to Amethyst for support. "You understand that, don't you?"

Amethyst shook her head, just a fraction, barely a movement at all, but it was enough to let them both know where she stood.

"I'm doing what's right," Mrs. Shepherd insisted. "One day you'll understand."

"I've *got* it!" crooned Poppy, jangling the keys triumphantly as the door creaked open. "All right, girls, let's go have a look at your new home."

"Give it a chance," Mrs. Shepherd pleaded. "I know you'll come to love it."

Abby spared another glance at the overgrown trees, the broken window, the sagging porch. She had a sinking feeling that her mother had never been more wrong in her whole life. Abby and Amethyst weren't going to love this new house at all.

Not even a little.

# 2

## Music of the Night

"**C**ome *on*, Robby, it's now or never!"

Piper Finch tugged at Robby's hand. Towering cornstalks swayed at the edge of the Halloween fairgrounds, their rustling louder than the distant carnival rides and crying toddlers. Piper tugged again, trying to get him to join his friends in line for the corn maze. As the line shuffled forward, Robby peered over the tops of heads for Abby and Amethyst, then checked his phone again. Still no sign of them.

"They're not going to let us in if we wait any longer," insisted Piper, an owl-eyed Black girl with springy dark curls. She was all but dragging him toward the maze entrance now. "Our tickets are time-stamped."

Robby allowed himself to be dragged back toward the group. His girlfriend, Becca, wrapped her arms around him, pressing close for warmth. Chestnut-haired Daisy Green and her pale, bookish twin Delphi stared off at the flashing lights of the midway, both craning their necks toward the carnival rides. The giant Ferris wheel at the opposite end of the fairgrounds was a rainbow blur in the distance.

The twins and Piper were half of the coven that also included Abby and Amethyst. Shouting erupted behind him, and Robby turned to see the final member of his friends' coven, Olivia Edwards, arguing with another girl called Sarika Swann. A prickly blonde cheerleader, Olivia usually pretended not to know any of them whenever they in public. Tonight, Robby didn't mind it so much.

"You go ahead," he told his friends, checking his phone again before pocketing it. "Becca and I will wait for Abby and Amethyst. They're almost here."

Delphi cocked her head at him, her expression curious. "Maybe we should all wait?"

"We haven't the time," said Daisy in a broad British accent she'd picked up at a theater camp in England a few summers earlier. "We'll miss our turn if we stay here any longer."

"That's what I've been saying!" yelled Piper, glancing at her smartwatch.

Robby steered Becca back a few steps. "Let's all meet by the giant pumpkin in half an hour. We can do the haunted hayride together."

"Better make it an hour. I've heard the maze is hard, and *someone*"—Delphi looked meaningfully in her twin's direction—"doesn't think we should use magic to solve it."

Daisy folded her arms. "It wouldn't be sporting."

"An hour it is." Robby pretended not to see Piper's don't-leave-me-alone-with-these-two expression as the trio moved toward the ticket taker. Waving goodbye, he waited until they were inside the corn maze, then said, "Abby just texted. She and Amethyst aren't actually coming. They had some kind of argument with Mrs. Shepherd."

Becca raised an eyebrow. "But you just said…"

"Maybe I'd rather it just be *us* for a little while," he told her.

Weaving her hands inside his jacket, Becca kissed him on the cheek. The subtle vanilla scent of her perfume mingled with the smells of fried dough and candy apples drifting in from the midway as she pressed close to him. "Maybe I'd like that too," she said, pink-cheeked and smiling, "but you'll have to promise to keep me warm. I'm not built for this cold weather."

"Says the girl from Wisconsin."

"Says the girl who *left* Wisconsin. The Venezuelan side of me isn't such a big fan of the fall weather." Still smiling, she raised her gaze above the corn rows to the colorful trees beyond the maze. "It is pretty, though. The reds and oranges and yellows. Reminds me of where we lived when my parents were still married."

"It's the carotenoids and anthocyanins that make the colors," Robby explained as they moved toward the ticket taker, a bored-looking high school girl with short black hair. "In the summer, the carotenoids are hidden by the green from the chlorophyll—"

Becca squeezed his arm, nuzzling closer. "Less science, more cuddling. I was promised warmth."

Robby pulled in tighter. "Better?"

"Much. Now, what's this about carotenoids?"

The high school girl suppressed a yawn as she checked their tickets and ushered them into the corn maze. Piper and the twins had turned right, so Robby went the opposite way on the mucky path. A boisterous wave of music and laughter briefly cut through the night when they rounded the first bend, but the deeper they moved into the corn maze, the more muffled the carnival noises became. Soon only the soft chirr of insects and the rickety rattle of an old metal windmill turning in the breeze filled the night.

When they stopped to get their bearings, a low fog was rolling in off the salt marsh, the wet air carrying with it the briny scent of the ocean. The moon slivered through a gap in the mist to reveal a gray corn silo rising above the cornstalks, and when it vanished again the night seemed suddenly darker. The carnival rides were well behind them now, the haunted hayride far ahead and through the woods, so that put the old burying ground somewhere to their left, just out of sight beyond the ridge. Not far away, the creaky windmill poked up through the swaying corn, working hard with some unseen purpose.

The further they got from the fairground, the darker it became, until even the fog thickened to blackness. Robby had to turn on his phone's flashlight to avoid tripping on fallen corn.

"We could hide in here for weeks," Becca said wistfully. "No one would ever find us."

"Think of all the homework we could skip," he said, playing along. But something in her expression caught his eye through the dim glow of his phone. The dusting of freckles on her cheeks parted into a weak smile when she spotted him looking at her.

Twirling the Star of David pendant she wore at the nape of her neck, she said, "Robby, there's something I need to tell—"

"Hold on, is that Zeus?" he asked, tilting his phone's light through the cornstalks. Even in the shadowy mist, there was no mistaking the bulky dark-skinned figure with the football player's frame for anyone other than their friend, Zeus Madison.

*Former friend*, Robby corrected.

Robby, Zeus, and Becca had become thick as thieves while working together to solve the mystery of Miss Winters and her connection to Abby last year. Eventually Zeus had even worked up the courage to reveal his crush on Abby and ask her to the winter dance. But over the summer, something had changed, something Robby couldn't even begin to guess at. Lately, every time he or Becca tried to talk to him, Zeus found a way to avoid them.

Becca pursed her lips as she followed Robby's gaze. Twining her fingers through his, she said, "He's all by himself. Let's go talk to him."

Zeus's eyes narrowed when he spotted the two of them. He shined his flashlight in their direction, then lowered it as recognition dawned on his face. For a moment none of them said a word. Finally, Zeus spun on his heels and started down the path without them.

"Zeus, hold on!" Robby called.

Becca let go of Robby's hand and sprinted ahead. "It's us, Zeus!"

His shoulders sank with a sigh as he stopped and spun again to face them. Becca reached him first. "Are you all by yourself?" she asked.

"My sisters got scared by a clown, so mom took them home." His voice was low and sullen. He sank one hand into a pocket and looked at the ground. "Dad's on duty at the police station, but he'll pick me up later."

"Come do the maze with us," Becca said.

"It's all right. I'm happy by myself."

"I promise I don't bite," Becca said, keeping her voice light. "It'll be just like old times."

Something caught her eye through the mist. Her voice trailed off. Robby saw it, too, a flicker of movement, a pale white face, eyes like glowing red embers. It could have been his imagination—a kid in costume, a trick of the light—but, somehow, he knew it wasn't. He could read it in Becca's expression. She'd seen the same thing.

She'd recognized that pale face.

"Lucinda Walker," Robby breathed. The missing girl. Becca let out a little gasp of confirmation. The two of them sprinted after her and Zeus joined them, grumbling but keeping up. Rough corn stalks scraped at their hands and feet. Wispy silk tickled their faces. They kicked up mud as they ran, and even though they were going as fast as they could, they were still falling behind with every twist and turn.

They rounded another bend and crashed into something—*someone*—else. Robby fell to the ground as Tommy "T-Rex" Rexman stumbled, then spun around, furious, to see who'd bumped him. Becca helped Robby to his feet, and Zeus pulled up short behind them both, hunched over and breathing hard. T-Rex wasn't alone. The ruddy-faced eighth grade bully and his best friend, Joey Swett, stood in the middle of the trail with another of their classmates, Margery Chen.

And something was very, very wrong with Margery.

Even as he wiped mud from his hands, Robby registered Margery yanking at her jacket collar, rocking back and forth and murmuring under her breath. Everything about her seemed frantic and unfocused.

T-Rex glared at Robby. "I—I didn't hurt her. She just started acting like this," he said, almost like a challenge. "It's not my fault!"

Robby and T-Rex had never gotten along, and things had only gotten worse last year when T-Rex made it known he had a crush on Becca, too. Robby wouldn't have put it past him to hurt Margery, but the expression on the bully's face was pure confusion. T-Rex wasn't smart enough to fake it that convincingly.

"There's something wrong with her," Joey echoed.

"Do you hear it?" Margery's voice was cold and inscrutable, not at all the warm tone she used at school. Her face was sweaty and paler than usual, almost bloodless. Her gaze flickered this way and that, unfocused and unsettling. She'd taken off her jacket to better claw at her turtleneck, leaving red scratches on her skin. "Do you hear the music? She's calling me… She needs me…"

Panic rose in T-Rex's voice. "What is she talking about?"

With a final tug, Margery ripped the turtleneck's collar at the stitches. Her neck was bare and exposed, and Robby recoiled at the sight of it. There were two angry welts, red and raw like a bitemark.

"She needs to go to a hospital," Becca breathed.

T-Rex and Joey both backed up a step. "You take her!" T-Rex ordered. He shoved his friend into the next row of corn. A moment later the pair was gone, their frantic footfalls squelching in the mud as they disappeared.

"Cowards!" Becca yelled after them. "Come back here!"

"I'll—I'll call emergency services," Zeus said, fumbling for his phone. "She definitely needs a doctor."

"She needs *me*," came another voice, barely more than a low animal growl. "My friend. My Margery." Somewhere in the dark, a cornstalk bent and cracked. Lucinda emerged through the neighboring row, her eyes glowing red and bright.

Zeus dropped his phone.

Becca pulled Robby back a step.

An oversized gray sweatshirt hung loosely from Lucinda's shoulders, tattered and streaked with something reddish brown. In the darkness she might have been anyone, only Robby was sure he'd seen Lucinda wear that same sweatshirt before—was sure he'd seen her doodling the same grinning anime cat on the front of it in her algebra notebook a few weeks ago. Her face was whiter than snow, and even her blonde hair seemed to have lost its color. Faster than lightning, she took Margery by the hand and dragged her back the way she'd come. Into the rustling corn stalks. Into the fog and darkness.

"What—what just happened?" asked Zeus, breathless. "What was that thing?"

"That thing was Lucinda!" cried Becca.

Zeus shook his head. "That was *not* Lucy Walker. Not any-more."

"We have to go after them," Robby said, shining his phone into the corn.

Zeus stared at him. "What? Why?"

"Because Lucinda isn't missing anymore and she just took Margery with her," Robby said. "And we're the only ones who know."

# 3

## Night Walkers

In the back of the minivan, Abby lowered her window as they reached the exit for Willow Cove. A damp breeze and the familiar mucky smell of the mudflats greeted her. Amethyst slumped against the other window, still snoring. Mrs. Shepherd stared straight ahead at the road, hands at three and nine o'clock on the steering wheel. The radio played low in the background. It was pitch black outside, and Abby was still stewing on the fact that there wouldn't be time to go to the Halloween fair with her friends. Another lie from her mother, right up there with "we're just going apple picking."

Glancing at her phone, she sighed and shook her head. Nothing from Robby since she'd let him know they weren't coming. Her mouth felt dry when she tried to imagine telling him the rest of the story. "We're moving," she whispered, closing her eyes, practicing. "Mom is selling the house. Amethyst and I have to leave."

Amethyst stirred beside her, and Abby's chest tightened a little with guilt. The whole drive home she'd been thinking about how Amethyst was being dragged away from her home, too. If

Abby hadn't pushed so hard for her mother to complete the adoption, Amethyst might have been able to stay in Willow Cove with someone else in the coven.

"Who are you talking to?" Amethyst asked, yawning.

"Myself. You. Robby."

Amethyst rubbed her eyes. "That sounds complicated."

"I'm just thinking out loud. Maybe you still have some options." When Amethyst stared at her blankly, Abby explained, "Do you think Piper's parents would let you move in with them?"

"Don't even joke. We're in this together. Best friends."

Abby gave her a bittersweet smile. "Sisters, legally."

"Sisters whose mom has lost her mind."

"I can hear you," Mrs. Shepherd chimed in from the front seat.

"I can fix that." Sitting up straighter, Amethyst slipped a hand inside her jacket and retrieved the thin willow wand she used for casting spells. She flicked her wrist, then whispered, *"Obscuro,* Mrs. Shepherd."

"Amethyst, no!" Abby yelled, too late. Three wispy strands of light shot from the tip of her friend's wand toward the front of the minivan. Her mother couldn't see them, but Abby still flinched when the colorful threads wrapped around the driver's seat and her mother's expression slackened to a vacant stare. Mrs. Shepherd would hear nothing but idle chitchat the rest of the way home and remember none of it by the time she went to bed. It was one of the few spells their mentor, Robby's stepmother Tina, allowed them to use without supervision, but only in emergencies.

"Sorry, had to," Amethyst said, tucking the wand back inside her jacket. "When I was asleep just now, I dreamed about that new house. Something's bothering me, Abby. It's been bothering me since the minute we saw it." She took a deep breath and leaned in. "Did it seem… familiar to you?"

Abby tried to picture the house again. The sagging porch and overgrown trees. The chipped slate roof. The dark, narrow rooms, the creaking stairs, the stuffy attic. She shrugged. "It looked like every other old farmhouse."

"Not every farmhouse. Just *mine*."

Abby blinked. "What?"

"The overgrown trees and bushes disguised it, but the more I think about it, the more I'm certain. It's an identical copy of my old house."

Mrs. Shepherd slowed to a stop near the outskirts of town. A dangling traffic light pierced the darkness above the road in a way that had always reminded Abby of a giant floating eyeball. She pulled her gaze away and turned back to Amethyst. "A copy?"

"Maybe that's normal. Maybe all Victorian farmhouses are the same," Amethyst said, though she didn't sound convinced. "But that realtor, Poppy Delacroix, made a big deal about showing us the roof deck." Amethyst let out a quick breath. "Like she *knew* we'd appreciate it, Abby. Like she knew we'd used the roof deck at my old house to take off on our broomsticks."

The traffic light changed to green, and Mrs. Shepherd continued through the intersection. A soft rain misted Abby's face through the half-open window as they passed the old colonial burying ground. Moonlight filtered through the clouds, brightening the barren stretch of road ahead. A few stray leaves floated on the breeze.

"The whole thing is weird," Abby agreed. She removed her glasses and leaned into the night, feeling the mist on her face, in her hair. She wondered how her mother had picked that house in particular, how she'd found Poppy Delacroix.

Or had Poppy been the one to reach out to her?

Abby wiped her cheeks and replaced her glasses. The quickest way to end the *Obscuro* enchantment was by directly addressing the subject of the spell, so she said, "Mom, how did you meet Poppy Delacroix?"

In the rearview mirror, Mrs. Shepherd's expression sharpened. She blinked once as the colorful threads of Amethyst's spell dissolved around her. "What was that, sweetie?"

"Your realtor, Poppy Delacroix, how did you meet—"

Mrs. Shepherd slammed on the brakes and the minivan fishtailed on the wet road before coming to a stop on the narrow shoulder.

"Mom!"

The squeal of brakes was still echoing in Abby's head when she saw the two girls frozen like deer in the headlights. The closest one had ghostly white skin, luminous blonde hair, and deep red lips like blood on bone.

*Lucinda Walker…?*

Their eyes met for a moment across the misty night. It *was* Lucinda Walker, but somehow it wasn't her, either. At least not exactly. The pallor of her skin was different from the girl Abby had known since kindergarten. Her eyes were different, too. Her tattered sweatshirt was soaked through, but Lucinda showed no sign that she noticed. Rolling the window all the way down, Abby peered at the other girl with her. Another familiar face—Margery Chen. The pair were holding hands, but Margery seemed to be in some kind of trance, drifting and directionless.

Mrs. Shepherd opened her door and stepped into the street. "Are you girls all right? Do you need help?"

Illuminated in the headlights, Lucinda's mouth curled into a horrible smile. Her canine teeth were grotesquely long and so white they seemed to glow almost as intensely as her eyes. She stared at Mrs. Shepherd for a heartbeat, her red eyes narrowing in calculation, then she darted into the trees along the side of the road. Margery stared directly at Mrs. Shepherd for another beat before taking off after Lucinda.

Abby tried her door, even though she knew it was still locked. "Mom, that was Lucinda Walker!" she yelled. "The missing girl. Let us out!"

Mrs. Shepherd slipped back into the car and slammed her door shut. "I'm not letting either of you out of this car!"

"We have to go after her," Abby repeated.

Mrs. Shepherd shook her head. "Under no circumstances, Abigail." Fishing around for her cell phone, she added, "I'm calling the police."

Amethyst motioned to her wand, a questioning look on her face. Abby considered their options, but she couldn't think of any other choice. Lucinda Walker was out there, right now, and whatever had happened to her, whatever had changed her, it looked like the same thing might be happening to Margery, too. Tilting her wand at the car door, Abby sprang the lock and scrambled into the street. Amethyst was right behind her.

"Abby! Amethyst!" Mrs. Shepherd yelled. "Get back in the car right now!"

Abby took a deep breath. They had to move quickly or risk losing track of Lucinda and Margery. It was an emergency. Tina would understand—she'd have to understand. With a fluttery feeling in her chest, she tilted her wand at the open window.

"Abby?" Mrs. Shepherd said.

*"Obedio,* Mom!*"*

Her mother's face went slack.

The wand shook in Abby's hand as she knit the threads of the obedience spell. "Mom, drive straight home," she said, not quite holding her voice steady. "Lock all the doors and go to bed. Don't look for us until morning. Forget this ever happened."

"I'll drive straight home," Mrs. Shepherd repeated. "I'll lock all the doors. I'll forget this ever happened."

The car drifted down the road and disappeared. Abby's stomach churned and she felt as if she might puke. *I can't believe I just… I shouldn't have…*

Amethyst gripped Abby's shoulder, pulling her back into the moment. Her gaze darted to the woods. "You did the right thing. Something isn't right with Lucinda. Did you see…?"

Abby nodded. "I saw it. Those eyes. That smile."

"Fangs, Abby. She had *fangs*! Did she always have fangs?"

"That's definitely new."

"I'll summon backup and catch up with you." Amethyst raised her wand and a shuddery raven leapt off the tip, fluid as a shadow. A winged messenger waiting for instructions.

Abby took off for the dark woods. Wet leaves squished underfoot, and the moon hung like a crooked yellow claw through the tangle of branches. Something thorny nicked her face as she raised her wand. The soft blue glow of her wandlight illuminated the pale figures of Lucinda and Margery vanishing beyond an incline.

Abby sprinted after them. A moment later, Amethyst was at her heels again, breathing hard. They crested the hill and skidded to a stop. Rising from the ground at the bottom of the incline was a black iron fence marking the boundary of the old colonial burying ground. A maze of slanted headstones weaved in and out of the misting fog on the other side. Lucinda and Margery were nowhere to be seen.

Abby led the way down and they both squeezed through a small gap in the fence. Tiptoeing through the wet grass on the other side, they moved between the grave markers, searching for any sign of Lucinda or Margery. A handful of old-growth trees crowded close together, dowsing the cemetery in shadow. Somewhere, an owl hooted. Abby's gaze flitted toward the noise, her skin prickling.

Anything could be hiding in those branches.

Anyone.

A flicker of movement caught her eye. Squinting into the rain, Abby raised her free hand and mouthed for Amethyst to listen. Heavy footsteps. Twigs snapping. Then a trio of familiar voices reached them through the fog.

"Which way did they go?"

"Did they always move that fast?"

"What if they doubled back toward the corn maze?"

Robby. Becca. *Zeus?*

Abby swayed where she stood as the three of them burst into the open. Robby raised a hand to shield his eyes from Abby's wandlight. Becca and Zeus pulled up short behind him, disoriented.

"Abby?" Robby blurted.

"What are you doing here?" they both said at the same time.

"We saw Lucinda Walker," Abby told him.

"So did we." Robby wiped a rusty wet curl from his eyes. "She took Margery Chen. We have to find them."

"Something tells me that won't be a problem," Amethyst cut in, pointing at a pair of crooked headstones just past Robby, Becca, and Zeus. Two pale figures crouched in the tall grass, both of them staring straight ahead.

Lucinda Walker. Margery Chen.

And their fangs were bared.

"Get behind us!" Abby shouted.

Amethyst positioned herself opposite Abby while Robby, Becca, and Zeus squeezed together between them. Wind whistled through the cemetery. The trees shook in the breeze. Abby's heart was still thudding from all the running and her face was slick with sweat, but she had a tight grip on her wand and an idea that they might be able to put an end to this—whatever *this* was—fast.

"What's the plan?" Amethyst called.

"You take Margery. I'll deal with Lucinda. Defensive spells only?"

"For now."

"We need to get them help. We need to find out what's going on." Abby pointed her wand at Lucinda. *"Suspendo!"*

The binding spell rocketed from her wand in a flash of blue light. Lucinda leapt into the trees—impossibly high, impossibly fast—and Abby's spell fizzled as it struck a headstone. Hissing, Lucinda dropped to the ground again, her head tilted to one side, her scarlet eyes narrowing as she moved another step closer. Abby tried again. Lucinda dodged to the side, still too quick for the spell to catch her. Her lips were peeled back in a wicked smile. Her fangs glistened in the lingering glow of wandlight.

Amethyst didn't seem to be having any luck either. "Time for Plan B," Abby called over her shoulder.

"What's that?"

"I was hoping you had one, actually!"

Lucinda and Margery were moving in and out of the fog, and the only sign of them from moment to moment seemed to be Lucinda's glowing eyes, first here, then there—then right on top of them. Abby twisted around just in time as Lucinda sent her rolling onto the wet grass. Lucinda lunged for her neck, but Abby kicked free and snapped her wand back like a whip, discharging what little energy she had left. It was enough to send Lucinda flying out of sight again.

Scrambling back to her feet, Abby wiped mud from her glasses. Robby and Zeus were still with Amethyst, still holding back as Amethyst swept her wand back and forth to keep Margery at bay. Closer to Abby, Becca crouched against a slanted grave marker, then hurried to Abby's side.

"Margery was half mad when we found her in the corn maze, but not like this, not—"

Abby forced Becca down as Lucinda leapt toward her again. This time Abby's spell grazed the girl, and Lucinda let out an angry hiss before vanishing again into the darkness. "Not like what, exactly?" Abby asked.

"She didn't have fangs a few minutes ago!" Becca stared wild-eyed at the trees and grave markers ahead. "She was sick—unfocused, muttering, helpless."

"That's a pretty sudden transformation," Abby said.

"But she had marks on her neck, Abby. I saw them. Maybe this wasn't so sudden. Maybe it had already started."

Before Abby could consider the idea, Lucinda swept into view again. Margery was there too, the pair of them darting between headstones, quick as cats. Abby leveled her wand. She had a spell on her lips when the two girls pulled up short a few paces from her.

"You are the witches of Willow Cove." It was Lucinda's familiar voice, but gravelly and raw from disuse. "The ones the Shadow Lady spoke of. She will complete her circle of blood. She will have her revenge!"

"Abby, something's coming!" yelled Amethyst.

"Something *else*?!"

A sudden gust ripped through the graveyard. Leaves swirled, the mist parted, and Abby turned her gaze toward the commotion just as the rest of her coven burst through the fog, wands aglow. All at once, the night blazed blue with wandlight.

"Enter four witches, stage left!" shouted Daisy.

Amethyst raised a hand in triumph. "You got my raven!"

"Next time just text us. It's easier!" shouted Olivia.

Delphi and Piper skidded to a stop near Robby and Zeus. Olivia completed the defensive circle, the six witches now forming a protective wall around their nonmagical friends. Abby had never been happier to see her coven in her life.

Piper adjusted her glasses. "What are we dealing with here?"

"Lucinda Walker and Margery Chen," Abby said.

"With fangs!" added Amethyst.

"'Tis now the very witching time of night,'" said Daisy in her practiced accent, "'when churchyards yawn and hell itself breathes—"

"Save the Shakespeare for later, Daisy!" shouted Amethyst.

Abby waved her wand at the darkness. "Daze and Delphi, you two take Margery. Amethyst and I will go after…" Her voice trailed off. Far away, the two lithe figures dipped beyond a shadowy incline and vanished. Abby stumbled forward, half a mind to pursue, but then Becca's hand was on her shoulder, squeezing, holding her there. Abby let out a breath, then another, longer one. She loosened her grip on her wand. Her friends were all there, all safe. Lucinda and Margery were too far away to catch. She slipped her wand into her back pocket.

"Did we scare them off?" asked Piper.

Abby shook her head. Nothing about the way Lucinda had carried herself suggested fear. *You are the witches of Willow Cove,* she'd said. *You are the ones the Shadow Lady spoke of. She will have her revenge.* What did it mean? Who was the Shadow Lady? What could she possibly want revenge for?

Zeus's gaze roved from side to side. "Can we get out of here?"

"I wouldn't mind someplace a little less… *cemetery,*" Amethyst agreed.

"But we won," said Piper.

Abby shook her head. "We were lucky. Something tells me we're going to need more than luck the next time."

"Why does there have to be a next time?" asked Amethyst.

"One way or another," Abby said, "there's always a next time."

# A History of Vampires

**Z**eus lifted open the creaky first-floor window to his bedroom, then raised a finger to his mouth as the others began to clamber up the side of his house. He lived closest to the cemetery, but already he looked as if he were having second thoughts about inviting them inside. Standing in the dewy grass, Abby tapped her phone to call Tina. It went straight to voicemail again. Halloween was the busiest night of the year for pet seances at her veterinary clinic.

Her stomach fluttered as Zeus looped his hands together to give her a boost. Why did she still get this way around him? Why couldn't she just turn off that little thrill of excitement when he was around? *He dumped you*, she reminded herself. *He doesn't like you anymore. You shouldn't like him either.* But even with everything else going on, her body wouldn't listen. Pushing her sneaker into his hands and scrambling over the windowsill, she did her best to ignore the way her skin crackled at the contact with him.

The rest of the group was already squeezed together around Zeus's desk when Abby scrabbled between Robby and Becca. She gave them each a nervous smile while Zeus spilled in behind her. The sporadic croak of a bullfrog from the pond behind his house punctuated the silence in his bedroom.

"Who else saw their fangs?" Amethyst asked, still breathing raggedly from the long run out of the graveyard.

Zeus pulled the window down to just a crack. "Not so loud."

"You'll wake the triplets," Abby explained, catching Zeus's eye and then looking away. His eight-year-old sisters shared the bedroom next to his. Back when he and Abby were dating, they'd spent a lot of summer afternoons here babysitting the girls. Abby missed them almost as much as she missed him.

Amethyst lowered her voice. "Lucinda had fangs!" she insisted.

"Margery had them too," Becca said.

"Were they vampires?" Amethyst's gaze passed over them all. She ran a hand through her hair. "Is that what we're dealing with here?"

Olivia snorted. "Vampires aren't real."

"I suppose you don't believe in witches either?" snapped Amethyst.

"Are they… dead?" asked Piper. "Vampires are supposed to be dead, aren't they?"

"Undead," said Robby.

"Is there a difference?"

Robby shrugged. "I have no idea."

Even with the window cracked open, it was hot with the group all crowded together. The floor radiator cranked away. Abby wiped steam from her glasses, pacing the small room while she considered what they knew so far.

"Becca, you said Margery had marks on her neck when you saw her in the corn maze. We know Lucinda disappeared a few weeks ago, then she turned up tonight looking like"—she waved her hands for lack of a better term—"like a vampire. And she came after her best friend Margery, who started sporting fangs right after Lucinda found her."

"It was dark," said Zeus. "It was scary. Who knows what we really saw?"

"I do," said Daisy. "I think we all do if we're being honest. We've seen plenty of supernatural things before. Some of us *are* supernatural. Vampires don't seem like much of a stretch to me."

"Since when do we have vampires in Willow Cove?" Zeus's tone was almost desperate. "Why would anyone turn Lucy into a vampire?"

Abby thought of Lucinda's strange, raspy message in the graveyard. "'You are the witches of Willow Cove,' Lucinda said to me. Like she knew us—what we are, I mean, all six of us." Her gaze passed slowly over the other girls in her coven. "She said something else, too. Something about a shadow lady and a circle of blood and…"

"And what?" prompted Olivia, leaning forward.

"And revenge." Abby tried to picture the scene again. "'The Shadow Lady will complete her circle of blood. She will have her revenge.'"

"I don't like the sound of that at all," muttered Amethyst.

Daisy's face went pale. "'My revenge is just begun. I spread it over centuries, and time is on my side.'"

"Enough with the Shakespeare," said Olivia.

"It's not Shakespeare," Daisy whispered. "It's *Dracula*."

Piper reached into her pocket and took three deep drags on her inhaler. "Why would anyone want revenge? What did we *do*?"

"Nothing," Abby said. "Obviously nothing."

"A shadow lady," said Robby thoughtfully.

"*The* Shadow Lady," Abby corrected. "I think she meant it like a name or a title."

Zeus was shaking his head again. "I still don't get why any of this would be happening in Willow Cove."

His tone was almost a challenge, like if he pushed back hard enough it couldn't be true. But if he'd shown Abby anything by breaking up with her, it was that sometimes things happened whether you wanted them to or not. And you didn't always get an explanation for it, either.

Becca, who'd been staring out the window, suddenly brought her gaze back to the group. "Actually, this might not be the first time it's happened in Willow Cove. I spent a lot of time researching the town's history last year when we were trying to understand what Miss Winters was up to. I remember coming across something about vampires in an old folklore book from the library. Let me see if I can find anything about it online." She tapped her phone, searching for something, and after a moment her voice went triumphantly up a note. "Here it is. The Great New England Vampire Panic."

In the hallway, a shadow slanted beneath Zeus's bedroom door. Soft footsteps padded by. Becca waited, then read quietly, "'Two hundred years after the witch trials, people all over New England became convinced the dead were returning from the grave to feed on their surviving loved ones.'"

"There were really vampires here?" Piper asked.

Becca was still scanning her phone. "I think mostly it was a disease called tuberculosis. It made people sick all over the region, and the bereaved took to cutting off the heads of their loved ones after they died to make sure they didn't come back. I never mentioned it because it didn't seem relevant to what was happening last year. But maybe in Willow Cove, it really *was* vampires."

Zeus threw up his hands. "This town is cursed."

Becca's brow creased. "That's even what they called it here. 'The Curse of Willow Cove.'"

"To understand the future you must first understand the past," said Delphi.

Olivia let out a forced laugh. "Thank you, Nostradamus."

"No, I think she's right." Robby was staring at his phone now, too. "It could be connected to what happened back then. It says here the first suspected vampire in Willow Cove was a teenage girl named Julia Morrow in 1889."

"What happened to her?" asked Delphi.

"She came down with a wasting sickness," said Becca, scrolling fast. "The family doctor thought it was tuberculosis, like I said before, but the local priest called it a curse. She became very ill—no, wait, sorry, I think I misread that—it was Julia's twin sister Briony who got sick first, but Julia was the one later accused of vampirism. It says her first victim was a boy named Elijah Woodward, her cousin."

"So, history is repeating itself," said Amethyst.

"Why now? Why then?" Robby asked. "What about all the time in between? What's the common denominator?"

Becca scrolled a little further, then swallowed hard. "I don't know, but I think we'd better figure it out fast. If it happens the same way as in 1889, then things are about to get a lot worse. Once the disappearances started, they came faster and faster."

"Maybe if we understood what happened then," Abby said, peering over Robby's shoulder at his screen, "it would help us understand what we need to do now. Why it started. Why it stopped. How *we* can stop it."

"That part's easy," said Amethyst. "We introduce them to the pointy end of a stick."

"We need to cure Lucinda and Margery, not stab them!" said Piper.

"How did it end in 1889?" Abby asked.

Becca bit her lower lip as she scrolled and read. After a moment, she shook her head. "It's pretty vague. The vampires just… disappeared at some point."

"Whatever happened, Julia Morrow is the key," said Robby. "Someone had to turn her into a vampire just like Lucinda. Maybe it's the same person doing it now."

"The Shadow Lady?" Becca suggested.

Robby crinkled his nose, deep in thought. "There's got to be newspaper articles or church records we can look at. Anything we can find about what happened here."

Abby caught her reflection in the window and looked away. It was as if everything had caught up with her all at once—the vampires, the farmhouse her mom had bought, the forbidden spell she'd cast to keep her mother safe. Her voice shook from exhaustion. "I agree we should find out as much as we can about Julia Morrow," she said. "Something tells me Lucinda won't stop at just one victim, so I think we'd better do it fast."

# 5

## Summoned

That night, Abby and Amethyst talked quietly in Abby's bedroom until sleep finally took them. When the Sunday morning sunlight finally spilled in through a crack in the curtains, they both lay squinting at the world, awake and not entirely happy about it. Amethyst's raccoon, Spooks, raised a drowsy eyebrow at them from inside a laundry basket, then turned his head and settled back to sleep on top of Abby's dirty soccer clothes.

The hazy dreams Abby remembered had been haunted by memories of the graveyard, of Lucinda's red eyes and Margery's bloodless face, the two of them moving like wolves through the rolling mist. There was something else, though, some jagged piece of memory Abby couldn't quite fit with the others—a piece of the puzzle she could sense but not quite touch, not yet. Whatever it was tugged at her consciousness but refused to come into the light.

What a day she'd had. What an awful end to her fourteenth birthday. Letting out a deep breath, she pushed that last thought from her mind. At least she'd had a birthday. Would Lucinda or Margery ever have another one? Were they dead now… or were they *undead* as Robby had suggested? What did it even mean?

"Next time," said Amethyst, rolling her shoulders as she sat up, "*make* me go back to my own bedroom. Your bed is not comfortable."

"I like a firm mattress," Abby said.

"Cement," Amethyst growled. "You like a *cement* mattress." She climbed to her feet and pulled the window shade up, flooding the room with more of the midmorning light. Something caught her attention outside, and she frowned. "Here comes trouble."

Abby joined her at the window. Outside, Tina was marching from her yard to theirs with her usual limp, a determined scowl on her face.

"Tina doesn't look happy," Abby said.

Amethyst pursed her lips. "Does she ever?"

"Not lately." There'd been a time when Robby's stepmother's eyes twinkled with a sort of childlike mischief, but something inside her had changed over the past year. She was angrier now. Her voice rasped, and her hands, once so sure and nimble, betrayed the occasional tremor, as they did this morning while she pressed the doorbell on the back steps outside the kitchen. For all the time that had passed, Abby sometimes thought their mentor had never entirely left the tiny cell beneath Whispering Hill where she'd been imprisoned last year.

By the time they dressed and made it downstairs, Tina was already sitting at the kitchen table alongside Mrs. Shepherd, who smiled and cleared a spot for the girls to join them. Abby's gaze passed over a stack of papers, and she let out a groan as she realized what they were—real estate documents, bank records, and photos of their new house sprinkled in with yesterday's mail.

More proof that it was really happening.

She took a deep breath and slid into the chair next to Tina just as her mother rose to switch off the radio. A pair of newscasters were speaking in serious voices about a student's disappearance, and Abby caught Margery Chen's name just before the radio was silenced.

"I was so tired I don't even remember coming home last night." Her mother topped off her own mug and extended the coffee pot in invitation to Tina, who shook her head with a grim smile. "There's pancakes warming in the oven, too."

"Thank you, Carolyn. Don't let me keep you from your writing. I'll talk to the girls about that overnight volunteer opportunity."

"What opportunity?" Abby asked.

Tina silenced her with a look. In addition to being Robby's stepmother and the coven's mentor, she also ran a veterinary clinic where the six young witches sometimes volunteered. It was a handy excuse whenever they needed to train in one of the back rooms she'd set up for them. Abby had a bad feeling Tina hadn't actually come to discuss new volunteer opportunities this morning, though. Her stomach clenched as she thought of the obedience spell she'd cast on her mother. A few faint threads of it still trailed Mrs. Shepherd's movements like silky white cobwebs visible only to those with the sixth sense like Abby or Amethyst.

Or Tina.

The moment Mrs. Shepherd was out of earshot, Tina's eyes narrowed. "What were you *thinking*?" she demanded. "And don't try to deny it, Abby, that spell has your signature written all over it. A wand remembers every spell it's ever cast, and I'll bet if I were to check yours—"

"It was an emergency!" Abby said.

Tina waved a hand at the real estate paperwork. Her gray-gold curls shook with her unhappy laugh. "This is just life, not an emergency. You can't solve all your problems with spells. It's against witch law, for one thing. Have you forgotten everything I've taught you?"

"I didn't want to do it, Tina."

Tina pressed her elbows to the table. "Then why did you?"

"Vampires," said Amethyst.

Tina's gaze shot to Amethyst. "What do you mean?"

"Vampires," Amethyst repeated. "Formerly classmates of ours, now firmly in the *I come to suck your blood* camp. Two of them."

"The missing kids," Tina breathed with sudden understanding. "Oh, those poor girls."

Abby placed her hand on Tina's. Her mentor's skin was thin and rough, like crinkled wax paper. "We have to do something, Tina. They're still out there. We tried to stop them, but—"

"No." Tina removed her glasses and rubbed her eyes. "I understand the temptation to get involved, but you can't do that. Especially not right now. The Council—"

"—put you in charge of us, and we have to do as you tell us," Abby cut in, repeating a mantra she'd heard more than a few times in the nine months since Tina had begun instructing them. The Council of Witches was a group of six powerful elders who set witch law. Abby had never even met them, and already she'd begun to bristle against their restrictions. "I know we're not supposed to use our magic around other people without permission, but this is our town we're talking about. Our classmates. We have to do something."

"I'll look into it. I promise I will."

Abby pulled her hand from Tina's. "Look into it? People are in danger right now!"

"I need you to trust me on this, Abby. I haven't told you everything about witch law yet. I haven't told you nearly enough about anything. I thought we had more time."

Amethyst rocked forward in her chair. "What do you mean, *more time*? What's going on?"

Tina joined her hands together on the tabletop. "That's the real reason I'm here. You've been Summoned—all six of you—to meet the Council."

"What? Why?" Abby sputtered.

"The Summoning is a witch's first call to stand before the Council. It's a rare opportunity to meet them face to face and an important rite of passage. It's a great honor, normally, but I'm afraid there's more at stake for the six of you. Your coven is unusual. At your Summoning, the Council will determine whether you will be allowed to remain a coven at all."

"What?" Abby repeated.

"Why would they want to break us up?" Amethyst asked.

Tina's eyebrows drew together. Her features softened just a fraction. "The events of last year interfered with your development as witches. My task was to watch you girls for signs of magic. Yes, I was sent to teach you, but I was also meant to make recommendations about where to place you. No one could have imagined the six of you would form your own coven without the permission of the Council."

Abby frowned. "We needed permission to form a coven?"

"It's the role of the Council to assign each witch to a coven. It has been that way for generations beyond count. The Council puts complementary skills and personalities together. A coven of six blood relations sharing a single ancestor such as yours is— well, it's unheard of. The Council decides what's best. In all things," Tina added meaningfully. After a quick glance into the living room where Mrs. Shepherd was staring at her laptop screen with a strained expression on her face, she continued, "We'll meet at the clinic after school tomorrow. Pack an overnight bag because we won't be back until the following afternoon. You don't have school on Tuesday anyway, so your mother already said yes."

"Why don't we have school?" asked Amethyst.

"Because it's the first Tuesday of November." When both girls stared at her blankly, Tina said, "Election Day? The middle school is a voting place, so it's closed to students. Honestly, what are they even teaching you kids in Civics these days?"

"I could say the same about you and witch law," Abby complained.

"Abby, *please* take this seriously." Tina cleared her throat and scraped her chair back from the table. "I've taught you everything

I thought you needed to know. I'll explain more tomorrow. In the meantime, I meant what I said about the vampires. There's no room for discussion. No snooping around after dark." She lowered her glasses to meet their eyes directly. "No vampire hunting."

# 6

## Nancy Drew Stuff

F at chance of that," Abby said as Tina disappeared down the driveway. "I don't care what the Council says, we can't just ignore the fact that someone is turning our classmates into vampires."

"I mean, we *could*. It would probably be safer."

"Amethyst, be serious."

Shuffling the real estate papers on the kitchen table, Amethyst's expression creased into a frown. "I don't like it any more than you do. I don't like the part about the Council possibly breaking up our coven, either. If Tina is worried about it, then maybe we should be worried, too." Her fingers caught on something in the pile and stopped. She held out a sealed envelope for Abby to see. "This one's addressed to me. What's the Omaha Fire Insurance Company?"

"Probably something to do with your grandfather's farm." Abby waved away the thought as another occurred to her. "Tina said no snooping after dark. Nothing about daytime. I think we should see if we can find any clues we might have missed last night."

Staring hard at the envelope, Amethyst shook her head. "I'll leave the Nancy Drew stuff to you today. I smell pancakes in the oven, and I just want to hang back and eat my feelings all day, maybe try to talk some sense into your mom."

"She'll never change her mind."

"Abby, *darling*," Amethyst trilled in a passable imitation of the realtor Poppy Delacroix, "you haven't *seen* me turn on the charm yet!"

As she slipped into the woods behind her house, Abby thought about knocking on Robby's door but decided against it. She knew she'd have to tell him about moving and she wasn't ready for that yet. She ignored a group message from Piper, too, clicking her phone dark and slipping it back into her pocket along with her wand. If she were being honest, her unsettled mood wasn't just about the move or the Council. Something from last night was still niggling at the back of her mind and she needed space to think about what it might be.

It was a cool and blustery morning, crisp but still bright with the sun. She took the long way through the woods to avoid going by Zeus's house, because she didn't want to start thinking about him either. Normally she loved fall days like this—the smell of wood smoke in the air, the wind-stirred branches whipping leaves onto the muddy trail—but today everything felt wrong. Even the stray candy wrappers and smashed jack o' lanterns along the edges of the trail seemed vaguely sinister this morning.

When she finally came back to her thoughts, she realized she'd gone the wrong way where the old carriage road through the woods split between the Heights and the Hollows. Her feet had taken her to the salt marsh instead of the old burying ground, and if she looked hard, she could see the crown of Willow Hill in the distance. The billowy trees were blowing in the breeze in the same spot where Miss Winters had taken them on the day she'd become their history teacher last year, back before her plan to use the coven as vessels for resurrecting her sisters was even a suspicion in any-one's mind.

A thought occurred to Abby just then, sharp as a pinprick. Becca said the first mention of vampires in Willow Cove was in the year 1889. Abby turned a half-forgotten memory over and over in her mind, then pulled her sweater tight against the cold and started toward the distant hill. She was remembering something else that had happened near the end of the nineteenth century, the reason why the year 1889 sounded so familiar in the first place. That was the first time Miss Winters had tried to bring back her sisters using *another* young coven.

Tried and failed.

It was probably a coincidence. It almost had to be a coincidence. Still, her subconscious mind had brought her here for a reason. She might as well follow it all the way through to the top of Willow Hill and see where the idea led.

Puffing into her hands as she walked, Abby wished she'd worn gloves when she left the house. The barren hill wasn't steep, but the tall grass was still crunchy with the season's first frost and the wind was bitter without any trees to soften it on the climb. Behind her, a jumble of athletic fields stretched out like a mismatched quilt, and beyond them the brick-and-ivy walls of the middle school loomed quiet and empty. A handful of chimneys puffed smoke into the air from the school.

The world was so quiet Abby could almost believe she was the only one in Willow Cove, but as the hilltop drew closer, she saw someone at the top watching her approach. Her heart caught in her throat at the sight of dark hair and a scarlet cloak flapping in the wind, and for just a moment she imagined Miss Winters looming above her on the crest of the hill. Even as she reached for her wand, though, she realized the details didn't add up. This figure was shorter than Miss Winters, petite where her teacher had been tall and commanding, and the red cloak was just a scarf wrapped loosely around a knee-length wool coat.

Abby let out a little sigh and turned her head to the wind. Why did her thoughts keep coming back to Miss Winters this morning? Why did her mind keep looking for her former teacher around every corner? Deep down she thought she already knew the answer to both questions. Sometimes the mind sees what it's most afraid of seeing.

Or what it most wants to see.

*Don't trust the Council.* Miss Winters's final whispered words were either a warning or another manipulation. Abby knew where the other girls in her coven fell on that question, but she'd never been so sure herself, especially after what Tina had told her about the Summoning this morning. What if Miss Winters had been right about the Council all along? What if her coven couldn't trust the six elders of the witching world? What if, in her own way, Miss Winters had been looking out for them after all?

The red-scarfed figure was still there when Abby reached the top of the hill. Even after the surprise wore off, it still took her a beat to recognize her friend. Becca's nose and cheeks were a rosy pink, and she was hugging herself against the cold as Abby met her in the shade of the willow grove. Becca's dark hair was plastered to her cheeks in the stiff breeze. The tiny willow sapling they'd all planted last spring to mark Miss Winters's passing shook in the wind by her feet.

"Becca, what are you doing here?"

Becca sank her hands into her pockets and shrugged. "If I had to guess, probably the same thing as you."

"1889," said Abby.

"You made the connection, too?"

"Only just now," Abby said. "Subconsciously."

"I only realized the significance of the dates this morning. I guess I wanted to see for myself before I told anyone. See if there was anything *to* see, I mean." She nudged the hard dirt around the sapling tree at her feet. "I know it's crazy to think she could be involved in any of this, but I wanted to make sure her wand was still buried here, you know? That she hasn't come back and started using it again somehow."

*Would it be so bad if she did?*

Miss Winters had been different at the very end. All along she'd been as much a victim of history as anyone, and while it was true she'd done terrible things, she'd also cared about Abby and her friends—cared enough to spare them from her own spell when you came right down to it. But, of course, Abby had been the only one to speak with her as she died, the only one to hold her as she crumbled to dust and whispered her final warning about the Council into the wind.

"It was kind of stupid of me," Becca continued, shaking her head. "The ground is ridiculously frozen. It's not like I could dig it up and find out if her wand is still there anyway."

"Maybe there's an easier way." Abby blew into her hands again and crouched to the ground. The dirt around the sapling was as hard as rock, but as she touched the tips of her fingers to it, she could already feel a gentle pulse beneath the cold surface, steady as a heartbeat.

Becca dropped to her side. "Anything?"

"The wand is still there. Right where we buried it."

"She wouldn't have come back from the dead and left her wand behind," Becca said.

Abby was struck by how tired Becca sounded, tired and maybe a little sad. It was there in her friend's eyes, a far-off look Abby was certain had never been there before. "Is everything okay with you?"

The hint of sadness vanished like a magic trick. "I'm great," she said, too fast and too breezy for Abby to entirely believe her.

She squeezed Abby's cold fingers and stood up, stretching her arms over her head. Abby studied her again as she also rose to her feet, but it was as if Becca had already slipped on a familiar mask. The pretty smile, the bright eyes, the happy-go-lucky girl everyone liked.

"You're sure?" Abby asked.

Becca waved a hand. "Just the usual worries. You know, blood-sucking vampires, missing classmates, that kind of thing." Despite the lightness in her voice, she wasn't making eye contact. Something *was* bothering her. Abby wanted to remind her they were friends—they could talk about personal stuff, not just magic and vampires—but then she hesitated. Was that true? Were they close enough for her to keep pressing when Becca obviously didn't want her to? Or were they mostly friends because Becca was dating Abby's best friend?

The silence between them was growing uncomfortable, and Abby was just opening her mouth to say something—she still wasn't sure what—when her phone buzzed. She held it up for Becca to see that Amethyst was on the other end of the line, then clicked it on and switched to speakerphone.

"Oh good, you're there," Amethyst said without preamble. "I need you to come to my house and see something."

"It's our house," Abby corrected her. "We live together."

"My old house. At the farm."

"Why are you there?"

"I may have found something important. How soon can you get here?"

Abby looked up from the phone. Becca was watching her. "Becca's here with me. We were following a lead together."

A pause, and then: "Good. That's perfect. She might be able to help."

Amethyst was waiting for them on the bottom step of the burned-out farmhouse she'd shared with her grandfather until his death last year. For a few months after his passing, she'd lived on her own without anyone knowing there were no adults to care for her, but when her house burned down she'd come to live with Abby and her mother. Spotting Abby and Becca now, she hopped to her feet and led them toward what remained of the barn.

"It's over here," Amethyst said, stirring ashes into the air as she stepped over the barn's crumpled front wall. She'd already cleared the charred debris near the middle of the floor to reveal the painted hexagram stretching across the old foundation, once red and now almost entirely black. Abby recognized the hexagram immediately. It was the spot where they'd practiced magic together in the early days of their friendship.

Amethyst's parents had died when she was little, and she'd gone to live with her grandfather on the same farm where her mother grew up. Eventually she'd discovered hints of her mother's ties to the supernatural world, which included the six-pointed star hidden beneath the hay bales here in the barn. As Amethyst dropped to her knees and scraped away more soot, Abby realized the hexagram had been carved into the stone floor, not simply painted there as she'd always assumed.

"What's this about?" Abby asked, crouched beside her friend.

"I always thought the hexagram was just something my mom put there to look cool," Amethyst said. "Back then I didn't know what a witch's seal was or how it could be used, and I never really thought about it again after we started learning other things."

"What's a witch's seal?" asked Becca.

"It's like a door that can only be opened with magic. It's always in the shape of a six-pointed star. Witches can use them as portals," Abby explained.

"Or as a safe to keep things hidden," Amethyst said. "It never occurred to me that Mom might have locked something away for safe keeping right under *this* seal until this morning. I tried opening it before I called you… and I found something."

"What happened to leaving the Nancy Drew stuff to me?"

"You can be Nancy Drew. I'm more the Sherlock Holmes type."

Becca leaned forward. "What did you find?"

"This." Amethyst lifted a small wooden chest from the ground and positioned it between the three of them. "Once I discovered all the witchy stuff Mom kept here at the farm, obviously I assumed she was a witch like me. But I never knew for sure until today. Now I think there may be even more to her past than I suspected."

Abby stared at the chest. "What's in there?"

"Remember how I said there's something weird about that house your mom bought?"

Becca's face lost a few shades of color. "You guys are moving?"

"Not if we can help it," Amethyst said, flipping the lid to reveal a mess of old photographs, letters, and other mementos. She held one of the pictures out for Abby and Becca to see. Six young women were standing in front of an old New England lighthouse on a grassy windblown bluff, each of them pointing a wand at the camera and smiling from ear to ear. Everything about their body language suggested sisterhood and loose-limbed laughter.

"This is my mom." Amethyst tapped the head of a cute light-skinned girl with curly blonde hair. "I've seen other pictures of her when she was young, but never with a wand. Or a coven," she added meaningfully.

"Who are all these other girls?" Abby asked. "Are there any names on the back?"

"No need for names on this one." Amethyst dragged a finger across the photograph to another teenage girl with a wide rosy-cheeked grin. Something about the face looked familiar, but Abby couldn't place it. "Look closely."

Abby squinted, then looked up, wide-eyed. "Is that…?"

"Poppy Delacroix," Amethyst said, nodding. A vein beat a visible pulse above her left eye. "I'm positive it's her. She was in the same coven as my mom. She's a witch just like us."

"Who's Poppy Delacroix?" asked Becca.

Abby let out a slow breath. "The realtor who just sold my mom a decrepit farmhouse on the other side of the state. But she can't possibly be a witch, Amethyst. We would have sensed the spark in her."

"Unless she found a way to hide it from us," Amethyst countered.

"How would she do that?"

"I'm more interested in why." Amethyst replaced the photograph and closed the chest tight. "Becca, your mom's a real estate agent, isn't she?"

A flicker of hesitation crossed Becca's face at the mention of her mother, that same far-off look she'd shown Abby on Willow Hill. Then the mask was on again, the pretty smile, the pleasing expression. "Yeah, why do you ask?"

"There's almost nothing about Poppy Delacroix on the internet. Could your mom ask around about her? Maybe someone knows more about her than we can find on our own."

Becca's expression was skeptical, but she nodded. "I'll ask."

"I want to know why she hid the fact that she's a witch," Amethyst said.

Abby pressed her lips together, another worry suddenly crowding in alongside the others. "I want to know what happened to the other girls in your mom's coven," she said, "and why Ms. Delacroix seems to have turned up at exactly the same time as all these vampires."

## Puzzle Pieces

The school week arrived cold and wet, but Robby hardly noticed the lashing rain against his bedroom window until Tina knocked on the door to make sure he was awake. Hunched over a pile of mildewy old library books, he rubbed his eyes and blinked, frustrated that he didn't have more to show for a sleepless night of research.

Beyond what they'd already turned up, there was almost nothing about vampires in any of the local history books. Nothing about anyone called the Shadow Lady. Nothing about a vampire wanting revenge. He'd had better luck reading folktales and legends about warding off vampires—sunlight, garlic, and religious symbols came up often, and a stake through the heart would kill them—but there was still too much he didn't know, especially about the vampire panic in Willow Cove.

The door cracked open, and his stepmother inched into the room. "I'll give you a ride to school today. It's raining cats and dogs out there, and that's my official opinion as a veterinarian." When Robby still didn't look up from his desk, Tina ruffled his hair until he finally lifted his head. "At least your father laughs at my jokes. I'd remind you to make your bed, but it looks like Einstein is the only one who slept in it last night." Robby's iguana wagged his tail at the sound of his name. Seeing the books spread across his desk, Tina swallowed hard and lifted a leatherbound volume called *Crowley's Creepy Compendium*. "Where did you get this?"

"It's Amethyst's," he told her. "It belonged to her mother."

"Well, it doesn't belong to *you*. It's a witch book." Thumbing through the yellowing pages, she said, "If the Council ever found out you were reading this—"

"Who's going to tell them?"

"That's not the point."

Robby pulled the book back from her. "'Once sired, the newly turned vampire is compelled to go after the person they hold closest in the world,'" he read aloud from a dog-eared page. "That's *exactly* what happened with Margery. Lucinda came for her best friend. She turned Margery into a vampire."

Tina squeezed his shoulder. "I asked you to stop, Robby."

"'Vampire bites are not like that of any other animal. We do not simply fear an infection. The bite *is* the infection—a kind of primitive blood magic that begins the process of transformation from living to unliving. It takes two encounters to fully turn a victim. The first bite drains them of blood and begins the infection. The second bite returns their newly infected blood to them, sealing their fate as one of the undead,'" he read, only meeting Tina's gaze again once he'd finished the passage. "Margery had bite marks on her neck when we saw her in the corn maze, but she wasn't a vampire yet. She only became one after Lucinda returned for her. Two bites. Is everything else in this book accurate, too?"

This time Tina pulled the book from him more forcefully. "I said to leave it alone. Trust me on this. It's dangerous."

"Margery will go after someone close to her next," he said.

Tina's expression was sympathetic but firm. "You're not particularly close with Margery. Just keep inside after dark and you'll be fine. This isn't a problem you need to solve."

"Someone has to!"

"I'm looking into it. And I'll keep you and your friends safe, Robby. It won't be like last year. I promise you that." Retreating to the hallway, she paused in the doorway. "Can I get you something for breakfast before we leave? You always like eggs and bacon."

"I'm not hungry."

"Robby, please don't be like that."

"Not. Hungry," he repeated, punctuating each word. "I think I'd rather walk to school today, too."

After she went back downstairs, Robby dressed and brushed his teeth. He grabbed his jacket and muttered a sullen goodbye as he headed out into the rain, half wishing he hadn't turned down breakfast after all. The smell of bacon followed him out the door, and at first he almost didn't hear the loud *thwack* over the rumble of his own stomach.

Then it came again.

*Thwack, thwack!*

A pause.

*Whack!*

The rain was coming down sideways and his first thought was of a wooden shutter banging against the side of the house. Then he saw Abby and her mother at the end of their driveway next door. He couldn't make out what they were saying, but Abby was waving her arms, and her school clothes were already soaked through. Someone in a yellow rain slicker was pounding a heavy realtor sign into their front lawn while Abby and her mother argued.

*THWACK!*

Shielding his eyes from the rain, Robby stared at the sign, not quite believing what he saw. For sale? Abby's house was *for sale*? When she spotted him, Abby stomped in his direction with a raw expression on her face. She had a duffel bag squeezed under one arm and led him under the cover of the birch tree between their two yards.

"I know I should have told you. I just didn't know how." Her teeth chattered. She shuddered miserably. "We're moving."

Robby stared at the wooden FOR SALE sign, then at her duffel bag. "Right now?"

"What? No, the bag is for tonight," she said, shifting the over-stuffed duffel in her arms. "The whole coven has been Summoned to meet the Council. Apparently, it's a sleepover."

"Summoned?" he repeated, running his hands through his hair.

She caught his dismayed expression and forced her face into a smile. "There's a lot going on. Let's just go to school. Amethyst will catch up with us, and I have more to tell you before we get there."

"But you're soaked."

"I'll dry out." Abby raised her voice in the direction of her mother. "I just don't want to be around *some people* for one more minute today!" Then she stepped out from under the branches and started toward the trail through the woods.

Robby shot one last look at the signpost in her front lawn, then at Mrs. Shepherd's stricken expression, before staggering after her. The rain felt more like drizzle under the cover of the trees, but a stubborn breeze still tugged at their wet clothes. Abby looked miserable beside him, pale and shivering. Robby slipped off his Spider-Man sweatshirt and gave it to her, waving away her pro-tests. Abby pulled it tight to her shoulders and Robby could almost see the tension leaving her body.

"I shouldn't have said that to my mom. I know she thinks she's protecting us. It's just that with Margery vanishing now, too, Mom's even more determined to move." Abby's expression dropped again. Her shoulders slumped. "The new house is far away, Robby. Really far—and that's not even the worst of it."

"What could be worse than that?"

"The whole thing is strange. Our realtor is a witch, for one thing, but she tried to keep it secret from us. She also might have belonged to the same coven as Amethyst's mother when they were younger. Becca is trying to find out more about her for us."

The knot in Robby's stomach clenched tighter. "You told Becca before me?"

Abby rubbed a hand over her face. "I'm sorry, I've made a mess of the whole thing. Don't be mad at her. Or me," she added, her voice losing some of its conviction. "I just didn't know how to tell you."

As they were talking, the old carriage road through the woods began to fill with kids with umbrellas and rain boots making their way to school. Robby's gaze fell back to Abby's rain-splashed face. She was watching him, waiting for him to react. Her expression all but begged him to just… *understand*. He gritted his teeth and nodded. He did understand. He wouldn't have known how to tell her, either.

Abby slung her duffel over one shoulder and together they trudged toward school, sneakers squelching on the mucky trail. He couldn't help thinking about everything going on at the same time, so many different crises all at once. Folktales coming to life. The Council of Witches summoning Abby and her coven. A mysterious new witch suddenly surfacing. They all felt like pieces of a puzzle, but he wasn't sure they belonged to the same puzzle. There were too many jagged edges that didn't fit together.

He was still thinking about it when Amethyst found them, breathing hard from rushing to catch up. "I almost forgot to put Spooks outside before I left," she told Abby, wiping wet hair from her face as she squeezed between them. "The last thing we need is your mom finding a raccoon in the house."

"You know he just sneaks into *my* house when you do that," Robby said.

"What's the problem? We're practically family now. Besides, I need you to take care of him for me tonight." She propped her own travel bag on one hip, shifting its weight. "Abby told you we've been Summoned?"

When Robby nodded, Amethyst said, "The rest of it too?"

"He's all caught up," Abby said.

Amethyst drew closer to him. "So, as you can see, the impending vampire apocalypse is but one of many delightful situations we're dealing with."

A few yellow school buses were already pulling away from the curb when the three of them arrived outside the middle school, dodging puddles as they made their way toward the main entrance. Of the kids still lingering in the rain, most were gathered near the front steps to gawk at the news vans ringing the driveway. A smaller group huddled under one of the maple trees, where the school gossip, Sarika Swann, was talking into a microphone attached to her phone.

Four umbrellas lifted to let them in as Robby, Abby, and Amethyst edged closer to hear what she was saying. Olivia and Piper were clustered together with the twins, all four of them listening in as they readjusted their umbrellas.

"Sarika has started some kind of podcast investigating the history of unexplained phenomena in Willow Cove," Olivia whispered, apparently feeling charitable enough to be seen with them this morning. "She's *still* trying to figure out what happened last year. She thinks it may be connected to all the new disappearances. Can you believe she actually tried to interrogate me about it?"

"You did repeatedly wipe her memory in seventh grade," Robby pointed out.

"She's such an attention grabber, though. It's just another form of gossip for her." Checking her phone, Olivia added, "It looks like she already has a few hundred subscribers, which I'm sure is all she really cares about."

"What's she saying?" asked Amethyst. "I can't hear any-thing."

Piper let out a low moan. "Two more people have gone miss-ing."

"Sarika says T-Rex and Joey Swett both vanished sometime last night or early this morning. The police haven't officially con-firmed it yet," Delphi said.

"They were both with Margery in the corn maze," said Robby.

Piper's mouth fell open. "She's had a crush on the two of them for a while now."

"'Oh, most false love,'" said Daisy.

"They're probably busy torturing animals or setting fire to someone's house right now," Amethyst said. "They do have a his-tory of doing that sort of thing together. They're like terrible twins."

Robby blinked. His thoughts snagged on something Amethyst had just said. *Twins.* His gaze drifted again toward Daisy and Del-phi, the two of them so different, so unlike each other in so many ways—yet still inseparable. The twins were never far apart, not even when they couldn't stand each other. Weren't most twins like that?

"Eyes up here," said Delphi, catching him staring in a way he hadn't meant to.

"What? No, I wasn't looking at… I was just thinking about something."

Olivia snorted. "I'll bet you were."

"Not *that*," said Robby, his cheeks flushing. Of course he'd noticed how Delphi had filled out all of a sudden, how she'd grown her hair long and started looking pretty in a nerdy sort of way—but that wasn't what he was thinking about right now.

Abby touched his hand. "You figured something out?"

"Maybe," he said, glad for the rescue.

"Tell me."

He shook his head, the idea still only half formed. "I need to check something in the library first. Let's meet after school."

Abby patted her duffel bag. "We can't, remember?"

"Fifth period, then. Study hall. The whole coven should come. I think we might have missed something important about how this started." He tilted his head to take in all six girls. "If I'm right, I might have figured out how some of these puzzle pieces fit together."

# 8

## The Tale of the Twins

Abby was still scribbling answers on her French quiz when the bell rang at the end of fourth period. While the rest of the class shuffled to the door, she lay her pencil down and looked up, feeling panicked. Madame Toussaint, her teacher, watched her from the front of the room. Sighing, Abby scooped up her things and dropped the quiz onto Madame Toussaint's desk, knowing it would take a small miracle for her to get a passing grade.

She was usually a good student, but it wasn't like she'd had time to study over the weekend. Or that she could have concentrated on conjugating verbs today even if she *had* studied. As she slung her duffel bag across one shoulder, her thoughts ran again to her coven's meeting with the Council later today. There was no use worrying about that just yet, she thought, waving au revoir to Madame Toussaint. Not when she had so many more pressing worries piling up.

Her overnight bag was bulky and uncomfortable, and she struggled with it into the crowded hallway. If she were being honest, she was almost glad none of her friends were in the same French class as her. Telling them about Poppy Delacroix and her mom's plans to move had been harder than she'd thought it would be. In some ways, it was a relief to have a break from their questions. Now the only person left to tell was…

*Zeus.*

She hadn't noticed him in the hallway until just now. He spun around when she pushed into him with her lumpy duffel bag, a frown still stretched across his face from whatever he'd been saying to Sarika. His expression dropped even further when he saw Abby rearranging her bag against her hip.

"Sorry," she said, pushing her glasses up to keep them from falling. Her cheeks were already scarlet and the last thing she needed was a pair of broken glasses to add to her embarrassment. Sarika drifted toward another group of students, but the girl's big brown eyes stayed on Zeus until she disappeared around the trophy case down the hall. Abby gritted her teeth. Were Zeus and Sarika together now?

She supposed it wasn't any of her business. It wouldn't change the fact that he didn't like *her* anymore. He'd made that clear enough by barely talking to her since their breakup. Not for the first time, she found herself wondering why he'd dumped her, what she'd done to deserve it, why he wouldn't even tell her. It had seemed so sudden—one minute they were together, the next they weren't—but she knew that wasn't right. He'd been pulling away from her for a while beforehand, even if she hadn't recognized it at the time.

Now that she really looked at him, though, she would have bet anything that smile for Sarika had been just a mask. And before she could stop herself, before she could think she shouldn't do it, she reached out and touched his hand. His eyes widened and she thought he would pull away. He *did* pull away. But not before his expression warmed a little.

"Everything okay?" she asked.

"Sarika thinks I must have some inside information about T-Rex and Joey Swett going missing." His gaze drifted in the direction where she'd disappeared around the corner. He shook his head wearily. "You know, because my dad is the police chief."

The hallway was clearing out around them. Most of the students had gone to wherever they were headed for fifth period, and the only sound was the steady tapping of Madame Toussaint's cane on the hard floor as she made her way to the breakroom across from them, opened the door, and disappeared inside. Abby and Zeus both watched her. It was easier than looking at each other.

"Is it true then?" Abby asked. "Did they really go missing, too?"

The warmth in Zeus's expression vanished. "Now you sound just like Sarika. She said she has information to trade with me if I can find out what the police aren't telling the public."

"What kind of information?" Abby asked.

"I don't know. I don't want to know. I only got involved because Robby and Becca dragged me into all of this in the corn maze."

"Because they're your friends, Zeus." He looked so miserable that Abby wanted to hug him, or touch his shoulder, or squeeze his hand again. Or kiss him…? No, she only wanted to comfort him, because just then it didn't seem to matter as much if he still liked her or not. It didn't even matter why he'd dumped her. Before all that, before things had gotten so complicated, they'd been friends. "We could *all* still be friends," she told him, "if you wanted that."

She'd never been great at reading people, at least not boys, but based on the way he looked at her now, it seemed like maybe he did still want to be friends. He let out a heavy sigh, but there was a sort of longing in his eyes she recognized, too. A hint of the old Zeus, before things had gone wrong.

"Zeus, come with me to the library. We're all meeting there now." She lowered her voice to a whisper, even though they were alone. "I think Robby has figured out more about what's happening here. About the vampires."

"Of course you think he has." Now there was a hard edge to his voice she recognized, too. Was he mad at her for some reason? At Robby? She hugged the damp Spider-Man sweatshirt Robby had loaned her in the rain and tried to meet Zeus's gaze with a smile. His scowl only grew harder as his eyes lingered on what she was wearing.

"You should come," she tried again. "Be a part of it with us."

"I don't think so, Abby."

"Look, I get it," she told him, even though she wasn't entirely sure she did. "You didn't want to be involved. Well, you're involved now anyway, aren't you? Your dad's involved, too. So, come with me and let's see what we can learn. I *want* you to come, Zeus."

She let out a deep breath and risked another look at his face. His brows drew closer. His expression tightened. He stared at her for a long moment, not saying anything as he weighed whatever reservations he had about the whole idea. About everyone in the group. About her? Then he pursed his lips and nodded.

"I'll come this time," he said, "but that still doesn't mean I'm getting involved."

Abby had one eye on her phone and the other on Zeus as they weaved through the bookshelves toward the back of the library. His mood had soured even more when she told him about her mother's plan to move across the state, so she kept her voice intentionally light as they rounded the last of the stacks.

"Robby says there's a hidden archive room on the second floor," she said, reading his message again. "I've never noticed any stairs here before, but—oh, it looks like he was right after all."

Becca was already peering into the shadowy recess in the wall-to-ceiling bookcase on the back wall when they came to a stop beside her. A pair of rolling ladders had been pushed aside to reveal a narrow stairwell spiraling up into darkness. "It's like a secret room," she said with a hint of awe in her voice, rolling one of the ladders in front of the opening to conceal it, then rolling it back to reveal the stairwell again. "Sometimes I love this creepy old school."

Muffled voices drifted toward them, and the smells of mahogany and musty books grew stronger as they climbed to the hidden room. Abby took the steps in a rush. At the top, Amethyst, Piper, and Daisy were talking in hushed tones by a giant stained-glass window, their overnight bags shoved into a small pile beneath the sill. Robby and Delphi were practically attached at the hip while flipping through a collection of books and maps at a dusty rectangular table. Seeing the two of them like that, Abby remembered Becca's strange mood at Willow Hill, the melancholy sadness that seemed so unusual for her. Was *this* why she seemed off? Did she think Robby and Delphi were…?

*No, not in a million years.*

Becca still lit up whenever she and Robby were together. Whatever had been upsetting her yesterday, it wasn't anything to do with Robby and Delphi. Zeus, on the other hand, *was* watching Robby with a pinched expression. The longer Abby looked, the more convinced she became that it was one of jealousy. Did Zeus like Becca? Did he like *Robby?* Before she could ponder further, the stairs creaked with the weight of footsteps.

Daisy poked her head down the stairwell, then made a sour expression of her own. "'Something wicked this way comes,'" she announced.

Olivia shot her a venomous glare as she emerged into the attic. "Charming as always, Daze. Haven't we all agreed it's time for you to move on from Shakespeare?"

"For your information, I was quoting Bradbury, *not* Shakespeare," Daisy replied, huffing to her full height. "It's hardly my fault if he borrowed that line from the Bard himself."

Olivia waved her hand at a phantom cobweb. "Was this ancient library room borrowed from Shakespeare too?"

"No, it's Victorian," Robby corrected without looking up from the table.

An icy draft crept in around the corners of an old brick hearth near the back of the room, shaking ashes and the dust of ages. Abby hugged her arms to her chest as she took it all in. Long cobwebs stretched from the stained-glass window up to the high-pointed ceiling. A bare lightbulb dangled above the table, its soft yellow glow not quite reaching the bookcases opposite the hearth. Abby suddenly realized where they must be in relation to the outside of the school, because she recognized the window from the original Victorian wing. She'd never guessed at the prowling shadows and old books behind it, though. "How did you even find this room?" she asked.

"Delphi dreamed about it last night," said Daisy.

"I had a premonition," Delphi corrected, "that what we'd need would be found here, so I helped Robby find it last period."

Daisy dropped a pile of books onto the table beside her twin. Dust billowed around her, and she waved it away, coughing. "*Someone* thinks she's some kind of oracle now because she predicted a few things correctly last year."

"Someone *else* still thinks she's William Shakespeare," Delphi retorted, "and for once I agree with Olivia. It's time to move on."

"'No prophet I will trust, if she prove false,'" Daisy spat, twirling a strand of chestnut hair between her fingers. "*Henry VI, Part I.*"

Delphi gave her twin a long-suffering eye roll. "See what I mean?"

Becca scraped a chair alongside the table while Abby dropped her duffel bag with everyone else's. Zeus loomed beside her, tall and dark, his body radiating heat. It was all she could do not to lean into him for warmth. Not too long ago she would have. She hugged Robby's sweatshirt tighter instead.

Now that they were all here and the rest of the group crowded around the table, Robby raised his gaze to meet them. "This morning I said I thought we'd missed something important about the 1889 vampire attacks," he said. "Now I'm sure of it."

Abby's breath misted between them. "What is it?"

"People don't just *become* vampires. Someone has to turn them. So, who turned Julia Morrow into the first vampire in Willow Cove?" His gaze flitted to Delphi, then dropped again to the books splayed across the table. "We know Julia Morrow had a twin sister named Briony. We also know Briony became ill before the first outbreak. But that's all we know about her. Briony's name never comes up again—not in the local histories, the folktales, anything."

"So, she dodged a bullet," Abby said, struggling to follow his logic.

Robby shook his head. "What if she *was* the bullet? When someone becomes a vampire, they feel a compulsion to turn the person they're closest to. Lucinda turned her best friend, Margery. Margery had a crush on Joey and T-Rex—"

"Well, then we're in luck," Amethyst cut in. "T-Rex doesn't have any other friends."

"There's Sarika," Abby pointed out. "He used to hang out with her."

"And Olivia," said Zeus.

Olivia made a gagging sound. "Ugh, no. We dated briefly. He was way more into Becca last year."

"Don't remind me," Becca replied.

Piper cleared her throat. "I still don't understand what this has to do with the Morrow twins in 1889."

"If the same pattern held true back then," Robby explained, giving her a grateful look, "then why didn't Julia Morrow try to turn her twin sister?"

"Because Briony had already turned her first...?" Abby said with dawning realization.

Robby grinned at her. "Exactly."

"Even if that is what happened, doesn't it bring us right back to the same question as before? How did Briony become a vampire?"

"That's why we're here in the school archives." Robby had started flipping through one of the old books while they were talking. His fingers finally stopped on a brittle yellow page speckled with mildew. "There's at least a century's worth of school records up here. Delphi helped me track down the school yearbook from 1889."

"Delphi *and* her sister," said Daisy.

"Mostly me," Delphi said, beaming at Robby. "I also found some contemporary accounts of the vampire scare and a Morrow family profile in the local newspapers that I read on microfiche. I had to sneak into the historical society building to find everything, but in my premonition I saw Robby looking at all those different sources, so I knew I should fetch them."

"You just wanted a reason to skip gym class," said Daisy.

"Yes, that too."

Robby repositioned the worn leatherbound volume so everyone could see. Most of the page was smudged or faded, and one jagged corner had been lost to time, but a black-and-white photo taken in the town's original schoolhouse remained undamaged. "Briony and Julia Morrow are posing here with some of their classmates," he said, tapping a spot just above a pair of identical light-skinned girls staring back at them from across the years. Both had dark eyes and slightly upturned lips. Like all of the other girls in the photo, Julia wore a long flowing white dress—all except her twin sister, whose high-necked dress was as jet black as her hair.

"A Victorian goth girl," murmured Amethyst with undisguised interest. Her eyes were glued to the picture like it had hypnotized her. "I may have finally met my soulmate."

"If you're into that sort of thing," said Olivia.

Amethyst leaned in for a closer look. "I think I might be."

"Gross, Amethyst. She's probably been dead for a hundred years."

"No, that's exactly what I'm trying to tell you," Robby said, plunging ahead. "I don't think she's dead at all. I think she's *undead*. Her father was some sort of prominent local figure back then—wealthy, respected, a town elder. You can see from this picture that Briony was a bit different from other girls, though. The Morrow family profile Delphi found talks about how Briony had an interest in spiritualism. Her parents would often catch her wandering around the cemetery after midnight or conducting seances—"

"That seals it," said Amethyst. "Definitely my soulmate."

Robby traced a circle around Briony's face with his finger. "If anyone could have summoned a vampire, or *become* one, wouldn't it be a disaffected teenager with an interest in the occult? I think Briony was the one who started the vampire attacks in 1889. Julia Morrow never tried to turn her because Briony was already a vampire. And if Briony Morrow really was the source of the original outbreak, there's no indication she was ever destroyed."

Delphi was nodding her head. "She doesn't register a single mention after the outbreak began. There's no record of her in any other yearbooks, nothing about a marriage or moving away, no birth announcements or death notices. It's like she ceased to exist at the same time as Julia."

"Maybe she just died from her illness," Olivia suggested. "Maybe she didn't warrant an announcement in the newspapers. Teen girls weren't exactly front page news back then."

"If that's the case," Robby said, "she'll have been buried with the rest of her family."

Abby's stomach clenched. She didn't think she was going to like wherever this was going

"We have to know if she's still there or not," Robby pressed. "If she isn't, then she might be back to finish what she started in 1889."

Becca's expression was thoughtful. "If the Morrows were a wealthy family, they would have had a crypt. The original cemetery records would probably be kept at the town hall. Or maybe the funeral home?"

"That's a good start," Robby said.

"I don't think anyone should go near that cemetery—"

Robby threw a hurt look in Abby's direction.

"—*until* we get back from meeting the Council," she finished. "We'll all look into it together. It's safer that way. Promise me you'll wait."

Abby held Robby's gaze until he nodded.

"I promise," he said.

But he didn't look happy about it.

# 9

## Betwixt and Between

When school let out for the day, Abby stuffed a few notebooks inside her locker and slammed the door shut, spinning the combination lock back and forth while Amethyst waited. They were meeting the rest of her coven outside the front doors, but for now Abby leaned into the cool metal of her locker and shook her head, mind made up.

"We can't just leave. What if something else happens while we're away?"

"We don't have much choice," Amethyst said between chews of bubble gum. "Tina was pretty clear about that."

"But we don't even know where we're going."

"It's one night, Abby. We'll be back tomorrow. In the meantime, we need to be on our best behavior. The stakes are too high."

"I know. I *know*." Abby shook her head. "Since when are you the pragmatic one?"

"Since Tina said the Council could break up our coven if we don't behave. Besides, aren't you even a tiny bit curious what they're like?"

"Maybe a tiny bit. I suppose if anyone knows how to stop what's happening in Willow Cove, it would be the six most powerful witches in the world."

"Tina wouldn't like us even asking about that," Amethyst pointed out.

"I'm just saying. Maybe we'll learn something useful."

Amethyst raised an eyebrow. "Now who's being pragmatic?"

Outside, Daisy and Delphi walked ahead as they turned onto the muddy path through the woods to Tina's veterinary clinic. Olivia loitered a few paces behind, inspecting her fingernails with a frown, hesitant as usual to be seen with the rest of them. Abby fell into step with Piper and Amethyst, shifting her overnight bag from hip to hip, still feeling a bit lost in her thoughts.

"Do you really think a teenage girl like Briony Morrow could summon a vampire?" Piper asked into the silence.

"I don't know what to think," Abby said, wrinkling her forehead. "Miss Winters opened a portal between time and space last year. It kind of feels like anything is possible."

Piper looked unconvinced. "She was a powerful witch, though."

"A powerful witch who warned us against trusting the Council," Abby said quietly.

Amethyst frowned at her. "She was also evil. Let's not overlook that part."

"Miss Winters wasn't evil, Amethyst. She was… complicated."

Amethyst shook her head but decided not to challenge Abby's point. They continued in silence. The sky was turning black through the treetops, and for a moment Abby almost wondered if she'd lost track of time, but a quick glance at her watch showed it was still late afternoon. The day was growing more overcast, the looming storm clouds low and dark with the promise of more rain.

Branches shook in the breeze and Abby zipped her borrowed sweatshirt, shivering. The whispering wind made the hair on the back of her neck stand up. She stopped in her tracks, suddenly alert. Amethyst and Piper stopped with her. Olivia opened her mouth but seemed to reconsider when she saw the expression on Abby's face. Listening hard, Abby heard it again—a flittering between branches, a soft crunch in the underbrush.

There was something in the woods with them.

Something more than just the rustle of the wind. A flutter of blonde hair, a flash of pale skin, a shadow that moved like the wind.

*Lucinda?*

Abby squinted into the woods. The clouds were dark and there was no sunlight to speak of now. Lowering her duffel bag to the ground, she reached for her wand and raised it defensively, the tip flaring blue at her silent command. The shadow darted again in the corner of her vision, and Abby spun after it, pointing her wandlight at a rush of darkness. *Revenge, revenge*, the swaying branches seemed to whisper. *She will have her revenge.*

"Vampires are only supposed to come out at night," breathed Amethyst, as if saying it out loud might remind the universe of this all-important rule.

"Somebody needs to tell them that!" said Olivia, pulling up alongside Abby with her wand raised. Suddenly they all had their wands up. They formed a defensive circle in the middle of the wooded trail, their training kicking in without the need for words, six points of wandlight cutting through the gloom.

In the dark woods, four pairs of red eyes burned like hot coals, and Abby knew they could only belong to their missing classmates. But already the whispers were growing softer, already the heavy clouds were rolling away again as gray daylight poked through the treetops. Before Abby could take a step in their direction, the red eyes vanished as quickly as they'd come. She kept her wand out, holding her breath, waiting. Listening. Nothing came jumping out of the woods at her. Nothing happened at all.

Piper eyed the woods uncertainly. "Are they… are they gone?"

"I think so." Abby lowered her wand. "You all heard it, too?"

"'*She will have her revenge,*'" said Olivia in a half whisper. "No mistaking that."

Abby scooped up her bag. "The sooner we get out of these woods the better."

Nobody spoke as they rushed the rest of the way to the veterinary clinic. Despite the chill, Abby was sweating by the time she clambered up the back steps and hurried inside to where Tina was waiting for them.

"You're late," Tina said, ushering the coven into the cramped back room they used for lessons. "We don't have much time. Leave your bags and phones in the crate by the door and take your places. Quickly now, girls."

"Tina, we just saw—" Abby began.

"Tell me later, Abby."

"In the woods, there were—"

"I said *later*! When you get back. There isn't time now." Thick pillar candles flickered at each point of a hexagram painted across the floor, and Tina strode to her usual spot in the center, looking harried as her gaze flitted between them. A few stray animal sounds spilled in from the front rooms. Piper's seagull, Flapper, who spent most days lounging at the clinic, sat up straight on a squishy cushion near the back wall, cooing loudly at the sight of her. Piper rushed over to him while the others dropped their things by the door.

"Why are we leaving our stuff?" Abby asked.

"I said quickly!" Tina pointed her wand at Abby's usual place in the hexagram. It was impossible to miss the irritation in her voice. "Your cell phones won't work where you're going, and your overnight bags were only necessary to maintain the illusion of travel for your parents."

"But you said we're spending the night."

"I said you'll be back tomorrow. There's a difference."

Abby blinked as she struggled with the logic. Then another thought slipped through. "That's the second time you said *you*," she observed as the rest of the coven hurried to their spots. "When *you* get back. Tina, you're coming with us, right?"

Tina removed her glasses and rubbed at the heavy bags under her eyes. "I've been directed to stay and monitor the portal. I will be right here when you get back."

"You're—you're not coming with us?" Piper stammered.

"What *portal*?" Amethyst asked.

Tina pursed her lips. Abby had known her long enough to read her different expressions. This one—the wrinkled brow, the darting gaze, the rapid blinking behind her horn-rimmed glasses— meant she was deciding if she should level with them or try to reassure them. Tina sighed and slowly unclenched her fingers. Abby knew this one, too. She was going to level with them.

"I thought I would be going with you. I had planned on it. There would have been plenty of time to explain how it all works when we arrived," Tina said, "but my instructions have changed. It's you six who have been Summoned—only you six. Not me." She let out another sigh. "My orders couldn't be clearer."

"But we need you," Piper said.

"Maybe we just shouldn't go," Abby replied.

"It's not that simple, Abby. Please remember that your situation is unique. The Council will break up your coven if you give them the slightest reason to do it. You need to do exactly as they instruct. As do I." Tina checked her watch and scowled. "Even when I don't like it."

"But where is the Council?" Piper peered behind Tina as if expecting to find the six elder witches hiding there. "Flapper gets tired if he has to fly too far."

"They are… betwixt and between," Tina said in a measured tone, appearing to choose her words carefully. "And I'm sorry, but Flapper can't go, either. He'll be quite happy here with me, I assure you." Abby wasn't sure who squawked louder at that, Piper or her seagull, but Tina was already shaking her head.

"He likes pizza for dinner," Piper said.

"Tina, what did you mean betwixt and between?" asked Abby.

"I'm getting to that part." Tina spread her hands to indicate the six outer triangles of the hexagram. "Everyone, please make sure you are inside the hexagram—yes, just like that—no, I said you won't need your overnight bag, Olivia. Leave it here." With a flick of her wand, she floated Olivia's backpack to the pile with the others. "The Council cannot precisely be said to exist where or even when. They are somewhere between the two."

"So, we won't be driving there," said Amethyst.

Tina looked to the ceiling, then blew out a long breath. "Be serious, please. Your first time using a portal is likely to give some of you an upset stomach, but it will pass shortly after you reach the castle. The most important thing—what is it this time, Amethyst?"

"Did you just say *castle*?"

Tina took in each of the girls in turn before her gaze finally landed again on Abby. Her voice was as serious as Abby had ever heard it. "I wish I weren't sending you anywhere at all, and certainly not by yourselves. As I said, I thought I'd have time to explain it all when we arrived. But the Council wills it, and that's that. In about thirty seconds"—she checked the time and frowned again—"perhaps less than that, your Summoning will begin. I've arranged for you to be met there by a friend of mine. Her name is Prena. I trust her."

"Wait, Tina, are you saying—" Abby started. Just then, the back room of the veterinary clinic began unstitching itself in a whirl of colors. The hexagram spun like a top, faster and faster until Abby's stomach lurched into her throat and her limbs seemed to peel away like taffy. She glimpsed Tina through a kaleidoscope of colors and called after her again. "Are you saying there are people there we *shouldn't* trust?"

The hard angles of the storage room blurred. Tina's mouth was moving but Abby couldn't hear the words. Then Tina was gone, the room was gone, the lights were gone. And only a suffocating darkness remained.

For a moment Abby was bodiless, shapeless, voiceless. When she screamed, no sound came out. An eternity passed before the world rushed back around her, and it felt as if she were coming up for air from deep underwater. All at once she swayed, stumbled, and dropped to her knees. Arching forward on all fours, gasping for air, she pawed for her glasses on the rough stone floor beneath her.

Wait, a *stone* floor?

The veterinary clinic didn't have a stone floor. She crouched for a heartbeat with her fingers around her frames, trying to get her bearings as the world continued to spin. When it finally slowed enough that she could slip her glasses back on, she blinked with relief. Her friends were wobbling on the ground beside her like they'd just been tossed from a merry-go-round. After a moment, Olivia retched loudly into the silence.

A few strips of light spilled from narrow slits in the distant walls. The whole room seemed to be round, like a lighthouse or a dome… or a castle tower? Abby's breath misted in tiny puffs. Shivering, she could just make out the pattern of a white hexagram on the stone floor. She touched a fingertip to it and pulled away, surprised—it was ice cold, but otherwise it could have been the same paint as in Tina's storage room. And were those the same half-melted candles? *We're still inside the hexagram*, she realized, *but the hexagram isn't inside Tina's room anymore.*

Abby's sneakers squeaked on the stone floor as she took a few tentative steps toward the distant slashes of light. The brittle air was so cold it actually hurt to breathe. She shivered harder the farther she stumbled from the candlelight, even with Amethyst and Piper so close on her heels that their breath warmed the back of her neck. The lights resolved into a row of windows a little higher than eye level, and Abby, Amethyst, and Piper stood on their tiptoes for a look outside while the twins found their way to another window just to their left.

No wonder it was so cold. Everything outside was covered in snow, a bleak and unending wasteland that only ended when it reached a horizon of twinkling stars. A few frozen lakes dotted the distant landscape like dark mirrors, but there were no trees, no buildings anywhere. Nothing at all beyond the unending white plain. Where *were* they?

"Does anyone else hear that?" asked Delphi.

Abby shook her head. "Hear what?"

"It's like a low hum." Delphi's brow furrowed as she took in her friends' confused expressions. "Really, no one else? It's so loud, it's… it's distracting. I can feel it in my veins, my bones, my inner ear—even the depths of my feet."

"That last one is probably frostbite," said Amethyst.

"The stars are different, too," Delphi continued. "Tell me you see that at least?"

Abby slid over from her window to Delphi's. "Different how?"

"I think—no, I'm sure—that cluster of stars is Centaurus." Delphi's expression darkened. She squinted at the night, then pointed. "This one looks like Hydrus."

"So what if it is?" Olivia had finally staggered over to join them. Her face was a splotchy sheet. "What's the big deal about a few constellations?"

"The big deal," Delphi explained with exaggerated patience, "is that they should only be visible in the Southern Hemisphere."

Abby was peering over Delphi's shoulder for another look when something caught in her sideways vision. A flash in the darkness, gold like sunlight and then… gone. She spun around, wand raised. The others did the same, their collective wandlight illuminating a slender figure in a gold cloak that rippled with movement. The figure dropped her hood to reveal a dark face with pale eyes and shimmery green hair cut to her shoulders. Abby thought she must be in her early twenties, if even that old. Her smile was so broad and welcoming that Abby found herself lowering her wand without meaning to.

"Very impressive." The newcomer spoke with a syllabic rhythm Abby associated with an Indian accent. Her boots clicked on the stone floor as she approached. Her hands were outstretched in greeting. "Not many witches would have spotted me so quickly, I think. It must be true what they say about you six being especially attuned to the magical world. Of course your mentor should be complimented as well."

*Our mentor should be here with us*, Abby thought. But she was so disarmed by the woman's smile that the thought didn't have much bite to it.

"I'm Prena," the woman said, joining them by the window. "How was your journey?"

"Nauseating," said Olivia.

"We're not even sure where *here* is," added Delphi.

"I will explain as we walk." Prena swept a hand across the dark chamber with the fluidity of a dancer. Her eyes were bright and entrancing. "But first, let me welcome you all to the Midnight Castle."

# 10

## A Visit in the Night

Rain lashed at the windows of Robby's bedroom, tap-tap-tapping like clawed fingers at the rattling glass. A thunderclap shook the house to its bones. Already the storm had knocked out power up and down the street, first with an uncertain flicker and then all at once, plunging the cul-de-sac into darkness. Robby and his father were getting by in the dim glow of a few emergency candles hastily retrieved from the basement.

The candle nearest to the window fluttered and Robby cupped his hands above the flame, trying not to shiver. Einstein peered nervously at him with puppy dog eyes from the foot of his bed. Amethyst's raccoon burrowed under a blanket, uninvited but not exactly unwelcome.

Another crack of thunder boomed overhead as Mr. O'Reilly appeared at the door. "The whole town's out," he said, juggling a pile of sleeping bags and a staticky weather radio between his arms. "Trees down everywhere. Streets flooded. The Heights are totally cut off from traffic."

He dropped the sleeping bags into a pile on the floor. The wind howled loudly through the curtains. The weather radio crackled indistinctly. "It's going to be a long night if we don't get the power back," Mr. O'Reilly continued, rubbing his glasses on his shirt. "You may want to use both of these sleeping bags if the heat doesn't come back on. I'll be downstairs reading if you need anything."

The glow of lightning lit the room again as he left. A long slow roll of thunder boomed soon after. Rain continued to beat at the window, tap, tap, *thump*, tap, tap, *thump*. Robby lifted his head. Something in the tapping caught his attention, something unsteady and irregular. He pulled back the curtain and squinted into the night. A pair of eyes glinted back at him. The rest of the form filled in around it, hazy but unmistakable.

*Becca!*

Prying open the window, he caught her as she spilled inside. Her clothes were soaked through, and she was shivering badly, but she had the presence of mind to paw at the window behind her until it slammed shut. Then she sank to the floor, her whole body shaking. Robby wrapped a blanket around her and peered out the window again. He saw nothing but raindrops against the glass.

"I'm s-sorry. You w-weren't answering—d-door…"

"The doorbell's broken." Robby's heart thudded in his chest. He pressed the blanket tighter to her. "Are you okay? What are you doing here?"

"Are you a-alone?" she asked.

"Dad's here. He was just in the basement looking for extra blankets. That's probably why he didn't hear you either. The power's out," he added, unnecessarily.

Becca's teeth chattered, but she seemed to be getting a little of her color back. "You weren't answering your phone. I c-came straight from the c-church because—because—"

"What were you doing at a church?"

Her eyes darted to the window; she blinked and looked away. "I would have just walked home, but it was dark, and your house is closer and—and I think someone was following me."

"Who?"

"I don't know, but it almost felt like…" Her voice trailed off. She shuddered. "Well, it doesn't matter now anyway."

"Who?" Robby pressed.

"T-Rex. It was just a feeling, though, and it doesn't make any sense. He wouldn't have any reason to follow me."

"What were you doing at a church?" Robby asked again. "You're Jewish."

"Half Jewish," she corrected as she unwrapped herself from the blanket. Her hair was still dripping wet, and raindrops beaded her face, but her familiar smile was inching its way back. "I'll explain about the church in a second, but first… could I borrow some dry clothes?"

Robby found a clean shirt and sweatpants, then grabbed a few towels from the bathroom while she finished changing. Drying her hair, Becca said, "Mom forgot to pick me up after school again, so I started walking home. I figured I might as well look into those cemetery records we talked about, so I stopped at the town hall. They sent me to the congregational church. After that it was pretty easy to learn the location of the Morrow family crypt."

"They just handed you the burial records?"

"Never underestimate the power of a pretty smile." She wrinkled her nose at her reflection. "Well, not so pretty now, obviously. But listen, there's something else. The minister told me someone had already been there looking for the same information. A girl about our age."

"Who? Sarika?"

Becca shook her head, then pulled out her phone and turned the screen to show him the picture of Briony Morrow from the old school yearbook. "He described her as dark haired, very pale, wearing an old-fashioned black dress. Sound like anyone we know?"

"Amethyst's Victorian goth girl," Robby whispered. His eyes narrowed as he stared at the image. More puzzle pieces that didn't quite fit together. "That doesn't make sense, though. If it is her, why would *she* be looking for the Morrow family crypt?"

"Maybe we got something wrong," Becca said, pulling her hair back. "Or maybe it's not really her. Either way, now we know we're not the only ones looking for that crypt." She tossed the towel onto her pile of wet clothes. "We don't have school tomorrow. We should go check it out."

Robby sat down beside her. "We promised we'd wait until the coven was back."

"It'll be daytime. Full sunlight. Totally safe."

"We promised we'd wait," Robby repeated.

Becca twisted a ring on her left hand, round and round, not meeting his eyes. "It's just that I want to solve this before I…" She shook her head and fixed her eyes on the floor, clearly having said more than she intended. "Never mind."

"Before you what?" he asked.

She took a deep breath and wrapped her hands around his.

"Before *what*, Becca?"

She squeezed his hand. Her fingers were ice cold. "Before I have to leave," she whispered. Her shoulders slumped. "You know the only reason my mom wanted custody was to beat my dad at something. Well, now Dad has a new job as the dean at some private school back in Wisconsin and he wants me to go there. He sued for custody again."

Robby's breath caught in his throat. "Maybe he won't win."

"He already did." Becca let out a long weary sigh. "I was hoping Mom would keep fighting it or something, but she doesn't even seem to care. I guess having custody was more work than she thought it would be."

The room had started spinning around the edges of Robby's vision. Outside, the rain continued to beat against the window. Thunder rumbled again, more distant than before. After a while Becca pressed her chin to his shoulder, and he realized he'd been silent for a long time.

"Say something, Robby."

He swallowed. "How soon?"

"A week, maybe two if I really drag my feet. Dad doesn't want me to miss any more of the school year than I already have. I'm sorry, Robby. I know it's awful, especially with Abby leaving, too."

Robby hopped to his feet and began pacing the room.

Becca rose, too. She stopped him, wrapped her arms around him, leaned her head against his shoulder. "I know I haven't lived here very long, but this town is my home. It's the only place that's ever really felt like home, and that's because of you. Because of our friends. I love it here, I love… the whole deal. And if I only have two weeks left, I don't want to waste any of it when I could be *helping*."

Robby blew out a breath and looked at her, really looked at her. The way her hair curled to her shoulders when it was wet. The way her lower lip quivered when she was sad. The perfect splash of freckles across her nose and cheeks, so faint you could only see them right up close. "You're sure you know where to find the Morrow crypt?" he asked.

"Positive."

"Then let's go look for it tomorrow."

She squeezed him again before he'd even finished. Then she kissed him on the cheek, and when she pulled back her smile was like the sun. "Robby, do you think your dad would let me stay here tonight? The storm's so bad and… there's no one waiting for me at home."

"Where's your mom?"

"At her boyfriend's." She stared out the window, running a hand through her hair. "I don't want to go home to an empty house."

Robby knew his dad would want to talk to Becca's mother first, even with the roads flooded, even with Becca's house in the Heights cut off from the rest of the town. He didn't want to risk it.

"Dad would have to say yes if he knew everything that's going on," Robby suggested. "So, we might as well not even bother him with it."

"My feelings exactly. We can just camp out here tonight." She picked up a candle and swept it across the room, tilting her head a little when the dim glow illuminated a pile of comic books he'd found in the attic. It was mostly old horror classics from his dad's collection, musty back issues with creased covers and pulpy titles like *Tomb of Dracula* and *Werewolf by Night*. Flipping through them, she raised an eyebrow. "This is what you were planning to do all night?"

"It's research," he protested.

"Well, in that case I'd better help," she said, hiding a smirk. "I'm very good at this sort of thing. Reading. Talking. Sharing ideas." Her gaze fluttered meaningfully to the sleeping bags on the floor. "*Just* reading and talking, though, okay?"

"Yeah, definitely," Robby said, flushing.

He handed her a stack of comics and lifted another one for himself, sorting the issues with the most interesting covers between them. They sat shoulder to shoulder, knee to knee, and when Becca smiled a little sadly and pushed her sleeping bag against his, he had to admit he didn't exactly want to *just* talk and read comics with her. Mustering all his willpower, he reached across the floor and plunked Einstein into the space between them. "I'm pretty sure Tina bribes him with treats to keep an eye on me," he said. "Let's make him our chaperone tonight."

"That," Becca said, leaning her head against his, "is a very good idea."

## 11

## The Midnight Castle

"It's inhumane!" yelled Piper, struggling into a heavy black cloak at least twice her size. The other girls hugged their own cloaks tight as Prena led them down the spiraling steps of the tower where they'd arrived.

Abby glanced over her shoulder to find Piper scowling. "What's inhumane?"

"These cloaks! I think they're made of *real* fur."

"Not enough of it," Olivia said between chattering teeth.

"Girls, girls," Prena cut in, her voice calm and placating. "You do all identify as girls?" When they nodded agreement, she continued, "These cloaks are nearly a thousand years old. I assure you we only use natural fibers for our newer cloaks. Things *do* change around here now and then."

A tall wooden door was ajar at the bottom of the stairs, beyond which a bright white glow hinted at the endless plain of snow Abby had seen from the window earlier. As soon as she stepped outside, though, Abby realized her initial impression had been wrong—on this side of the tower, the endless white expanse wasn't endless at all. A half dozen other freestanding towers formed a crescent shape, and thousands of floating lanterns lit a snowy path toward the outer wall of a distant castle, its turrets stretching toward the stars.

"Maybe I just have vampires on the brain," said Amethyst, huddling close and pointing at the walled fortress, "but does that not look *exactly* like Dracula's castle?"

Abby made a small noise of agreement. Snow was already collecting in thick clumps on her head and shoulders, but she tugged her hood down anyway to better see her new surroundings. She couldn't believe what she saw.

Everywhere she looked, there were witches.

Hundreds of them.

Thousands, maybe.

Some strode along the snowy paths in the same thick cloaks as Abby and her friends, but most were soaring across the night sky, their silhouettes blotting out patches of starlight. The smell of the ocean was strong here, and Abby could just make out the dark edge of the sea beyond the castle, but even as she took it all in, her gaze kept coming back to the witches. A pair of girls with Asian features waggled their fingers in greeting as they passed, and Abby wished she could ask who they were, how they'd come to be here.

"Are you even listening to me?" Amethyst asked.

"What? No, sorry." Abby shook her head, pulling her thoughts back to the here and now. "Something about Count Dracula?"

Amethyst jutted a thumb at the far off castle. "I'm just saying, what are the odds that place *isn't* some Transylvanian count's secret lair?"

"I think it looks more like Hogwarts," said Piper, her voice tinged with awe.

"Hogwarts is in Scotland, which this obviously isn't," Olivia replied. When the other girls gaped at her, she added, "What? I do read, you know."

"I *didn't* know that," said Daisy with something approaching respect.

"You could fill a whole book with the things you don't know about me," Olivia snapped.

Amethyst was still shuddering under her cloak. "Forget Scotland. It's like we landed in Antarctica."

"I think that's *exactly* where we landed," said Delphi, staring up at the night sky. "Look, that's the Southern Cross, and over there is—"

"Well spotted." Prena latched the door before joining them again beneath the shadow of the tower. Ice and snow crunched underfoot as she started down the path. Even at this distance, Abby could make out a narrow gap in the castle wall that must have been a drawbridge and gate tower. Prena seemed to be leading them toward it. "Here on the seventh continent, the Council of Witches governs from a seat of power that favors none above any other, a place of neutrality possessed by no nation on earth. Even that is not the entire story, however. We are also what you might call betwixt and between."

"That's what Tina called it, too," Abby said.

"She's exactly right. You've guessed the *where*, but the *when* is an entirely different matter."

"Do you mean we time traveled?" Piper asked.

"Think of it as a time pocket," Prena explained, walking faster now, her golden robes shimmering with every step. Abby couldn't help noticing that all the witches were giving her a very wide berth. "The Council wisely placed this sanctuary in a time before human exploration of the white continent, so that it may never be found or overcome. Every stone has been plucked from its original home and reassembled here for us. For you. The edges have been smoothed, but in effect, time does not pass here as it does elsewhere. Now and forever, the Midnight Castle is frozen precisely at midnight on a cold autumn day in the late seventeenth century."

"Time's not the only thing that's frozen," Amethyst said, still shivering.

"The weather is also a little betwixt, I suppose. At any given time, you might find a thousand other witches drawn to the pull of learning and sanctuary that is the Midnight Castle. We've found it best for us all to keep to the rhythm and routine of our daily lives, which includes the illusion of the passage of time—hence the changing weather. Through this gate we'll enter the outer bailey and continue to the keep," Prena added, leading the coven toward the long drawbridge.

Abby scrunched her frozen toes inside her sneakers, still a little damp from her walk to school in the rain. Was that really just this morning? The unreality of it hit her all at once and she forced herself to imagine Robby back home, the idea of him, the realness of him in his warm house and messy bedroom. The drawbridge stretched across a deep crevasse, and as Abby crossed it a strange feeling settled over her. She was frightened by how easy it was to feel so removed from the real world, how quickly it could happen if she let it.

There were more witches moving about in the courtyard, still more peering down at them from glowing windows inside the keep. A pretty young woman in a wheelchair rolled over as if she'd been waiting for them, the icy breeze catching her coppery hair as she leaned into a quiet conversation with Prena. The pair nodded while they spoke, then the girl drifted back the way she'd come, watching Abby's coven all the while.

The more Abby considered how different the Midnight Castle was from the outside world, the more her sense of unease tightened like a knot in her stomach. After a moment, she edged closer to Prena, and the golden-robed witch looked at her with an open expression, friendly and inviting. "I know why we've been Summoned," Abby said. "I mean, I know we're not like a normal coven. But is it possible we could also ask the Council for help with something back home?"

Piper shot her a look. "Tina told us not to even ask!"

"I'm afraid Tina was right about that," Prena said, not un-kindly.

"How can you know?" Abby pressed.

"Oh, I know the Council well enough. I have some idea of what's happening in Willow Cove as well. You'd get one or two votes from the Council, but no more—certainly not enough. You must remember you are here at their invitation. They would not take kindly to you turning their Summons into… something else."

"But you said things were changing here."

"I said things change *now and then*." Prena's smile seemed sadder now. "Progress is often slow and always difficult. Of course, you must already understand why the Council regulates the use of magic beyond sanctuaries like the Midnight Castle?" she added, then furrowed her brow at the blank expressions staring back at her.

"I don't understand it at all," Abby admitted.

"Wait, there are *more* places like this?" Piper asked.

Prena nodded. "It's easy for me to forget there are so many gaps in your education. Neither Tina nor I expected you to be Sum-moned so soon," she hastened to add. "The Midnight Castle is the capital of the witching world, but it is not the only such place. Every nation on earth has communities that are similarly betwixt and between. Yours alone is home to dozens of them. When witches—and warlocks, too—reach adulthood, most choose to live among our own kind."

"Tina has lived in Willow Cove for years," Abby pointed out. "She's married."

"A few members of the Order are selected to be the Council's eyes and ears in the wider world, some even when they are still apprentices. Tina worked hard to become one of them, for reasons that are her own. She has several responsibilities, including find-ing and training new young witches like you. There are others whose job is to protect those of us who move between the various sanctuaries. Still others help the Council enforce witch law."

"Like not letting normal people know about our magic," said Amethyst.

"Is that how Tina explained it? I'm afraid it's a bit stricter than that. Not only must we keep our powers secret, we are forbidden from using magic to interfere with the outside world beyond our own self-defense, *period*. Hunting vampires to protect a non-magical community would be strictly off limits, for example."

"That doesn't make any sense," Abby cut in. "Those are our friends, our families. If we have the power to save them—"

"Too often in the past we have revealed ourselves, Abby, only to fall victim to hate and superstition—and that was before the non-magical world developed more efficient ways to kill than hanging and burning. The Council believes we must remain separate. It's one reason most of us remove ourselves from the outside world entirely."

Abby shuffled in the cold beneath the strange foreign stars. The Antarctic wind tugged at her hair. "A year ago," she said, drawing out the thought as she tried to put a complicated feeling into words, "I could barely turn a soccer ball with a simple rotation spell. I used to fantasize about what I'd do if I became really powerful, you know? Like maybe I'd use my powers to put more spin on my corner kicks, or I'd get rid of all my stupid freckles, or—I don't know—I'd make it so all the cute boys at school liked me."

Prena said nothing, only tilted her chin, urging her to continue.

"But those were all childish things," Abby said after a moment's consideration. "I outgrew them because isn't that what growing up is supposed to be about? Not thinking only of your own wants and needs?"

"And now that you do have more power?" Prena prompted.

Abby could feel all her anxiety about this strange place crystalizing, her anger at the Council's laws rising to the surface, the strength of it warming her cheeks despite the chill. She shrugged uncomfortably. "I guess I just can't imagine using it to wall myself off from the world instead of helping people who really need it."

Prena didn't say anything in reply, didn't speak up when Abby and her friends shuffled deeper inside the courtyard to escape the wind. But when Abby snuck a glance back at the green-haired witch a moment later, she and the young woman in the wheelchair were deep in conversation again.

And for some reason, they were both smiling at her.

# 12

## Bound by Blood

Other than a few utility vehicles working on downed wires, the Hollows were quiet when Robby and Becca met outside his house after sunrise. He'd awakened to a burst of light from his desk lamp when the power came back on, and by the time he'd returned from the kitchen with a plate of toaster pastries, Becca was sitting up in her sleeping bag, staring at her phone.

"As predicted, Mom never even checked on me last night," she said, looking up long enough to smile at him and accept a Pop Tart. "She says she'll see me after school, which means she also forgot we don't have school today. I guess that means she won't be voting, either."

Robby had gone downstairs again to say goodbye to his dad while Becca changed and snuck out of his room the same way she'd come. Now the tips of her ears were bright pink from waiting and she hugged herself against the wind, only brightening when she saw Robby appear around the corner.

A stiff breeze whipped wet leaves and small branches across the trail when they reached it through the woods. It had stopped raining overnight, but the morning was still chilly and damp, and the air smelled like the ocean. They followed the trail to the edge of the cemetery, where a rusty iron fence circled the bottom of the hill and a few sparse tree branches poked through the iron pickets. Another path led up the hill to a gap in the fence, and Robby's backpack caught on it as he tried to slip through. He unzipped the bag and handed Becca a flashlight and a wooden garden stake—just in case—and joined her among the tall grass and slanted headstones on the other side.

"Does it feel like we've spent most of our time in cemeteries over the past year?" he asked, cinching his hoodie tight.

Becca's fingers were icicles when she squeezed his hand. "You're forgetting all the dark tunnels and spooky hilltops." Somewhere an owl hooted in the early morning shadows. The distant sounds of leaf blowers and chainsaws drifted briefly on the wind as the sun climbed slowly through the treetops. "Plus that one time we broke into the police station."

"*You* broke in." Robby grinned. "I was just an accessory."

Passing beneath the bower of a towering oak, they came to a stop where the shadows met a small patch of light. A damp breeze shook the branches. Becca scanned her phone and tried to get her bearings. After a minute she pointed in the direction of the old church, whose tall white steeple rose above the waving treetops like a ship on a choppy sea. She twirled her Star of David pendant absently. "The Morrow crypt is this way. We're close now."

They followed a rubbly path through the cemetery, sticking to the sunlit areas where they could. Becca's gaze darted again from her phone to the tombstones. Hurrying ahead, she reached a moss-covered granite building half sunk into the hillside. A heavy bronze door loomed over her, blue lichen flecking the hinges like crepe paper. Becca jangled a rusty chain lying discarded in the mud. "This is the crypt, but I think someone else got here first and cut the chain."

A chipmunk chirped and went silent. Wind rustled the long grass. Robby tugged at the bronze door and it scraped along the ground, heavy and awkward. He pulled again and it moved another inch. Inside, the crypt remained silent and still.

Her expression wobbling, Becca gripped Robby's shoulder. "I think I'm having second thoughts."

"I think I am, too."

They both stared at the door. Becca leaned so close Robby could feel her heart beating against him. "We can't stop this outbreak until we find out who's causing it," she said, holding his gaze, hopeful and uncertain. "One last adventure before I move?"

Robby met her eyes, nodding. A twinge of sadness twisted in his gut. "One last adventure."

Together they pried the door wide enough to slip through. Inside, they waved their flashlights at the silent darkness as a whiff of decay hit them. Holding his nose, Robby took a tentative step into the unknown. Becca's breath was warm on his neck behind him.

Another step.

Another.

Near the bottom of the stairs, something stirred, and Robby stopped in his tracks, his heart in his throat. A whirlwind of dust and cobwebs swept past him like a whisper. Just the warmer air from outside mingling with the cold of the crypt, he told himself. Just science. He inched the rest of the way down. Becca followed a step behind. The beams of their flashlights gleamed through cobwebs thick as sheets, revealing a dozen or more stone plinths in the murky darkness. Dust scattered the floor. Robby squeezed Becca's hand and pointed. Fresh footprints led the way deeper inside.

"Someone definitely got here before us," she said.

Robby's flashlight showed a raised wooden coffin on the nearest plinth, the form bent out at the elbows like something from an old monster movie. He wiped dust from the platform and read the words etched into the stone. "'Alpheus Morrow, 1652 to 1701.'" Scanning the chamber again, he made sense of the other shapes stretching into the darkness. Each held another coffin. "We'll have to check them all."

Becca moved toward the next one. "This one says Ezelda Morrow, 1666 to 1712."

"Libbeus Morrow over here," Robby said, moving deeper into the crypt.

"Here's one called Festus Morrow." Becca smiled weakly. "He sounds fun."

Shadows twisted all around them. Robby followed the footprints toward the rear of the crypt, his fingers tingling from the cold. "There are two more back here," he called over his shoulder. These plinths were different from the others—closer together, side by side. He ran a hand along the dark wood of the nearest coffin, then pulled it back. There was almost no dust. "This one's been opened recently."

Becca looked a few shades paler as she joined him. "This one, too."

Robby puffed away the remaining dust, squinting at the words on the plinth. "This is Julia Morrow. Hold on, there's something carved beneath her name." Repositioning his flashlight, he read, "'Sealed by stake and bound by blood, never to—to— '" He furrowed his brow. "'—never to curse the living again.'" Robby's heart thudded so hard his chest hurt. "We have to look inside the coffin."

Becca snapped a photo of the writing, then turned back to him, looking as if she might be sick. Robby clicked off his flashlight and set it on the ground. In his other hand, he clutched his wooden garden stake. "I'll open it. You shine your flashlight."

Becca reached for his arm. "I think I've changed my mind."

"It's the only way we can know for sure." Before he could doubt himself, he lifted the lid. Two dazzling disks glinted in Becca's flashlight beam, nearly blinding him. As Becca shifted the light, the disks became silvery coins in the eye sockets of a human skull with wisps of dark hair, dry and thin as spider silk. A wooden stake protruded from the skeleton's rib cage. Exhaling, Robby pressed at the skull's jaw with the tip of his stake. Two sharp fangs stood out among the top row of teeth, sharp and wolf-like.

"That's not normal," Becca breathed, clutching her own stake more tightly.

Robby's hands shook as he closed the coffin. "Someone wanted to make sure Julia Morrow stayed dead. 'Sealed by stake—'"

"'—and bound by blood.'" Becca's voice was low and frightened. "Robby, look at *this*."

He hadn't noticed it before, but as Becca swept her flashlight across the floor again, he couldn't miss it. A six-pointed star encircled the twins' coffins. It was a dark, rusty color, crusting at the edges from age and rot, but still unmistakable. A hexagram scrawled from blood.

Robby shivered. The puzzle pieces were rearranging themselves in his mind again, but if anything, the picture was even less clear now. "A witch's seal," he breathed.

"What could it mean? The hexagram, the chain that was cut—all of it?"

"That there's something else going on here. Something we don't understand yet."

Robby's gaze drifted to the other twin's coffin. Briony Morrow's name and date of birth were etched into it, but Robby's attention was drawn to the base of the plinth, where in the darkness he'd somehow missed a rugged canvas backpack.

Becca unzipped the top of it and peered inside, then let out a shaky breath. "There's a black dress in here. You don't think…?"

Clutching his stake again, Robby motioned for Becca to provide the light. Briony Morrow's coffin lid caught for a moment, then gave way with a soft creak. A body lay inside as if sleeping, pale and bloodless in the soft silvery glow of Becca's flashlight. Long dark hair coiled to her shoulders. Her eyes were shut. Her lips were sealed.

Her chest rose and fell.

Robby took a quick step back.

Becca's flashlight clattered to the floor. She retrieved it and shined it again at the pale girl. "That's not a skeleton," Becca whispered. "She's—she's—"

"She's a vampire." Robby swallowed hard. "We were right after all."

The pair exchanged a look. Robby's knees wobbled. Steeling himself, he raised his wooden stake above the girl's chest. He wasn't afraid, he told himself. He *wasn't*.

But of course he was.

The girl's eyes snapped open. Becca screamed. Robby dropped the stake. Faster than lightning, Briony Morrow sat up, her eyes wide and red.

"Run," Robby breathed.

"Okay," said Becca.

Neither of them moved.

Then he said it again, louder, grabbing her hand this time.

Together they ran.

# 13

## The Fatekeeper

"What do you think they're up to right now?" Abby asked, shrugging deeper into her cloak. A cold breeze whistled through the drafty halls of the Midnight Castle. The heat of all their bodies crushed together in the narrow corridor should have been enough to keep her warm, but she still felt a shiver as she followed Prena toward their meeting with the Council.

"Who?" asked Amethyst, her ears and nose both a bright shade of pink.

"Everyone back home. Robby and Becca. Tina. Mom."

Dormitories and private residences occupied the upper floors of the inner keep, but Prena had explained the lower corridors were the most direct route to the High Tower and Seat of the Council. She seemed concerned they were already running late and had kept conversation to a minimum since waving goodbye to the copper-haired witch in the wheelchair. There were hints of grander things inside the castle—wafting kitchen smells, a choir of voices, even a colorful garden bursting from one of the towers—but Abby had only seen a handful of other witches inside the castle itself, most of them trailing wet mops or bubbling cauldrons with minds of their own.

"I think you're asking the wrong question," Amethyst said.

"What should I be asking?"

"Is our now the same as theirs? All this betwixt and between stuff makes my head hurt."

"Mine, too," Abby admitted.

"Not as much as this cold makes my *whole body* hurt," said Daisy, edging between them. "There must be a thousand uninhabited tropical islands in the world. Two thousand! Why would the most powerful witches in the world build their castle in the coldest spot on the planet? It doesn't exactly inspire confidence."

Abby's teeth chattered. "Be serious, Daze."

"I *am* serious. Seriously cold, too. Delphi gets it, just look at her." Daisy gestured at her twin, whose already pale skin had turned worryingly white. Beads of sweat were frozen in her eyebrows. "Isn't that right, Delphi? Delph?"

Delphi blinked. "The embers," she whispered to no one in particular.

"*What* embers?" asked Daisy. "It's freezing!"

"You can light a fire… with a single spark…" Delphi breathed.

Abby touched a hand to Delphi's forehead. The girl's skin was burning.

Delphi's gaze focused on Abby. "Our blood is like fire. We are reborn in flame. Where even one ember still glows, an inferno may… may…"

Piper slowed to a stop beside them. "What's—what's wrong with her?"

Olivia arched an eyebrow. "Where do I even start?"

"I don't know," Abby said, ignoring Olivia's snark. The way Delphi was talking, the nonsense words—it was the same breathy whisper she used whenever she had a premonition. This time her tone tugged at the tight knot of anxiety already in Abby's chest. "I think there might be something really wrong with her. Like she's in a trance or something."

"AN INFERNO MAY FOLLOW!" Delphi yelled.

"Time to wake up," said Daisy, shaking her twin.

Prena stopped in her tracks, then hurried back in a whirl of golden robes and blazing wandlight. Delphi's lips moved soundlessly between outbursts. Touching Delphi's forehead, Prena glanced back at the other girls. "This has happened before? She has premonitions?"

"Never like this." Daisy's voice was high-pitched and panicky. "Do something!"

"I had hoped taking this route would avoid the worst of it for her." Prena lowered Delphi to her knees. "I fear we're still too near the Hall of Fates. The threads are overwhelming her."

"What threads?" Abby demanded. "What's the Hall of Fates?"

Daisy's gaze was focused on her twin. "Can you help her?"

"You'll be late to your Summoning," Prena said under her breath.

"The Council will have to wait," Abby told her.

Prena's gaze flitted back the way they'd come. "Well, yes, obviously you're right."

"Blood like fire," Delphi said into the quiet. "A single spark."

"You have to stop this!" Daisy shouted in that panicky voice.

"I can't, but Bree will know what to do." Prena waggled her wand toward the distant darkness. A winged shadow shot from the tip and was gone. Soon after, another witch hurried toward them as if summoned from thin air. Abby might not have recognized her so quickly if not for the wheelchair, but she knew this girl at once. It was the young copper-haired witch who'd smiled at her in the courtyard.

"She's even more sensitive than I suspected," Prena told the girl.

Bree waved a hand in front of Delphi's eyes. "Take my hand," she said in a soothing voice. "Let me tether you." Her voice was strongly accented with an Irish lilt that grew more pronounced with each word, but it seemed to be having some effect. Delphi's murmuring slowed, then stopped. The change was so sudden that for a moment Abby could hear her own heartbeat. Then Delphi's expression went slack, and Bree caught her as she collapsed into her lap.

Daisy let out a worried breath. "Is she all right?"

Delphi's eyes fluttered open. She returned to her feet, wrinkling her nose at the onlooking faces. "Why's everyone staring?"

Daisy hugged her. "I thought we'd lost you for a minute there."

"My brain was… fizzing. It's that psychic hum I mentioned when we arrived. It's overwhelming. It's almost as if—just now—I was—was—"

"You came too close to the Hall of Fates," said Prena kindly. "Its effects can be unpredictable on witches with precognitive abilities."

"What does that mean?" asked Piper.

Prena turned back to Delphi. "Tell me what you saw."

"I saw the Midnight Castle. There were flames and six silver thrones and—and a circle without end." Her eyes widened as they settled on Prena. "You were there, too. We were all there, but something was different—one of us was… not like the others." Delphi's gaze swiveled to Olivia, almost an accusation. "You."

"What about me?"

"You weren't like the rest of us. You weren't one of us."

"Finally noticed that, did you?"

Bree and Prena exchanged a wordless glance. Bree said, "Perhaps I should accompany you the rest of the way to the High Tower."

"Bree is a Fatekeeper," Prena explained, as if that solved everything.

"Fatekeepers are witches who've lost their magical abilities," the young woman added in a clarifying tone. "It lets us access the Hall of Fates without a… disruption. Being without magic also lets me act as an anchor when someone like your friend becomes lost in a premonition."

Delphi brightened. "*Some* people don't believe my premonitions are real."

"Oh, they're terribly real." Bree took Delphi's hand. "Walk beside me and I will see you safely to the Council."

Prena nodded. "We really must be going now. I'm afraid we're already late."

The others had already wandered ahead when Abby realized Olivia wasn't moving with them. Piper and the twins crowded to either side of Bree with Prena just ahead. Amethyst threw a questioning look back to Abby, who hesitated a moment before hanging back. Olivia trudged forward in her general direction.

"How can we be late," the girl asked, shaking her head as the others turned a corner, "if time doesn't even pass here?"

"I try not to think about it," Abby told her.

Olivia lowered her voice. "This whole place gives me the creeps."

They passed into an empty dining hall with an arched timber ceiling, but Prena was marching too quickly for Abby to study it. "We just have to make it through the Summoning," Abby said with forced optimism. "Then we can go home."

Olivia stared straight ahead at Delphi. "And what was *that* all about? Silver thrones, reborn in flame, a circle without end? It's all going to go straight to her head, you know. She's going to want to be treated like an actual oracle now."

"We all need to support each other," Abby said, "if we want to get through this without the Council breaking us up."

"Does it even matter what the Council decides? You and Amethyst are moving. You're already leaving us. How is that sticking together?"

"I never wanted that to happen!" Abby lowered her voice when Amethyst glanced back at them. "Anyway, don't pretend you're sad about that. I'm sure you won't mind us leaving."

"You don't know the first thing about what I would or would not mind," Olivia replied.

Abby gave her an evaluating look. Olivia stared back with hard, challenging eyes. "Maybe I don't. Why don't you tell me?"

"I will tell you *this*," Olivia said as they continued through the castle. "I don't like how many things I don't understand about this place. Fatekeepers? Hall of Fates? What else has Tina neglected to mention?"

"I don't like it here, either. I guess we finally have something in common."

"I guess we do." Ahead, Prena and the girls turned a corner, briefly vanishing from sight. Olivia glanced ahead, then back at Abby, her expression shrewd but guarded. "For the record, I'm a little bit scared of all this." Her gaze flicked to Abby, practically daring her to make fun. It wasn't exactly a secret between friends, but it still felt like the most honest thing Olivia had ever confided to her.

"I think you might be right to be afraid," Abby said.

"A *little* afraid."

"I think it's smart," Abby said, tiptoeing with her words, "but I also think we should try to learn as much as we can from Prena while we're here. About the Council. About all of it."

Olivia nodded. "That's not your worst idea."

When they pulled up alongside Prena, the witch's lips were parted, her expression open and inviting. Still, Abby hesitated, unsure where to start. "What you said earlier about the Hall of Fates," she finally began, "I was wondering what you meant? Tina has never mentioned it."

Prena's lips creased with apology. "She wouldn't have had any reason to. The Hall of Fates is—no, girls, please follow the brooms." She indicated a hovering bundle of brooms whose tips were bobbing left where two dim hallways intersected. "That way, please. We're nearly to the High Tower." A pair of seething cauldrons bobbled past and Prena let out an irritated sigh. "The Hall of Fates records the deeds of every witch in history," she continued. "All our secrets, every moment we've ever lived, every moment we've *yet* to live—all possible futures laid out before us."

*Every secret?*

*Every witch?*

Prena seemed to read Abby's startled expression. "Yes, even yours and mine. Fatekeepers follow all the possibilities of our lives like the threads of a tapestry. You can imagine why such a place is useful when the Council must make important decisions."

Abby's head spun. What Prena was describing sounded impossible—it had to be impossible. But what did impossible even mean anymore?

"Only those without magic can safely enter the Hall of Fates. That's why the Council relies upon Fatekeepers to advise them on such matters. For some especially sensitive witches like Delphi, even being too near the Hall of Fates is dangerous. There are too many possibilities, too many threads—you've already seen how it affected her."

"How can a witch lose her magic?" asked Olivia.

Abby shot her a surprised look. "You cut all of us off from our powers last year."

"That was only temporary." Olivia rolled her eyes. "I did apologize."

"It's a discussion for another time, anyway," Prena said as they stepped into the castle's snowy inner bailey. "Here we are."

The snow shone so brightly that for a moment Abby was forced to cover her eyes. When her focus returned, she followed a long shadow up to a spiraling black tower at the center of the yard. With no obvious entryway at eye level, the bundle of brooms tilted up like an arrow, its bristles brushing the snow. The brooms parted and one drifted toward each of them.

"The Council is just at the top," Prena said, waving a wordless goodbye to Bree. "We'll rise and meet them together." As Abby reached for a broom, Prena touched her shoulder. "Rise beside me, but slowly so we may speak before we reach the top."

Olivia waited for Abby to nod that it was okay before she took her broom and began to rise. Abby urged her own broom slowly upward. Prena's voice was not quite a whisper, but it was clear her words weren't meant to be overheard. "The Council is very wise but also very proud. They will expect deference from you, Abby, and you *will* need their approval if you wish to remain together. You must earn their trust."

Just then Abby felt Miss Winters's long ago warning about the Council like a shiver down her spine, so stark and sudden she almost flinched at the memory of it. Prena's eyes never left her as they lofted higher, and in that moment, Abby decided it would be no use hiding her concerns from her, at least. "Someone once warned me not to trust the Council," she ventured.

"Someone you trust?"

"I don't know," Abby admitted. "I guess I don't trust as easily as I used to."

"It's wise to be cautious, but if I could offer a word of advice? Remember where your loyalties are supposed to lie."

"I'm loyal to my coven. My friends."

"And to the Council," Prena reminded her. "To them above all others. Remember that, or at least"—her shimmering green hair swirled free of her hood as the pair crested the tip of the tower—"make them believe it."

"Why are you telling me any of this?"

Prena's smile was kind but sober. "Because already I sense you are a rare and powerful young witch. You put the wellbeing of others above all else. You do not crave power for power's sake. That makes you dangerous. People like you are not easily controlled."

"And the Council doesn't like people who aren't easily controlled?"

"Now you're getting it."

Abby's friends had already formed a semicircle around a pyre of red flames when Abby and Prena touched down. The flat tower top was open to the elements—no roof, no walls—and Abby's gaze was drawn to the six silver thrones on the other side of the pyre. The women who sat upon them were much younger than she expected. Adults, certainly, but not *old* adults, definitely not the aged crones she'd imagined. It wasn't just the Council's age or obvious power that seized her attention, though. Not just their fierce gazes, their raised seats that seemed designed to emphasize their position.

It was that one of the six thrones was empty.

Then Prena stepped through the flames, an apologetic smile creasing her face as she met Abby's open-mouthed stare. "Make them believe you," she mouthed before taking her place in the sixth and final Council seat.

# 14

## First Blood

Robby slammed the crypt door. The girl, the creature, Briony Morrow—whatever she was—was already hurling herself against it from the other side, pushing and pounding with all her fury. The broken door chain lay useless and discarded at his feet, and it took all of Robby's strength to hold the door shut while Becca scrambled for something to wedge against it. He threw his weight into it again, harder now. "She's too strong!" he yelled. "I can't hold her for long."

"Try this!" Stumbling under the weight of a heavy rock, Becca jammed it against the base of the bronze door, gasping. "It might hold her long enough for us to get away."

Robby switched shoulders. "It's going to have to!"

"It's daytime, Robby, maybe she can't—"

"We don't know for sure." His gaze flitted to the cold morning sun, the patchy clouds, the dark and overcast sky. "I don't want to find out!"

Becca ground the rock harder against the door. "Ready?"

"Now!"

He put all his strength into one last shove, then took off into the morning light with Becca just ahead of him. They ran without looking back until finally Robby had no choice but to drop to his hands and knees, panting for air. Branches weighted with red and brown leaves loomed over them at the cemetery's edge.

Leaning against a slanting grave marker, Becca said, "It still doesn't add up." Her breathing came fast and heavy. "The overnight bag. The chains cut from the outside. What if that wasn't actually Briony Morrow in there?"

"It looked just like her photograph." Robby shook his head. He could barely hear his own thoughts over the wind whooshing through the trees. "She was sleeping in Briony Morrow's coffin! Normal people don't do things like that. And her eyes—the way they glowed—did you see—"

"I'm *still* seeing them!" Becca forced his gaze back the way they'd come. The girl from the crypt was moving like a shadow through the dark patches beneath the trees. Her red eyes scanned the patchwork of gravestones for them.

"We have to keep moving," Robby huffed. "No, Becca, not *that* way! Not into the…" He trailed off. She was already too far ahead to hear his rasping voice.

Squeezing through a gap in the iron fence, she finally turned as Robby caught up to her. "Not into the dark woods," she realized, too late. "Sorry!"

It was nearly as black as night on this side of the fence. The early sunlight was all but gone beneath the thick tree cover, but they had no choice now but to keep going. Briars crunched underfoot, frosty and stiff, and as Robby looked back toward the graveyard he saw Briony Morrow already gaining on them. She was yelling something, but he couldn't make it out.

Shadowed by the woods, they had no choice but to hope for a gap of sunlight up ahead. They ran until their lungs burned again and all the trees began to look the same. The woods grew quieter as they came to another stop. Robby leaned into a slender birch and tried not to collapse as the world spun around him.

"I think… maybe… we lost her?" Becca said, scanning the woods.

Cold daylight filtered through the trees, dappling the woods with jagged slats of sunshine. Robby followed an old stone wall mostly swallowed by the woods until he reached a wider trail rutted with tire marks. Something about it seemed familiar. "This is part of the haunted hayride from the Halloween fair. We must not be far from the edge of the woods now." He waved a hand past the stone wall. "I think I see more daylight."

A branch snapped nearby.

Robby's head jerked up. Leaves crinkled nearby. An acorn plinked to the ground. Suddenly Becca's hand was like a vise around his, and a pair of red eyes glimmered back at him from the depths of the woods. He turned the other direction to find *another* pair of eyes in the woods. Then another and another.

"Is it her?" Becca asked.

Robby struggled to keep his voice steady. "No, I think it's Lucinda and Margery and… and…"

"T-Rex and Joey," Becca finished for him.

All four of their missing classmates crept into full view, fangs bared and eyes ablaze. In the weird in-between gloom of the woods, their transformation was even clearer than it had been at full dark. Their faces were bloodless, and something about the way they moved seemed different, too. Angry. Predatory. Hungry.

"Why aren't they bothered by the sunlight?" Becca whispered.

Robby risked a glance through the treetops. The morning sky was dense and moody, the air thick with the scents of the distant marsh. The sun was trying to poke through, but it was weak. "There isn't enough of it. Stay behind me."

"You stay behind me! I still have my wooden stake."

Robby scooped up a dead branch, desperately running through possible escape routes. None of them seemed very good. He crowded back-to-back with Becca as their classmates drew nearer. "We'll have to run for it. If you see a gap, don't hesitate."

"You, too," Becca said.

The four vampires drew into a tighter circle. Robby raised the broken branch like a baseball bat. Becca white-knuckled her wooden stake. Lucinda and Margery were so close now that Robby could have poked them with his branch.

"I—I loaned you my math notes last year," Becca called to Lucinda. "Remember?"

Lucinda took another step closer. "You will be next in our circle of blood."

Robby tried to draw her attention. "Lucinda, if you're still in there—"

"I don't think she is," said Becca.

"The noose grows tighter. The Shadow Lady will have her revenge."

Robby was so focused on Lucinda that he nearly missed Margery. Her matted hair snapped like a whip as she hurled him high into the trees. His backpack snagged around a branch, and he dangled helplessly while all four vampires trained their eyes on Becca. They hadn't even given him a moment's thought.

It was Becca they were after, only Becca.

Last night she'd been worried about T-Rex following her from the church. She'd rejected him in seventh grade, but what if that didn't matter? What if T-Rex wanted her for his first victim anyway? Robby yelled for Becca to run, but she seemed frozen in place now. He tried again to wriggle free, only catching glimpses as T-Rex lunged at Becca and swatted her stake from her hands. Joey came up from behind while Lucinda and Margery grabbed her by the arms. She flailed. She kicked.

But T-Rex was faster.

He went for her neck with animal speed and Becca screamed. Then T-Rex screamed too. As he recoiled, his scream became a wounded howl. His mouth was bloodied, and Becca's face was white as the grave, but he seemed to be the one in pain. The other vampires loosened their grips in surprise, and as Becca began to thrash again, something small and bright glinted against her collarbone—her pendant reflecting a sliver of light through the dense tree cover.

Robby lunged at the nearest branch and pulled with all his strength until the shaft of light widened a little more. Steam rose from Lucinda's pale skin and Robby yanked harder, this time catching Margery and Joey, too. The strap of Robby's backpack was sliding now, giving way, and then with a sudden burst he broke free and fell so hard it knocked the air from his lungs. Unsteadily, he clambered to his feet only to find the four vampires fleeing into the shadowy woods. Smoke hissed off their skin like a smoldering fire.

Becca rolled onto her back, moaning. There were two red puncture marks on her neck, round and raised like hives. An eternity passed as Robby shook her, calling her name. He was afraid of shaking too hard, but terrified she wouldn't come back to him if he didn't. Finally, her eyes fluttered open. Her Star of David pendant had broken off its chain in the struggle, but it glinted again in the sunlight when she opened her hand. "I'm—I'm okay," she said weakly. "I don't think T-Rex liked my pendant very much."

"Religious symbols," Robby said breathlessly. "Vampires are repelled by true faith."

Becca gave him an anemic grin. "Let's hear it for my… Jewish… superpowers." She rose to a sitting position, using his weight for support. Her color still wasn't right. Her strength was already fading again.

"We need to get you to a doctor," he said.

"No, I just want to… go… home."

"Becca, he *bit* you!"

"Just a nibble." Somehow, she managed another weak smile, but then her expression became serious. "Robby, you don't think—I'm not going to—to become like him…?"

Robby shook his head. "The transformation takes two bites, not just one. Now that we know he's after you, we're not going to give him a second chance."

Becca half-smiled at his reassurances as he helped her to her feet, but otherwise made no indication she'd heard him.

# 15

## The Council of Witches

"Prena?"

Abby's mouth hung open. She shivered at the stiff wind cutting through her cloak, the quickly falling snow on her head and shoulders, the dancing glow of the pyre flames. On her silver throne, Prena now wore the same impassive expression as the women seated beside her—the rest of the Council of Witches. She folded her hands and leaned back, showing no trace of her previous familiarity.

"You will address her as Sister Novus," said the woman seated to Prena's left. A fair-skinned witch with golden hair and a rigid posture, she was one of the most severe-looking women Abby had ever seen.

"Sister… Novus?" Abby croaked.

"And I am Sister Severitas," the golden-haired woman replied. "Also seated before you are Sister Constantia, Sister Prudentia, Sister Clementia, and Sister Veritas. We are the Council of Witches."

"Severitas, Clementia, Veritas," Amethyst muttered. "Tina forgot to mention there'd be a Latin test."

*Tina forgot to mention a lot of things.*

"'This royal throne of kings,'" breathed Daisy, taking it all in with wide eyes, "'this fortress built against infection and the hand of war...'"

"Six silver thrones," whispered Delphi, wide-eyed. "My premonition."

Abby had almost forgotten her friends were there. Without meaning to, she took a step toward the pyre, but the flames hissed and popped at her approach. Prena had walked right through the fire, but Abby couldn't see how. Backing up, she bumped shoulders with Piper, who gave her a queasy smile without taking her eyes from the seated witches.

It was impossible to take in all six of them at once, but as Abby's gaze passed over each throne, she tried to put names to the remaining faces. Sister Constantia was a plump dark-skinned woman with friendly eyes. Sister Prudentia had a narrow face and pink hair down to her shoulders. Sister Clementia and Sister Veritas both leaned forward in their seats, but that was where the similarity ended. Sister Clementia had high cheeks and a wand stuck through a tight hair bun, while olive-skinned Sister Veritas had hypnotic eyes that glowed like candle flames. Abby found herself looking away from them, and her gaze fell once again on Prena.

*Sister Novus,* she corrected.

"Do you girls have so little regard for this Council that you would come late to your own Summoning?" asked narrow-faced Sister Prudentia, her pink hair glinting briefly orange in the firelight. Her English was so sharply accented that Abby struggled to follow the flow of her words.

Catching Abby's eye, Prena tilted her chin almost imperceptibly toward the other witch, her eyes narrowed in warning. Abby fought the urge to ignore Prena's advice out of spite, to let her embarrassment at being deceived win out. But Tina had said they could trust Prena, so for her sake she would play along. At least for now.

"We're very sorry." Abby forced her voice into its sweetest register. "We were all just so impressed with the Midnight Castle. We lost track of time."

"The fault was mine," said Prena, speaking over Sister Prudentia before the other witch could reply. "I lingered too long before bringing them before this Council."

"Out in the cold," said Amethyst, shivering.

"Child, you speak when you should be listening." Sister Severitas glared until Amethyst looked away. To the whole coven, she said, "Despite your unusual beginnings, you girls show great potential. Many questions remain, however, and I will not tolerate further interruptions while we determine whether your coven shall be permitted to remain intact."

Prena leaned forward on her throne. "I myself have already seen enough to—"

"You will have an opportunity to address this Council at the appropriate time, young sister."

"I may be the youngest on this Council, but is my voice not equal to yours?"

A crease formed between Sister Severitas's eyes, but she nodded. "Of course, Sister Novus. The Council benefits from your wisdom in all matters."

"I was tasked with assessing these girls upon their arrival," Prena said. "If it is the aim of this Council to assign witches of complementary abilities and personalities to each coven, I have seen evidence that this coven is already such a mix. This one"—she tilted her chin toward Delphi—"possesses powerful precognitive abilities she has only begun to harness. Her twin provides the group with a touch of whimsy that augurs well for creative spellcasting in her future. The one called Amethyst speaks her mind with honesty and candor."

"Oh fun, it was all a personality test," Amethyst grumbled.

"Piper brings kindness and a connection with the animal world. Olivia possesses an independent streak that may serve them well in times of conflict." Prena's gaze settled on Abby. "And this one is both their leader and their conscience. A rare combination, wouldn't you agree, Sisters?"

An undercurrent of tension crackled between the thrones. Sister Severitas gave only the slightest clench of her jaw in response, there and gone in the blink of an eye. "Wouldn't *you* agree, Sister Novus, that we cannot know what ideas were placed in their young minds by the witch called Joanna Greylocke?"

Abby startled at the use of Miss Winters's real name, the name their former teacher had kept hidden from them until the moment she meant to betray them.

"But we can look to the past as a guide to what may befall such a chaotic assemblage," Sister Severitas continued. "Hangings. Burnings. *Disobedience.*"

"Perhaps you place too high a value on obedience," suggested Prena.

"Perhaps you do not value it enough," countered Sister Severitis, her voice rising to be heard above the wind.

The pink-haired witch with the pinched expression—the one called Sister Prudentia—stroked her chin, considering. Her gaze passed over Abby before landing on Olivia. "There may be other issues within this group as well. I fear this one will never thrive in such a coven. There is great strength within her, great potential for leadership—but not with these girls. The balance is off."

"We could pair her with that meek witch from Belarus," suggested Sister Constantia, "or the one from Guizhou province so in need of a firm hand?"

Sister Veritas nodded thoughtfully. "She would do quite well with that stubborn girl from Vermont, I think."

"Then we are agreed the one called Olivia would be better placed within another coven," Sister Severitas replied. "Time and distance are no obstacle to the formation of a coven better suited to her—"

"No!" The word surprised Abby even as it slipped from her lips. Her heartbeat raced as the eyes of the Council turned on her all at once and she stood mesmerized, unsure where to look or who to address. Risking a glance at Olivia, she found the other girl staring back at her, too. Olivia's typically expressive features were a mask this time.

"Let's not be hasty about such a decision," agreed Prena.

"A coven can have only one leader, Sister Novus." Folding her arms, Sister Severitas allowed a sly smile to cross her face. When she spoke again, she addressed Abby. "Would you deny Olivia the opportunity to reach her full potential? Would you hold her back simply to keep that which is comfortable and familiar intact?"

"No, I… Of course not."

Abby thought of Delphi's premonition. *You weren't like the rest of us. You weren't one of us.* She thought about her conversation with Olivia just before they'd reached the High Tower, too. Maybe she really *didn't* know the first thing about what Olivia wanted. Her cheeks flushed at the memory of it. Did any of them really know Olivia that well? "I wouldn't want to speak for her," Abby told Sister Severitas, "but I think Olivia should have her own say."

Olivia met Abby's gaze. Her cheeks were apple red in the chill air. Her blonde hair and dark cloak whipped in the phantom breeze. Her expression was indecipherable. "What I really want," she said, "is to—"

"Want, want, want!" cried Sister Clementia, removing her wand from her tight bun and shaking her head until her dark hair fell free. "This is precisely the problem with young witches today. It's always about what you want. Never mind what serves the greater good."

"Whose greater good?" Abby cut in.

"Abby, that's quite enough." Prena's voice had another warning edge to it.

But it didn't feel like enough to Abby, not now that she'd finally found her voice again. She was tired of her coven being talked about as if they weren't even there. Tired of being at the Midnight Castle, period. "Aren't you the ones making decisions based on what's comfortable and familiar? Don't you have the power to make things better in this world if you really wanted to? Back home there are people in danger. You could help them. Or you could just step aside and let *us* help them. Instead, you've called us here to decide if we're even allowed to be together? Why do you get a say?"

For a moment there was only silence on both sides of the pyre. Abby let out a halting breath, already regretting her outburst. Her arms prickled with gooseflesh at her own audacity. Her friends stared at her wide-eyed. She'd done the one thing Tina had warned about, and it had felt good, even necessary. But what if she'd ruined it for everyone, not just herself?

"Nice job keeping your cool," Amethyst whispered to her.

Abby blew out a worried breath. "I know."

"Calm and collected," Olivia said through gritted teeth.

"I said I know!" Abby hissed.

After a moment, the witch with the hypnotic eyes made a soft wheezing noise.

"Something amuses you?" asked Sister Severitas.

Sister Veritas chuckled again. "We have a saying where I am from. *Hora pars vitae.* 'Every hour is part of life.' What seems important now is but one moment in an eternal tapestry. But of course that wisdom can only come with age. Abby, do not assume the worst of this Council simply because we choose caution as a matter of course."

Sister Severitas's nose twitched. "Do we need further proof that the taint of their rogue mentor's bloodline is too strong? She too once stood before us in such a fury—"

Abby's mouth fell open. "Miss Winters was *here*? At the Midnight Castle?"

"Joanna Greylocke was here," Sister Severitas corrected. "Long, long ago."

"One does not easily forget an untrained witch who slipped through the cracks so regrettably. She found us, not the other way around, and came before us quite uninvited," replied Sister Veritas with a note of irritation.

"It had never been done before," agreed Sister Constantia.

Sister Prudentia nodded. "Nor since."

"Nor shall it ever happen again," said Sister Severitas.

"What—what did she want with you?" Abby stammered.

"To *complain*," said Sister Severitas with a scowl. "To rage that we did not help her sisters. But they weren't even her real sisters, were they? Not even witches. I will tell you what I told her. This Council does not concern itself in the affairs of common people. For your sake, we can only hope you learn the lesson better than her. When we would not give her what she wanted, she left and we never saw her again."

"Because she didn't let you," Abby blurted, and somehow—absurdly—she felt proud that Miss Winters had evaded the Council of Witches so thoroughly. "You looked for her, I know you did. She lived three hundred years without being caught by you. She must have been even more powerful than you knew. Even without your training."

Sister Constantia's lips twitched in a smile. "I think I may like this one."

"She's reckless," said Sister Severitas. "Hot headed. Impetuous."

"But brave," countered Prena.

"Rude, though," said Sister Prudentia.

Prena cocked her head. "Yet courageous."

Sister Severitas leveled her unkind gaze at Abby. "And angry. What do you have to be so angry about, little girl?"

"For starters, maybe she doesn't like being called a little girl," Amethyst snapped before Abby could reply.

"They're *all* quite spirited," said Prena, leaning forward now as if she could sense the turning of a tide. "None can argue with that."

A smile crept to the corners of Sister Veritas's mouth. "With small risks there are but small rewards. Perhaps they would each do well if we split this coven, but only in an ordinary sort of way. United, they might be exceptional. I vote to keep them together." The tip of her wand glowed green as she directed it toward the pyre. "For now, at least."

"As do I," said Prena, also pointing her wand at the fire.

"And me," added Sister Clementia and Sister Constantia at the same time. The pyre had been flickering between red and green with each new vote, and as Sister Severitas and Sister Prudentia lowered their wands, it grew brighter until at last the flames glowed entirely green.

"The Council has spoken," said Prena triumphantly.

Sister Severitas looked upon the six girls gravely. "Indeed it has. You may remain together, though I do not think it wise. Sister Novus will see you returned to your home. But remember this: You will be watched with great interest by this Council from this day forward."

Amethyst sighed and shook her head. With a whisper just for Abby, she said, "Well, that's not super convenient, is it?"

# 16

## Homecoming

When they reached the bottom of the High Tower, Prena brought her broom down directly in front of Abby. "What were you thinking?" she demanded. "I warned you to be humble before the Council, Abby. Courteous and smart, not whatever that was supposed to be."

"I'm more interested in what you didn't tell us." Abby was still angry at herself for losing her cool in front of the Council, but even angrier at Prena for deceiving them. "We had no reason to think you were on the Council."

Prena's shoulders slumped. "I needed you to trust me."

"By lying to us?" Abby asked, while the rest of the coven looked on, nodding their agreement.

"I never lied to you."

"A lie of omission is still a lie," Abby snapped.

"Fair enough, but I was giving you good advice."

"Strange how you wanted our trust without ever giving yours," Abby told her. "It all worked out in the end anyway, though, didn't it… Sister Novus?"

Prena's eyebrows flashed up. "That's the name they gave me, not one I chose for myself. It means young and fresh—new, to be more precise. The rest of the Council thinks to remind me of my age, which is much closer to yours than theirs. It's a way to keep me in my place. Sound familiar?"

Abby made a noncommittal noise in the back of her throat.

"You were lucky today because your performance amused the others, but do not think that means you won over any hearts or minds. You merely entertained an audience. I wouldn't advise you to make a habit of it."

"I never want to come back here again," Abby said, shaking her head. "I just want to go home and see my friends." Prena threw her hands into the air, looking at once both exasperated and already spent of anger. She let out a deep sigh and looked ready to say something more, but Abby chose not to give her the opportunity. "You heard the Council. It's time for us to go home. So, let's go home."

Sighing again, Prena led the coven out of the castle in silence. Abby still felt the flush of heat on her cheeks, the rush of anger at having been treated like a pawn in some game she didn't understand. But beneath all that was a deep embarrassment. Prena *hadn't* lied, really. She hadn't had to lie because Abby had filled in all the blanks with her own assumptions.

Keeping their heads down against the driving wind, the coven crossed the creaking drawbridge and emerged onto the lantern-lit path to the tower where they'd first arrived. Abby tried to pull Olivia aside on the way, but the girl shook her off and kept walking. "What were you going to say?" Abby called after her, undeterred. "Back there with the Council? What you really want is...?"

"For you to mind your own business," Olivia replied, lowering her head again and marching resolutely onward.

When they reached the tower, Prena heaved open the heavy door and the girls spilled through it in a rush to get out of the cold.

On the upper floor they shed their cloaks and took their assigned places in the hexagram, shivering in the clothes they'd worn to school that morning.

Abby tried to look busy while Prena said goodbye to each of them one by one. Coming to her last, Prena laid a hand on Abby's shoulder and leaned close to whisper. "I am sorry for deceiving you," she said, her short shimmery hair brushing Abby's cheek. "I'm new to the Council, and I don't share their old beliefs, but we all must play the hand we're dealt until one day we hold the better cards. Rest assured that day will come."

Abby frowned. "What do you mean?"

"I think you can see that the Council seeks only to preserve how things are rather than how they should be. You and I look at the world differently." She swept her hands apart, flashing the same quick smile that had made her seem so approachable when she'd first appeared. "I want to change the Council, and to do that I need allies that Sister Severitas can't control—allies who share my vision of a world where witches live and work among mortals rather than hiding from them out of fear or superiority. I believe we have gifts to offer the wider world, and that we should share them. Tina told me I could rely upon this coven, but I needed to see for myself if our beliefs were truly aligned. So, yes, I evaluated you. I tested you. You passed."

"You told me not to even ask the Council for help," Abby replied, feeling another rush of indignation. "I don't see how you're any different than they are."

"What would you have me do? Tear it all down? Lead an uprising? Start a civil war among witches?"

"No, obviously not! But people are in danger right now. People that matter to me. So what if you want to change things at some point in the future—that doesn't help right now."

"How we make a change is just as important as the kind of change we hope to make. Victory means changing minds. It means changing from within. It's easy to believe in simple solutions when you're young, but many problems do not have simple answers. Real change is slow and difficult and often very frustrating, but I believe it's the only way that's morally acceptable." Prena leaned closer. "I wonder, though, if you look more closely at your situation, whether someone is already trying to help."

"What's that supposed to mean? Who?"

Prena shrugged. "Something for you to consider. As to the larger picture, please know there are others who feel as you and I do, but for now we must be patient, we must be clever, and we must wait for the right moment. In the proper environment you can start a fire with a single spark."

Abby looked up, surprised at her words. "What did you just say?"

"Only that if we wait for the right moment, it may simply take—"

"No, the part about a single spark," Abby said impatiently. Her gaze shot to Delphi, who was deep in hushed conversation with her twin. "That's what Delph said during her premonition. 'You can start a fire with a single spark.'"

"Is it? How interesting." Prena's face was guileless. "Well, she's quite perceptive. Perhaps we should both think on that until we meet again." Prena retreated a step, her hand slipping from Abby's shoulder. She pushed something cold and small into Abby's hands. "The Council will be keeping an eye on your coven, but if you need me for anything in the meantime—anything I can do without compromising my position, you understand—use this. I would still like to prove to you that our interests are aligned."

Abby's gaze dropped to her palm. Prena had given her a small colorless crystal, ordinary and forgettable. "What is it?"

"A keystone. Think of it as a back door into the Midnight Castle. It will not allow anyone with malicious intent to enter, but something tells me you and your friends could still cause mayhem quite by accident, so keep it secret and keep it safe. This is me trusting you, Abby. I hope someday you will choose to trust me again as well." Prena raised her voice to the group and said, "It's time to send you girls home."

Delphi was peering at the starry sky through the tower windows. "What time will it be when we get there?"

"That depends on the position of the earth, the moon, the stars. This is complicated magic and not to be trifled with." Prena held a thumb to the open window as if measuring. A strong breeze ruffled her green hair. "With Mercury in retrograde, some spacetime interruption is to be expected." She paused, pursing her lips. "It should be late afternoon in Willow Cove. You'll have been gone a full day."

Piper reached for her inhaler. "We are time travelers."

Prena snapped her wand like an orchestral conductor, and all at once Abby's stomach lurched into her throat. The sharp angles of the tower blurred to softness. Her fingers stretched and grew as long as tree branches. Her body flattened like a paper doll, and she squeezed her eyes against a swirl of colors. There was a moment of absolute stillness—no sound, no light, no sensations at all—and then the world righted itself and she collapsed to the floor, blinking and wobbling on her hands and knees.

Color returned around the edges of her vision. The animal smells of Tina's veterinary clinic reached her next. Then came the sounds—barking and mewing, the caw of a hungry bird—and then her friends gasping and groaning inside the hexagram.

"Oh, that *cannot* be good for us," Amethyst said.

Abby stumbled to her feet, instinctively patting her arms and chest and face to make sure they were all where they were supposed to be. The candles at the tips of the hexagram had burned to waxy nubs, and Tina's desk lamp was dark, too. Only the glint of fading sunlight outside the clinic lit the room. There was no sign of Tina herself. Hadn't she promised she'd be waiting for them when they returned? Abby fetched her duffel bag from the corner and reached inside for her phone. Prena had been right about one thing, at least—an entire day had passed during the short time they'd spent at the Midnight Castle.

Piper, who'd gone into the hallway in search of Flapper, suddenly burst back into the room holding the seagull to her chest like an overprotective mother. "He's starving!" she declared. "Hours, it's been hours since he ate—"

"Why don't you ask Flapper where Tina went?" said Daisy.

Piper clicked her tongue at the seagull, then nodded and listened as he squawked back. "He says Tina left in a hurry this morning. Hours ago! She never even gave him the pizza she promised."

Abby's heart beat faster. "Piper, why did she leave in a hurry?"

"I'm getting to it, jeez. Tina got a phone call from Robby." Piper clicked her tongue again and tilted her head as the seagull replied. Her forehead creased. "Some kind of emergency."

Abby's breath caught in her throat. "What happened to Robby?"

Piper's eyes widened as Flapper's squawks grew more insistent. She clicked her tongue again. The seagull let out another indignant squawk, then turned his attention toward her springy dark curls. "Oh no," Piper said.

"What?" asked Abby.

"It's Becca. Something terrible has happened to Becca."

Yellow streetlights twinkled in the dark November sky as Abby and her coven zipped toward the Heights on spare broomsticks borrowed from the clinic. Wood smoke puffed lazily from the chimney of the two-story colonial where Becca lived with her mother, but inside they found her lying with her eyes closed in her bedroom. Tina was tinkering with an IV drip she'd brought from the veterinary clinic. Robby hovered at Becca's bedside with one of his sleeves rolled up and a white bandage around the crook of his elbow. His face was so much paler than usual that Abby wondered if he'd just donated blood.

She stashed her broom against the wall and crowded around Becca's bed with the others. There was a tight bandage wrapped around Becca's neck. Her face had turned ominously white. "What happened? Did she lose a lot of blood?" Abby asked. She began rolling up her own sleeve. "I can donate, too."

"I would not advise it," said Tina, squirting disinfectant onto her hands and shooing Flapper away from the bed. "Witch blood is a tricky thing. Besides, it's not so much what she lost as what she may yet become if we aren't vigilant." Placing a hand on Abby's shoulder, she managed a weak smile. "I'm sorry I had to leave the portal before you girls returned. Thank goodness you're all home safe."

"Was that ever in question?" asked Piper.

"You should've told us about Prena," Amethyst said.

"I told you everything I was at liberty to say," Tina replied.

"I want to hear all about your meeting with the Council as soon as possible, but for now there's still a great deal to be done if we're to keep Becca safe through the night."

"What happened?" Abby repeated.

"It was daytime," Robby said, running his fingers through his tangled curls, "but there wasn't much sunlight. We were surrounded by—by our classmates. They were able to move around in the shadows somehow, and now she's—"

"*Fine*," Becca said, coughing a little as she struggled to sit up. "I'm totally fine."

"You were bitten by a vampire. You are the very opposite of fine," Tina said gravely.

"Well, I *feel* fine. More embarrassed than anything."

Tina clenched her jaw. "Please lie back down."

"I'm fine," Becca mouthed again as she sank obediently back into her pillow.

Tina brushed a hand against Becca's forehead. "In time your body will correct the imbalance on its own," she conceded, "but only if we prevent a second bite. Medically I've done as much as I can." Turning to the others, she added, "What Becca needs now is protection. You may be certain the creature who did this will return tonight to finish what it began. You girls must be ready."

Piper reached for her inhaler. "Us?"

"I'm afraid it's my turn to visit the Council now, and I could be gone several days." Tina raised a hand to cut short the coven's protests. "It's a direct order. Surely I don't need to explain again how one does not simply decline a Summons. Before I leave, I've got to take Becca's mother somewhere safe. I've used the *Obscuro* charm on her, but it's too dangerous for her to be here tonight, especially in that compromised condition. Abby and Amethyst, you two will stay here in this room with Becca and Robby. Piper and Olivia, I want you both on the front porch. Daisy, Delphi, back of the house—you'll form a perimeter guard. Wands out the moment any of you even suspects something is wrong, understood?"

"Understood," they all said together.

"Vampires cannot enter a home without an invitation, but vampirism is a powerful branch of magic, and vampires have many tricks—hypnosis, telepathy, just to name a few. You must all keep your wits about you. This is likely to be the longest night of your lives."

"So much for my nice warm bed," said Amethyst, shaking her head as Tina vanished down the stairs.

Olivia rolled her eyes. "At least *you'll* be inside. Piper, bring your seagull and let's go. We're on porch duty."

"He has a name!" Piper squawked.

When the twins had gone, too, Abby closed the bedroom door and returned to Becca's side. An owl hooted somewhere in the dark beyond, its deep-throated call so loud that Abby's gaze flicked to the window to check that it was closed. Windswept branches scraped against the glass. Treetops slanted in the breeze. Robby sagged into a seat by the window, resting his head in his hands.

"It was T-Rex," he said. "He went straight for her."

"Vampirism has not improved his breath," Becca rasped. She scratched at the bandage around her neck as if it itched.

"What else can you tell us," Abby asked as Tina's car pulled away from the driveway, "now that we're alone?"

"We were looking for the Morrow family crypt in the grave-yard—"

"Robby, you promised!" Abby blurted, unable to help herself.

"We only meant to find it, not go in," he said, "but someone else had already gotten there first. The chain on the door had been cut from the outside. We couldn't wait for you, Abby. We had to find out what was going on."

"The sun was up," Becca added, reaching for her neck again. "We thought it was safe."

"We found the remains of Julia Morrow inside. She was definitely a vampire, but someone staked her a long time ago." Robby clicked his phone and held it up for Abby and Amethyst to see. "Whoever did it used some kind of magic to seal her inside the crypt, too. Look at this."

"'Sealed by stake and bound by blood,'" Abby read aloud, "'never to curse the living again.' That sounds like blood magic."

"What's that?" asked Robby.

"Most spells weave magic from the world around us—air, wind, fire, that kind of thing. Blood magic comes from within us. It's supposed to be more powerful, especially when it comes to creating new spells, but also more taxing. Tina hasn't taught us much about it, but Miss Winters used it last year when she tried to bring her sisters back."

"Definitely not an experience I'm eager to repeat." Amethyst squinted at the photo. "Who would have used it to seal Julia Morrow in her crypt?"

"If they were trying to protect the people of Willow Cove, it probably wasn't someone who was working for the Council," Abby said.

Becca struggled to sit up straighter. "We found Briony Morrow, too, only she was a lot less dead than her twin sister. She chased us into the woods, where T-Rex and the others were waiting."

"You're sure it was her?" Amethyst asked.

"It was definitely your Victorian goth girl," Becca said, rubbing again at her bandage. "Briony is the piece that doesn't add up for me. I think she's the one who broke into the crypt. Why would she do that if she was the one who started the vampire plague in the first place? What would she be looking for—*ugh*, this bandage!" Becca slid her fingers under it and scratched until her neck grew splotchy. "I wish I could just take it off."

Robby was looking at her with concern. "Better not."

Becca pulled her hand away from her neck, embarrassed. "I don't know what's come over me, honestly. I feel fine otherwise." With effort, her face brightened, and she reached for her phone. Her eyebrows slanted in concentration as she tapped and scrolled. "Being bedridden all day did give me time to do some more research on your situation," she told Abby and Amethyst. "You asked me to look into that realtor for you, Poppy Delacroix?"

Abby sat up straight, her breath catching. "I'd almost forgotten about that."

"Don't tell me she's a vampire, too?" said Amethyst.

"No, it's even weirder than that. I couldn't find anything useful about her, so I started looking into your new house instead. It's not just an exact twin of your old farmhouse, Amethyst. It's one of *six* identical houses."

Amethyst leaned forward. "What?"

"They were all created by the same architect. They have the same design, the same floorplan, square footage, everything. Three of the six houses are currently unoccupied. Yours burned down last year," Becca told Amethyst, "one was just bought by Abby's mom, and the final one"—she turned the screen for Abby and Amethyst to see, a look of undisguised triumph on her face—"is owned by Poppy Delacroix herself."

"That can't be a coincidence," said Abby.

"I was actually pulling for the happy coincidence theory," Amethyst said, "just this once."

"What could it all mean?" asked Becca, letting out a little groan as she repositioned herself against the pillows.

"That we need to arrange another talk with our realtor, for starters." Abby crossed her arms. "Add that to our to-do list, I guess."

"Slay evil vampire sire, cure undead classmates, confront sketchy realtor," said Amethyst, ticking them off on her fingers one at a time. "Did I miss anything?"

"Deal with intrigue at the Midnight Castle," Abby said.

"What's that?" asked Robby.

"A very long story." Abby pulled up another chair alongside the bed. Outside the wind continued to whistle. Through Becca's bedroom window, a streetlight played tricks with shadows on the walls. Abby twirled her wand between her fingers, considering. Then after a moment she said, "I suppose we have time." Her gaze drifted to the bandage around Becca's neck, then back to Robby. "Tina did say it's going to be the longest night of our lives."

# 17

## The Longest Night

A cold breeze flicked at Abby's face some time later, stirring her gently from her thoughts. She didn't remember turning out the lights, but somehow Becca's bedside lamp had gone dark, and the only illumination came from the soft glow of a hallway light peeking in from under the door. Blurred shapes assembled around her as she adjusted her glasses: Becca's bed, solid and square in the inky darkness; Robby hunched in his chair across from her; Amethyst snoozing with her mouth open and her head on his shoulder.

Why didn't she remember any of them falling asleep?

Turning her gaze to Becca's bed, Abby sat up sharply, suddenly alert. The bed was empty. She fumbled to her feet, opening her mouth to sound the alarm when she spotted Becca looming before the window with her back to the room. Heat seemed to rise off her in waves. Her neck bandage had been tossed to the floor and her loose pajamas fluttered in the breeze of an open window that Abby was certain had been closed earlier in the night.

*Vampires have many tricks.*

Her heart pounding, Abby called softly to Becca. When there was no response, she placed a hand on Becca's shoulder and gasped. Her friend's skin burned hot to the touch and her cotton top was soaked through with sweat. The two small wounds on her neck were raised and angry, and the skin around the bite marks had a puckered redness to it, as if she'd been scratching.

"Becca, did you turn out the light? Open the window?"

"I—I don't know," Becca said in an airy half whisper as Abby turned her away from the window. Her face was slack, her expression almost trancelike. "I thought I heard music. Do you hear the music?"

Abby strained to hear but detected nothing beyond the indistinct voices of Piper and Olivia on the porch below. A bright red light flashed once in the distance, but after a moment Abby recognized it as a nighttime beacon for airplanes flying near the water tower on the other side of the Heights.

"You're burning up," she told Becca. "You should be lying down."

Becca shook her head and resisted being directed back toward the bed. "It's like an undertone," she said, "there but… not there? Like a siren call. Remember the sirens from our Greek mythology unit in Western Civilization?"

"They lured sailors to their death with enchanted singing," Abby said. "You're not going to hurl yourself out the window, are you?"

Becca's smile was strangely muted. "No, I… I shouldn't do that. I feel strange, though. I'm not sure what's come over me. You really don't hear the music?" Becca craned her neck toward the open window, then spun back to it so quickly Abby nearly lost her grip. "If I could just go outside for a second…"

Abby's gaze darted to where Robby and Amethyst slept huddled together, and with her left hand she freed her wand from her back pocket and pointed it at the bedside lamp. A quick spell illuminated the room in a burst of bright light.

"What's going on?" Robby asked, blinking awake.

Abby guided Becca toward her bed while Amethyst moved to the open window, peering into the darkness beyond.

"I think she's in some kind of trance," Abby said, pulling open the covers and easing Becca onto the mattress. "Lie down again. We'll watch over you."

"You're a good friend, Abby. I'm going to miss you when I… when I…" Her face had that bloodless pallor again, even in the bright light of the bed lamp. "I don't want to go, but the music… the voice… she wants me to go to *him*."

"Whose voice?" Robby asked.

Becca snapped upright, her eyes wide open. It took all of Abby's and Robby's combined strength to keep her in the bed. "The Lady of Shadows."

"You're not going anywhere, Becca," Abby said.

"I don't want to go to T-Rex. Don't let me go to him!" Becca cried, louder now.

Robby stared frantically at the window. "They're trying to lure her out."

"Then they're going to be very disappointed." Abby cast a restraining spell on Becca's wrists and ankles. Her friend's body snapped back to the mattress with a sudden *whoomph* that startled them both. "We won't let her go. I promise we won't."

At the window, Amethyst sucked in a loud breath. "I see red eyes."

"It's the beacon from the water tower," Abby told her. "I saw it, too."

"Did this beacon also have arms and legs? Because otherwise I think we're looking at two different things."

Abby checked the pattern of her restraining spell to make sure it would hold for at least a few minutes, then crossed to the window. Robby was right on her heels. In the thick maple tree across the street, a figure dressed all in black leapt between branches with animal grace, slipping from shadow to shadow as if she were made from the darkness itself. Her face was white as ivory, her eyes like glowing cinders. Long dark hair swirled about as she settled onto the next branch in a balanced crouch.

Robby dropped his hands to the windowsill. "That's her. That's Briony Morrow."

"My Victorian goth girl," Amethyst said with something like admiration. "Look at the way she moves."

Becca struggled against her restraints. "There's a wooden stake. I stashed it… under… the bed."

Abby remained glued to the window, but Amethyst dropped to her hands and knees, using the blue glow of her wand to peer under the bed. "Got it!" She leapt to her feet, then back to the window.

Briony Morrow was still moving from tree to tree. Abby shouted a warning to Olivia and Piper on the porch below. Piper moved right below Briony's perch, wand out but searching straight ahead into the woods, not up in the branches—not anywhere near the girl.

Abby shouted again, louder. "Piper, look *up*!" Piper's gaze shot upward, but her eyes were drawn to Abby's voice from the window instead of the branches. "The trees!"

The pale form leapt to another branch, then leapt again, further away. Amethyst looped the garden stake through her belt while Piper and Olivia searched below, always two steps behind.

"I'm going after her!" Amethyst yelled, snatching her broom and lifting the window screen.

"Amethyst, wait!" Abby yelled, but her friend was already out the window.

"You have to go help her," Robby said.

"I can't leave you and Becca alone."

"You can't let Amethyst face Briony Morrow alone, either."

Abby swore sharply and called to her own broom. "Get Olivia up here the second I leave. She's the strongest witch in our coven. She'll keep Becca safe!" Abby shouted as she took to the night, her hair whipping wildly behind her. Amethyst was already a blur and Briony Morrow was only visible in glimpses through the trees, a shock of pale white in the distance. Abby leaned harder on her broom and sped after them.

The last of the neighborhood houses glittered like jewels behind her as she careened along the rocky spine of the Heights. Slanted branches leapt at her hands and face. Jagged boulders scraped the tips of her shoes. At the edge of the cliff, the old water tower loomed like a slumbering sentinel over the Hollows far below.

Briony leapt to the grassy field around the tower, then found some kind of animal track and followed it back into the woods. Even on foot she was faster than Abby would have imagined possible. Ahead, Amethyst's wand exploded in a burst of bright light as she aimed for the girl, who easily dodged it. Abby swooped through the disintegrating threads of spellwork and finally pulled alongside her friend.

"What's the plan?" Abby shouted.

"No plan, exactly."

"Why does that not surprise me?"

Pushing ahead of Amethyst's broom, Abby closed the gap between her and the vampire girl. When she'd pulled nearly alongside, she thrust her wand out and cast a restraining spell, but Briony dropped and rolled beneath Abby's broom with lightning speed. The spell fizzled as Abby yanked the head of her broom up and reversed direction. Already the girl was pinballing back toward Becca's house with Amethyst in close pursuit. Putting her shoulders into it, Abby swooped alongside Amethyst again, every muscle in her body screaming from the effort. "Force her to the right," she yelled, dodging sharp branches along the trail. "Keep her headed that way no matter what."

"What's the plan?" Amethyst yelled.

Abby grinned. "No plan, exactly!"

But she did have an idea, and it involved getting Briony Morrow out into the open where she'd have fewer opportunities to get away. Yanking the broom hard, Abby lofted above the treetops and into the clear night sky. She hoped she was making the right decision, hoped that Amethyst could handle herself until she found—*there!* Pale moonlight danced against the top of the water tower. Tall grass rippled like ocean waves in the clearing below it. Just the kind of open space she needed.

Abby's eyes watered as she cut through the wind. A heartbeat later, Briony Morrow burst into the clearing with Amethyst rocketing just behind. For an instant the girl froze in the tall grass, then she scrambled up the water tower's thin metal ladder with hands and feet that barely touched one rung before leaping to the next.

Exactly as Abby had hoped.

Soaring higher, Abby circled the water tower again as the girl reached the top. It was only a matter of seconds now—she had one chance before Briony Morrow could jump back into the cover of the trees. Swooping above her, Abby shoved her wand between her teeth and leapt from her broom. The impact knocked them both to the metal surface and they rolled in a tangle until Abby freed herself with a desperate kick. "Now!" she yelled, ducking to give Amethyst a clear shot.

Amethyst hit the girl head on with a restraining spell and spun around the tower top again and again, pulling the spell's gossamer threads tight as a lasso. Scrambling to her feet, Abby knit a second spell around the girl while Amethyst dismounted.

"Nice work," Abby told her.

"I'm just getting started." Amethyst pulled the garden stake from her belt. "I take no pleasure in slaying my dream girl, but—"

Briony Morrow's eyes bulged. "You would not!"

Abby grabbed her friend's shoulder. "We should question her first. If only Tina were here—"

"Yes, call Tina!" the girl rasped through her restraints.

Abby loosened the weave just a little. "What did you say?"

"Tina… brought me… here," Briony said, still struggling against the spells.

"What are you talking about?" Abby demanded. "She would never—"

"I am here because of her." The vampire girl's voice seemed to grow stronger. She spoke with a British accent in a soft, confident tone. "She's the one who brought me back to this cursed village."

Abby pulled the restraining spell tighter. "No, your name is Briony Morrow and you—"

"Worked that part out for yourself, did you?"

"—you died in 1889—"

"I did no such thing!"

"—and you're lying to us," Abby continued, "because Tina would never bring a vampire to Willow Cove."

Briony's pale features creased in exasperation. Even struggling against her invisible bonds, she forced a laugh. "I'm not a vampire, you idiot."

Amethyst inched closer, raising the stake between them. "Then what exactly are you?"

"A vampire *slayer*." Briony stood straighter, mustering her pride. "And unless you want your friend Becca to join the ranks of the undead, you'd better let me get back to it right away."

# 18

## The Shadow Lady

Abby gaped at the girl. A hundred years might have passed before she found her voice again. "A vampire slayer?" she repeated.

"That's right." Briony bristled against the restraining spell. "A bloody good one, too."

Amethyst shook her head. "But you're so… so…"

"Preternaturally fast? Inhumanly strong?" suggested Briony.

"Pale," said Amethyst. "I was going to say pale."

"One doesn't tend to get much sunlight stalking vampires."

Abby peeled back the girl's upper lip with the tip of her wand. "No fangs."

"Are you *quite* finished?" Briony snapped.

Abby lowered her wand, breaking her hold on the restraining spell. Amethyst did the same and Briony stumbled forward, nearly dropping the pair of them off the side of the water tower together. "If Tina brought you here," Abby asked, "why did you run from us?"

Briony let out an unhappy breath. "Because you chased me!"

"Then why did our friends find you sleeping in a tomb?"

"It was a crypt, not a tomb," Briony corrected. "My *family* crypt, as it happens. One tends not to have much luck finding hotel rooms when you're cursed to look fourteen years old for more than a century."

Abby shook her head. "But if you're really not a vampire…"

"Then the Shadow Lady and her pack are one step closer to your friend," Briony replied. "Every second you waste questioning me puts her in greater danger."

"We thought *you* might be the Shadow Lady," Amethyst said.

Briony's red eyes narrowed. "Then you're even dimmer than I supposed."

Abby's skin prickled in the midnight chill. Something was off, she realized. Not with Briony but with the air itself. "Do you smell…?"

"Smoke," said Amethyst, alarmed. "Fire."

"We must get back to your friend's house," Briony said. "Quickly now!"

Abby mounted her broom and caught the wind without another word. Amethyst pulled Briony onto her broom with her and leapt after Abby. An eerie orange glow illuminated the night sky above the treetops, and the smoke grew thick as they approached the homes along the ridge. Soon Abby's eyes watered from the sting of it, and she cried out as she brought her broom to a stop at the top of Becca's driveway. The house was engulfed in flames. *No, no, no,* she thought, *this can't be happening!* Any one of the girls in the coven could have extinguished a natural fire no matter how quickly it spread.

"That's spellwork!" Amethyst shouted, bringing her broom to a stop beside Abby. "Look at the threads around those flames, Abby, that's sophisticated magic. Who could have done that?"

Abby didn't stop to consider it. Her mind worked frantically in search of a spell to untangle the house fire, but then Amethyst gripped her wand arm and pulled it down. "Save your strength. There's no one in there."

"How can you be sure?"

"Because they're all over there now." Amethyst pointed through the smoke to the streetlights across the way. Even as she spoke, a half dozen figures materialized through the haze. Blue wandlight. Red eyes. In the harsh glow of the firelight, witches were fighting vampires while somewhere in the distance, a discordant symphony of sirens grew louder.

"They were flushed from the safety of the house," Briony breathed.

Abby sprinted toward them through the haze. At the end of the street, Olivia and Piper had cast a protective bubble around Becca, Robby, and themselves, the telltale threads of their warding spell keeping T-Rex and the other vampires at bay. Trancelike, Becca was probing at the edges of the spell, with only Robby's firm grip keeping her inside it. Not far from them, Daisy and Delphi had their wands raised against someone else in the shadowy darkness.

"Who is that?" murmured Amethyst.

A stake materialized in Briony's left hand. Another slithered down the inside of her opposite sleeve and she gripped them both like daggers. "The Shadow Lady," said Briony. "She reveals herself at last."

Abby eyed the chaos uncertainly. T-Rex and Joey nipped at the edges of the warding spell. Lucinda and Margery poked and lunged in search of gaps. Piper and Olivia seemed to be holding their own for the moment, and even Flapper was doing his best to antagonize the four vampires. Abby's gaze darted back toward the twins and the shadowy figure that occupied them.

"Pincer movement," she shouted to Amethyst, making her decision. "Double envelopment, just like Tina taught us."

"I'll take the right flank," Amethyst huffed.

Nodding her agreement, Abby tore to the left side. If they timed it right, they'd come upon their opponent from both sides at once. But Abby had only made it a few paces before a streetlamp crashed to the pavement in front of her, blinding her with a blur of white sparks. She felt the impact in her bones, and by the time her eyes adjusted, the lamplight had fizzled to darkness and Daisy lay motionless on the ground, struck down by another light pole. Abby rushed to her friend's side while Amethyst and Briony steadied Delphi a few paces back.

Then a woman emerged from the darkness with a mane of raven black hair coiling around her like a coat of shadows. Her eyes glowed terrifyingly red, and her lips parted to reveal fangs as sharp as needles. Abby's eyes were drawn to the roiling filaments all around her, their swirling patterns both familiar and obscure. It was spellwork—the woman was surrounded by spellwork. Which could only mean one thing. The Shadow Lady wasn't *just* a vampire.

She was also a witch.

"Abby, look out!" Delphi's warning came just in time. Abby wove a flimsy shell around herself and Daisy as the Shadow Lady lunged for them. Amethyst and Delphi lifted their wands to reinforce Abby's spell, but the threads dissolved before they could fully knit together. Abby's wand shook as she tried to reinforce it herself. Instead, another spell pried at her protective barrier like claws tearing paper. Abby's wand arm fell to her side and all at once a narrow slit appeared before her. The Shadow Lady was through.

The woman's lips stretched into a menacing smile. "Where is it?" she demanded with a hiss that made Abby's limbs go limp with fear. "Not here, but near… so near I can taste it…"

"What do you want?" Abby yelled.

"Revenge."

"We've never… never… done *anything* to you!" Abby stammered.

"My circle of blood closes around you like a noose, young witch."

Abby had only an instant to raise her wand again as the Shadow Lady lunged. This time her spell held long enough to send the vampire witch spinning away, and Abby's heart surged as Briony appeared in her line of vision. Yet even as the slayer plunged toward the creature, her stakes burst into flames. With barely a second thought, the Shadow Lady knocked Briony Morrow aside and returned her gaze to Abby.

"Soon your secrets will be mine," she said in that terrible hiss-purr. "Soon I will have what I need." The last threads of Abby's warding spell fell away as the woman loomed above her. Clawed hands tore at her sweatshirt. The Shadow Lady's lips parted, and her mouth pressed so tight to Abby's neck that she could feel the warmth of the woman's breath. "Yes, you will do nicely…"

"We'll have none of that!" came a voice from the distance.

The Shadow Lady howled in surprise as Tina stepped through the haze and lassoed restraining spells around her arms and legs. Abby gaped as Tina raised her wand again. Her hair hung in thick wet curls around her shoulders. Her expression was grim, but her body crackled with a power Abby had never even guessed at.

"T—Tina?" she gasped. "What are you doing here?"

"Change of plans."

"But the Council—"

"I decided some things are more important than a direct order!" Tina tore the wooden stake from Amethyst's hands. "This ends now," she growled, raising the sharp tip to the night as she approached the vampire witch.

"It has only just begun," the Shadow Lady taunted, "and you are already too late."

Somewhere, Piper screamed. Tina's focus faltered for just an instant, but that was all it took for the vampire witch to reverse the flow of Tina's spell like a river suddenly changing direction. Now the restraining spell was stitching itself around Tina's arms, tighter and tighter until she screamed from the shock of it. Her wand and stake both fell to the ground. The Shadow Lady raised herself to her full height again.

The smoke cleared just long enough for Abby to see Piper on her knees with the small broken form of her seagull cradled against her chest. Olivia was still holding the four vampires away from Robby and Becca, but only just—without Piper the spell would never hold. Abby's gaze flicked back and forth with indecision.

"Go!" grunted Tina, already countering the Shadow Lady's spell.

Abby and Amethyst staggered toward Olivia, but not before T-Rex slipped through the barrier. Then he was at Becca's side, his mouth open, his fangs shimmering like polished ivory.

"No!" Abby yelled.

"My noose grows ever tighter." The night shook with a heavy breeze as the vampire witch swirled into shadow and vanished, a final message reverberating in her wake like an echo. "Soon all will know my wrath…"

Robby lay motionless on the ground. T-Rex's eyes gleamed as he pulled away from Becca at last, his face bloodied and grinning. Knees buckling, Abby raised her wand again—unsure what to do, what spell to cast—but there was nothing left to do. Lucinda, Joey, and Margery leapt to the trees and were gone in the blink of an eye. T-Rex lifted Becca's limp body and plunged into the darkened woods after them.

"Becca!" Abby called, staggering after her.

Then Tina was at her side, head hung low. "We can't help her," she said with a whisper, "we can only help those who remain."

Olivia and Amethyst hurried to Piper, whose eyes were wild as she cradled Flapper to her chest. Daisy and Delphi were wrapped in each other's arms, bruised and unsteady. Rushing to Robby's side, Abby rolled him onto his back, yelling, crying, desperate. Her voice belonged to someone else, some other girl she'd never been before. Tina crouched beside him, too, stroking his head, checking his breathing. Becca's silver pendant lay loose and broken between his fingers. His eyes were clouded, his voice a thin rasp.

"I—I lost her," he said.

"We'll get her back, Robby. I swear we will. We'll fix this."

The smoking remains of a few old Halloween decorations floated in the night like falling stars. The distant sirens were getting closer. Briony shook her head at them. Her watchful gaze followed the direction Becca had been taken.

"Some things cannot be fixed," she said darkly. "Not ever."

# Part Two

# 19

## After the Storm

In the predawn darkness, Robby's flashlight cut a dim path through the storm-tossed woods behind his house. His face felt blue with cold, and he was still limping from his fall out of the trees, his sneakers dragging in the mud as he parted the branches of a weeping hemlock and staggered into the small grove that backed up to the rocky hillside. Slick granite glinted on either side of a gap in the bedrock as the beam of his flashlight passed over it, barely noticeable unless you already knew to look for it.

Most of the caves dotting Willow Cove were natural fissures in the hillsides, but not this one—at least not entirely. Carved with the help of magic centuries earlier, it honeycombed with other secret tunnels and chambers all across town. Robby and the coven were among the few people in Willow Cove who even knew about it. Becca was another. *She could be hiding in there*, he thought, kicking at a pile of leaves as he moved closer. It was low on his list of possible hiding places, but she hadn't been anywhere else he'd searched, and he was running out of ideas. Branches shook in the wind all around him when he stepped into the darkness.

"Robby, don't."

He froze, then turned back toward the grove. The green-blue glow of Abby's wand lit her slight form as she shouldered through the branches. Her nose and ears were pink from the cold. Her voice was hoarse. "Don't go in there."

"What are you even doing out here?" he asked, irritated.

"Looking for you. Tina said you weren't in your room when she checked. Have you been out here all night? Did you even sleep?"

"Can't."

"We're all worried about you, Robby. Everyone's out searching."

Robby let out a dismayed breath. "You just happened to guess where I'd be?"

"It's not that hard. You're my best friend," she reminded him, "which means sometimes I know what you're going to do even before you do. I know what you're doing *now*. You're going to turn this town upside down until you find Becca. But you can't. It's not safe. You'll be next now that she's changed."

Robby stepped back into the grove and ducked under a low branch to keep out of the rain. "What if Becca didn't change?" It felt good to say it out loud. He wanted it to be true. It *could* be true. Margery's transformation had been different—she'd walked through the corn maze hand in hand with Lucinda. She hadn't fought it at all. Becca had never stopped fighting. "It's been hours now and there's no sign of her. She could be trapped somewhere. We need to find her. Maybe she won't change."

"We both know that's not possible."

"We don't know what's possible! She's different from other people, Abby. She's—she's *good*. She's kind. It's not just a part of her, it's who she is. How could something like that just go away? She might be able to fight it. She might need us right now."

Abby joined him under the cover of the trees. She lowered her gaze. "I don't think anyone can fight it."

"Well, I do."

Waving a helpless hand at the cave, Abby said, "What if you find her in there? What then? Would you stake her?"

"No!" Robby stared defiantly at her, but his hands were shaking so hard he nearly dropped the flashlight. "I would never do that."

"I wouldn't either. I couldn't. I don't know what I'd do, and I don't think any of us should go looking for her until we do." She moved closer to him, wiping away a smudge of blood from his forehead. Her hand was warm and steady, but up close he could see she had scratches all over her face. Her glasses were bent and one of the lenses was cracked down the middle. She was still wearing the same clothes she'd worn for days, and in the glow of her wandlight, she looked thin and pale and tired. He realized she must not have slept very much in the past few days. "You're in shock, Robby. I think we all might be. We need to stick together now, not wander off alone into dark caves. Promise me?"

He shrugged miserably. "I made a promise to Becca, too. I let her down."

"We all did."

"She's moving away," he explained, his voice shaky even to his own ears. "*Was* moving, I guess. Whatever. She was being forced to leave Willow Cove to live with her father again. That's why we went looking for the crypt in the first place—one last adventure. Except it really was one *last* adventure."

Abby pulled him into a hug until his breathing calmed, and he felt a little more settled. He wondered if she'd been hurt more than she let on last night because she grimaced as she pulled away, then tried to hide it with a little self-conscious smile. The sun was coming up now, the early sky revealing streaks of pink and red through the golden fall leaves.

Abby's eyes were wide and serious. "Becca was exactly where she wanted to be, I know that much for sure."

"We need to find her," he said again with less conviction.

"With all the recent disappearances, and now the fire at Becca's and no sign of her this morning, the superintendent decided to cancel classes again today," Abby told him, "but the school will be open for anyone who wants to meet with grief counselors."

Robby crossed his arms. "I don't need a grief counselor. Becca is still out there somewhere."

"You should be with friends, though. We're all meeting there later, Tina and Briony, too. We'll come up with a new plan together. I just want you to wait until we can all help, okay?"

Robby's throat felt tight at the mention of Briony's name. He remembered Abby saying something last night after the attack about the Shadow Lady being a witch and Briony Morrow being a vampire slayer, not a vampire—but his memories were all jagged edges now, a jumble of shapes that didn't fit together.

"Are you sure we can trust her?"

"Tina says we can," Abby replied with a nod. "I keep wondering why she wouldn't have just told us about her in the first place."

A muscle clenched in Robby's jaw. One thing he knew for certain was he'd had enough of his stepmother's secrets. "I wonder about a lot of things she's done lately," he said, letting Abby lead him away from the cave, "and I agree it's time we finally get some straight answers from her."

Abby bought him breakfast at Hex-Mex, the local café where they sometimes hung out on weekends. He hadn't felt much like talking, so instead he sat mostly in silence as the day dawned cold and bright, grateful she understood him well enough not to force another conversation. Now as they made their way toward the middle school, Robby jammed his hands into his pockets to keep from shivering. He'd left the house before sunrise with no jacket—with nothing but his flashlight—and now it all seemed to be catching up with him. Wind whipped his hair and pried at his clothes like greedy fingers.

He shivered and leaned into her for warmth, and as he did her free hand went involuntarily to her side. She *had* been hurt last night, he realized. Bruised or broken ribs, maybe. She let out a pained breath but didn't say anything, didn't complain, and kept close even after they slipped inside the school. Her muscles were tensed, and she seemed ready to grab him at the slightest hint he might bolt. She had it wrong, though. He didn't want to run away—he wanted answers from his stepmother.

There were news vans parked out front again and a helicopter buzzing overhead. Ms. Bancroft, the vice principal, was directing students toward grief counselors in the auditorium, but the halls were mostly empty. Five students going missing seemed to have put a damper on school attendance in Willow Cove.

They made it all the way to the library without seeing anyone but Sarika Swann lingering by her locker and whispering breathlessly into her phone as she recorded another podcast episode. They found Piper standing watch at the bottom of the shadowy stairway leading up to the hidden archive room. Flapper was bundled in a sling against her chest, but the injured gull managed to raise his beak expectantly at their approach.

"How is he?" Robby asked.

Piper's expression brightened. "Better this morning. His wings are still mending, but his appetite is back. How are you, Robby?"

"How do you think he is?" said Amethyst, suddenly peeking over Piper's shoulders on the creaky steps.

Piper bit her lower lip and murmured a soft apology as they all climbed the stairs and emerged into the dusty old room together. The light squeezing in through the stained glass window was so dim it almost looked like nighttime again outside. Olivia and the twins were crowded close to Tina over a stack of books on the long wooden table.

They all looked up as Robby arrived. He shrugged away when Tina moved to greet him with a hug. Then Amethyst's quick sideways glance alerted him to the presence of Briony Morrow, who stood alone near the cold hearth, twirling a wooden stake in the shadows. Today she wore a black hooded sweatshirt with jeans and high-top black sneakers, and she might have blended into the darkness entirely if not for the hazy glow of her eyes and the quick movements of her bone-white fingers. Robby's breath caught in his throat at the memory of her sleeping in the crypt.

"This time I'm the one holding the stake," she said to him. Her voice was gravel and honey, sweetness tinged with steel. Her smile was a challenge.

Tina cleared her throat. "We're all in this fight together."

Robby took an involuntary step back from her, his knees suddenly unsteady. He bumped into a battered suitcase he recognized as Tina's and understood immediately what it meant. She was going to the Midnight Castle after all. Even with Becca missing and her community in tatters, she'd simply put off her Summoning by a day. When he needed her most, she was still leaving. It was too much for him, all of it too much. His cheeks burned with fresh anger as he thrust a finger in her direction. "Are we actually in this together?" he demanded. "It seems like one of us has been keeping a lot of secrets from everyone else."

Tina opened her mouth to respond, but Robby's pulse was already pounding. His voice quavered like a taut guitar string. "Aren't you tired of keeping so many secrets? If you'd just told us about Briony—"

"I told you to stay away from the vampires. If you had listened—"

"Both of you, stop!" Abby moved between them and gripped Robby's arm hard. "We're here to figure out what to do now, not argue about what's already happened."

Briony's gaze darted between them. "I was angry like him once. His feelings need an outlet, even if they are misplaced. Without anger I would never have survived losing my sister to the Shadow Lady."

"Tina owes us an explanation," Robby said through clenched teeth.

Tina's voice was softer when she finally spoke again. "I do get tired of all these secrets, Robby. Of course I do. But I also had reason to fear that if I shared what I knew with any of you, the Council would ferret it from the coven during their Summoning."

She shook her head, a picture of exhaustion in the faint dusty light of the archive room. Her blonde curls hung limply at her shoulders, and for the first time Robby noticed her nose had gone crooked, as if it had been broken and hastily healed at some point in the night. "They're more perceptive than you can imagine, and if they found out I'd become involved—or that one of their own had helped me track down Briony—"

"Prena," Abby said with what sounded like dawning realization. "Prena helped you?"

Tina nodded. "She thought it best to keep our plans secret and I agreed. I would have been expelled from the Order for interfering. Or worse. I couldn't risk that."

"'Kindred spirits are not so scarce as I used to think,'" said Daisy, blinking in the bare glow of the lightbulb above the table. "Lucy Maude Montgomery, *Anne of Green Gables*." She touched Robby's shoulder. "We're all on the same side."

Tina cleared her throat. "Yes, precisely. Thank you, Daisy. Now that we're all here—"

"Not all of us," said Delphi, raising a hand to cut her off. "Not yet."

There was a heavy creak on the stairs and Delphi tilted her head, the corners of her mouth creasing into a told-you-so smile as Zeus walked through the doorway. He scowled as his gaze took in Abby and Robby standing shoulder to shoulder with their arms locked for support. Shuffling his feet and looking away, he said, "Becca was my friend, too. I came here as soon as I heard what happened. We both did." Behind him, Sarika Swann craned her neck into the room like a lion who'd stumbled onto a herd of antelopes.

"What are you doing here?" demanded Olivia.

"I knew it. I knew you were hanging out with these freaks!" Sarika squealed.

Olivia rolled her eyes. "So you followed me?"

"No, I followed the story. You and your new friends just happen to always be where the story is." She thrust her phone in Olivia's face. "Care to comment on that?"

"I'd rather just wipe your memory."

"I think you all need to hear what she has to say," Zeus cut in. "Sarika, tell them what you told me."

With a lingering glare at Olivia, Sarika elbowed her way to the table and leaned her phone against a stack of old books. "All of this is on the record for my podcast," she said, clicking a button and turning back to the assembled group. "It'll be the perfect follow up to last week's episode." When no one said anything to that, Sarika sniffed with wounded pride. "Do you mean to say none of you listen to my podcast? Like not *one* of you? No support from my own classmates? You know I have almost five hundred subscribers now, right?"

Olivia crossed her arms. "Get on with it, Sarika."

"Fine." Squinting to make sure the phone was recording, she said, "Everyone thinks this all started when Lucinda Walker vanished, but it goes back further than that. A lot further."

"We know that already," said Robby. "The Great Vampire Panic."

"First it was some mysteriously slaughtered chickens at Lucinda's farm," Sarika continued as if Robby hadn't spoken. "Then two sheep were found drained of blood. Then a cow went missing, then their goat and one of their horses. The police investigated every time. It kept happening anyway."

Robby looked questioningly at Zeus, who shrugged. "Don't look at me. I didn't know."

"How do *you* know?" Piper asked Sarika.

"Lucinda didn't have many friends, but she talked to Margery, who talked to Joey, who told T-Rex, and eventually it all got back to me—like it always does."

Olivia waved a hand dismissively. "Still the queen of gossip."

"This queen of gossip knows something else you don't know, too."

"Tell them," Zeus insisted. "Tell them when this really started."

# 20

## Briony's Story

Sarika's smile was easy and broad. She knew she had it, her favorite thing in the world—a captive audience—and she meant to draw out the moment as long as she could. "It didn't start when Lucinda disappeared. The animal mutilations began almost a year ago," she said, standing taller. "You all remember that night with the weird lights and strange noises coming from Whispering Hill? Something very odd happened that night, something that's never been properly explained by the authorities. If you ask me, I think something *arrived* that night."

Robby's thoughts had been ping-ponging around, his mind still scattered and unfocused. But he straightened as the meaning of Sarika's words registered. Everyone in the room seemed to understand at the same moment. The strange noises and mysterious lights on Whispering Hill were the result of the spell Miss Winters had cast to bring back her lost sisters—a ritual designed to carry the lost souls of the Winslow sisters from the seventeenth century to modern day. A ritual that had briefly torn a hole in the fabric of time and space.

Abby leaned forward and turned off the recording on Sarika's phone.

"Hey, you can't do that!"

"What if the portal opened in both directions?" Robby whispered. "What if it was a two-way street? When Miss Winters opened the portal to the past—"

"—the Shadow Lady found a way to come through from wherever she was," Abby concluded, nodding.

Tina rubbed her temples. "I should have guessed."

"But Miss Winters was trying to pull her sisters back from the seventeenth century," Piper said, blinking behind her thick glasses. "Are you saying the Shadow Lady was there, too?"

"When you open a portal to the past, anything can come through," Tina explained. "Anyone, I mean, if they know how to do it. If the Shadow Lady sensed the weakening of spacetime, wherever she was—*whenever* she was—it's possible she could have pried it open and crawled through."

"This makes at least some things clearer to me now as well," said Briony. "The witch you called Miss Winters cast the very same spell long ago."

"Her first attempt to resurrect her sisters was in 1889," Abby said. "The same year as the vampire panic in Willow Cove."

"I knew it had to be Miss Winters's fault somehow!" Amethyst said.

Briony lowered her hood. Her skin was so pale it seemed to glow as she stepped into the flickering light. "You would not say such things if you'd known her as I did."

"We all got to know her pretty well when she tried to put her sisters' souls in our bodies, thank you very much," countered Olivia.

Robby was running his fingers through his hair, pacing the small room with a slight limp. "You knew Miss Winters?" he said to Briony. Well, of course she did, he realized. The timing fit— Briony would have been one of her students back then too. "It all makes sense now. The witch's seal in the crypt, the epigraph by her body, 'Sealed by stake and bound by blood.' We knew it had to have been made by a witch the Council couldn't control."

"It was Miss Winters who stopped the last outbreak," Abby said into the silence.

"She went by another name in those days," Briony explained. "But yes, your Miss Winters is the reason Willow Cove did not succumb to the vampire plague in my time."

"Also the reason it was even a possibility to begin with!" said Amethyst, throwing up her hands in exasperation.

Briony's face remained impossible to read. "The Shadow Lady was weak and fed off small animals and livestock when she first came through the portal. I was alone in the room I shared with Julia on the night she came to me. Because of my interest in the occult, I had some familiarity with her… *type*. I knew what she was when she fed off me that first night. But when she returned to finish what she had begun, it was my twin who met her in the dark of my room. Always, she protected me. She believed she could surprise the Shadow Lady, but instead she became her servant— the one who spread her contagion far and wide."

Adjusting Flapper in his sling, Piper took a long drag from her inhaler. "Just like Lucinda today," she said.

Briony nodded gravely. "Joanna—your Miss Winters, I mean—had already left town by the time it began. I can only assume she learned what was happening in Willow Cove and chose to return and set things right. She saved my life. She saved the entire town."

"She always had a conscience," Abby said.

Olivia scoffed. "It didn't stop her from trying to body swap us with a bunch of doomed Puritan girls."

"It stopped her from actually going through with it," Abby snapped back.

"I was still sick when Miss Winters returned," Briony went on. "Still suffering. The Shadow Lady's bite gave me a sort of psychic link with her, though, and when Miss Winters healed me, we worked together to end the contagion one by one until only my sister and the Shadow Lady remained."

"We thought you were a vampire," Robby said. "We thought you must be because you haven't aged."

"Hunting vampires is the work of centuries, not months or years. I begged Miss Winters to make me this way until I slay the vampire queen once and for all. It is my gift and my curse that I will remain as I am until she is no more."

"Why didn't you slay her then? Why kill your own sister and not her?"

"You think I wanted to slay my twin?"

"I've considered doing it now and then," Daisy said. The quip died on her lips as Briony's red eyes bored into her.

"Miss Winters believed the Shadow Lady's victims were neither living nor dead, but rather somewhere between life and death. She believed if we were to sever the blood magic that bound them, the victims might yet be restored. Yet the Shadow Lady evaded us at every turn until one day she simply vanished, gone without a trace—gone forever, or so I thought."

"How?" Robby asked. "Where?"

Briony shrugged. "Some other time, some other place. Somewhere unreachable to me. Back to wherever she came from, perhaps."

"But if she did arrive in Willow Cove during the ritual," Abby said, her face pinched with concentration, "the portal would have closed again when it ended. She couldn't have gone back through it."

Now it was Tina who shook her head. "Miss Winters tore a hole in time and space, Abby. Yes, she put it back together when the spell ended, but there might well have been tiny cracks left behind. Hairline fractures. Like a piece of pottery that's been glued back together—even if it looks right to the naked eye, it would not be as strong as before. A witch as powerful as this Shadow Lady would be able to pry the fractures wide enough to slip through."

"Then maybe she did the same thing again this time," Robby suggested. "Maybe we can follow her."

Tina's expression was grim. "If the Shadow Lady felt threatened enough to retreat to wherever she came from, she would certainly have found a way to seal her escape route behind her."

"That was what Miss Winters believed as well." Briony looked down at her hands. "So, we did the only thing we could. Now I wander this world in search of the Shadow Lady and her kind, praying that someday we will meet again so I may avenge my sister."

"There are other vampires out there?" asked Piper.

Briony nodded. "They are her spawn, every one of them. Since those first days, however, the Shadow Lady has not surfaced again. Until now."

"Who is she? Where did she come from? What's her real name?" Abby asked.

"The legend of the vampire dates back millennia to Babylon, to Sumer, to Mesopotamia and the cradle of civilization itself. In all those years, the Shadow Lady has been called by many names. Lilith. Glámr. Morana. To some she is the Red Queen, to others the Blood Countess—a hundred names for a hundred different bogeymen, all of them *her*." Turning her attention to the dusty table, Briony opened a thick leatherbound volume with the words *Vampira Historica* curled like thorns along its spine.

"Here," she said, tapping a colorful illustration spread across two opened pages. With coiled raven hair and glowing eyes, the figure staring back was unmistakably the same as the creature they'd come face to face with last night. "Persia, three thousand years ago." Flipping to another page, Briony pointed again and said, "Hungary in the Middle Ages." With every turn of the page, another illustration, another name. But always the same face staring back from the mottled pages.

"It's the same creature every time, but as for her true name, I do not know. I suspect it no longer matters. She is who she is whether we name her or not. For a thousand years, she turned up roughly once a generation. With patience and a skill for languages, it's possible to trace her movements across the continents until one night in particular."

Briony spread the book open to another page. "The legends record it as the Night of Blood and Shadows because it coincided with the rising of a Blood Moon above the Carpathian Mountains in the year 1614, a total lunar eclipse when the full moon appeared red in the sky—and an apt metaphor, because the ground ran red with blood that night as well. It was her greatest rampage, whole villages consumed in a single night. Until *something* happened. When the sun rose, she was simply… gone. Vanished. Silent for nearly three centuries. The histories say she was masquerading as a Hungarian noblewoman in those days, but today there's no trace of her left behind. Her castle fell into such ruin that I can find no evidence of it, not one single stone. Some say it was always a myth, but her path of destruction is very real."

"That was the last time she was seen until 1889?" Robby asked.

Briony bobbed her chin. "And after that, she vanished again— until now."

"If what you said about the undead is true, we need to find the Shadow Lady and slay her. We can still save Becca. We can save everyone. If we start looking right now, we'll—"

Briony's expression darkened. "My psychic link with her has gone dark again. Wherever she hid from me over the past century, I fear she's gone there again."

"Why would she go *back* into hiding?" Olivia asked.

"Dracula did." Daisy coughed, then said quietly when all eyes fell on her, "In the book, I mean. *Dracula*. That's exactly what he did. He fled back to Transylvania when he thought the vampire hunters were getting close. They had to chase after him."

"That's what we need to be doing!" Robby said. "We need to find her. We need to check every building, turn over every stone, look inside every cave. If she's hiding somewhere then we'll find her, we'll—"

"We cannot," Briony placed a hand on his shoulder. "Haven't you heard a word I've said? Wherever she's gone, we can't follow. The only thing we can do for your friend now is destroy her before you become the next victim."

Robby brushed her hand aside. "You don't know Becca the way I do. She would never do that to me. She wouldn't."

"With respect, you do not know vampires as I do, either. The vampire's only imperative is to make other vampires. None can fight the hunger forever, no matter how good they were in life. A vampire needs blood to live. Any blood will do at first—squirrels, rats, dogs—but it will not satisfy them for long. Soon enough it will be human blood or true death. She will come for you, Robby. She will beg and plead, she will lie, she will do anything to gain your trust. And then she will turn you into a twisted mirror image of yourself, hungry and evil. It is a certainty."

"There has to be something we can do." Robby's gaze cast about the room for support. "Just tell me and I'll do it. Anything."

"Anything?" Briony's red eyes drew together. "Then make it this: Stick to the problems you can solve. Leave the vampires to me."

# 21

## A Journey North

"Leave the vampires to me," Amethyst muttered under her breath three days later, not for the first time. Abby stood beside her on the elevated train platform, watching the coastal express train grow larger on the horizon as it approached. The mid-November day was dull and dark, and Robby and Zeus leaned against the railing a few paces back, gloomy and silent.

"Of all the arrogant, ignorant, *idiotic* things to say," Amethyst continued. Her lips were tinged a similar shade of purple to her hair. A small smattering of freckles on her face stood out in starker relief than usual. "I don't know why I ever thought Briony was so cool."

"Because she's mysterious," suggested Abby. "And pretty?"

"I guess." For maybe the first time in her life, Amethyst blushed. "Too bad she shows such poor judgment."

Robby and Zeus joined them, tapping their phones to call up their train tickets. Abby shifted the thick manila folder she carried to her other arm and raised her voice to be heard over the distant rumble of the engine. "Why do you think Briony has poor judgment?"

"You heard the way she talked about Miss Winters. She's more than a hundred years old—you'd think she'd be less naïve."

"Only chronologically," Robby said, engaging in their conversation for the first time since leaving his house this morning. Abby lifted her head at the sound of his voice, still so gruff and somber. His mood had been as bleak and gray as the weather since Becca's disappearance. "Physiologically, maybe not so much."

"What do you mean, physiologically?" Amethyst focused on him with a thoughtful expression. There was something new in her eyes, Abby realized, something that suggested her budding crush on Briony wasn't so easily squelched after all.

Robby shrugged. "Some people think aging is mostly about physiology. Just because she's lived more than a hundred years doesn't mean she's not still a fourteen-year-old on the inside. She only seems older to us because we know her chronological age." A note of bitterness crept into his voice. "I mean, *we're* listening to her. Even Tina treated her like she's some kind of authority figure."

The train whistle cut short any defense Abby might have made on Tina's behalf. She clutched the thick folder in one hand and stepped over the gap between the station platform and the train, piling into a nearly empty car with wan fluorescent lighting and bench-style seats along both sides. After Abby chose a spot with a window near the front, Amethyst and Robby spilled in behind her, selecting the row opposite hers. She suspected this was by design, as it left the seat next to her open for Zeus, who pressed his lips into a tight smile and sat beside her like it was no big deal.

An electric prickle ran up and down Abby's leg where their jeans touched. It might not be a big deal to Zeus, but apparently it still was to her. She blew out a breath to clear her head. Whatever her lingering feelings about him, however they were betraying her, they weren't why any of them were here on this train. So, with an effort she slid her leg away from his and studied the folder in her lap instead. Because Robby was right, they *were* listening to

Briony's advice and focusing on a problem they could solve—or at least one she hoped they could.

*There are six identical houses,* Becca had explained when she'd researched the connection between Amethyst's old farmhouse and the one Poppy Delacroix had sold to Mrs. Shepherd, *and one of them is owned by Poppy herself.* It was too much of a coincidence, Abby thought now as she leafed through the printouts and photocopies on her lap. Discovering how it all fit together was the last thing Becca had done, and Abby didn't intend to let that effort go to waste. Not if they could actually visit Poppy Delacroix's house and find out what she was really up to.

*Stick to the problems you can solve.* Well, this was one of them. It wasn't like they'd stopped looking for Becca, either. They'd searched every cave, every cemetery, every square inch of Willow Cove they could think of, but there was no sign of her or their other missing classmates—or the Shadow Lady. It was almost as if they'd *all* gone into hiding. The fact that Becca hadn't come for Robby or anyone else had to mean something, though. Abby just didn't know what.

"Can I look?" asked Zeus, indicating the folder. Abby slid it onto his lap, watching as he flipped through the legal documents, deeds, and land surveys before settling on the satellite images of each of the six houses. There were two in Massachusetts and one each in New York, Vermont, Connecticut, and Maine. It was this last one that belonged to Poppy Delacroix. Zeus squinted at the image. "It's really identical to Amethyst's old house?"

"And our new one," Abby reminded him. "Weird, don't you think?"

Zeus nodded, then returned his attention to the folder.

*Say it,* Abby thought. *Say you don't want me to move. Say you shouldn't have broken up with me and you don't know what you were thinking and it's not too late to fix it.* He didn't say any of that, though. He just sat there in silence, and after a while the train conductor came by and scanned their tickets. The train rumbled on with only an occasional horn or the sound of brakes punctuating the quiet. Abby snuck a glance at Robby, who still had a dazed look about him, and then at Amethyst, who'd had an angry set to her jaw since the other night, too. They were all sad and miserable and lost in their own thoughts.

Abby hadn't expected her mother to say yes when she'd proposed taking the train to the Maine coast with her friends, but Mrs. Shepherd had agreed as long as they checked in with her when they arrived and departed for home. Abby suspected her mom was happy to have a Saturday to herself to sort through all the paperwork for the bank and their new school and the movers and everything else that went along with moving. Abby had all but forced Robby to come so she could keep an eye on him, but Zeus had volunteered as soon as he heard the plan.

When Zeus had finished leafing through the photos, Abby closed the folder and tapped Poppy's address into her phone. It was just a reflex at this point—she already knew the house was about four miles from the train station, a long but doable walk— but she needed something to do that didn't involve looking at Zeus.

Finally, she popped her earbuds in and settled on watching the scenery zip by, first the familiar gabled roofs and church steeples of the towns near Willow Cove, then the fallow fields and sparse yellow marshes a little further north. The ride was smooth and there were few stops on the express train, so after a while she found herself drifting in and out of sleep. She woke at one point as they crossed a bridge into New Hampshire to find that her head had drifted onto Zeus's shoulder. Blushing, she changed positions.

The next time she woke, Zeus's head was pressed against *her* shoulder, his breathing slow and regular, his skin warm through her sweater. The overhead lights blinked. She thought about moving him, or waking him, or just rearranging her shoulder a little. In the end, she didn't do any of those things, and they stayed that way until the train pulled into the station an hour later.

Away from the platform, the wind buffeted them as they navigated a warren of cobblestone streets along the coast. It was another brisk morning, the air thick with the smells of the ocean and the sky gray and drizzly above the harbor.

Abby texted her mom to say they'd arrived, then hung back a little to walk beside Robby. Ahead of them, Amethyst checked the walking directions on her phone, frowned, and changed course at a traffic light that only blinked red. The smell of fried fish wafted down the street, reminding Abby she'd been too nervous this morning to eat breakfast. Now her stomach grumbled as they passed the tourist shops and restaurants just beyond the station. A few of the storefronts were already decked out with Christmas lights. One of the cafe windows looked so much like Hex-Mex's winter display back home that Abby steered Robby away before he could see, knowing it would remind him of the morning after Becca had been taken when he and Abby had eaten breakfast together.

The red brick buildings and narrow cobblestone streets soon turned into one worn road, the houses and buildings growing sparse. Even if they'd brought their brooms, Abby wouldn't have wanted to risk flying in broad daylight, and she figured it would only take about an hour to reach the old farmhouse and another to walk back, which would leave them most of the day to talk to Poppy Delacroix and get to the bottom of whatever she was up to. If she was even there when they arrived. If everything went according to plan.

Robby shivered inside his jacket as they crossed the town line, the hood of his coat shuddering in a cold breeze. There were fewer buildings and more trees here, and in the distance a storm cloud hung low and heavy above the ocean, threatening rain. Abby had never found it hard to talk to him before, but more and more since the night Becca was taken, she realized she didn't know what to say.

"You'd think Delphi could have predicted we'd need rain jackets," she said, settling on a lame joke rather than continue in silence.

Robby kicked an invisible rock down the road, which was now just a narrow dirt track between two slanting fences, while Amethyst and Zeus turned a corner and disappeared. Robby managed an appreciative half smile and Abby bent her head close to his in quiet commiseration. He was like a rail beside her, thin and wiry, and she wondered when he'd last eaten anything. They walked like that for a long time until she felt the tension inside him begin to loosen.

Amethyst and Zeus had come back to look for them, and Zeus had a funny look on his face that Abby couldn't read as he watched her and Robby coming around the corner. He turned and walked ahead again before she could say anything, and by the time she caught up, he and Amethyst were well into the wooded backroads. A grassy field stretched across a hill in the mid distance. There was another dirt road, barely passable for a car but easy enough for the four of them, and they followed it together past an old cemetery with a walking path cutting directly through it. A rusted sign above the gate read "South Hill Burying Ground." It would have been quicker to cut through, but they chose to go the long way around, having had their fill of graveyards for a while.

"Poppy's house is just on the other side of that hill," Amethyst said a few minutes later, clicking off her phone and shoving it into her backpack. "I thought maybe we should avoid being seen until we can get a sense of the place, so we'll need to cut through this field rather than walk down her driveway."

It was a more difficult climb than Abby expected, icy in a few spots where the sun was shaded by scraggly trees, but when they crested the hill, she let out an appreciative sigh at the view. The few trees on the slope below had shed their leaves and she could see all the way to the ocean from the summit. Any last doubts she might have had about the similarities between the farmhouses were erased as she squinted down at the sprawling estate. It was identical to the others, right down to the winding stone staircase in the hillside and the long, slanted barn set just off to the side. An expensive black car was parked in the driveway and there was a light on in one of the third-floor bedrooms.

"That's her car," Abby said. "She must be home."

Amethyst pointed to a whitewashed old lighthouse on a small island a few hundred yards off the coast. "Does that look like…?" Amethyst let her voice trail off as she crouched and unzipped her backpack. Producing the old photo of her mother's coven, she held it in front of her, eyes narrowed. Abby and the others shuffled behind her for a closer look. The photo flapped in the wind, but Amethyst clutched it tight.

Abby looked from the lighthouse to the photo of the six smiling girls, then back again. "It's the same place," she agreed, feeling a chill that couldn't be entirely attributed to the weather.

"Mom and her coven stood here," Amethyst said, "maybe *right here* when they posed for this picture." Her jaw was even more set than usual, her skin splotchy with emotion. "This is so messed up. I don't have a single picture of me and my parents together, nothing from when we were a family because it was all destroyed in the fire. And the one photo I do have"—she waved dismissively at the picture of her mother's coven—"is from a part of Mom's life she never got to tell me about."

For as long as Abby and Amethyst had been friends, Amethyst had avoided talking about her mother, who died when she was very young. Now it all seemed to be surfacing again whether she wanted it or not.

"I'm sure your mom would have told you when you were old enough." Abby rested a hand on her shoulder. "Let's look around some more before we talk to Poppy." She turned to Robby and Zeus for support, and both nodded.

Slowly, Amethyst nodded, too. "Where to first?"

Abby had thought about this already. She pointed to the barn. If it were the same as Amethyst's old house, there would be a hexagram carved into the floor. Now that they knew the hexagram in Amethyst's barn had been used as a witch's seal, she wondered if they might find another clue inside this one.

The clouds had moved inland from the ocean while they discussed their next move, further darkening the sky. Abby and Amethyst lit the tips of their wands as they scrabbled down the hillside with the boys in tow. The day suddenly felt menacing, and Abby had a shivery sort of feeling about what they might find.

She thought of the morning she'd gone to see Amethyst last year looking for advice about being a witch: hay bales had lined the walls of the barn and a giant red hexagram had been freshly painted across the floor. This barn wasn't like that, though. Inside, it was cold and mostly empty and there was no hexagram painted on the floor. Abby's wand revealed only a few moldering hay bales. Amethyst was already on her hands and knees, brushing at dust. Robby and Zeus dropped beside her, panning out, puffing at the cold stale air.

Abby floated to the hay loft and peered out one of the smudged windows to the outside world. The light was still on in Poppy's third-floor window. The rest of the house looked silent and empty. Breathing a cautious sigh of relief that they still hadn't been discovered, she returned her attention to the scene below her—and gasped. Scrapes and scuff marks punctuated each of the six points of a hexagram carved into the floor, more easily spotted here than at ground level. Drifting back down, Abby pointed out what she'd seen.

"I don't know if I really believed it until now," Amethyst whispered.

Abby dropped to one knee beside her. "Should we open the seal?"

In the open doorway, a floorboard creaked. The four friends glanced toward it in unison. Poppy Delacroix stood backlit by the gray morning sky with a stark expression on her face. Abby and Amethyst both raised their wands, slipping into a defensive stance in front of the two boys. Poppy's eyes narrowed. Shadowed in the doorway, she seemed stern and menacing now, not at all the cheery façade she'd put on for Abby's mother.

"I know what you girls are up to," she said, tilting her chin at the hexagram, "and I would not even think about doing it if I were you."

# 22

## Poppy Delacroix

"That just makes me want to do it more," Abby said.

"Of that I have no doubt." Poppy's smile revealed a mouthful of blindingly white teeth. It was a humorless expression, though, never quite reaching her eyes. "Your mother did say you're a feisty one."

Abby tightened her grip on her wand, probing for signs of magic within the woman opposite her. There was still nothing. No aura, no lingering wisps of spellwork, no wand. But Abby knew Poppy was a witch—the photograph in Amethyst's pocket proved it—so why would she continue with the deception even now, when faced with two witches who had their wands pointed right at her?

"Keep my mother out of this," Abby finally said when Poppy made no further move. "Why don't you want us to open the seal? What are you afraid we'll find?"

"Afraid? I'm not afraid of anything you could do to me." Poppy wrinkled her nose as her gaze passed over Zeus and Robby. "This is a loose thread I can't quite figure, though. Two non-magical boys who clearly know you're witches. Has the Council relaxed its rules so much these days?"

Behind her, Robby sucked in a breath and seemed about to speak. Abby cut him off with a sharp sideways glance. "We'll ask the questions," she said. "You know about the Council, so you *are* a witch. Why hide it from us? What is it you want? And what is this place—what are all these places? The six identical houses."

This time there did seem to be actual amusement behind Poppy's smile. "That's a lot of questions." She shivered in the doorway, jangling a pair of heavy bracelets, hugging herself theatrically. "Why don't we take this conversation inside? I'll make tea. You'd all enjoy something warm, I'm sure."

"I could go for a hot chocolate," said Zeus.

Amethyst glared until he lowered his eyes.

"Talk," Abby said to Poppy. "Now."

Poppy made a clucking noise, then shook her head. That smile again. Those teeth. "I *was* a witch. Past tense. The Council put an end to that years ago, as you can surely sense."

Abby snuck a glance at Amethyst, whose grip on her wand had gone so tight her knuckles were like white marbles. "You charmed my mother," Abby said to Poppy, her voice less certain now. "You convinced her to move all the way across the state. You're saying that *wasn't* magic?"

"Power of suggestion only." Poppy raised her hands, palms out. "My magical days are long since over, but I am still a very persuasive realtor. I made a promise to *your* mother, Amethyst, that I would look after you if the Council ever showed the same interest in you as it showed in our coven. These houses"—she swept a hand to indicate her own house, and Abby presumed the identical houses as well—"they can help with that."

"My mother knew about the Council?" Amethyst asked uncertainly.

"Of course she did. And she wanted to keep you safe from them. Safer than our coven ever was." Poppy's bracelets clinked as she pointed at the hexagram. "That seal hasn't been broken in many years, but I'm quite certain the Council still monitors it. Are you girls going to put those wands down now? You can see I'm no threat."

"Would you admit it if you were?" asked Amethyst.

"No, I suppose I would not."

Neither girl lowered her wand, but with her free hand Amethyst reached into her back pocket and waved the photo of her mother's coven between them. "What happened to your coven? Where are the rest of you now?"

"I loved your mother like a sister," Poppy said.

Amethyst's voice cracked. "That's not an answer."

"We were close, all of us. Closer than the Council approved of, that's for certain. When we were Quelled—"

"What does that mean?" Abby asked. "Quelled?"

"This." Poppy wiggled her fingers. "No more magic."

Abby blinked in horror. "The Council *took* your magic?"

"I don't believe that," Amethyst said with a sideways glance in Abby's direction.

"I do," Abby said, lowering her wand and thinking back to a stormy winter night last year when Miss Winters had first told her about the Council. First *warned* her about them. "Don't you remember? Miss Winters told me basically the same thing."

"She was a liar, Abby. I wouldn't trust her, either."

"They cut me off from the source forever," Poppy continued, "and they did the same to your mother, Amethyst, and the other girls in our coven too. Just as they do to anyone who disobeys them. Which is why I've been a bit wait-and-see with you two. I thought it best to understand your relationship with the Council before blundering in like a bull in a china shop."

Abby's mouth dropped. Beside her, Amethyst's breathing had gone ragged, the color all but gone from her face.

"But why?" Amethyst finally managed. "Why would they—how could they...?"

In the doorway, Poppy shivered. "A tale best told indoors," she suggested again, taking a step back, waving her bracelets in the general direction of the farmhouse. "Maybe now I can convince you all to join me for some hot cocoa?"

"With marshmallows?" Zeus added hopefully.

Abby blew into her hands, wincing at the pins and needles in her extremities as the group spilled into the kitchen. Robby and the others tucked their hands under their arms, shivering while Poppy busied herself in the pantry. The room was both similar and different than how Abby remembered Amethyst's old house. There weren't any rotting floorboards or peeling strips of wallpaper, but the bones of it were the same right down to the layout of the counters.

"This was my great grandmother's house," Poppy trilled over her shoulder, reclaiming the piercing singsong voice of their first meeting as she emerged from the pantry with a box of hot chocolate mix and five mugs. "She was a witch, too, and not the sort to blindly obey rules she disagreed with. In those days one did not choose one's own coven, the Council chose for you—"

"They still do," Amethyst cut in. "We're the exception. We became a coven before we'd even heard of the Council."

Poppy rapped her fingers against the counter, waiting for the kettle to steam. "It's times like these I miss magic the most," she said, shaking her head. "Would you mind…?" Abby waggled her wand at the kettle until it whistled, and Poppy continued, "I suppose it was that business with your history teacher that mixed things up."

"You know about Miss Winters?" Amethyst asked.

"I did promise to keep an eye on you," she reminded Amethyst as she divided the water between the five mugs. "You didn't seem to be involved with the Council, which I took as a good sign.

It's why I finally decided to make contact with you through Abby's mother."

Abby caught a glimpse of the lighthouse through the back window, where she could make it out better than before. It was worn and weather-beaten, with overgrown grass brushing against its whitewashed walls, and it reminded her of the lighthouse where Miss Winters had trained them back before everything went wrong. It made her feel wistful in a way she couldn't quite explain, other than that she'd felt safe and happy back then, and somehow everything seemed to have changed in the year since.

She would never admit it to her friends, but there was a part of her that missed their old teacher even now, even after everything Miss Winters had done—or intended to do. Abby was struck by a feeling of loss, too, a nagging belief that if only Miss Winters had chosen to stay and make amends, things might have been different over the past year.

Better, somehow.

"The past year has had its ups and downs," was all she said in response to Poppy's statement.

"Well, it at least explains how the Council allowed a blood coven to form right under their noses. It never seemed very like them. Self-selected covens are hard enough to control, but I would imagine blood covens are even more dangerous."

Abby searched her memory but couldn't recall ever hearing the term. "What's a blood coven?" she asked.

Poppy looked at her with surprise. "You're all from the same bloodline, of course."

"That can't be too unusual," said Amethyst.

Poppy's eyes were wide, her expression eager. "Oh, but it is, it truly is. The same magic runs through all of your veins"—she waved away the surprise on Abby's face—"oh, don't be surprised, I told you I've been keeping an eye on you. I know all about the others, too. It's a rare thing, blood covens. Dangerous, even."

"Dangerous to who?" Amethyst asked.

"Anyone who doesn't like strong, opinionated girls." Poppy handed each of them a mug, then raised hers in toast. "So, I would imagine that includes most people."

"I like strong girls," Zeus said into his mug.

"You like to dump them without explanation, you mean," said Amethyst pointedly. Abby snuck a look at Zeus and his expression crumpled. For half a heartbeat it looked as if he wanted to say something, to defend himself or maybe even apologize. Instead, he seemed to take an intense interest in the bottom of his mug and the moment passed.

The table quieted as they all sipped their cocoa. Gulls cried in the distance. Waves shushed against the rocks. The rhythm of it was as much a feeling in Abby's bones as a sound. There was something about this place, she thought, something powerful. She decided she liked it. "You said your great grandmother didn't blindly obey the Council's rules?"

"In those days," Poppy said, nodding, "when a witch reached maturity, they would be assigned to a coven and moved to a sanctuary space beyond the wider world."

"Like the Midnight Castle?" Abby suggested.

"Yes, exactly. At sixteen, my great grandmother was given the same choice as every other witch: Remove yourself from your old life, or be Quelled and return to the way you were before your powers manifested. I think you'll find the choice is much the same today, once you get a little older."

Amethyst rubbed her temples. "I thought moving to the other side of the state was bad."

"It is bad," said Robby.

"This is worse," Abby said, feeling a little sick to her stomach. "Tina never told us any of it."

"Tina is your adult mentor from the Order? Adults often keep unpleasant truths from children."

"We're not children anymore," Abby said.

Poppy shrugged. "That may be true, but sometimes it takes a while before adults realize that. It sounds as if she has been protecting you from a choice you don't yet have to make."

"What rules did your great grandmother break?" Amethyst asked.

Poppy snorted. "All of them! She formed a coven with her closest friends from the Midnight Castle."

"Why didn't the Council stop them?" Abby asked.

"Because they couldn't find them. That was the brilliant part of it all. You've heard of ley lines?" When the four shook their heads, Poppy said, "They're mystical lines imbued with deep power that crisscross the globe. The details don't matter. What's important is that ley lines were her particular area of research, and she came to believe these invisible lines also created tiny but immense pockets of energy—so much energy that it would be nearly impossible for the Council to detect the workings of smaller magic happening within them."

"Like a smokescreen," said Robby, holding his mug with both hands. He still had a sunken look to him, but at least he seemed interested now, more engaged, like he was thinking about something other than his girlfriend being a vampire.

Poppy bobbed her chin again. "My great grandmother mapped out safe havens for herself and the other girls in her new coven."

"The locations of the six houses?" Abby said.

"Exactly!" Poppy smiled her supernaturally white smile. "Making them identical was her own flourish, something about sisterhood and unity and all that. Their coven was a bit spread out, but for a very long time it worked to keep their secret. First my great grandmother, then her daughter, then my mother—three generations lived in the shadows outside the control of the Council. Avoiding notice. Doing as they pleased. Passing the safety of these havens to their own children or successors. It was enough for them." Poppy stared into her mug. "But not for us. Not for my coven."

"What happened?" Amethyst asked.

Poppy waved another dismissive hand. "It hardly matters anymore."

"It matters to me," Amethyst pressed. "My mother never got a chance to tell me. If there's anything you can share with me about it… about her…"

Poppy steepled her fingers, considering. "We were like sisters in every way that matters. We bickered and got on each other's nerves, but there was love there. Your mother loved you very much, too, Amethyst, I can tell you that. It's why she made me swear to look after you before she passed, and it's why I led Abby's mother to the one remaining house where you can still evade the Council's notice. They know about the others, but we did manage to keep the two in Massachusetts secret. I suppose giving you someplace to hide from the Council if you ever need to is my way of fulfilling my promise."

Despite the warmth of her mug between her fingers, Abby shivered a little at the thought of hiding from the Council. Of ever needing to. "How was your coven discovered?" she asked.

"We were reckless. Arrogant. Young. I suppose it's all the same. The point is we were found out and brought before the Council. Imagine six young witches like us, awed by the power of the Midnight Castle—"

"Not so hard to imagine," Amethyst said under her breath.

"In some ways it was like discovering a new purpose, a new community, but we bristled at their restrictions. Their way of doing things. Their forced obedience. We thought—well, I suppose we thought we could just ignore the rules we didn't like and keep doing as we pleased. What was the worst that could happen?"

"You didn't know you could be Quelled?" Abby asked.

"Oh, we *knew*, but we didn't believe it. Why would they strip away our powers for a few minor acts of disobedience? We were young. You never believe it will happen to you when you're young."

"A few minor acts of disobedience," Abby said, turning the words over in her mind.

Amethyst caught her meaning. "We're not the obedient sort."

"Neither is Tina," Robby said, lowering his mug and looking to them both.

"We've been so careless," Abby said. "Back home, there's a… a situation. Tina told us not to get involved, but we did anyway. One of our friends was in danger, so we tried to help, but things went wrong. Tina had to use battle magic to try to save us and now… now…"

"Now she's been Summoned by the Council," Robby said.

"Is she in danger?" Abby asked, fearing she knew the answer by the way Poppy's expression grew serious.

"If it's as you say it is, then yes, I think she might be in grave danger. The use of magic in self-defense is one thing, but to use it in defense of a non-witch is certainly against witch law."

Abby slouched back in her chair, cheeks burning. "Everything she's done lately has been to protect us from our own actions. We can't just leave her to face punishment for something she only did to keep us safe."

"But what can we possibly do about it?" Amethyst asked. "She's already at the Midnight Castle."

Abby rubbed her eyes, conjuring a vision of Prena, green-haired and smiling. Her hand fell to her pocket, and she ran her fingers over the keystone, considering. *Think of it as a back door into the Midnight Castle,* she'd said. Abby looked up again at her friends, a half-formed plan already stitching itself together.

"I don't know yet," she told them, "but I think I know where to start."

# 23

## The Knock at the Window

The sky had turned menacing by the time the express train rolled back into Willow Cove late that afternoon. At the station, Zeus's mother hurried them into her minivan with a furtive glance at the streetlights, which were casting wide yellow halos across the parking lot. It was full dark when they pulled to the curb between Robby's house and the one Abby and Amethyst shared next door, and Mrs. Madison waited until all three of them were safely inside before driving the short distance home with Zeus.

A few stray leaves swept into the kitchen as Robby opened the front door and kicked his sneakers in the general direction of the shoe rack. His father looked up from grading papers at the table, smiling guiltily as he stuffed a piece of leftover Halloween candy into his mouth.

"Dinner is some kind of casserole again tonight," he mumbled between chews, waving a hand to indicate something cheesy burbling on the stovetop. "Go clean up and I'll get it ready. You can tell me all about your day over dinner."

Tina made a habit of leaving pre-cooked meals whenever she was called away, probably because last year Robby and his father had lived on takeout food for months after her disappearance. But now it only reminded Robby that Tina was probably in danger again, this time with the Council, and he couldn't muster an appetite for it despite not having had anything but Poppy Delacroix's hot cocoa since breakfast. A pang of guilt pulled at him for having lost his temper with Tina in the library. Everything she'd done must have been with the knowledge that she was putting herself in danger with the Council, but she'd done it anyway. And all he'd done was yell at her about it.

Mr. O'Reilly scooped the casserole onto a pair of dinner plates while Robby washed his hands at the kitchen sink. Across the yard, the light switched on in Abby's bedroom and he looked away as her shadowed shape drifted toward the window. No light came on in Amethyst's room, which probably meant she'd slipped back outside to keep Briony company on patrol—something she'd started to make a habit of these past few nights, despite her protests about Briony's many flaws. Robby couldn't see either girl through the kitchen window, but he knew the vampire slayer would be out there somewhere, keeping an eye out for Becca in case she came for him.

"I know it smells like a lot of garlic," Mr. O'Reilly said with a rueful shake of his head. "Everything Tina makes lately is loaded with garlic. Not that I'm complaining." He grabbed silverware and glasses, then set two places for them at the table, pushing aside the school papers to make room. "You might want to let it cool for a bit. I snuck a few bites before you got here. It's still pretty hot."

"Do you mind if I take mine upstairs tonight?"

Mr. O'Reilly wiped his glasses on his sleeve, then took a careful look at his son. "Everything okay?"

They both knew it wasn't, but Robby played along anyway. "It's fine. We had a good time today. I'm just kind of tired now."

His father nodded, but Robby could tell he was disappointed. He *was* tired, though, even if what he was most tired of were the secrets he had to keep, like the fact that Tina hadn't just been called away on some emergency work trip. Or that most of his best friends were witches. Or that Becca was out there somewhere in the night, changed from who she used to be.

Robby balanced a plate and silverware as he climbed the stairs to his room, then set them on his nightstand and sank into his desk chair. The radiator hissed and gurgled. Wind rattled the panes of his window. As he'd done every night this week, he turned his lights down low and rolled his chair over to the window. Then he waited, and watched, and hoped, though he couldn't have said what he was hoping for, exactly. That Becca wouldn't come for him… or that she would?

The first night had been the worst. Pacing his room. Sitting at his desk. Lying in bed. It didn't matter what he did, every scrape and scratch of a tree branch against his window had him on alert. Not just the sound of it, but the sense it gave him that she was outside watching him, waiting for him, wanting to be let in. But every time he'd looked up, no one was there.

She wasn't herself anymore, that was what everyone said. If she came to him, it wouldn't really be her at all. It would be someone else, *something* else—something with a compulsion to turn him into a vampire like her. Only he couldn't bring himself to believe it.

The scent of woodsmoke from a neighbor's house drifted in through his drafty window, mingling with the garlicky scent of Tina's casserole. Outside, Briony and Amethyst passed beneath the penumbra of the streetlight, the two girls deep in hushed conversation. It had started to rain, little icy flecks like hail, and the girls huddled close together as they moved out of sight. Robby reached for his dinner, but then his head snapped up, suddenly alert to a tap at the window—and Becca's face on the other side of the glass.

He sat up straight, knocking his plate to the floor.

It wasn't his imagination.

Becca's face was so pale she looked like a streak of snow in the night. She touched the window again, rapping softly again with her knuckles.

*Tap, tap.*

Robby swiveled the lamp by his window toward her, shining it like a spotlight. His hands shook. His throat felt tight. Becca didn't blink. Her eyes were like glowing red jewels, her gaze sharp and unwavering.

*Tap, tap.*

"Becca?" he breathed.

It wasn't Becca, he reminded himself. It was a thing that looked like Becca. But his heart was still pounding and his limbs felt heavy as rocks, because what if everyone was wrong? What if Becca was different?

He moved the lamp until it illuminated the entire window. Becca clung to a branch just on the other side of the glass. Her face was all strange shadows and sharp angles, her dark hair tangled and wet. She still wore the pajamas she'd been in the night she'd been taken, now dirty and wet and ripped just below her collarbone. Her feet were bare, and the exposed skin was white as ivory.

*Tap, tap.*

Robby fumbled for his phone, the idea somewhere in the back of his mind that he should call Abby, that he needed her to come quickly.

"Robby?"

It was *her* voice. He didn't know what he'd expected, but he hadn't been prepared for her to sound just like the real Becca. She said his name again, not a question this time, just his name. A statement of truth—*I know you, I remember you*. Her lips moved, but the sound seemed to reach him not through the glass but in his head. "Robby, I'm so cold." She did look cold. She had to be cold because it was freezing outside. But she didn't shiver or quake even a little as the tiny flecks of freezing rain pelted her face. She barely moved at all. Just sat there staring with those wide, mesmerizing eyes. "I want to come in. Will you let me in?"

*She will beg and plead.*

*She will lie.*

*She will do anything to gain your trust!*

Briony's warning was still echoing in his thoughts when Becca spread her fingers wide across the rain-smeared window, five pale points where the tips pressed against the glass. Robby touched his hand to hers, reminded of another stormy night not long ago when she'd come to his window. A happy night, the last one they'd had together.

He shouldn't let her in. He knew he shouldn't. But somehow his hands were unlatching the window anyway, opening it a crack, then wider, wider still, until finally he and Becca were face to face with nothing between them but the mist of their mingling breath. Without the glass between them her face had changed. She was still porcelain-pale, still speckled with rain drops, but the angles seemed softer. She looked like Becca again, the real Becca, his Becca. Her face—it *was* her face—was sad and desperate and lonely.

Just like him.

"I—I shouldn't come in," she whispered. "I want to, but I shouldn't."

The distant sting of woodsmoke was gone. The air smelled of damp and decay. Her lips parted and her teeth gleamed in the lamplight, two long fangs exactly where he knew they'd be. Her eyes were pleading with him. "You have to say the words. I can't come inside until you say the words." Her expression changed to one of horror—at herself, at the world. She shook her head, nearly in tears, her gaze still locked on him. "Please *don't* say the words, Robby. It's not safe for you."

He raised his hand again and their fingers touched. It was too much. She was right there, she was cold, she was alone. She needed him. She would never hurt him. He closed his eyes and let out a deep breath. "Come inside," he told her.

But when he looked again, she was already gone.

An hour might have passed. A lifetime. Still he stood at the window as the rain soaked his shirt and puddled on the floor around him. He knew he should tell someone. Abby, Briony, *someone*. But he already knew what they would say, and he didn't think they would understand, not really. He'd invited Becca in. He'd invited a *vampire* into his house.

And she'd refused.

He forced himself to breathe as Amethyst and Briony moved in front of the open window again. His heart was still pounding like a runaway train. He shoved his hands into his pockets and paced the room, not knowing what it meant that Becca had come to him, that he'd told her she could come in—and she'd chosen not to. He didn't think it was a trick. And if it wasn't a trick, then what *did* it mean?

She didn't want to hurt him. That was the only explanation. He'd given her the chance and she'd resisted. Becca was telling him that she was still in there somewhere, still fighting. He had to find a way to fight with her. "Where would you go?" he wondered aloud.

Einstein raised his head and gave him an uncertain wag of the tale, then settled back into his nap. Robby had already looked everywhere for Becca. She couldn't have gone home because her house had burned down. It would be too risky to hide inside the school or library with so many people coming and going, but they'd searched there anyway. They'd searched the caves and the cemeteries, too. Next, they planned to search the old state hospital on Whispering Hill, though Robby couldn't imagine Becca choosing to hide there after everything that happened last year. She would need to go somewhere she wouldn't be found during the day, though, and if she really was fighting her instincts then it would have to be somewhere Lucinda and the other vampires weren't already hiding.

He closed his eyes as something shifted in his memory. Was it something she'd said? Somewhere they'd gone? He heard the rattle of hay wagons at the Halloween fair, saw the light of the moon, the trees swaying in the distance. No, not the trees—the cornstalks. And suddenly he knew where Becca must have gone.

*We could hide in there for weeks*, she'd said. *No one would ever find us.*

The corn maze. She was hiding in the corn maze. He slammed the window shut and gathered up his flashlight and phone. Then he stopped, shaking his head. It would be stupid to go out there alone. He clicked on his phone and his fingers hovered over the screen, typing, pausing, typing again. He took a deep breath and changed his mind. It would be stupid to tell anyone, too. They'd only try to stop him.

After listening for his father downstairs, he took the stairs quietly, then slipped into his jacket and sneakers and creaked open the front door. Just visible across the hallway, his father stood in the kitchen with his back to the sink, dishrag in hand, staring at nothing in particular. Robby was no stranger to being outside after dark, but as he tiptoed onto the front steps and then the wet grass, the world felt strangely empty around him. Nothing ahead, nothing behind. The streets were deserted, the few houses on their cul-de-sac lit sleepily from within, as if the entire town had already surrendered to the night.

Ducking into the woods before Briony and Amethyst could spot him, Robby made his way to the trail through the Hollows, only clicking on his flashlight once he was sure he was clear of them. The path ahead was thick with darkness, and even with his flashlight he couldn't see more than a few feet. He felt a feathery tickle at the back of his neck that told him he was being watched, but every time he stopped and waved his flashlight at the trees, he saw nothing.

A branch snapped nearby, and Robby's head jerked up. A few stray brown leaves twirled through his flashlight beam like wobbly parachutes. Somewhere, an animal moved through the bushes and away. He took a deep breath and swallowed, then picked up his pace until he reached the edge of the fairground, where a lone police car patrolled the parking lot near the west entrance. Covering his flashlight, Robby crouched low behind a stone wall and waited. A moment later, the headlights vanished as the car turned back toward town.

He ducked beneath the flimsy parking gate and past the darkened ticket booth. The agricultural tents were gone. The midway rides had been packed up and moved to some other fair in some other town, too. All that remained were wide puddles and stray branches on the paved pathways, a few wet hay bales, a handful of toppled trashcans spilling candy wrappers into the breeze. It was like a scene from the apocalypse, he thought, the day after everything ended. Or maybe the night before.

Shaking the thought away, he lowered his flashlight and made for the corn maze. He was nearly at the boundary when a slash of red caught his eye and he pulled up short, that uneasy feeling in his neck and shoulders again. But it was just a balloon, red and deflated and snagged on something in the rustling in the wind.

Wisps of cornsilk brushed his cheeks as he navigated the maze. His sneakers crunched the icy mud underfoot, occasionally sinking into softer muck. He called Becca's name, pausing long enough to listen for an answer, then continued until he found himself on the same path he'd already stumbled onto at least twice before. Turning back, he spotted the outline of a silo poking above the cornstalks and decided to make for it, picking up his pace as the tall corn scratched at him.

The maze walls seemed to grow thicker as the minutes ticked on, and after the third or fourth wrong turn he began to wonder if he'd imagined the silo entirely. But then he pushed through a thicket of corn, and it was in front of him, an old metal silo marking the center of the maze. He spun his flashlight through the dark, searching and calling for Becca again.

Corn swayed for acres in every direction. He kicked at an empty husk. Angry at himself, angry at everything, he suddenly felt the effects of the cold and drizzle all at once. His nose was running, his fingers and toes tingling and numb. He cinched his hood and leaned back against the swaying stalks in defeat.

And there it was.

In the weak beam of his flashlight, something pale and pink glowed like moonlight against the silver-gray silo, so out of place that his gaze was drawn to it. A scrap of torn cotton pajamas caught on a loose screw. Quickly he ran his fingers along the metal until he found a door latch. With his heart in his throat, he pulled it open.

That was where he found her. Huddled and unmoving, Becca lay on the floor of the silo. He dropped his flashlight and rushed to her side, calling her name again and again. Her eyes flickered open, the red glow suddenly bathing the darkness with crimson light. Her mouth parted. The tips of her fangs protruded just beyond her upturned lips, more vulnerable than threatening.

"Robby?" she croaked.

He slipped an arm beneath her and tried to help her sit up. "I'm here."

"Did you bring a stake?"

"No, of course not!"

She pushed him away. Her eyes grew brighter. She sat up under her own strength, though it seemed like a great effort. "Don't come any closer! I won't be able to stop myself."

"Let me help you," he said.

"You can't. No one can help me. I need…" She coughed and her whole body shuddered. She closed her eyes and sat back, fading again. "I tried small animals… rats… squirrels… but I'm still so hungry…"

Her torn pajamas hung like rags against her skin. There was almost nothing left to her. He inched closer to her again. "You didn't come into my house. You're still in control."

"I'm so hungry, though. You have to go."

His pulse quickened as her hands felt for his and she leaned closer, too, her breath cold on his neck. They were only inches apart now.

"You have to leave before I can't stop. *Please*, Robby. Please go."

"I came here to help you." He wove his fingers through hers and leaned closer. "I'm not going anywhere."

# 24

## Lost in the Maze

"Would you *please* just let me pay for it?" Amethyst's breath misted into puffy clouds as she shivered inside her overnight robe. The morning sun had brought little in the way of warmth to their house, something Amethyst emphasized by rubbing her hands together, then blowing into them and rubbing again. "It's my money. I want to pay for it. I've almost forgotten what it feels like to be warm!"

"Amethyst, don't be so dramatic," said Abby's mother between sips of coffee.

Abby's hair was wet from a rushed and very cold shower after breakfast, and she could feel it freezing to her scalp the longer she stood in the kitchen trying to make sense of the argument she'd walked in on. "What money?" she asked.

"It doesn't matter. Apparently I can't be trusted to spend it."

"I'm not going to let you waste it, that's all," said Mrs. Shepherd. "I may not be your real mother, but I am your legal guardian. It's my responsibility to help you make good decisions. We are a single income family, and times are tight. Throwing money away on unnecessary repairs is not one of them."

Amethyst shook her head. "Even Spooks is cold, and he's covered in fur."

"Who is Spooks?" Mrs. Shepherd asked.

"Forget about that. My point," Amethyst said, still shivering, "is that I am literally freezing to the kitchen floor as we speak."

"You are *figuratively* freezing to the floor, Amethyst. It's sixty degrees in here."

"What money?" Abby repeated, feeling inclined to agree with Amethyst even without knowing the details. The house was so cold Abby had tossed and turned all night, her toes never fully warming despite two layers of socks. All that tossing and turning had only led her to dwell on Poppy's warnings and worry even more about Tina, to say nothing of her constant fears for Becca.

*Stick to the problems you can solve*, she reminded herself, curling her fingers around the tiny keystone in her pajama pocket. She hadn't dared let their only ticket back to the Midnight Castle out of her sight even while she slept.

Amethyst waved an official-looking envelope in Abby's general direction, pulling her back into the conversation with her mom. "Fire insurance payment from my grandfather's house," she said. "I'm the recipient. For all the good it does me!"

"You will thank me when you're older," Mrs. Shepherd said.

"Not if we all freeze to death first."

Mrs. Shepherd's expression was sympathetic but firm. "The furnace has been on the fritz since we lost power during the storm a few days ago. I don't have the money to replace it just yet, so we'll all just have to bundle up tighter until the heat decides to kick in again. Things will be better when we're in the new house..." Her voice faltered on the last word. Peering out the kitchen window, her face wrinkled into a frown. "What's going on next door?"

A police cruiser had pulled into Robby's driveway and Chief Madison, Zeus's father, was clambering out. Abby cast a worried glance at her mother, whose expression didn't make her feel any better. Mr. O'Reilly opened the door to his house and ushered the police chief inside. Abby fired off a text to Robby and waited, but there was no immediate response. His window shade was pulled down and the bedroom looked dark from where she stood. He might still be sleeping on a normal Sunday, but probably not if his father had called the police.

A knock at the door startled her from her thoughts. Mrs. Shepherd jumped from the table to open it and Zeus appeared on the other side, breathing hard. "When did you last talk to Robby?" he asked between huffs. He must have run all the way from his house around the same time his father drove away in the cruiser.

Abby's glasses fogged as Zeus ducked inside. Closing the door behind him, she said, "Same as you. Last night when your mom dropped us off." A pit was forming in her stomach. Her throat felt tight and scratchy. "What's going on?"

"He's missing," Zeus said.

"He can't be missing. I *saw* him go inside his house. We both did," Abby added with a look to Amethyst, who nodded.

"He's not there now. Did he call, text, anything?" asked Zeus.

Abby shook her head. Nothing since yesterday.

Mrs. Shepherd, who had briefly left the room to grab a jacket and shoes, returned to the kitchen. "I'm going next door," she said, zipping her coat. "You three stay here."

Amethyst waited for Mrs. Shepherd to leave. "You don't think Robby—"

"No," Abby said. "No."

Amethyst and Zeus both gave her a dubious look, and even as she said it Abby knew he'd gone looking for Becca again. Or worse, she'd come looking for him.

Her phone buzzed. She jumped, then looked down at the screen.

"What is it?" asked Zeus.

Abby read the message twice. "It's... Robby," she said, relieved.

"Where is he?"

"The fairgrounds." She held up a hand to silence Zeus and Amethyst, who'd both started talking at once. "He says I need to come right now."

"I'll go tell my dad," Zeus said.

Abby shook her head, tilting the phone so he and Amethyst could both read it. "He says it's important. And he says I need to come alone."

"He must know that's never going to happen," Amethyst said as she and Abby slipped out the back door together a moment later. "You and I are a team."

Abby could hear Zeus curse under his breath and sprint after them. Thick clouds curtained the morning in darkness and the sun was just an indistinct smudge in the sky when they made it to the fairgrounds. Amethyst walked side by side with Abby, pretending not to notice Zeus.

At the corn maze, Abby plucked her wand from her back pocket and stepped inside. The tall rows of corn swayed a little in the breeze. Abby stopped at an intersection where the path cleared enough to see deeper into the maze. The grayish dome of the silo poked above the cornstalks. "That's where Robby said to meet," she told her friends.

Zeus touched her shoulder. "Are you sure it's not a trap?"

"Of course it's not," Abby said, giving her voice a note of false bravado. She knew it could be a ruse. She knew that if Robby had somehow been turned by Becca, he would probably come for her next. They all knew it. Abby felt a heavy weight pressing on her chest, and her throat ached with dread, but it wasn't like she could just ignore his message. She'd texted him again and again, but he hadn't replied. Finally, she'd made the decision to go to him. Now that they were inside the corn maze, she was having second thoughts—not that she was about to admit any of that to her ex-boyfriend.

She considered the two diverging paths at the next intersection before choosing the left. Zeus's hand brushed against hers, and when she looked questioningly at him, he pointed the opposite way. "This way's more direct. I'm actually really good at mazes," he added defensively when Amethyst shot him a questioning glare.

Abby let him take the lead. Soon a rustle up ahead stopped the three of them in their tracks. Something snapped around the bend, a branch or cornstalk, then silenced. Abby raised a finger to her lips and moved ahead of Zeus. Amethyst spun backward to take up the rear. Creeping silently forward, Abby turned the corner… and a flash of blue light blinded her. She cried out and stumbled backward into Zeus, seeing stars.

"Watch it!" said Olivia.

The rest of the coven materialized behind Olivia's outstretched wand, all four of them crowded close beneath the narrowing cornstalks. Olivia lowered her wand as Piper and the twins rushed forward to meet Abby, Amethyst, and Zeus. Strapped into a sling against Piper's chest, Flapper cawed irritably.

"What are you all doing here?" Abby managed.

Delphi tapped her right temple. "Psychic, remember? I had a vision last night."

Abby's head still buzzed. "Do you know something I don't?"

"Often, yes, but this time it's more of a gut feeling."

"Not exactly a detailed premonition," muttered Amethyst.

"I have lots of those, too." Color was rising in Delphi's cheeks. She crossed her arms, but her expression showed hurt. "See if I tell you when you get your first kiss."

"My first… really? When? *Who*?" asked Amethyst.

"Briony Morrow," Delphi said, turning away from her.

Amethyst's cheeks flushed crimson. "What? No, it's just a little crush—"

But Delphi was motioning toward a shadowy gap in the corn wall ahead. "Briony Morrow is here, too," she explained as the vampire slayer emerged onto the trampled path, crunching cornstalks underfoot. Grim faced, Briony carried a long, pointed stake.

"Did you follow us?" Olivia demanded.

Abby took a step backward as other voices joined Olivia's. There were so many people here now. Too many people. Her gaze drifted down to her phone screen and the last message Robby had sent her. *Come quickly. Come alone.* She didn't know what was waiting for her at the center of the maze, but her gut told her bringing her whole coven and a vampire slayer wasn't what Robby had in mind. She slipped another step backward. Zeus tilted his chin toward a slight opening between two rows as if reading her mind.

"Follow me," he whispered.

The path narrowed and turned a quick corner, and the last Abby saw of her friends as she snuck away was the purple shimmer of Amethyst's hair. Her fingers brushed Zeus's hand again before her brain could catch up. This time his expression curled to a quick smile, and he picked up the pace, but his fingers were still brushing hers. She hastened to keep by his side.

The maze was so thick that when they reached the old corn silo it came upon them without warning, suddenly there as they rounded a bend. The metallic paint was weathered and faded, a remnant from many corn mazes past—the one permanent structure in the corn field over the years. A creaky ladder led to the rounded top. A small square door stood shadowed just off the main pathway, only evident because Robby had told her to look for it. Abby pushed it lightly. The door creaked an inch, revealing only darkness.

"Robby?"

Silence at first, then the sound of someone shuffling in the shadows. "Are you alone?" It was his voice, but weaker than usual, dry and cracked. He'd been out in the cold all night. That was to be expected.

"Zeus is with me," she said, squinting. She couldn't see anything. "The others are in the corn maze somewhere, too. They followed us but we lost them for now. Can we come inside?"

"Just you."

Abby met Zeus's gaze. He shook his head.

"All right, just me." She squeezed her wand. "I'm coming in."

"Close the door behind you."

Zeus held her back. "I don't like this."

"That makes two of us." She pushed the door open before turning back toward Zeus. "Give me two minutes, then get the others."

Inside, a few dull shafts of light drifted down from cracks in the ceiling, but still the darkness threatened to overwhelm the glow of her wand. She felt around blindly and sniffed at something unusual in the air, something decaying and sour.

"Put your wand on the ground," Robby said.

Abby spun toward his voice. She still couldn't see him. "What?"

"Do you trust me?"

That was the million dollar question, wasn't it? "Of course," she said, and he clicked on his flashlight, illuminating half his face. A layer of sweat beaded the side of his forehead she could see.

"Then I need you to put your wand down," he told her again.

"Why?"

"Please. Just do it."

She tilted her head, considering, searching the small space for some scrap of understanding. It was no use. The darkness was too thick to make out even basic shapes. The desperation in his voice was clear, though, the raw need. She crouched to the floor and placed her wand on the cold dirt. She rose again to her full height and held both hands in front of her, palms out. "Okay, I did it. Now are you going to tell me—"

Robby rotated his flashlight to reveal more of himself. Tiny shapes swirled in Abby's eyes as she adjusted to the light. He was wearing just a thin t-shirt and jeans. His arms were pale and covered in goosebumps. Where there had been only darkness and shadow, now a second figure came into focus beside him. She had dark hair and crimson lips and a face both familiar and foreign. Abby lurched for her wand.

"You were specifically warned!" she yelled.

"Please don't be afraid of me," Becca said. "Please, Abby."

Abby raised her wand defensively. "Robby, are you—did she—?"

"She won't hurt you. I promise."

Robby's hand was covering his neck, but even in the dim light Abby could see the skin beneath his hand was raised and raw. She let out a horrified gasp, more a whimper. "Omigod, Robby, you didn't—she didn't—*please-please-please,* say she didn't—"

"Becca has something important to tell you."

Abby took another step back. Her eyes were misting. Her voice haltered. "She—she bit you…"

"There was no other way." Robby dropped his hand from his neck. There they were, the two telltale marks on his skin. "She was going to *die* without blood. It was the only choice. She didn't want to do it. I made her."

Abby wanted to run. She wanted to cry. She was almost to the door now and Zeus was right outside, Zeus and her coven and sunlight and Briony, just one more step. Her hand touched the door. Her fingers curled around the handle.

"I promise I won't do it again," Becca told her. "I won't need to because I—*we*—have a plan."

"It's not a trick," Robby said.

Abby let out a shaky breath. "It sure sounds like one!"

"Tell her," Robby urged Becca. "Tell her what you told me."

"I know the Shadow Lady's real name, Abby."

Her real name? What did that matter? Who cared about the Shadow Lady's real name? They needed to find her, not name her.

But Robby was grinning as if it did matter, as if it was the only thing that mattered.

"She knows her real name," he repeated, "and I think I know how we can use it to find her."

# 25

## Revelations

Abby bit back a yelp as the door handle twisted between her outstretched fingers. Light from outside flooded the silo and she danced back, reflexively covering her eyes. Having forced the door open, Briony marched inside with Zeus and the coven close on her heels.

"Back away from that creature!" yelled the vampire slayer.

"I tried to stop her," Zeus sputtered, bowling past Briony before pulling up short when he took in the scene. A smattering of other voices spoke over him—Amethyst, Olivia, Piper, and the twins all talking at once—and every wand but Abby's was raised toward Becca. Briony moved with shocking quickness, and Robby only just pushed away her stake in time.

"Don't try it," he said.

Briony's eyes flashed as she took him in. Her brow creased; her jaw clenched with recognition at the marks on his neck. "I can see your judgment is compromised."

Robby's grip tightened around Briony's stake. "Don't. Try it."

It was the steel in his voice that finally snapped Abby back into action. She didn't like what he'd done, but she understood it. It was stupid—God, was it stupid—but it was also loyal and caring, which were two of the qualities she admired most about him. And maybe, only maybe, he'd been right to do it. She laid her fingers over Robby's hand and slowly pushed the tip of Briony's stake toward the ground. "No one is staking anyone right now," she said.

"Becca isn't dangerous," Robby told the group. "She's our friend."

Briony shook her head. "That creature is no one's friend."

"I can't believe I'm saying this, but I agree with her," said Olivia, nodding at Briony.

Amethyst's gaze darted between Abby and Briony, her face shadowed and unreadable in the wandlight. The twins stared at Becca with wide unblinking eyes. Piper dragged deeply on her inhaler. Zeus hovered close to Abby, one hand still on the heavy silo door.

"I'm not dangerous to you. I promise I'm not," Becca said in a whispered voice.

"The promise of a vampire." Briony sniffed with contempt. Wind rattled the metal walls. The smell of decay filled the air. "The sooner we stake this one, the sooner its lies will end."

"You think that's the solution to everything," Robby said. "You think because you had to do it to your sister that we don't have any other choice either, but you're wrong. Becca needed blood to survive, so I gave it to her. She didn't take much, just enough to satisfy her hunger."

"She will turn you as surely as the sun will set tonight."

"You're wrong, Briony. I feel fine. She wasn't trying to hurt me. She's fighting it." Robby's color was rising, his voice growing stronger with every word. Abby had to admit he didn't seem anything like Becca had after T-Rex's first bite. "I spent the night here—the whole night. She only took enough blood to keep herself alive. We can trust her."

"You're really able to resist the… the hunger?" Abby asked Becca.

"I'm trying."

"How is that possible?"

"It's not possible," said Briony.

"Where have you been since the night you were taken?" Abby asked.

"I was disoriented when I woke up. I was somewhere dark, that's all I remember, and the others were still sleeping when I crept away. I stumbled until I found light, but it burned me, so I stuck to the shadows after that. I've been hiding ever since."

"A fairy tale," Briony muttered.

Abby ignored her. "What do you eat if not… you know…?"

"Squirrels. Chipmunks. Small animals." Becca attempted a smile. The flash of her teeth sent a shiver running down Abby's back, but Becca's gaze drifted to Piper, her expression apologetic. "I know you wouldn't approve, but it… seemed better than the alternative."

Abby let out a little laugh. "It's really you?"

"It really is." Becca opened her mouth wide to reveal two long fangs in the wandlight. "I think I'm going to need braces when this is all over, though."

"Oh, Becca."

Abby pushed Briony aside until she and Becca were inches apart. Her mind screamed in warning, but she slipped her wand into her back pocket anyway and wrapped her arms around her friend. Becca was cold and stiff, and Abby found herself holding her breath until Becca pulled back. Abby touched the smooth skin of her neck. No wound, no blood, no bite. She looked to the faces of her friends. "I think you can lower your wands."

"Or we could leave them up," said Amethyst, unblinking. "Just in case."

"Thank you for trusting me," Becca told Abby.

"You should not," warned Briony.

Abby ignored her. "The Shadow Lady told you her real name?"

"Not *told*, exactly. It's more of a feeling I get from her thoughts, a kind of... sense of self? Most of what I hear in my mind is like whispers, stray ideas, words or phrases repeated again and again. You know, the usual greatest hits—she will complete her circle of blood, she will have her revenge, all that stuff. But there's something *else* too, something underneath it I don't think she meant to share with me. The name she uses is Ereshkigal."

"What is that, like, Transylvanian or something?" asked Olivia.

"According to the internet, it's Sumerian," said Robby.

"Like in Russia?" asked Zeus.

"No, that's Siberian. Sumerians were one of the earliest known civilizations in the world." Robby met Briony's gaze. "You said the legend of the Shadow Lady stretches all the way back to Mesopotamia. Doesn't this confirm it? Her name, her sense of self, it matches what we know about where she came from—*when* she came from."

"Whatever you think you're learning about her, you can be certain it's only what she wants you to know. Perhaps she's laying a trap for you with this"—Robby tensed as Briony waved her stake in Beca's direction—"and like mice you are nibbling happily on the cheese while your doom looms quietly behind you."

"Shouldn't we at least consider the possibility it's not a trap?" asked Piper.

"I don't see how it could be," Abby said, running a hand through her hair, "because it still doesn't get us any closer to knowing where she's hiding, what she's doing now, or what she even wants with us."

Robby grinned. "It does when you consider what else we know about her. She's not just a vampire, she's also—"

"A witch," Delphi jumped in excitedly.

Abby's understanding clicked into place all at once. She couldn't contain a grin of her own. "The Hall of Fates?"

Robby nodded. "You told me about it the night you returned from the Midnight Castle. The Hall of Fates records the actions of every witch who's ever lived."

"Every secret laid bare," whispered Delphi. "Past, present, future."

"It could tell us where she is," said Daisy.

"And how to stop her," said Piper.

Robby glanced at each of them. "We could save Becca. We could save our classmates. We could undo everything the Shadow Lady has done here. We just need the Hall of Fates to help us find her."

Briony slammed her fist against the wall. "You know I want to destroy the Shadow Lady, but this"—she waved her free hand in Becca's direction—"this is not the way. You must never trust the word of a vampire, not even when it takes the form of someone you care about. Especially not then." She sighed wearily and raised her stake again. "Let me do what you cannot."

Abby leveled her wand in answer. One by one, the others joined hers. "You're not touching our friend," Abby told the slayer. "So I suggest you lower your stake—"

"—or one of us turns you into a toad," Daisy cut in.

"Toads do possess a sort of natural nobility," agreed Piper.

Briony's glare burned hot as coal. She let out another long breath, then retreated a step. Something in her expression made Abby's breath catch in her throat—the twist of her lips, maybe, the tiny crease between her eyebrows. The absolute conviction that Abby was making a horrible, irreparable mistake. The moment seemed to stretch on forever until finally Briony turned toward the door.

"Whatever follows now," she said, "will be on your conscience, not mine."

The silo door creaked on its hinges behind her.

Silence hung over them as the vampire slayer vanished into the swaying corn. Amethyst stared out the door, tense and open-mouthed, as if she were half considering going after her. Abby felt like she couldn't breathe, let alone speak, but she didn't have to because all at once the voices of her friends filled the echoing silo. She raised a hand to silence them.

"Briony made her decision," she finally said. "We've made ours. Now we have to see it through."

"It's not that simple." Olivia's voice cut across the others. "Am I the only one who remembers Prena saying witches can't enter the Hall of Fates?"

"We can't even get back to the Midnight Castle," said Piper.

"Actually, we can." Abby pulled the crystal keystone Prena had given her from her pocket, letting it catch the glow of their wandlight in her outstretched hand.

"What—what is that?" asked Delphi, blinking.

"Prena called it a keystone. A back door into the Midnight Castle. She told me to use it if we ever needed her." Abby stuffed the crystal back into her pocket. In a few halting words, she then recounted what Poppy Delacroix had told her about the Council the night before—about what they did to disobedient witches. "We know Tina ignored a Summons when she helped us fight the Shadow Lady. We know the Council will be even angrier when they find out why. Even if we didn't need to sneak into the Hall of Fates, I still think we'd need to use this keystone to find Tina and save her."

"You just can't help being the hero," muttered Olivia, rolling her eyes. "Maybe Tina doesn't need our help. Maybe we shouldn't be messing with things we don't understand. *Maybe*," she added, meeting Abby's rising glare with her own, "we should stick to the original plan and stay as far away from the Midnight Castle as we possibly can."

"You don't have to come." It was Delphi who'd spoken, and they all stared at her as she rubbed her forehead, considering an idea. "In fact, you shouldn't."

Olivia sniffed. "Oh sure, leave me behind. I'm not really one of the group anyway," she said with something like bitterness. "Is that it?"

"No, that's not what I mean at all," said Delphi. "Don't you remember my vision about the Midnight Castle? We were all there, all six of us, but you were different, Olivia. *You weren't yourself.*"

Olivia rolled her eyes. "Then who was I?"

"Me," said Robby.

"What are you talking about?" Olivia demanded,

"What if you were me? Or I was *you*, I guess." Robby straightened to his full height. His eyes had a new gleam to them, a look Abby knew well. "Daisy, what you said earlier about turning Briony into a toad, could you really do that?"

"Perhaps not me personally."

"But someone could? Someone powerful?"

Daisy nodded uncertainly. "Someone very powerful."

"And what about turning me into Olivia? Just my appearance, obviously, and just long enough for me to sneak into the Midnight Castle with you. I'll go to the Hall of Fates while the rest of you find Tina."

Amethyst's mouth dropped open.

Abby shook her head. "Robby, you're talking about transmogrification. It's difficult, almost impossible on such a complex scale. If something went wrong—"

"Last year you turned a rope into a python," Amethyst pointed out.

"That was an accident!"

"Think how much better it might go if you're doing it on purpose," Robby argued. "Only nonmagical people can enter the Hall of Fates, right? That's me. They'll never know I shouldn't be there because I'll look like I'm a witch." He wiggled his fingers. "Without any powers."

"We'll need a strand of your hair," Delphi said to Olivia. "A drop of your blood, too. The transmogrification will be stronger with your genetic material. Maybe it would help if you both—"

"I haven't agreed to this," said Olivia.

"Me either," said Abby.

Delphi gave them both a knowing smile. "You will, though. I know you will because I've already seen it happen. As for the spell, transmogrification will change every cell in Robby's body, but only for a short time. We'll need every advantage we can get to make it last, though of course if all goes well, we'll only be gone a few minutes."

Abby's stomach fluttered as she considered the possibilities. "What if it doesn't?"

"Let's try not to think about that."

"It's worth the risk," said Robby.

"Even if we find the Shadow Lady and slay her," asked Zeus, "how do we know for sure that will help Becca?"

"Briony said Miss Winters believed severing the tie between the Shadow Lady and her victims could restore them," Delphi reminded them.

"We're trusting Miss Winters now?" asked Olivia.

Becca cleared her throat. Her voice was soft and raspy when she spoke. "I can feel the Shadow Lady's dread. Her thoughts, her fears… She's scared of losing everything she's worked toward. I think if we stake her then I *can* be saved, just like Briony said.

That we can all be saved, Lucinda and Margery and the others, too."

Olivia wagged a finger in Becca's face. "That's another thing. I don't entirely trust you, either! Briony seemed pretty sure this is a trap."

"I don't trust myself either, Olivia. I can feel it inside me, this—this *urge*. I don't know how much longer I can fight it, but I know it's not forever." Becca spoke softly, shuffling her feet, not meeting anyone's eyes. "Sending Robby far away from me might be the safest thing for everyone. And having you stay here with me might be good, too. Maybe I need to be watched over by someone who doesn't trust me."

Abby looked at the faces of her friends. "If we do this," she said, already resigning herself to the possibility, "we'll only have one chance to get it right."

"I'm in," said Robby immediately.

When Olivia remained silent, Abby said, "What about you?"

Olivia let out a long, tortured breath. "I suppose," she said after a moment's hesitation. She looked to Robby, then quickly away. "But just for the record, I think it is super gross."

# 26

## Transformation

Robby tapped the keypad to the back door of the veterinary clinic until the lock made a soft click. A few barks and squawks met the group when they pushed inside, but the coven's training area was otherwise quiet. The hexagram on the floor came into focus as the dull fluorescent lights whirred to life. It was still early, but somewhere in the depths of the building, one of Tina's vet techs was probably busy cleaning cages or tending the overnight patients. The rest of the staff wouldn't be in for hours.

Sunlight was beginning to creep in through the shuttered windows, forcing Becca to sink into the shadows against the back wall. After letting her feed off him last night, the walk through the woods had been more exhausting for Robby than he'd let on, but he could tell it was even worse for her. She already looked weaker than she had just before they'd left the corn maze. Less like herself again, too. Her eyes still glowed unnaturally red, but as she watched Amethyst and the twins gather candles and replace the melted nubs at each point of the hexagram, her gaze was distant, almost vacant.

Abby touched Robby's shoulder, pulling him from his thoughts. "You should call your dad before we do this," she said, her expression all kindness and concern. "He's worried sick. The police are still out looking for you."

Robby had considered this, but there would be too many questions, too much time devoted to explanations about where he'd been, what he'd been doing, why he'd left the house in the first place. "You said we'll only be gone a little while," he told Abby.

"I mean, *hopefully.*" Brushing hair from her eyes, she leveled a serious look at him. In the harsh glow of the overhead lights, she looked overtired too. "Robby, time works strangely at the Midnight Castle. We might be gone hours. I don't think any of us knows how long it will be, exactly."

"Then we probably shouldn't waste any more time talking about it," he said, more sharply than he intended.

Abby bit back whatever reply she planned to make as Olivia approached with one of Tina's thick spell books clutched in one hand. Her finger marked a spot between the covers. "I think I found the most appropriate transmogrification spell," she said, pulling the book back from Abby when she reached for it, "and I think I should be the one to do it."

"What about what I think?" asked Robby.

"Isn't Abby the only one who's ever done it before?" asked Zeus.

"Again, that was an accident," Abby said. "Olivia, are you sure you want to do it?"

Robby was too tired to hide his skepticism. "Are you sure she *can?*"

"I'm the one who's sacrificing my individuality," said Olivia.

"And I'm the one whose body will be completely rewritten on a cellular level," Robby countered. "You can understand why I'd rather trust Abby with this."

Olivia dropped a hand to her hip. Her nostrils flared, but with obviously forced patience she said, "I appreciate you two have a special relationship"—at this, Zeus's expression became suddenly miserable—"but this is not an easy spell. In fact, it's very difficult."

"You're making my point."

"It's *so* difficult," Olivia cut over him, "that if Abby casts it, then the best case scenario is it drains most of her strength. You want her to be at her strongest inside the Midnight Castle, not totally exhausted. Right?"

Robby blew out a breath. "Right," he agreed reluctantly.

"Then let me do this."

Robby caught Abby's eye. She nodded. "She's just as good at magic as me."

"Better, if we're being honest," said Olivia.

"All right. Thanks, I guess. It's good of you to offer."

"Next time don't act so surprised."

They stood awkwardly until Abby pulled the keystone from her pocket and began inspecting it. "I should probably go figure out how this thing works," she said. Then with a reassuring smile she drifted across the room toward the rest of the coven. Zeus followed after her, hands in his pockets.

Becca remained slumped against the back wall, the crimson glare of her eyes growing dimmer until Daisy appeared beside her. "I found you a little snack from the canine blood bank," she said, unzipping her backpack. "You're looking a bit peckish."

When they'd all moved out of earshot, Olivia opened the spell book and scanned the page she'd bookmarked again. Her expression did nothing to give Robby encouragement. He tried to peer over her shoulder, but she elbowed him aside. "For an identical transmogrification," she told him, looking up, "it says we'll need to start with some of my hair." She plucked a few long blonde strands, wincing anticipatorily before each tug, then wove them into Robby's rusty curls with surprising tenderness. Peering back at the page once more, she wrinkled her nose. "Now comes the mixing of the blood."

"Mixing…?"

"Believe me, I don't like this any more than you do." Olivia placed the spell book on a small table. She traced the tip of her wand across her palm and a thin red gash opened in her skin. When a few scarlet drops pooled inside her hand, she turned her wand on Robby, whose hand was shaking. "Stop fidgeting, I told you this isn't an easy spell."

"Are you sure we shouldn't just ask Abby?"

"This is challenging enough without your whining." She leveled her wand at him, squinting as if eying him through a telescope, then slowly waved the tip above his palm. The skin split, but the wound was slight and painless. Robby and Olivia were about the same height, and she met his gaze as she twined her fingers with his and pressed their bloodied palms together. "I just realized that if this works—"

"If?" he asked.

"When," she said, smiling half-heartedly, "when this works, you'll be the only other person in the world who knows what it feels like to be me." Her blue eyes were bright and vulnerable, and when she squeezed his hand, there was a whole universe in her expression whose meaning Robby couldn't begin to guess at. She raised a questioning eyebrow. "Ready?"

He sucked in a deep breath. He wasn't ready. He couldn't imagine ever being ready.

"I'm going to count down from three," she told him. "Close your eyes and don't open them again until I say so or things could get interesting."

"What kind of interesting?"

"The bad kind," she said. "Okay, *three.*"

His left eye twitched as Olivia whispered a few words in Latin.

His lips swelled and grew numb.

His nose itched.

"*Two.*"

He grunted and the sound was unfamiliar, the voice not entirely his own.

The muscles in his arms and legs tightened.

His stomach cramped.

"*One.*"

His whole body felt like it was folding in on itself.

His clothes grew loose.

His limbs contracted.

Then his breathing grew shallower, and he could feel his hair and fingernails lengthening so quickly it made his skin itch until—

"*Done.* Open your eyes."

He did as he was told and found that the group had closed in around him, all except Becca who remained in the shadows, hood drawn tight against the creeping sunlight. Color had risen in Olivia's cheeks and her face was peppered with sweat. Abby and Piper stood to either side of her, mouths agape. Amethyst's mouth was a dark circle, too, and Zeus looked uncomfortably away from him. The twins both held their hands to their cheeks in what might have been shock.

"Did—did it work?" Robby asked. His voice was high and soft, not his voice at all. He held out his hands and studied the fingers—long, smooth, and definitely not his either. He made a fist and long fingernails bit into his palms. His eyes traced the contour of his hips to his knees, his ankles. His clothes were still his own, but the body inside them was not.

It was Olivia's.

"This is—I'm—" he breathed. His gaze fell to his chest, stunned. "I have—"

"*Those* are mine," Olivia said, nudging his chin back up to eye level.

He stumbled back a step. He would have collapsed if not for the twins, who each took an arm and propped him back up.

"Now you really are an honorary witch," said Daisy.

His legs wobbled. "Why is it so hard to walk?"

"Olivia's weight is distributed differently," Abby said, staring. "You'll get used to it."

"But not too used to it." Rising to her feet, Olivia unfurled her ponytail and removed a hair elastic, which she used to pull his now-blonde hair from his eyes. Lips pursed, she then unzipped her jacket and stuffed his arms inside it. "Don't even think of peeking at anything private, are we clear?"

Robby rolled his eyes in his best Olivia imitation. "Like I would *ever*."

"Oh, very good. You might actually pull this off."

Piper was still staring at Robby with her mouth half open. "She—he, I mean—doesn't need your jacket. We're going to have to find some of those awful cloaks again if we want to blend in."

"Yes, well, in the meantime I do not enjoy seeing myself in a *Star Wars* t-shirt," Olivia said, frowning at Robby's whole outfit.

"I think it rather suits you," said Daisy.

Pulling her gaze away from him at last, Abby tapped her watch. "I know this is a lot to process, but there's no telling how long the spell will last. We should get going."

"Could I just have a minute with Becca?" Robby asked.

Abby nodded, and all the witches but Olivia filtered to their respective points of the hexagram. Hands in his pockets, Zeus nodded once at Robby and then feigned interest in the floor pattern to give him some privacy. Olivia hovered close by, watching as Robby crossed the room to Becca.

"I really am the prettiest girl in Willow Cove," she said appreciatively as he moved.

"We could use a moment alone, Olivia," Robby said.

Some color had returned to Becca's cheeks, but it was her lips that drew his attention when he dropped to his knees beside her. They were the deep scarlet of blood. Twin puncture marks scarred the blood bags Daisy had brought her, both discarded on the floor by her feet. Robby was startled all over again at the stillness of her heartbeat as she pulled him close for a hug. She leaned back against the wall, half-smiling in a way that made Robby think she was holding back so her teeth didn't show. "Is it weird that I can still tell it's you even though you look like her? It's like you're still *you* no matter what you look like on the outside."

"So are you," he told her.

Her smile evaporated. "It's not the same, Robby. It's not just what I look like that's changed. Everything about me is different now. I'm never going to grow old. I'll never go to high school or college. I'll never have a job or get married or—or anything." She kicked at the empty blood bags, her face pale and miserable. "I'll just be *this*. Forever."

"Don't say that. We're going to find a way to fix it."

She leaned forward to kiss him on the forehead. "It's enough that you're trying."

Olivia coughed loudly, and when Robby looked up, she'd moved within a few feet of him. "The others are ready," she said, not unkindly this time. "Zeus and I are going to stay here with you, Becca."

"And Flapper!" called Piper from across the room.

Olivia rolled her eyes and returned her focus to Robby. "Look, I want you to take this with you," she said, pressing her wand into his hands. "We don't know how closely they'll look at you if you run into other witches before you get to the Hall of Fates. It'll be weird if you aren't carrying a wand. Bring it back in one piece, okay?"

"I will," he said, rising to his feet.

"Remember, you have my body—"

"I get it, Olivia, nothing creepy!"

"Just shut up for a second, will you?" She laid a hand on his shoulder. "You have my body, but *not* my powers. This could be dangerous. So, just… be careful, okay?"

"You'll stand in Olivia's spot," Abby told him, indicating the point of the hexagram opposite her. "It's going to feel really weird when you go through the portal."

"It feels weird already," Robby said under his breath. It was strange hearing Olivia's voice when he spoke. He was still unsteady on his feet, too. Even his posture was different, and he couldn't stop looking at himself—his fingers, his hands—or sneaking the occasional glimpse of his reflection in the window. *Olivia's* reflection.

Daisy took him by the elbow. "I'll walk with him. Her. They?" Her forehead creased. "What pronoun do you prefer right now?"

"I'm still *me*, Daze."

"Well, come this way," she said gently, guiding him toward the hexagram. It felt like every pair of eyes was staring as he moved.

Abby placed the keystone at the center of the hexagram before retracing her steps to her spot. She smiled at him encouragingly. "If all goes well, we'll be back in the blink of an eye."

"Be careful, Abby!" called Zeus. "I mean… everyone. Be careful, everyone!"

In the back of Robby's mind, he couldn't escape a vague worry that the portal might not open for him. But then the room began to spin. Colors exploded everywhere, and just like that he was like a kite in the wind, turning, whirling, rolling… and slamming to a halt. His breath caught in his throat and there was a *thump* that might have been his body falling to the floor. Everything was black all around him. Bile rose in his throat as he scrambled to his hands and knees, terrified that he was alone in the darkness. Alone somewhere he shouldn't be.

*Abby!*

He must have yelled her name because a heartbeat later she answered in a haltering voice. "I'm here. I—I can't see anything."

"Me either."

"I'll find you. Keep talking."

"Over here," he called.

"There's something poking into my back," came Piper's voice.

"I think that might be me," said Amethyst.

Robby reached out a hand to steady himself. "I—I'm going to be sick."

"I think Delphi already was," said Daisy.

"Yep, that was me."

Somewhere to Robby's left, Abby's wand shot to life, revealing herself and her coven in blurry blue lines. Amethyst, Piper, and the twins were all tangled together like they'd been caught in a game of Twister. Robby rolled onto his back, knees bent, and tried not to throw up. Abby crawled toward him.

"Wherever do you think we've landed?" asked Daisy, igniting the tip of her wand to reveal four rough square walls. "It doesn't look like the Midnight Castle."

"It doesn't look like anything," said Amethyst.

"Something is *still* poking in my back," said Piper, perturbed.

Abby and Daisy swung their wands in Piper's direction. The pooling of both their lights made Piper blink and rub her eyes, and she made another anxious noise as she climbed to her feet. Delphi scrambled to stand beside her. A pile of broomsticks shone back in the wandlight.

Abby grinned. "It's a broom closet."

Robby pointed to a thin strip of light on the wall behind Piper and the twins. "That must be the way out."

"First order of business is to figure out where exactly we are in the castle," Abby said.

Amethyst helped Robby to his feet. "No, the first order is to get away from the lovely smell of vomit," she said, stepping around a suspicious puddle near her feet. "*Then* we can come up with a plan."

# 27

## Separate Paths

Outside the broom closet, the chamber resolved into a wide windowless room with six narrow beds pushed close to a central stone hearth. Soft furs stretched across the floor like steppingstones, and a blazing fire gave everything a cozy warmth that almost made Abby sigh with pleasure. She hadn't realized just how cold she was until now.

The beds were neatly made, but there were other signs beyond the fire that suggested recent occupation—melted candles on the bedside tables, a pair of tall boots by the hearth, shirts and pants and socks flung across the bedchamber—and Abby was reminded of Prena's description of the castle's upper floors housing dormitories for visiting covens. Although the fire was invitingly warm, it also made the skin on her neck prickle with unease. The longer they lingered, the greater the risk of being discovered by someone who wouldn't expect them here.

A wave of cold air rippled the flames. Abby looked up to find the twins pulling open a thick oak door set into the far wall. Shivering, she followed them to a balcony with a low railing looking out over the distant white plains. Spiraling towers glistened beneath pinpricks of starlight, and a river of witches on brooms flowed between the many towers. The Council's High Tower stood at the center of it all, darker than the night itself.

Robby dropped his hands to the rail, shaking his head. "It's… it's a castle. An *actual* castle," he said, his whole face lighting up with a kind of wonder in spite of everything. Well, Olivia's face, not his, but Abby couldn't recall ever seeing such an awed expression from Olivia.

"It loses its charm real fast," Amethyst told him, heading back inside with Piper and the twins to escape the chill.

Robby pulled away from the ledge, rubbing his arms the same way Olivia did whenever she was cold. Still trying to get her bearings, Abby studied the skyline a moment longer before retreating inside to warm her hands by the fire. The crackling flames only reminded her of Delphi's premonition from their first trip to the Midnight Castle, and she wondered again what it could mean. "Where even one ember still glows," she repeated in a low whisper, "an inferno may follow."

Her gaze slid to Robby again. Delphi had been right about Olivia—she was both here and not here—so did that mean the rest of her vision would come true, too? Would they understand what it meant in time for it to be useful? It had something to do with the Council, Abby recalled, the six silver thrones and… a circle, maybe? She tried to remember Delphi's exact words, but the details were too fuzzy, and in the end it felt a little bit like trying to make sense of someone else's dream.

"How do I get to the Hall of Fates?" Robby caught himself twirling his ponytail around a finger and stopped, looking sheepish as he stuffed his hands into his pockets. "Can one of you teleport me there?"

"When have you ever seen us teleport?" Abby asked.

"Other than just a minute ago?"

"Portals are different. Anyway, the whole point of the Hall of Fates is that no one with magic can get in. Even if we could teleport, we couldn't teleport *there*."

"Which is why we'll need these," said Delphi, returning from the closet with a stack of brooms hovering behind her.

"And these," added Daisy, wrestling with a pile of fur cloaks piled up to her chin.

Robby blew out a deep breath. "We're flying?"

"When in Rome," said Delphi.

"Rome is a lot warmer," said Piper, accepting a cloak from Daisy with a conflicted expression on her face.

"You do know I can't fly," Robby pointed out.

Delphi raised her broom. "That's why you're going to ride with me while everyone else looks for Tina."

Abby had been wriggling into her cloak. Now she dropped the hood and said, "It can't be you, Delph, you react too strongly to the Hall of Fates. The last time we were here—"

"The last time we were here, I was the only one who even sensed the Hall of Fates. I'm our best chance of finding it exactly *because* I reacted so strongly to it. In fact, I'm almost positive I've already worked out where it is. We're better off splitting up."

"Haven't you noticed we've been living in an actual horror movie lately?" Amethyst protested, looking up from the hearth. "It never makes sense to split up."

"You can't know what kind of story you're in until it's over. We did just stumble out of a closet into a frozen fantasy land, which is very *The Lion, the Witch, and the Wardrobe* of us, if you ask me," said Daisy.

Abby didn't like it. "We need to stick together."

"I'll go with them," offered Daisy. "I can take care of Delphi and make sure Robby gets to the Hall of Fates. Divide and conquer and all that."

Robby shuffled his feet, impatient to get going. He looked so vulnerable just now, so out of place in his own skin—Olivia's skin. He was scared, that was obvious, but the tilt of his chin practically dared anyone to try to stop him. Abby supposed they were all taking risks. The stakes were too high to reject an idea just because it made her scared for him. Pulling Robby and the twins aside, she said, "Meet us back here when you're done."

Abby watched in silence as the trio made their way back to the balcony. Robby mounted the broom behind Delphi and wrapped his arms around her as they lifted off into the night, Daisy following close behind. Abby's gaze lingered until they grew small and indeterminate, just another speck in the starry night.

"Now what?" asked Amethyst.

"We should find Prena," Piper suggested.

Abby pulled her cloak tight against the chill. "We'll have to be careful. I don't want to make things more complicated for her. She's—"

"She's quite curious why you've come," interrupted a familiar voice. A shadow rippled at the edge of the room and Prena emerged into the firelight. Her wand gleamed to life, a red slash in the darkness, and in that brief glimpse Abby was reminded of her power—and of the Council's power, too. Of how much stronger these elder witches were than her.

"I think you'd better explain what you're up to," Prena continued, "and then *I'll* decide what happens next."

# 28

## A Glimpse of Things to Come

"Robby, could you—*oof*—move your hands—*oof*—a little bit—higher?" Delphi called over her shoulder. The back of her head bobbed up and down. "I can't breathe!"

"Sorry!" he yelled. "Better?"

"Not *that* high!"

"Sorry!" he yelled again.

He'd never flown with anyone but Abby, and only now did he appreciate just how hard she worked to make sure he didn't fall off. The broom bucked as Delphi swerved to avoid an oncoming blur of witches, and despite her protests he wrapped his arms tighter around her midsection. The Antarctic cold was unlike anything he'd ever experienced before, a cold that seemed to cut right to the bone. His breath froze to his cheeks. His teeth chattered, drowning out nearly every other sound. Delphi's dark hair whipped wildly around his face.

Veering hard to the right, Delphi brought them into a quieter flight path, and they drifted level with a snow-capped tower. Robby's heart was still pounding, but at this slower speed he was finally able to adjust his hands and legs. Some of the tension he'd been carrying melted away, even if Delphi seemed to be having a different reaction. Starlight reflected off her glasses as she looked over her shoulder, her breath billowing in thick gray puffs between them. "We're never going to reach the Hall of Fates if you asphyxiate me mid-flight," she said. "You have to squeeze the *broom*, not me!"

"This isn't—exactly—a smooth ride!" His fingers were like ice picks digging into her cloak, but he could still feel her muscles going rigid as she urged the broom forward again. The icy breeze hit him square in the face and he gripped harder. "How much f-f-farther?"

"I think we're almost there," Delphi called back to him. "I can feel the psychic hum getting louder."

"I can't feel it," said Daisy, flying alongside them.

"I can't even feel my face anymore!" Robby shouted over the whooshing wind.

Delphi pushed her broom past the long, crenellated wall encircling the Midnight Castle, then drifted toward the ground. The trio flew above the frozen plain until the castle was just a distant smudge on the horizon. Ahead of them, a bright aurora lit the night.

Pulling alongside a tall snowdrift, Delphi brought them to a stop and hopped to the ground. Robby rolled off the broom into knee-deep snow, his legs wobbly. It wasn't only the way his weight was distributed that threw him off. He knew Becca had taken as little blood from him as she could manage, but it was still a lot—and more than he'd told his friends. He took another moment to steady himself and when he looked up, Daze and Delphi were already bickering about something.

"Here, Delph? Really?"

"Yes, really." Delphi planted her broom in the snow bristle-end up, then pulled her cloak tight and clomped heavily through the deep powder, leaving a trail of white footprints behind. "Are you two coming or not?"

Robby and Daisy looked at each other.

"Where?!" Daisy yelled, panting hard as she and Robby struggled to catch up.

Snow was already riding up inside Robby's jeans. He gasped at the shock of it. Another minute and his ankles and feet would be as numb as his face.

Delphi flicked a finger toward the glowing sky just beyond the crest of a hill. "That's not a natural aurora. The psychic hum is—*unhhhh*—actually quite a bit louder here than inside the castle. The closer we get"—she slowed to a standstill and lowered her hood to take in the scene—"the more difficult it is for me to—*oof*, yep—to maintain my focus. I'm starting to feel it again, like a tingling in my eyes and ears, a pressure in the back of my skull. Like I'm on the verge of another episode."

"Then we should stop right here," Daisy cut in. "The last one was scary enough."

"It'll be all right now that I know what to expect. It was the surprise that got me before."

Robby and Daisy exchanged another glance. "You're sure?" he asked, touched that she would put herself through this for her friends.

Delphi gave him an encouraging smile. "Of course."

Robby was beyond cold now. It was all he could do to put one foot in front of the other, but another quick peek at Delphi put an end to any thought of complaint. Snow was collecting on her shoulders, in her hair. Still, she marched ahead with a determined smile when their eyes met again. He looked back at the spot where they'd landed, their brooms barely visible now. "Are you sure we can't just fly over the hill?" he asked.

"*They're* flying," Daisy agreed, pointing skyward to a half-dozen witches circling like vultures just beyond the snowy crest.

"They're patrolling," Delphi countered, "and I don't think we want to attract their attention."

Now that he'd noticed them, too, Robby couldn't help but agree with her.

"Definite flying monkey vibes," Daisy conceded.

After a few more steps, Delphi slowed to a stop, her eyes going wide and unfocused. Robby reached out to steady her, but the stupor seemed to pass just as quickly as it had come on. "I'm— I'm all right," she said, shaking cobwebs from her head. "It's just getting to be a little more than I was ready for." She tucked her shoulders together like she was trying to outlast a brain freeze. "You really mean to say neither of you can feel that?"

"Nothing," said Daisy.

Robby shook his head.

"Well, I think we're very close now."

They hunched together as they crested the hill. Six domed towers formed a circle across the snow white valley beyond, crackling with multihued lightning and flooding the night with color. A complicated web of columns and bridges and passages connected them to a seventh tower at the center of it all, soaring higher and brighter than the others. Something about the columns made Robby think of a shrine or sanctuary or... *oracular temple,* he decided, recalling a half-remembered lesson on ancient Greece. "What's a Greek temple doing in Antarctica?" he whispered, his breath catching in his throat.

"You think that's the weird part? Not the medieval castle we just left?" asked Daisy.

"It's all weird," he agreed. "How did Prena say the Midnight Castle got here?"

"Lifted stone by stone and reassembled here for all the witches of the world," Daisy told him, repeating what Abby had told him. "I guess that must be how the Hall of Fates got here, too—though obviously from somewhere *else*. It's definitely Greek, right, Delph?"

Delphi murmured softly in agreement.

"Like the Acropolis? Or is it the Parthenon? I can never remember which is the temple and which is the—oh, no!" Daisy's voice grew sharp with worry. "Not again!"

Robby tore his gaze away from the illuminated domes. Delphi stood rigid like a statue beside him, her eyelids flickering open and shut, open and shut. Staring at her twin, Daisy was practically paralyzed, too. Robby waved a hand in front of Delphi's face and spun her away from the view below.

"You... and me..." Delphi whispered, her eyes snapping open, her gaze fixing on Robby.

"What about us?" Robby asked.

Her voice grew breathy and urgent. "We... we're... together..."

Delphi's hand darted to his. Robby pulled away, but Daisy said, "No, let her—please, take her hand—you can be an anchor, I think Prena called it. You can pull her out of this. Only you, only someone without magic!"

Robby did as she told him. Delphi's hands were surprisingly warm, her grip like a vise, sudden and crushing. "What do you mean, together?" he asked her, mostly to keep her talking, to keep the sound of his voice in her ears. To anchor her like Daisy wanted.

"We... we're going to..."

"Delphi, come back. Tell me what you're seeing. We're going to *what*?"

All at once her eyes shot open and she stumbled into his arms. He barely kept his balance as he caught her. With Daisy's help, he propped her up, and this time Delphi's gaze followed him like a spotlight. She blinked as if startled at the sight of him. "Robby?"

"I'm here."

She pressed her hand to his again. Still warm. "I—I saw *us*. We were together at the winter dance, and then later, we were..." Delphi pursed her lips, looking as if she were trying to outrun a fading dream. "We were in high school and we—*oh*."

"Oh?" said Robby and Daisy at the same time.

Delphi lowered her gaze. "Never mind."

"Tell me," said Robby. "Please."

Almost to herself, Delphi whispered, "I guess it makes sense. I'm surprised, obviously, but not totally opposed… I mean, it's not like the thought hasn't crossed my mind before."

"Whatever are you talking about?" asked Daisy.

Delphi fixed her gaze on Robby again. Little flecks of ice melted against her cheeks. She smiled at him uncertainly. "In my vision, I saw us at the dance. I can still see it right now, almost like it's already happened. The streamers in the gym, the music playing—we're both happy, we're having fun. The next part is fuzzier, but I think—no, I'm almost positive—in high school we're going to get… even more friendly with each other. If you know what I mean."

Daisy let out a dismissive snort before Robby could respond. "I think Becca's going to have something to say about that," she said.

Then her voice trailed off. Her face went white.

"Becca wasn't in any of my visions," Delphi said in a small voice.

Robby pulled his hand away from hers. "That doesn't mean anything."

"You're right," Delphi assured him, her voice apologetic. "You're totally right."

"She gets things wrong all the time," Daisy added. "She's not perfect."

Delphi looked past Robby, focusing on the aurora. "There are so many different possible fates," she said after a moment's consideration, "I don't know how *anyone* could ever really… really…" Her voice trailed off as she lost the thread.

Then all at once she was darting back toward the crest of the hill, kicking up snow as she moved. Robby caught her wrist before she could get too far away. Gently, he guided her away from the lights again. Over his shoulder, he called, "Daze, you have to get her away from here."

"We can't leave you!"

"You can't get any closer. It's not safe for her. Take Delphi back to the brooms and I'll meet you there as soon as I can."

Daisy waved a hand in the general direction of the circling witches. "What about the flying monkeys?"

"I was always going to have to get past them somehow," he reminded her. "You know I have to do this alone."

Making his way into the valley, he tried not to think about Delphi's visions or what she thought it meant for the two of them. It didn't matter right now. None of it did. If he was going to save Becca, he needed to focus on the Hall of Fates.

Everything else would sort itself out later.

# 29

## An Agreement

Abby's heart was still thudding in her chest, but she tried to keep her voice light as Prena drew nearer. "You scared me," she said, lowering her wand. Amethyst and Piper did the same. "We didn't expect you to just… appear."

"You *should* be scared. This is a bad time to be in the Midnight Castle. Very bad for you girls in particular."

Prena's eyes had a scarlet sheen to them in the glow of her wandlight, and Abby was briefly reminded of Becca, of the glowing alienness of her friend's eyes. Prena's expression softened as she took in Abby and her friends. The obvious question about where the rest of their coven might be was clear on her face, but she didn't ask, and Abby decided not to volunteer the information. It was probably better for everyone involved.

"You said you could help us if we ever needed something," Abby said instead. "I think we need something."

Prena waved her wand until four stiff wooden chairs materialized by the fire. "None of you appear to be injured. That's good news at least. Now, sit down and explain to me what's going on before anyone else learns you're here."

Abby shook her head. "There's no time—"

"Sit down, Abby." She sighed apologetically. "Please sit down, I mean. Time is the least of your worries at the Midnight Castle. I need to know what's going on before I'll know how to help you."

"*If* you can help us, you mean." Prena tilted her head in question and Abby continued, "You said you'd do anything you could to help, as long as it didn't compromise your position."

"So I did," Prena replied, sinking into a chair beside the fire and sweeping a hand toward the other seats. Reluctantly, Abby and her friends joined her. Prena's face was golden in the firelight, but her expression remained guarded. "Let's find out whether or not I can be of help. What brings you back here?"

"We're worried about Tina. We spoke to someone who told us—"

"—what the Council does to disobedient witches," Amethyst jumped in. Her nostrils flared as she wagged a hand at Prena. "Witches like my mother."

Abby placed a warning hand on her friend's shoulder, but Amethyst brushed it off. Abby could have kicked herself for not realizing Amethyst might react this way. Of course she was angry! She had every right to be. But right now, they needed to focus on saving Tina, not on something that happened a generation ago, no matter how horrible.

"Amethyst, I did nothing to your mother." Prena sat forward to address her directly. "You must realize that. I've wasn't even on the Council when your mother was Quelled. I hate that it happened to her. I hate that it's happened to anyone. That it's still happening."

"Have you done it to other witches?" Amethyst pressed. "You personally?"

"We just want to know where Tina is," Abby said at the same time. She knew she was speaking over Amethyst, steering the conversation away from the answers her friend wanted, but they needed to be smart—to compartmentalize their anger—if they were going to help Tina. She looked meaningfully at Amethyst until her friend sat back in her chair.

"We're worried about Tina. That's why we're here." Abby almost added, "It's the only reason," but that wasn't entirely true, and she worried Prena might sense the lie if she pressed it. "If you could just tell us where to find her, we'll go, and you'll never have to hear from us again."

Prena turned her eyes upward as if staring at something only she could see. "I'm afraid the situation has become more complicated. I cannot allow you to skulk about the Midnight Castle until we've set some ground rules. Are we agreed?"

Abby and Piper both snuck a glance at Amethyst. Having said what she needed to say, Amethyst's posture seemed looser now, her expression a little less intense. When all three of them nodded their agreement, Prena continued. "You're right about the Council. About what they do to disobedient witches. But not me. Not happily, at least."

"You're still complicit," Amethyst whispered under her breath.

Prena did not quite meet any of their eyes when she replied. "The Council has done terrible things. I suppose I am complicit because I've done terrible things as well. I've had no choice. That's what I'm trying to change, girls. I told you before that our goals are aligned. I do believe that, just as I believe that if you work with me, we might change things even faster. I didn't claw my way onto the Council to sustain the status quo. I want to lead a Council that does what's right instead of what benefits the privileged and powerful. I can't do it alone."

*I want to lead the Council,* Abby repeated to herself. Was that really what this was about for Prena? Was all her moral certainty just a smokescreen to hide her real desire to be in control, even if only subconsciously? Abby wasn't sure, but she hoped not, because more and more she was coming to believe there was a good person in there—that Prena's heart was in the right place, at least mostly. Tina certainly seemed to believe it. Hadn't she said Prena was the one who'd sent Briony to help them?

"What exactly do you want from us?" Abby asked.

"At the moment, nothing. The pieces are still not in place. I simply want to be able to count on you when the day comes."

"If we agree," said Piper, "you'll tell us where to find Tina?"

"I'm not entirely certain she would want me to tell you," Prena said.

Abby sat forward in her chair. "We're going to find her whether you help us or not. If you want to prove we're on the same side, this is how you do it. This is how you get us to help you when the time comes."

Prena closed her eyes, breathing slow and deep. A moment later, she turned her palm up and conjured a three-dimensional map of the Midnight Castle above her outstretched hand. "This is where Tina is being held," she said, pointing with her other hand, "and this is where we are now. Please understand, you must leave the Midnight Castle in the same manner you arrived. When you're done, return to the broom closet and use the keystone. Anything else will be… less precise."

*Back through the wardrobe and home from Narnia*, Abby thought.

Prena seemed to consider her next words carefully. "You understand I have no choice but to preserve my position on the Council for the larger conflict to come. I can't risk everything I've worked for to help you." Their eyes met and she held their gazes, solemn and serious. "If you're caught going against the will of the Council, I cannot protect you. I *will* not."

"We understand," said Abby.

Amethyst nodded. "We'll risk it."

Piper groped inside her cloak for her inhaler. "Tina would do it for us. She already has."

"It will be very dangerous," Prena reminded them.

Abby shrugged more confidently than she felt. "What else is new?"

"You're certainly brave." Prena's smile was warm, even affectionate. "I only hope you don't come to regret it."

# 30

## The Hall of Fates

Racing down the snowy slope, Robby risked a glance at the witches circling overhead. They hadn't seemed to notice him yet. His tracks were already hidden by the snow and his cloak was practically white with ice, so it wasn't impossible to think they'd *never* notice him. He hoped not, anyway.

He slowed to wipe snow from his face and accidentally poked himself in the eye with one of Olivia's long fingernails. So far, the transmogrification spell was holding, but for how much longer? He let his gaze linger on the distant spot where he'd last seen the twins, worried for them. Worried about a lot of things, if he were being honest.

*You and me, together,* Delphi had said.

No, that wasn't going to happen, and he needed to stop his thoughts from circling back to it, because the most important thing right now was finding his way into the Hall of Fates. With a final look to the sky, he forged ahead to the first tower and tried the handle of a door coated with ice. It didn't budge.

He tried again and something hissed at his feet like escaping gas. He darted back but was too slow to stop a tendril of dark mist from wrapping around him, prodding him, poking. His skin fizzed like Pop Rocks as the mist scraped along every inch of his body—Olivia's body—and then seeped *inside* him, through his mouth, his nose, his ears. He could feel it pulling at the stitches of Olivia's spellwork, tugging at every loose thread. But her spell must have been strong, because almost as quickly as it had started, the fizzing ended.

The coiling mist fell away.

The door swung open.

The light on the other side was warm and golden, almost welcoming. Robby spared a final glance at the witches overhead—they *had* noticed him, he decided, they were watching him even now—and he hesitated at the doorstep. *If it was a test*, he thought, *did I pass?*

"I know how you're feeling," said a voice from somewhere beyond the threshold. A moment later a lightly freckled face appeared before him, peering intently in his direction. It was a girl, maybe a young woman, in a flimsy white robe that ended just below her bare ankles. A braided golden rope encircled her waist like a decorative belt. Staring up at him from her wheelchair, she met his surprised expression with a sympathetic smile. "Part of you hoped you'd be found wanting, because at least that would mean they didn't take it all."

Her accent was thick and hard to understand. It took him an extra beat to make sense of her words. "All of what?" he asked with Olivia's voice, higher than he intended.

"All your magic, of course. You can't enter the Hall of Fates if you still have the spark, but don't worry, they'll have scooped out every last bit, I promise you that. You're safe here. I'm Bree, by the way."

She extended a hand. Robby shook it, blinking.

"Brie," he repeated uncertainly. "Like the cheese?"

She corrected him with a laugh. "Bree, from the Celtic *briganti,* meaning powerful or exalted. And I've heard all the jokes, so you needn't bother saying it—oh, how the mighty have fallen. It's true. But you'll know all about that, too, I suppose."

"I—I will?"

"Every new Fatekeeper feels the same way at first. It's not like any of us choose this path, and you never entirely get used to it. Of course, I was told you'd be a full-grown woman, but we do get the odd mix-up here and there, even with all the prophecies and oracles swirling about." When Robby didn't say anything to that, the girl narrowed her eyes, studying him closer. "You do look young for a Fatekeeper, though. Familiar, too. Have we met?"

*Had* they? Robby closed his eyes, thinking hard. All at once it came to him. Abby had never told him the girl's name, but the thick accent, the wheelchair, the kind green eyes—it all added up to the same young Fatekeeper who'd saved Delphi from her vision on their first visit to the Midnight Castle. Of course she'd recognize him. She thought he was Olivia. She thought they'd already met.

There was a note of surprise in Bree's voice as she came to the same conclusion. "I do remember you now, but what have they done? You're too young for this. It isn't right. Come inside, we'll get you taken care of. You're with a friend now." The concern in her voice only grew deeper as she rolled back and caught sight of him in the full light. "They haven't even given you a proper robe!"

Taking him by the hand, she all but dragged him across the threshold. Sconces lined the rounded walls and a winding ramp led upward toward an eerie glow that must have come from the shining dome high above. Most of the light inside the chamber spilled in through a series of passages, the widest of which acted as a long window to the central tower.

What had looked like lightning from the outside now seemed more like tangled, shimmering threads. It was so bright that Robby couldn't stare directly at it for more than a heartbeat. Wispy strands twined onto the bridges and walkways like technicolor vines; others were threaded through a shining loom, where a dozen women dressed like Bree hurried like bees in a hive, many of them clutching scrolls. Tendrils trailed behind like kite strings.

"The Loom of Fate," Bree said matter-of-factly, as if that explained everything. She snapped her fingers when she caught Robby staring at it. "Best not to look too long. Come on, we'll get you a robe and maybe a good cuppa before we get started."

The air inside the tower was shockingly warm compared to the weather outside. Robby's hands and feet tingled from the sudden change, and he might have stood there forever if Bree hadn't gently nudged him with her wheelchair. With a friendly smile, she led him up the ramp to the next level, where she began sorting through rows of shelves in a crowded storeroom. She looked him up and down and then produced a flimsy robe and belt like her own. "Knock when you're dressed, then I'll show you where to— what is it?"

Robby's cheeks flushed. He was not going to strip down, not even with his eyes closed. Olivia would never forgive him. "I can't change into this."

"You're just a slip of a thing. Of course it'll fit." Her expression grew concerned as he pushed the robe back into her lap. She ran a hand through her copper curls and considered him with a tilt of her head. "But is that all you're worried about, I wonder? I've never seen such a pretty girl look so uncomfortable in her own skin."

Robby's heart beat fast, but something about the way she looked at him with those bright green eyes made him wonder about her.

*It's not like any of us chooses this path,* she'd said.
*You never entirely get used to it.*
*It isn't right.*

Those weren't the words of someone committed to the Council. He didn't think she'd turn him in, at least not right away, not until she'd heard what he had to say. "What if I told you it's not really… my skin?" he asked.

Bree wheeled to the door and pushed it closed behind her. "Whose might it be, then?"

No going back now.

"Her name is Olivia. She's a—a witch. I'm not."

"You weren't sent here to be a Fatekeeper," Bree said flatly.

Robby shook his head. "Someone I care about is in danger. The Hall of Fates might have information that can save her. I thought…" He closed his eyes, praying he'd read her right. "I thought maybe you could help me."

"What's your real name?"

Robby took another deep breath and told her.

Bree's laugh was so loud he half-expected the rest of the Fatekeepers to burst inside and see what had caused it. Instead, the girl sat back in her wheelchair and shook her head, eyes still shining with amusement. "You're a boy."

Robby nodded.

"The cheek of it," she said, grinning. "How did you get here, Robby? And I don't mean the Hall of Fates. I mean the Midnight Castle. How did you get *here*?"

"My friend was given a keystone from someone named Priya, I think? Perna?"

"Prena," Bree corrected.

Silence stretched between them, but after a moment Bree pressed the white robe back into his hands. "You can't afford to stand out here. Close your eyes and I'll help you change. You've not got any bits I haven't seen before," she added with another shake of her head. "Anyone else might have turned you in, but lucky for you I've got no love for anyone on the Council except Sister Novus."

"You'll—you'll help me?"

"I'll help." Her green eyes sparkled mischievously. "Just as soon as you tell me whose fate it is we're here to find."

The ramp was narrow and switched back and forth at each new level, but Bree seemed to have no difficulty navigating the tower in her wheelchair. "I've been doing this for longer than you've been alive," she said, catching Robby's gaze as she wheeled over the uneven flagstones. "Try to look like you're supposed to be here or we'll both end up before the Council. Hunch a little if you need to, but make sure your robe conceals your trainers."

"Trainers?"

"Shoes, sneakers, whatever you call them."

Robby wasn't sure why she seemed so concerned. The other Fatekeepers were so absorbed in their duties they rarely even made eye contact. As far as he could tell, Bree was the only one who seemed to be curious about anything. "Do you ever wonder about your own fate?" he asked when they reached the top floor.

She touched his elbow to indicate he should keep to the shelf-lined outer walls, avoiding the center where a crackling red ball hovered beneath the curve of the dome. Jagged filaments dangled beneath it. A stout-looking Fatekeeper wound them into a scroll and left the chamber. "Truth be told, I'd rather not know how it all turns out for me," Bree said under her breath, watching the other woman leave. "I want to believe I have a better second act coming. If I knew for certain my story ended here, I'm not sure how I'd find the strength to keep going."

She rolled forward to block his view of the hovering ball, bringing her face into stark relief. The glow revealed a pretty constellation of freckles that reminded him a little of Abby. "It's safe to look at individual fates, but don't look directly at that tangle," she warned with a grim twist of her mouth. The shelves were bent under the weight of so many scrolls, and she rolled back and forth between them, opening one, discarding it, and repeating the process again and again. "Can you reach that one for me? No, the other one, little to the left—yes, perfect, that one."

Robby slid the scroll toward him, then handed it to Bree and waited. A slight frown creased her lips as her eyes passed over its arcane script.

"What is it?" he asked. "Not the right one?"

Bree was quiet for a moment. "What did you say the name was again?"

"Ereshkigal. The Shadow Lady."

Bree handed the scroll back to him. "I was worried about this. It *should* be here, if the witch you're looking for is truly one of the ancients. The thing is, I've been a Fatekeeper for"— she did the math, her forehead creasing—"well, it's hard to keep track of how long it's been in the outside world. How long has it been since the Allies took Berlin?"

Robby gaped at her. "You mean World War II?"

"Back home we just called it 'the War,' but yes, exactly. My point is I've read all the ancient fates and I've never come across that one. What else can you tell me about this witch you're looking for?"

"She's also a vampire."

"Buried the lead there, didn't you?"

Robby explained how the Shadow Lady kept turning up with new names at different points throughout history. "But we have reason to believe her real name is Sumerian," he added. "Dating all the way back to the Bronze Age."

Bree listened carefully. "Maybe… No, that can't be right. But what if…?"

"What if *what*?"

"You'll have seen all the towers outside. Each one records the fates of a different era. We're in the Tower of Ancient Fates right now. There's also Prehistory, the Middle Ages, Modern times, and the Tower of the Unborn, which is where all the future fates are recorded. But I wonder…"

Thinking hard, she held up a finger to forestall his next question. "Every fate falls into one of three categories. Type one:

You're born, you die, you move only in one direction. That's most people. Type two: You move through time in stops and starts, but the weave follows along with you. That's witches, mostly, but one trip to the Midnight Castle will do it, so that'll be you now, too."

"Stops and starts?"

"Time can be a bit dodgy here. You'll see." She waggled three fingers at him. "The third type of fate is what we call Untethered. That's someone who's run loops around the weave so many times the threads snap right off. Type three fates break free of the weave, so to speak. They're not tethered to it anymore." She made a cutting motion with her fingers. "Unlike you or me, their final fate is so tangled we can't decipher it. If this Ereshkigal is a type three, we'll need to go to the Tower of Untethered Fates to learn anything. But that area is monitored."

Robby's gaze drifted to the hovering red ball. He shivered and looked away. "Will you take me?"

"A friend of mine used to say fortune favors the bold. I've come to believe she was probably right."

"I always preferred, 'Chance favors the prepared mind.'"

"Yes, well, that particular ship has already sailed, don't you think?" Bree raised an amused eyebrow at him. Her face shimmered in the iridescent light. "Are you coming or what?"

# 31

## Untethered

"Follow me. Don't say anything," Bree whispered as they slipped into a corridor that followed the circular curve of the six outer towers. Empty sconces dotted the walls where lights might once have been, and the red glow from the Tower of Ancient Fates thinned the farther they moved from it. Soon only a few crackling wisps drifted like seaweed near their feet, barely lighting the way.

Robby's footsteps echoed on the rough stones. Bree rolled silently ahead. The air grew frigid and still, but after a few minutes the darkness took on the quality of predawn light, and then the passage opened into a mirror image of the first tower. Here the light from above was green instead of red, and a hint of warmth returned.

"Is this—?"

"Shhh, I said don't say anything." Bree smiled at another Fatekeeper rushing past. "This is the Tower of the Unborn. We're not supposed to be here, either, but it's not strictly off limits. The Tower of Untethered Fates is around the next curve. Act like you belong."

Looking this way and that, Bree rolled into the adjoining passage. Robby hastened to keep up. Away from the greenish glow, the air again grew cold and his fingers and toes tingled with pins and needles. He gazed jealously at his clothes in Bree's lap. Then his thoughts drifted to Daisy and Delphi waiting out in the snow and he picked up his pace. The sooner he found what he needed here, the sooner they could all warm up at home.

The passage darkened as before, then thinned into a purplish haze when they drew near the next tower. They passed a pair of Fatekeepers coming down the ramp, but neither woman questioned them. Robby watched them disappear around the bend, mystified. "If this is a restricted area," he asked in a low voice, "why didn't they stop us?"

"When you act like you're supposed to be somewhere, people often assume you are. That's a little trick I picked up in the War."

"That actually works?"

"Sometimes." She flashed him a rueful smile. "Not always."

Rounding the final switchback, they emerged at the top of another domed chamber, this one dominated by a hovering tangle of purple lights. Where the first tower's walls had been lined with thousands of scrolls, here there were only a few hundred, maybe even less. Each was sealed inside a heavy cylindrical case—some of them leather, some wood or metal. Bree wheeled back and forth until something caught her attention. She bent to the floor and presented him with a scroll case that hissed like an overheated tea kettle.

"I do love being right," she said with a note of pride. "You read. I'll keep watch."

He broke a nail fumbling with the leather strap, but finally the lid flipped open. The light inside it seared flashes in his vision, and he had to look away, blinking. When he looked again, a scroll shimmered back at him. Wisps of light gleamed like frayed strings as he unspooled it, as if both ends had been roughly torn from some larger parchment. Writing moved across the page like ants marching from margin to margin. Robby swayed where he stood, unsure where to look. Unsure *how* to look.

"Take your time, of course," Bree whispered sarcastically from the doorway. "We've all day if you need it."

Even when Robby followed the words across the page, he still couldn't make sense of them. "It's in Latin."

"Of course it's in Latin. That's the language of witchcraft."

Robby shook his head. "I can't read Latin."

"What kind of witch can't—" Bree started, then cut herself short. "I almost forgot in all the excitement. You're not a witch at all." Rolling back to him, she held out a hand, palm up. "What is it you want to know?"

"Anything. Everything."

Bree laughed. "Let's narrow it down. Tell me what you *need* to know."

"Where's the Shadow Lady hiding now?"

"It doesn't work like that. Time isn't moving in a straight line for her. There is no *now*." Bree tapped the purple writing with one finger. "Use those wits of yours. What can it still tell you?"

"I don't know! I don't even know how she became a vampire."

Bree's face lit up. "Maybe that's a good place to start." As her fingers traced the words, a few loose tendrils curled around her hand like roots. She shooed them aside, whispering while she read. "Even as a child, Ereshkigal was curious about blood. Its taste. Its power. Especially the power of blood magic." Her gaze darted between Robby and the scroll like a metronome. "That's how she became a vampire."

"I don't understand. Who turned her?"

"That's what I'm trying to explain—no one did. She was the first of her kind, the mother of all that have followed. Witches draw magic from the natural world, you understand? The five elements. But not *this* witch. She fuels her magic with the blood of others." Bree looked as if she might say something more, but a low steady thump in the distance brought her up short. She stared at the doorway until the noise faded. "After a few millennia, even the Council of Witches tired of her. They banished her to—well, that can't be right."

"Where?"

Bree pursed her lips. "*Here*. The Midnight Castle." She traced the shimmering letters again, reading and re-reading. "I don't understand what it means. She's here but also not here. The threads are so tangled. You said she appears at different moments in history. When was she last seen before now?"

"The nineteenth century."

Bree wrinkled her nose at the scroll, then shook her head. "What about before that?"

"The 1600s," Robby said, trying to remember how Briony had described it. "She was living as a Hungarian noblewoman. On the night of a total lunar eclipse, she attacked entire villages—but by morning she was gone. Vanished without a trace. Even her castle seems to have disappeared." He looked up suddenly, startled.

"What is it?" asked Bree.

"'Lifted stone by stone and reassembled here for all the witches of the world,'" Robby said, thinking of what Daisy had told him. "Isn't that the story of the Midnight Castle?"

"It's *her* castle," Bree whispered, understanding his meaning. "The Council banished her and took it for themselves."

"Then she must be here somewhere," Robby said, his eyes darting about the tower.

"Here but not here," Bree reminded him. "Robby, I think they imprisoned her in a time pocket just like this one—locked away in a single moment forever. At least until she escaped."

Robby peered over Bree's shoulder as if the writing might somehow make more sense now. "We know she used the portal created by Miss Winters's blood magic to come into the modern world, but we could never figure out where she was coming from—or where she went afterward. Briony couldn't find any trace of her."

"Who's Briony?" asked Bree. "Who's Miss Winters?"

"Vampire slayer. Rogue witch."

"You have all the excitement, don't you?"

Robby nodded. Like a Rubik's Cube snapping into place, his thoughts were rearranging around a new idea. Briony thought the Shadow Lady had retreated to wherever she'd come from, somewhere no one could ever find her. "Here but not here," he repeated, catching Bree's eye. "Not just where but also *when*."

Bree let out a slow breath. "The time pocket."

"Her secret prison is her castle in the Carpathian Mountains," Robby said. "A single moment in time, frozen forever on the night they banished her in 1614. The Night of Blood and Shadows."

"That's how her weave became so tangled," Bree said. Before Robby could offer anything further, the sound of footsteps grew louder again. More determined. "Speaking of time, I think ours may be almost up," she said, quickly rolling the scroll and stuffing it back into its case. The light in the room dimmed fractionally as she banged the lid closed.

"Who is it?" Robby whispered.

"Probably someone who figured out we're not supposed to be here." She glanced about the room, doing a quick calculation. "Run back the way we came. Don't stop until you're well clear of the Hall of Fates."

Robby hesitated. "Come with me."

"I'd only slow you down, and I'm needed here anyway." She raised a hand to quiet his protest. "There's change coming sooner than those old crones on the Council suspect. Sister Novus needs people here. Loyal people."

"But they'll catch you."

"I can talk my way out of anything. It's you who sticks out like a sore thumb." She pushed his bundle of clothes into his arms. "Off you go!"

Urgent voices joined the footsteps in the distance.

"Thank you," Robby said. "Good luck, Bree."

He sprinted down the ramp, knocking into another Fatekeeper as he turned. He continued running without a backward glance while somewhere ahead, more voices rose in protest. The way was still clear as he neared the outer temple area and he sprinted for it. In the shadowy darkness of an empty corridor, he pulled Olivia's jacket over his disguise and tugged his cloak over that.

Breathing hard, he made it a few steps into the snow before stopping short, not quite believing his luck. He wouldn't need to find the twins again—somehow, they'd found him. They were leaning against each other in the rainbow glow of the lighted domes, their hoods down and their hair whipping behind them in the wind. Robby took another few steps in their direction before stuttering to a stop.

"Run," Daisy said through clenched teeth.

"Daze?"

"Run!" she repeated, louder this time.

But it was too late to run now. Another figure was emerging through the snow behind the twins, tall and lean and with hair the color of ash. She frog-marched the girls toward Robby until they were only a few paces apart.

"Sorry, Robby," Daisy croaked. "The flying monkeys caught us after all."

# 32

## Into the Depths

"I had my hopes set on never coming back here," Amethyst said, tracing the full length of the High Tower with a miserable gaze. Cold and apprehensive herself, Abby crowded close to her friend for warmth. Piper moved in step with them, her gaze on the ground rather than the distant glow of the pyre at the top of the tower.

"I never noticed how much it looks like the Eye of Mordor," Amethyst said.

"Sauron," Abby corrected.

"What?"

"In *Lord of the Rings*, it's the Eye of Sauron, not Mordor. And don't say nerdy things like that right now. It makes me think of Robby and I'm already worried about him."

"I'm a bit more worried about us, if we're being honest."

"Breaking into the High Tower isn't exactly what I had in mind," said Piper, reaching for her inhaler, "when I agreed we should rescue Tina."

Prena's warnings still echoed in Abby's mind, but she reminded herself they'd still be searching blindly if not for her help.

At least now they knew where to find Tina, even if it meant climbing into the lion's den—or below it, because Tina was being held deep beneath the High Tower. With any luck they'd be in and out before the Council even noticed. Everything after that was a problem for later.

Up close the High Tower wasn't quite the smooth spiral it appeared to be from a distance. In the glow of her wandlight, Abby noticed little chinks between some of the inlaid stones. Prena had told them to look for a simple hexagram pattern that would open into a doorway, and dragging her fingers along the wall, Abby could already feel the faint hum whispering just beneath the surface.

The stones to either side of her were cold to the touch, but directly in front of Abby the subtle outline of a hexagram teemed with energy. "At least we know Prena was telling the truth about one thing," Amethyst said while Abby traced the shape of it with her fingers. She pressed the tip of her wand to the center of the hexagram and exhaled as the seal crackled with release. A circular opening materialized, black and uninviting. The faint outline of a spiraling staircase revealed itself through the darkness.

"So, we're in a castle full of witches," Amethyst said hesitantly, her breath misting between them, "and the door to the maximum security dungeon can be opened by any fourteen-year-old with a wand? Doesn't that seem like a glaring oversight?"

"Or a trap," said Piper, taking another long drag on her inhaler. "My vote's on a trap."

Abby stared into the darkness. "Maybe the Council is just arrogant."

"That tracks, too," said Amethyst.

The stairs curved both up the tower and down. Abby's skin prickled with goosebumps as she led the way into the depths, Piper and Amethyst close behind. The air grew colder and thicker as they descended. A thin layer of ice had formed on the inside walls, and Abby's glasses fogged when she puffed into her hands for warmth. When she held up a hand to slow her friends, the faintest hint of a moan drifted up from the depths.

*Tina?*

Abby could tell by their faces that her friends heard it, too. She doused the glow of her wandlight and waited another moment until her eyes adjusted to the darkness. Except it wasn't dark anymore, not entirely. A faint orange light illuminated the steps farther below. Continuing down, Abby realized the glow was coming from a pyre at the very bottom of the tower, nearly identical to the one high above. And just as above, six thrones were arranged around the fire. Another mirror image.

Abby's breath caught in her throat. Beside the flames were three, maybe four witches lying face down in the orange glow. One of them was Tina, Abby was sure of it, but who were the others? How many other witches were in trouble with the Council? How often did this happen?

Clambering the rest of the way down, Abby dropped to the nearest witch's side. She rolled the woman onto her back, relieved and horrified to find it *was* Tina. Her mentor's face was gaunt, her lips opening and closing in silent misery. "Seems like I'm always rescuing you," Abby said lightly, thinking back to the night almost a year ago when she'd discovered Tina imprisoned beneath Whispering Hill. "Can you stand? Are you hurt?"

Tina moaned again, the sounds confused and unfocused, but her eyes flickered in recognition at Abby's voice.

Abby slipped an arm beneath her. "I'll help you."

"It could be worse," Amethyst said. "I half expected Mother Superior to be waiting for us down here."

"It's Sister Severitas," corrected Piper, her voice high and tight, "and I think we may have an even bigger problem."

It was Piper's tone that made Abby glance suddenly in her direction. Piper was kneeling over the other shadowed witches, two or three of them tangled together in a pile of dark cloaks. Leaving Amethyst to support Tina, Abby scrambled toward Piper, only pulling up short when she recognized the bodies tangled together at the girl's knees.

Daisy. Delphi. Olivia.

Abby didn't know where to look, who to focus on. She searched each of them for a pulse, then crawled back toward Amethyst just as her friend looked sharply up. Even in the darkness, Amethyst's face was white as snow.

"Abby, I think they already did it," she croaked.

"Did what?"

Amethyst's voice was barely a whisper. "You know what."

Cradling Tina in her arms, Abby searched for her pulse, too. It was there, but Amethyst's face was still a mask of horror, so Abby closed her eyes and focused again, this time on the magical spark unique to Tina.

It was gone.

"They wouldn't," Abby said, blinking hard into the darkness.

Amethyst's voice was a thin rasp. "They did."

This wasn't happening, Abby told herself. It couldn't be. She squeezed Tina's hand, but it was her own hand that wouldn't stop shaking. Tina had only gone against the Council's wishes because Abby had given her no choice.

"I'll make them change their minds," Abby whispered, maybe to Amethyst, maybe to Tina. Maybe just to herself. "I'll tell them what happened. I'll explain it was our fault—my fault. They'll listen, they'll *have* to listen."

"I'm afraid it's far too late for that," said a cold voice from above.

Abby's gaze shot upward. The Council of Witches floated down from the void, their luminous wands spinning dark shadows as they settled onto their thrones. Sister Severitas, their leader, pointed her wand at Abby, whose heart beat a thunderous symphony in her chest. For the first time in her life, Abby thought she might know what it felt like to suffocate. She wanted to cry, but she knew that wouldn't get her anywhere. That wouldn't make the

Council undo what it had done. They responded to strength, not mercy.

Abby raised her own wand and pointed it right back at Sister Severitas.

To her relief, Amethyst and Piper did the same.

Sister Severitas stepped toward them. Another few paces and she would be close enough to touch. "Your teacher willfully deceived this Council. She violated our laws and intervened where she had no right to do so. In keeping with custom, Tina O'Reilly has been Quelled for the betterment of all."

Abby's vision was blurry with anger. "She was only trying to help people," she said, finding her voice, holding it steady despite her fear. "That's her real crime. She cared and you don't!"

"The only question that remains," Sister Severitas continued, "is what to do with the six of you. I charge you three"—she waved her wand at Abby, Amethyst, and Piper—"with attempting to corrupt the course of justice. I charge these three others with trespassing in or near the Hall of Fates."

Pink-haired Sister Prudentia stepped forward, joining her wand with Sister Severitas's. "The whole coven is rotten. They deserve the same fate as their mentor."

Sister Clementia made a clucking sound as she raised her wand as well. "They are too green to become Fatekeepers, but they cannot be trusted as witches."

"Insolent, each one of them," agreed Sister Constantia, whose expression bore no resemblance to the warm smile she'd flashed at their first meeting.

Sister Veritas stepped forward next. "No respect for the old ways," she declared, leveling her wand beside the rest.

With a pleading look, Abby tried to meet Prena's eyes—only to find that the woman's gaze was not directed at her at all. It was on the body at Piper's feet.

Robby's body.

His *actual* body, not Olivia's. The transmogrification spell
was unraveling before Abby's eyes. Most of Robby's body was
still hidden beneath his cloak, but his nose and cheekbones were
already more pronounced, his rusty hair sprouting through the center part between Olivia's blonde curls.

Abby's mouth formed a wide circle, but no one other than
Prena seemed to have noticed anything yet. Abby released Tina's
hand and inched toward Robby. Sister Severitas was speaking
again, but Abby barely heard her as she dropped the hem of her
cloak to cover Robby's face. She didn't know what would happen
if the Council discovered him, but if they couldn't Quell him, if
they realized who he was—she couldn't shake the fear that they
might kill him.

An unfamiliar pressure pushed against the back of her skull,
a buzzing that grew stronger and louder until Abby could no longer
ignore it. Her gaze flashed to Sister Severitas, certain that this was
it, this was the Quelling, but the elder witch was still speaking.
Then another presence was beside Abby in her mind. Knocking on
a door. Asking to be let in.

Prena tilted her chin, the message clear. *Let me in.*

*Prena?* Abby thought. *What is this?*

*What is this, what is this,* Abby's voice echoed.

"—must be Quelled—" came Sister Severitas's voice, distant
now.

*You must listen carefully, Abby.* Prena's outward expression
remained unchanged, but her voice seemed so close Abby could
almost believe she was whispering in her ear. *Remember what I
told you once before. You can light a fire from a single spark. You
can rekindle a flame in the same way. Do you understand?*

*No!* Abby yelled with such force that she might have toppled
over if not for Piper, who caught her as she began to slip. When
Abby shot a glance at Prena, the other witch's chin tilted almost
imperceptibly toward Sister Severitas. *Remember,* her expression

seemed to say. But that was all it was now—an expression. The voice in Abby's head was gone.

Abby shivered as she became aware of other sensations around her again. The cold cutting through her cloak. The ragged sound of her own breathing. The dancing glow of the pyre, the flames so fierce and bright. *You can light a fire with a single spark,* Abby repeated. It was meaningless, every word of it meaningless.

"What say you, Sister Novus?" asked Sister Severitas.

Prena stared at Abby dispassionately. "There can be no disagreement. These six are guilty."

"No!" Abby yelled. Her friends were yelling, too, but Abby was too disoriented to untangle the sounds. The back of her throat ached, and when she rose to beg for her friends to be spared, her voice broke. "*Please,* no."

"Rotten," Sister Prudentia cut in. "The whole lot of them."

"To their very core," said Sister Severitas.

"It is decided," Sister Veritas added.

Abby stared in horror as Prena joined her wand to the others. "We are unanimous. They must be Quelled."

"They must be Quelled," repeated the Council.

A searing heat snapped across every inch of Abby's body. Her hands shot to her temples. Her back arched and she was thrown into the air as if struck by lightning. Her blood felt electric, and the screams of her friends joined hers until at last Sister Severitas lowered her wand. One by one the other witches on the Council did the same. Dropping back to the floor, Abby fumbled for her own wand, directing every ounce of anger she'd ever felt at Sister Severitas.

Nothing happened.

She tried again.

Nothing!

There was nothing. *She* was nothing. A hollowed husk, discarded and broken. Powerless. Helpless. Useless. "My—my powers…"

"Mine, too," gasped Amethyst.

Daisy and Delphi stirred beside her. Piper stared at her hands, moaning wordlessly. Robby looked confused but alert beneath the folds of his hood.

"Consider yourselves fortunate that is all we took from you," Sister Constantia told them.

"Break their wands," said Sister Severitas, "and send them away.

# Part Three

# 33

## Powerless

Abby opened her eyes to blinding snow. Her first thought was that the Council had cast them back to the courtyard, because all around her was the bright white haze of a blizzard. But as her vision cleared, the familiar shape of Tina's veterinary clinic came into focus: the old couch pushed into the corner, the stacked animal crates, the half-melted candles at the outer points of the hexagram, burned to the nub and… covered in ice?

She'd landed in her usual spot within the hexagram, but as she rolled onto her back she could see that most of the floor was layered with snow. An enormous drift had formed beneath a broken window, and the outside wind howled through it, a piercing wail even higher than the cries of her friends. There was no sign of Zeus, Olivia, or Becca. No sign of anyone at all.

The enormity of what had just happened hit her all over again. They hadn't saved Tina. They'd lost their powers. Or maybe they hadn't? Maybe it was only a warning meant to scare them? She dropped her gaze to her hands and willed her fingers to give off a spark, even a small one, anything to prove there was something still inside her—some little ember of magic. There was nothing, though.

Her magic was gone.

Her eyes watered and she would have fallen back to the floor if not for Robby, who steadied her until she could stand on her own. One by one he went to the others and helped them up.

They'd failed in every possible way, Abby realized. How stupid had she been to think they could break into the Midnight Castle and not get caught? How thoroughly, totally, *unforgivably* stupid? She hurled the broken pieces of her wand at the wall and gave into a scream, half in anger, half in disbelief. She'd been warned. Again and again, she'd been warned, yet she'd blundered ahead anyway.

"Abby?" croaked Amethyst, staggering to her side. "Did they really do it…?"

"They can't have," said Piper.

Abby buried her head against Robby's shoulder, the tears coming so fast now that she couldn't stop them. Tina had never entirely woken up. She'd been so dazed; she might not even remember they'd tried to save her. She might never know what had happened to her students. And Prena had stood there and watched and—no, it was worse than that, she'd *joined* the rest of the Council in stripping them of their powers.

"It wasn't supposed to happen this way," whispered Delphi.

Amethyst spun to face her. "Did your crystal ball forget to mention this part?"

"It was always a possibility, but I didn't think—I never really believed—"

"You might have considered mentioning that!" Amethyst screamed.

"Of all the possible futures to keep secret from us," Daisy said, thrusting an angry finger in her twin's face, "*this* is the one you didn't tell us about?" Shivering in the breeze, she pulled her cloak tight to her body. "Why is it so bloody cold in here, anyway?"

"It's because of how they sent us back." Delphi's voice was still low, almost inaudible as the wind from outside picked up again in intensity. "We didn't come home through the same portal we arrived in. Prena warned us."

"Don't say her name," growled Abby.

Robby's head snapped up and he met Abby's gaze with alarm. "You told me time works differently at the Midnight Castle. How differently?"

Piper was digging their phones out from beneath the snow drift. She held hers up and said, "I had a full charge when we left, but now the battery's dead."

"Mine, too," said Daisy, taking hers from Piper.

Abby didn't even have to look at her screen. She already knew. The broken window, the snowdrift—they'd probably been gone for weeks. Months, maybe. She dropped her head into her hands. "It's winter out there."

"It's winter in here, too," Amethyst said. "What happened to this place?

Daisy swayed back and forth. "What about our parents? They'll think something's happened."

"Something *has* happened!" Amethyst yelled.

Abby's throat tightened. *Mom.*

"If it's winter now then we've been gone for weeks," said Piper with rising panic. "Who's been feeding Flapper? Where *is* Flapper?!"

Robby stumbled to the other side of the room, his long cloak carving a trail through the snow. He pried open the door to the hallway and disappeared before Abby could call to him. When he returned a heartbeat later, his face was pale as a sheet. "Something's gone wrong."

Amethyst rolled her eyes. "You think?"

"There's no one here," he continued. "There are papers scattered everywhere. Filing cabinets toppled. More broken windows. And all the animals—"

"What about the animals?" asked Piper.

"They're gone, too. Their cages are empty and some—some of them…" He shook his head. "Crates smashed. Broken. Ripped apart like plastic."

Abby spied an old broomstick leaning against the wall, the long handle white with ice. She had a momentary urge to take it and fly home faster than she'd ever flown before. But it was only a broomstick now, useless and discarded. Just like her. She let out a low despairing sob at the realization that she would never fly again, never cast another spell again. None of them would.

Piper and the twins had rushed to the hallway after Robby. Now they shook their heads, too. "There's no signal on the landline," Delphi said. "The storm must have taken out all the phones."

Robby wiped a fresh layer of snow off the clothes he'd carried home through the portal. "I'm going to get changed, and then we need to find Becca. If it's been weeks or months—"

"She'll be with Olivia and Zeus," Abby said. "We need to find them all."

"And Flapper!" said Piper.

"All of them," Robby agreed, "and we need to hurry. It'll be dark soon and we won't be safe without…" His voice trailed off, but the unspoken word hung heavy between them.

"Without our powers," Abby finished for him.

The sky was still a hazy blur when they staggered out of the clinic, and only dim sunlight poked through the lowering tree branches. It was dusk already. Full dark wouldn't be far behind. Marching through the parking lot in knee-deep snow, Abby barely noticed the unlit Christmas lights flapping like loose sails on a few nearby houses. She hardly registered that all the houses were shuttered and dark, too. It was only when they reached the center of town that it began to pry through her stupor. "Willow Cove is a ghost town," she murmured.

"Maybe everyone's inside because of the storm," said Piper.

Olivia's house was not far from where Becca had lived, and the fastest way there would take the coven through Abby's neighborhood. As they turned away from the main street onto the trail through the woods, it was difficult to ignore that none of the chimneys poking through the treetops seemed to be puffing smoke. No television screens glowed through the windows, either. Nothing stirred anywhere they went. Abby's sense of worry only grew stronger when she realized the only tracks in the snow were their own.

She picked up the pace the closer she came to the trail behind her house. Her mom would be there, probably worried sick, probably still a little mad that Abby and Amethyst had left the house to look for Robby after she'd specifically told them to stay. But she *would* be there. She had to be. And that would make some of this all right, even if only for a little while.

Robby hurried after Abby and soon they were both bursting through the woods into their shared backyard. As one, they skidded to a stop. Like every other house on the cul-de-sac, the windows in both their homes were dark. The FOR SALE sign at the end of Abby's driveway shook in the snow and a second placard clattered against it, a single word piercing the winter gloom in bright red letters. Piercing Abby's entire world.

"Sold...?" she whispered in disbelief.

She broke into a full sprint. At the front stoop, she banged loudly on the door. Nobody answered. No lights clicked on inside. No one was home. She tried the handle but found it locked, so she darted to the living room window, half a mind to break the glass and climb in. By now the others had caught up to her. Robby and Amethyst both restrained her while she yelled for her mother.

"She's not here," Amethyst said, her own voice thick with disbelief.

"My dad's gone, too. The house looks empty."

"Mom wouldn't just leave. She'd be out looking for us, you know she would." Abby lurched free and shouted again, louder this time. *"Mom!"*

"Maybe it means she's somewhere safe," Amethyst said. "Maybe it means we can… can…" Her voice dropped to a whisper. "Oh, no. No, no, no."

Abby followed her gaze back to the woods. The sky had darkened during their walk from the clinic. A sliver of moonlight peered through the snowy trees, and a figure with glowing red eyes was staring back at them through the branches. Then two figures. Then three, four, *ten*. Abby recognized Lucinda and Margery right away. Joey and T-Rex, too. They were far from alone. Madame Toussaint, Abby's French teacher, was among them. So was Ms. Bancroft, the school's vice principal. Her skin was gray-white, her eyes a malignant shade of scarlet that grew deeper with each step toward them. Her gaze was angry and hateful.

And hungry.

"We have to go," said Amethyst, yanking Abby back a step, "right now!"

Abby's feet were moving but she wasn't in control of them. Robby took her other arm and dragged her toward the glowing streetlights in the cul-de-sac, where Piper and the twins had already retreated. The red eyes were all around them now. Not just in the bushes and trees, but in the windows of her neighbors' homes, on the street ahead of them, anywhere and everywhere, a noose closing tighter and tighter.

"Death by a thousand vampires," said Amethyst. "So much for going peacefully in my sleep."

Abby reached instinctively for her wand. She pulled her hand back, empty, just as something pale and red-eyed dropped from a streetlamp and landed in the snow before her. When the creature raised its eyes to meet hers, Abby let out another despairing sob. Lithe and dark-haired, it was Becca in shape only. The vampire wore a wicked expression. Her eyes glowed like two searing coals.

Too much time had passed, Abby realized.

They'd been gone too long.

It wasn't really Becca anymore.

Robby stiffened, and now it was Abby's turn to grab *him* by the arm and turn hard the other way. Except there was nowhere else to go. The night was aglow with the deep red of a thousand eyes as the gathering advanced from the woods. Abby spun again, and in that instant Becca lunged for Robby, lightning fast. Thrown to the snow, he lay dazed and unmoving, too stunned even to yell as Becca fell upon him. She went for his neck, and all Abby could do was scream.

# 34

## Sanctuary

At first Robby didn't recognize her. The girl's limbs were too thin, too long, and in the flickering streetlight her face was so sunken that Becca never crossed his mind. For a split second after she dropped to the ground, she was just another pair of red eyes. Then her dark hair flew behind her like a shadow and she bared her teeth, and he knew.

He had just enough time to protect his neck before her fangs could find him. Her momentum carried them both to the ground and suddenly he was rolling, wrestling, and beside him someone else was screaming. There was snow everywhere. With all his strength, he shoved until finally he pried free of her grasp and scrambled back to his feet.

Becca was already on her feet again, too. "You failed me, Robby. You left me here too long." Her voice was low and raw, an animal growl thick with human emotion. Her eyes spun like tops, magnetic and mesmerizing. "Soon you will be like me. Soon you will join the Shadow Lady."

"I'll—I'll join you…" It came out like a grunt, a whisper.

"You will complete our circle of blood. Together, we'll—"

"Not so fast!" came a voice from above. Shouts rang in the distance and then a blonde figure on a broom swooped down through the snowy night. Hurling blue light from her fingertips, she sent Becca staggering with three quick blasts, one after another until the vampire girl fell to the ground again. Robby scurried the rest of the way to his feet.

"Come with me if you want to live!"

Robby gaped at the girl on the broom. "Olivia?"

Olivia hopped to the ground. Blue light spun like a globe between her palms and grew around them until the night crackled with heat. Grunting, she added a second spinning ball to the mix and launched it above the treetops like a flare. Her eyes darted toward Abby and the others. "Where's Tina?"

The girls stared at her wordlessly. Robby steadied himself with a hand on Olivia's shoulder, pressing his other hand against the old wound on his neck. The skin throbbed where Becca had bitten him once before, but it was still scabbed over and unbroken. He was dizzy and disoriented, but Olivia's spellwork seemed to be holding the vampires at bay.

"A little help, maybe?" she yelled at the coven.

"They—they can't help you," Robby rasped. "They don't have—have…"

Olivia cut him off with an exasperated sigh. "Fine, I'll just deal with this whole vampire horde myself, no problem! But we are all going to have an *extremely unpleasant* conversation when this is over!" she shouted, loud enough for the assembled coven to hear. A pale halo crowned her forehead as her gaze swiveled left, then right. "Anyone see our ride?"

"What ride?" Robby asked.

Olivia exhaled as two bright headlights flooded the night and then a white van careened down the snow-slicked street. Robby couldn't make out the driver, but the sea of red eyes parted as the van screeched to a stop beneath the streetlight.

"Everyone, get in!" Olivia yelled, throwing open the side door. "Now!"

Robby staggered toward the door, but dropped to one knee as a pressure grew in the back of his head, sudden and sharp.

*Come back to me, Robby.*

It was as much a feeling as a sound, a buzzing he couldn't ignore. His friends were making for the van, but Robby was paralyzed as Becca's face came back into focus before him. Her eyes were like kaleidoscopes.

*Be one with me.*

"Becca!" he called to her.

Then someone was clutching at him, dragging him.

"Becca!" he yelled again, reaching a hand toward her.

"Robby, *no*!" yelled Abby. It was the way she said his name that finally pulled him back, the desperation in her voice and the note of fear. He scrambled again to his feet and then Abby dragged him inside the van. Someone else slammed the door behind him.

"Floor it!" Olivia screamed, scrambling into the front passenger seat.

Abby pressed a hand to Robby's neck. Her eyes were wild with worry. "Omigod, Robby, she almost got you," she cried, cradling him between the rows.

The world spun as he tried to sit up. "I'm fine," he protested. He wasn't fine, he was the furthest thing from fine—but he knew it could have been worse. He turned his arm for Abby to see where Becca's teeth had scraped the skin. "It looks worse than it is. She didn't change me. Who—who's driving?"

"Buckle up!" shouted Zeus from behind the steering wheel, slamming the gas pedal as the van rocketed into the night. Robby had more questions, but his strength was fading fast. It was all so much. Too much. He sank back into Abby's arms and stared silently as the last glimpse of his house disappeared in the rear-view mirror.

"Wake up, Robby."

Somehow, he'd fallen asleep, and now someone was shaking him. His arm throbbed. His thoughts were sluggish. He called to Becca, but when he opened his eyes, it was Abby who loomed over him. The van slid as Zeus took a corner too tight and a wave of red clouded Robby's vision. Abby swatted her hair away from his face, and with her other hand pressed hard against his wound. "It's still bleeding," she shouted over her shoulder. "Olivia, you'll need to cast a healing charm."

"I'm a little busy over here!" Olivia shrieked from the front. She had the side window down and was hurling blue fire into the night behind them. "Why don't you make yourself useful and do it yourself?"

"Because I *can't*, that's why!"

"None of us can," echoed Amethyst.

Muffled cries escaped from Piper and the twins as the three of them huddled together in the back row with Amethyst. With a weary sigh, Olivia leaned in to face them all. "Robby, at least give me my wand first."

Robby shook his head.

Abby said, "Olivia, we lost—"

"YOU LOST MY WAND?!"

"No," Abby tried again, "we lost our—"

"Save it." Olivia's fingertips glowed from within, shadowing her expression as she touched them to Robby's arm and whispered a few words under her breath. "That should help a little," she said through labored breaths. "Do you have any idea how taxing it is to cast all these spells without a wand?"

Robby took a breath and let it out. When he breathed again, the pain in his arm seemed to have loosened. He sat straighter, his muddied thoughts coming together again. Becca's voice felt like a distant star, unseen but omnipresent. He whispered her name. Abby hugged him tighter in response.

"Try not to think about that right now," she said to him.

"I agree. Robby, you need to rest." Olivia waved a hand in the direction of the back rows and added, "You've all been gone for six—no, *seven* weeks! You have no idea what I've been dealing with since you left."

Piper's head shot up. "We missed Christmas?"

"Trust me, it wasn't very festive this year."

The van rolled on past row after row of darkened houses. "Where did everyone go?" Daisy asked. "They aren't all… vampires?"

"A lot of people left. Moved out, went on vacation, whatever. The whole town's still in denial about what's really happening. Or it was, anyway. It's pretty hard to deny it for those of us who are still here." Olivia stared past them, then seemed to remember something. "What happened at the Midnight Castle? Where's Tina? Why are you all suddenly so useless you won't even cast a simple healing charm?" Her gaze shot to Robby. "For that matter, where's my wand?"

"They took it," said Daisy. "They took… everything."

Olivia threw up her hands. "Who took what, exactly?"

"The Council. Our powers." Abby's voice was barely a whisper. "We got caught, Olivia."

Silence hung in the van between them. The lonely road zoomed by. Without a word, Olivia extinguished the last blue light from her fingertips, and as Robby's eyes adjusted to the new shadows, he noticed the circles around her eyes. Her face looked haunted.

"What do you mean, caught?" she asked.

"It was already too late for Tina when we got there," Abby said tonelessly. "When the Council discovered what we were doing, they stripped us of our powers, too. They Quelled us and then they just… just…"

"Discarded us," said Delphi.

Olivia's mouth formed a dark circle. "Why would they do that?"

"I never thought they would." Abby's voice hitched. "Even after Poppy warned me, even after she told me what happened to her coven, I guess I never… really believed it."

Olivia blinked. Her shallow breathing was the only sound between them. "Why didn't they send Tina back with you?"

Piper let out a hopeless little sigh. "Who knows?"

"I think I might," Robby said. At first, he wasn't certain he'd spoken aloud. Then he felt everyone's eyes on him, and he spoke again, louder. "They were waiting for a new Fatekeeper to arrive at the Hall of Fates. Someone just stripped of her powers."

"You think they meant Tina?"

"I think it's possible."

Olivia sank into her seat, suddenly deflated. "So, no one's coming to help," she said, blinking back some raw new emotion. "I knew something had happened when I felt the transmogrification spell snap. I *knew* it, but I hoped it just meant you were finally coming home. By the time I got to the clinic you'd already gone. I followed your footsteps here, and—"

"We were trying to get to your house," offered Daisy.

"My house isn't safe anymore. My parents…" She shook her head. "The whole town is overrun."

"No, really? We hadn't noticed," snapped Amethyst.

Olivia sat up straight again, her eyes flashing with anger. "Yeah, well, I'm the one who's been dealing with it for the past seven weeks. You all need to take a good look around. Look at the people in this van, because this is pretty much who's left. Night after night, the vampires multiplied while you were all gone, and then one night it finally just"—she let out a long sigh, defeated—"spiraled out of control."

"Explosive amplification," Robby said under his breath. "Like a virus."

Abby dropped her head into her hands. "I only ever wanted to do the right thing," she said, her voice so soft that Robby knew he was the only one to hear. Outside, the snow continued to fall, and more houses rushed by without any lights in the windows. Abby's voice caught in her throat again as she whispered, "Instead I've made everything worse."

The streetlights had gone dark somewhere behind them, and now only trees and snow were visible through the van's headlights. "Everyone, hold onto something!" Zeus yelled into the back seat. "Things are about to get bumpy!"

"Where are we going?" Robby asked, struggling to sit up.

"The safest place in Willow Cove," Olivia said grimly.

Zeus hit the gas again. The van rocketed forward, and everything swayed as he overcorrected, then thundered to a stop when it struck something low and hard. A thick tree branch shook loose, heavy with snow. A cloud of smoke billowed out from under the hood. Crawling into the middle row, Olivia flung open the side door and pointed at Zeus, already outside the van. "Follow him, no questions!"

Robby gaped at her. "But—"

"No! Questions!"

Olivia hung back to guard their flank while the rest of the coven spilled out of the van. Slanted grave markers stuck out from the snow like jagged teeth. Robby stumbled until Abby and Amethyst looped their arms under his and dragged him deeper into the night. When they caught up with him, the muscles in Zeus's neck bulged as he pried at the door of a crypt half swallowed by snow.

"*This* is the safest place in Willow Cove?" asked Amethyst.

"Inside," Zeus said, breathing heavily, "now."

Down the steps, someone else was waving them inside. Shrouded in shadow, she held a small fiberoptic Christmas tree like a lantern, and its battery-operated lights illuminated a long trail of potato chips and candy wrappers leading deeper into the crypt. Raised coffins disappeared into the thickening darkness beyond. Dirt, leaves, and a trail of slush glinted green and red in the artificial glow. Robby's gaze shot from the girl holding the Christmas tree to the shadowy crypt and back again. "Sarika?"

Zeus huffed hard behind him. "She's one of us now, too. One of the living."

"But she—"

"—was spying on Zeus and Olivia the night it all fell apart," Sarika cut in. "I knew I was on to something with that podcast."

"We couldn't just leave her out there with a town full of vampires," Zeus said.

"Where exactly are we?" breathed Abby. "And why?"

The deeper they pushed into the crypt, the more certain Robby became that he already knew. There were more multihued Christmas trees between the coffins, but even without their glow he couldn't have missed the coppery outline of the hexagram near the back of the crypt. Three ruffled sleeping bags and a familiar backpack were pressed together inside the circle. "The Morrow family crypt," he said.

A blurry black shadow scurried just beyond the glow of the Christmas lights, disappearing before Robby could make sense of it. The rest of the girls rushed in while Olivia backtracked to make sure no one was following them. When they were all accounted for, Zeus heaved the giant door back into place. The wind outside squelched to silence. "Home sweet home," Zeus said, sinking to the floor with a loud sigh.

Piper gaped at him. "You actually sleep here?"

"When we can," Olivia said.

"She stays up all night reading graphic novels," Zeus replied. "She's kind of a nerd now."

"I've been busy keeping us alive, thank you very much." Olivia stuck her thumb in Zeus's direction. "He's the one in charge of entertainment. It's not my fault he raided the comic book store instead of someplace practical."

"She made me go back for more," Zeus whispered conspiratorially.

"You're sure it's safe here?" Piper asked with a shiver. "We're literally surrounded by the dead."

"Better dead than undead."

"Why here?" Abby asked again.

Taking the artificial Christmas tree from Sarika, Olivia tilted its glow toward the outer ring of the hexagram. "Miss Winters put that witch's seal here to keep Julia Morrow locked inside the crypt if she ever rose again. 'Bound by blood' and all that. It was Briony who realized the seal might also keep other vampires *out*. As long as we sleep inside it, we're safe."

"Where is Briony?" Amethyst asked, her eyes probing the shadows.

Olivia waved at one of the coffins. "She sleeps in there sometimes, but she's out searching for vampires right now. There's no shortage of them."

"What about Flapper?" Piper's voice was tense and high-pitched.

"Who do you think's been eating all these potato chips?" Olivia cast her light down the row of coffins, where the parting shadows revealed Piper's sleeping seagull huddled with a raccoon and iguana. Piper crossed the chamber in a heartbeat. Amethyst followed on her heels, dropping quickly to hug Spooks. Robby stroked Einstein's scaly neck until the iguana's eyes opened and he wagged his tail.

"You kept them safe," he said, full of wonder. "Olivia, thank you."

"It's Sarika's job now," Olivia said. "She needed something to do other than spread more rumors."

"Those rumors were all true," Sarika protested.

"Shh!" Piper swatted them both to silence. Her expression fell as she clucked softly at Flapper, and he cooed back at her.

"Don't let him tell you I haven't fed him," said Sarika.

Piper shook her head. "He can't—I can't—"

"You won't be able to understand him without your powers," Amethyst said while Spooks rolled onto his back for a belly rub.

"What? No, that's not it, that can't be true. Flapper, listen to me, listen to Mommy…" Piper scrounged in her pockets for a snack to offer him. The seagull clucked again. Louder, more insistent. Piper's springy curls shuddered back and forth. Her whole body shook with a kind of magnetic desperation. "He's clucking, but I don't—I can't—" Her mouth made a wide oval. "I don't know what he's trying to say!"

"'O, that I knew thy heart, and knew the beast,'" said Daisy in a shaky voice.

Piper quaked with annoyance as she spun on Daisy. "Have you ever had a single original thought in your life? ENOUGH WITH THE STUPID QUOTES!"

"I—I only meant that—that—" Daisy's practiced accent frayed around the edges. "'I quote others only in order the better to express myself.' That's from Michel de Montaigne, and it's true, it's why I always—"

While Daisy sputtered, her twin thrust an angry finger in Piper's face. "Do you think you're the only one who's hurting right now? The rest of us have actual human beings we care about. Parents and siblings and friends, not just some dumb bird who won't talk to us anymore."

"He's not a dumb bird! You take that back!"

Amethyst slammed her fist on a coffin, startling Spooks and Einstein and sending Flapper squawking. "Let's all listen to the psychic who just happened to overlook the fact we could lose our powers! I'm with Piper on this one. I've had enough of you and your sister both, and if we're being perfectly honest—"

Robby's gaze slid to Abby, expecting her to step in and stop the arguing, but she didn't even look up. He took a long breath and turned to the others, shaking his head. "We need to stick together, not argue with each other."

"What do you suggest?" asked Amethyst. "In case you haven't noticed, it's basically the End of Days out there."

"But we can still undo all of it."

Amethyst stared at him as if he'd lost his mind. "With our bare hands? Because, again"—she wiggled her fingers sarcastically—"no powers, Robby."

"I know how to find the Shadow Lady now." With everything coming at them so suddenly, he'd almost forgotten. "I know how we can save everyone."

"You… you do?" asked Olivia.

Robby cleared his throat. "In the Hall of Fates, I learned where she's hiding—*when* she's hiding, I mean. The Council imprisoned her inside her castle on the Night of Blood and Shadows. That's why Briony could never find her. She's hiding in another time pocket."

"In the Carpathian Mountains? In the Middle Ages?" Amethyst pressed her back against the wall, shaking her head. "If only we hadn't left our TARDIS at home."

"God help me, I actually get that reference now," Olivia said.

Robby looked to Olivia hopefully. "Can you get us there?"

"Robby, I don't know any time travel spells. I don't even have a wand." Olivia slid to the floor next to Zeus, looking defeated. "Something that complex, I'm not sure it's even possible. You'd have to be more powerful than all six of us together." At that, Piper let out a small choking sound, quickly stifled. Olivia sighed. "So, unless one of you has another idea…?"

Abby looked up sharply. She opened her mouth as if to say something, then shook her head and looked down at her feet again. No one else said a word.

"Then it looks like the vampire apocalypse is here to stay," Olivia said.

# 35

## Friends

Abby woke to the soft nuzzle of a raccoon snout against her chin. Pressing into her chest like a lead weight, Spooks stared at her with expectant eyes while Abby reorientated herself to the dim lights inside the crypt. She groaned and gave the raccoon a dutiful scratch behind the ear, then nudged him back onto Amethyst, who lay curled beside her on the cold hard floor. Robby was snug against Abby's other shoulder, his injured arm draped across her. Einstein curled like a comma in his lap.

Everyone else had packed together on a makeshift mattress of fur cloaks inside the small hexagram. If you could somehow ignore the coffins and the bodies of the ancient dead all around, the crypt might have been comfortingly crowded, even cozy. Abby could almost imagine it as just another slumber party with her friends.

Almost.

Rolling onto her side, she pressed a hand against Robby's neck. No matter how hard she tried, she couldn't unsee the moment Becca had lunged for him. She'd thought for sure Becca had turned him with a second bite. His breathing was fine, though, and he didn't appear to be in any pain—any more than the rest of them, at least. The marks from Becca's first bite were still puckered and angry, but nothing had changed since then. He was still Robby. Olivia's healing charm had probably saved him a lot of suffering, too.

Abby's gaze flicked to where Olivia lay sleeping across from her. Her head was resting on Zeus's shoulder. She was wearing his jacket like a blanket. The tips of their fingers were touching as if they'd fallen asleep holding hands.

As if they were together now.

Abby blinked and did a double take.

*Were* they together now?

Zeus's eyes shot open as if he could sense her staring. He didn't react at first, but as his gaze focused on Abby, she knew instantly from his guilty half-hidden expression that she'd guessed right. They were together. Well, *of course* they were. Olivia was beautiful and she still had her powers. Why wouldn't the universe also give her Abby's boyfriend? Well, ex-boyfriend, but it had definitely seemed like something was kindling between them again before Abby had left for the Midnight Castle.

Zeus whispered her name, but she purposely didn't meet his eyes. Her jealousy would flash like a neon sign on her face, and she didn't need him to see that on top of everything else. But then he said her name louder and she was afraid he might wake the others if she didn't acknowledge him. Why couldn't he just let her be humiliated without drawing attention to it?

"Can we talk?" The words seemed to rattle around the crypt as if he'd shouted them. Zeus winced. "It's not what you—well, it is, but we never meant for it to happen."

Abby realized she'd been holding onto a little shred of hope that she'd gotten it all wrong, but now even that was gone. She let out a deflated breath. "It's fine, Zeus. We were broken up. You don't owe me anything."

"I still want to explain."

"I think I get the picture pretty clearly." Beside him, Olivia's peaceful face was haloed by the red and green glow of Christmas lights. Abby lowered her voice. "Look, I'm happy for you. Congratulations."

"Abby."

"I said it's *fine*, Zeus."

"Can we just—"

"Keep your voice down," she cut in, practically hissing. It was embarrassing enough they were even having this conversation, but what if her friends overheard? She hated that she was letting these dumb feelings claw their way back to the surface at all, especially now, because there were so many other things she should be worrying about. But she couldn't change how she felt.

"If you'd just let me explain," Zeus insisted.

"Explain what? Why you're with Olivia? It's none of my business."

Zeus blew out a frustrated breath. "That's not what I mean."

"Then what?"

"I've had seven weeks to think about what happened between us. Seven weeks of not knowing if you'd ever come back. It's like the end of the world out there, Abby, and I feel like I owe you an explanation because I may never get another chance."

"Maybe it's been a few months for you, but it's been one day for me. One day," Abby repeated, "and when I left, I thought we were..." She let her voice trail off. Thought they were what? Going to get back together? No, not exactly. But she'd felt *something* between them again. Something mutual. A longing for what they'd once had, maybe, their friendship and their more complicated relationship all rolled into one.

"I thought we were, too," he said into the quiet between her thoughts.

Abby let out a low sigh. "And now you want to explain why you dumped me at long last," she whispered back to him. "I thought I needed to know, but I don't. I have bigger things to worry about. We all do. Obviously."

"I didn't know how to explain it before," Zeus said, his voice low and earnest. "Being with Olivia helped me understand what I was feeling all this time."

Abby snorted. "You chose the pretty blond cheerleader over me. What's left to understand?"

"Everything!" he said, his voice rising again. Olivia nuzzled back into him.

Abby waved a hand. "I think I get it loud and clear."

"You're not listening to me."

"Oh, was that the problem? I didn't listen?"

"No."

"Then what? What was so wrong with me?" she blurted. It was the question that had been eating at her for months, the root of all her self-doubts. He'd dumped her and hadn't said why. All she'd been able to do was fill in the blanks with her own answers. She'd had plenty of material to consider.

"It was never about you, Abby. It was never even about us." His eyes cut into her, then he lowered them as if embarrassed by his own feelings. "It was you and Robby. The way you are together. I was… jealous."

What? *What?*

Zeus shook his head. "With Olivia, it's just me and her. With you, there was always Robby, too." He let out a deep sigh and tilted his chin in the direction of Robby's arm, still draped around her where they lay. "I couldn't handle it. I still can't. I'm *still* jealous."

Abby was so stunned she didn't bother to lower her voice. "You broke up with me!"

"Not because I wanted to. Because I didn't know how to not be jealous. Because—"

"Because I'm friends with Robby? You know that he and I aren't—that we've never—"

"I know what I felt."

"You don't know anything!" Abby crawled to her feet and scooped up one of the loose cloaks. This conversation was over. She wanted out of the crypt, and she didn't care if she woke the whole group to do it. She couldn't believe she'd ever really liked him—that some part of her *still* liked him—and the whole time he'd been jealous of her closest friendship. There was a pressure building in her chest, a kind of certainty that maybe Zeus was right about one thing, at least. They were never going to work out if this was how he felt.

"I never stopped liking you, Abby. I still want to be friends, I—"

"How does it feel to want something you can't have?" She hurled the question back at him, feeling a kind of unfamiliar power over him, apparently the only power left to her. At least she could deny him the one thing he seemed to want from her. "You and I are not going to be friends, Zeus. We're never going to be friends again."

She turned away from him to pry instead at the heavy door to the outside. She wanted to storm out, but the door wouldn't budge no matter how hard she pushed or pulled—not when she grunted so loudly it might as well have been a shout, not even when she kicked it so hard she ended up dancing back in pain. *Stupid*, she thought, she'd been so stupid about everything! The door was never going to budge for her. Nothing was ever going to move again just because she wanted it to, not anymore, not without her powers.

Except somehow the door did move.

Abby took a quick step back as the door scraped open another few inches. Hazy morning light spilled down the steps. She stared at it through tiny clouds of dust, then looked back at her hands. It wasn't possible, was it? Did she still have…?

No.

There wasn't any spellwork clinging to her fingertips. No subtle shifts in her perceptions, no sense that the world around her was somehow *more* again. She felt a certain quiver in her stomach, but it wasn't from the strain of wishing something into being—it was just the pangs of hunger because she hadn't eaten in ages. So, if the door had not opened by her command, then how? She spun back toward the sleeping bags to find Olivia sitting up, her eyes closed, her lips moving in the slow language of magic.

Mystery solved.

Olivia to the rescue again.

Abby didn't wait for her to finish her spell. She couldn't wait. Already she imagined the smug look on Olivia's face when she'd finished, the unspoken reminder that she wasn't the one who'd failed at everything. Abby kicked up dust and snow as she stumbled up the steps and into the cemetery, hoping more than anything that Olivia would get the hint and leave her alone with her thoughts.

It was early morning, bright and bracingly cold after the night's snowstorm. Long shadows stretched away from the crypt in the low winter sun. A few lingering snowflakes drifted down from a sky that threatened more to come. Not far from their van, Briony Morrow stood pale and alone in the early light, her telltale red eyes like a slash of blood against the snow. Spotting her, Briony took a step in Abby's direction, then stopped when Abby made her own expression hard as steel and turned away.

"Sometimes she keeps watch until the sun comes up," Olivia said from the crypt steps, startling Abby as she came up behind her. Apparently she had not gotten the hint.

"Go away, Olivia."

"Come back inside and let's talk. We need to figure out—"

"There's nothing left to figure out!" Abby yelled, spinning to face her. "There's nothing more to do. We are literally powerless."

"I still have my powers."

"Thanks for the reminder! You always said you were as strong as me, but now there's no question about it. You have my boyfriend, too, so hurray for you."

Olivia's cheeks went scarlet. "*Ex*-boyfriend."

"You didn't waste any time swooping in while I was away, though, did you?"

"Do you think—hold on, do you actually think I'm enjoying this? Any of this?" Olivia pulled herself to her full height. Her whole face quivered with anger. "I have been holding on by a thread since the moment you left me behind. Scared and exhausted and—and—" She let out a low, shuddering laugh. "—and just waiting for you to come back, hoping you had a solution to all this, and why? Because you always have a solution! That's the only thing that's kept me going. I've been counting on you."

Briony eyed them in the distance but made no move to approach. Abby blew out another breath and sank to the snow with her back against an old gray headstone, feeling suddenly very tired again. "So, I let you down just like everyone else," she said, her voice low and dull. "Believe me, I know."

Olivia slid down beside her. "Is that what you think?"

"You don't?" Abby buried her head in her hands to hide what she felt sure were going to be tears. She would not cry in front of Olivia Edwards. She wouldn't. That much she could still control. Her shoulders shuddered from the effort of holding back her emotions.

Olivia was quiet for so long that Abby finally snuck another sidelong look at her, only to find that Olivia was staring intently at *her* with an expression that was so unexpected—so full of kindness—that Abby had to look away.

"What I think is it's not like you to just give up," Olivia said. "That it's only really hopeless when we stop trying. That's what I think."

Abby stared at her hands. "What am I without my powers?"

"The leader of our coven. Still. Always."

Abby pressed the back of her head against the grave marker. "We're not much of a coven anymore. You heard us all last night. We were at each other's throats. Everything's come apart and I let it happen. It *is* hopeless."

Olivia gave her a frustrated shake of the head. "That doesn't sound like the Abby I know. You've always been hopeful, not cynical. That's why everyone follows you and not me. It's what keeps us all going. Yes, even me," she added when Abby looked at her sideways. "Hope beats cynicism every time."

Abby considered her for a moment longer. "I thought you hated me."

"You are frequently insufferable."

Abby managed a weak smile. "Frequently, but not always?"

"Don't fish for compliments." Olivia let out a breath. "I used to hate you. Last year, I mean. I guess it's been easier to let you think I still do. Easier than admitting the truth, anyway."

"Which is what?"

It was Olivia's turn to look away. Abby nudged her until finally she raised her chin again. Maybe it was Abby's imagination, or the wind and cold, but Olivia's eyes were wet when they met each other's gaze. "When we were at the Midnight Castle, the Council thought I wanted to lead my own coven, but they didn't understand me at all. None of you did. All I really want is to be part of this one. To actually fit in, I mean." She shrugged miserably. "But I don't know how."

"Olivia, you already do."

She shook her head sharply. "I know what I did last year, Abby. I still feel guilty about it. I turned you all over to Miss Winters and she almost—"

"She manipulated you," Abby said firmly. "You need to forget about that. Put it behind you. I have." A thought floated into her head like a stray breeze, faint and ephemeral. An idea she'd had once or twice before and quickly stamped down. Now it begged to be asked. "Don't you ever wonder…?"

"What?"

Abby cleared her throat. "Well, I guess *I* sometimes wonder if we could have become friends. Under different circumstances, that is. If Miss Winters hadn't purposely driven a wedge between us."

"Friends have a way of disappointing me," Olivia said. A tight smile wavered across her face. "I suppose it might not be the worst thing in the world. Being friends with you."

"You're not quite as awful as I used to think, either," Abby conceded. She tried to soften it with a smile of her own, but when she finally looked up, Olivia's gaze remained fixed on her in a strange and unsettling way. "What?"

"I want to tell you something, then," she said. "As a—a friend? You need to go easier on yourself. We all make mistakes."

Abby stared at her powerless hands. "Not like this."

"You gave me a second chance after I sided with Miss Winters over all of you. No one else would have done that."

"That's not the same."

"It is. When it really mattered, you believed in me. Even though I screwed up. Even though I *repeatedly* screwed up." Olivia waved vaguely in the direction of the crypt. "Everyone in there still believes in you. I still believe in you, too. The truth is, I kind of admire you. You're stubborn and annoying and self-right-eous—"

"That doesn't sound like admiration."

"—and you're kind and clever and loyal. You're persistent. Determined. You're never boastful even though you could be, and you always try to make people feel included. Even people like me. When you do something, it's only ever because it's the right thing to do. I see things in you that I know I'll never possess."

"That's not true," Abby said. "What you did here while we were away? Keeping Zeus and the animals safe the whole time, holding out hope for us, coming to our rescue when we got back— it's incredible, Olivia."

Olivia shrugged, then kicked at the snow. "Fine, maybe we're both awesome."

Abby found herself grinning. "All it took for us to admit it to each other was the end of the world."

"Well, about that. There's one more thing." Olivia hesitated, clutching her knees to her chest. "I think you lied to us last night. I don't think you're out of ideas at all. I think you're afraid of failing again."

"That's not it, Olivia."

"It's Liv, actually." She held Abby's gaze, one eyebrow arched like a question. "I always wished my friends would call me Liv."

Abby's heartbeat quickened. "What makes you so sure I have an idea?"

"Because you *always* do."

Abby crawled to her feet and extended a hand to Olivia, suddenly feeling lighter than she had in days. "There might be something we could try," she admitted.

"I knew it!"

"There's only one way it'll work, though." Abby shook snow from her cloak and peered back toward the darkened crypt to make sure no one else was coming. "The others won't understand at first, so we'll have to do it together, just you and me... Liv."

# 36

## The Wand Remembers

"It probably *won't* work," Abby said as they left the cemetery behind. Wet snowflakes were collecting on their heads and shoulders, and already the trail of footprints behind them was vanishing beneath a gauzy film of new snow.

"What is the plan, exactly?" asked Olivia.

"It's actually a very bad idea."

"As usual, then."

"It's just that something you said last night made me think." Abby brushed a few snowflakes from her nose. "No time machine and no wands, right?"

"Right," Olivia agreed. "That's still true."

"Is it, though?" Abby cracked a smile, even though her shoulders were tense and inside her stomach was churning. She did have an idea, maybe even one that could work, but there were risks— and that was if she could even get the others to go along with it. She snuck a look over her shoulder. Briony was just a speck in the distance now, the crypt long gone from view.

"You're enjoying this way too much," Olivia said. Her cheeks were apple red in the early morning chill. Her expression held both anticipation and uncertainty. Abby couldn't escape the fact that it felt strange talking to her like this, like a friend. Stranger even than talking with Robby when he had Olivia's face.

"Are you going to tell me what you're thinking, or…?"

"You said you trust me. Did you mean it?"

"Well, yeah." Olivia pressed her lips together. "I mean, mostly. Some of it was obviously just a pep talk. Why?"

Abby hesitated. Her mouth was dry. She took another moment to adjust the clasp of her cloak rather than meet Olivia's gaze. "If I'm wrong, things could get… I don't know… worse?"

"Worse than the vampire apocalypse," Olivia deadpanned.

Abby nodded. "Maybe."

"You're really selling it."

Abby answered with her most disarming grin, the one she reserved for when she knew she'd done something wrong but still hoped she could charm her way out of it. Olivia rolled her eyes, and they walked in silence for a while longer. Even against the snowy sky, the full light of the sunrise bathed the rolling hills in golden light. It could almost pass for a pleasant winter morning if she didn't know what they'd all been through—and what she was about to suggest they do about it.

Olivia's hugged herself against the wind. "I should have gone back inside for my broom. It would have been much faster to fly to"—she waved an annoyed hand—"wherever it is you're taking me."

"We're almost there." Abby pointed toward the sloping hill ahead of them, a steady unbroken stretch of wind-driven snow that ended at a summit of bare-branched willow trees. "That's where we're going."

"Willow Hill?" Olivia's voice was puzzled. "Why would we—oh, no."

"Yes."

"*No*, Abby."

"We need a wand, Liv."

Olivia slammed to a halt and crossed her arms. "Not *her* wand."

"Yes, hers. Miss Winters's wand." Abby crossed her arms, too. Olivia had called her stubborn as if that were a good thing, so let her see a little bit of that stubbornness in action. "It actually has to be her wand. The plan doesn't work without it."

"Then it's a bad plan!"

Abby grinned. "I did tell you that."

"She tried to kill us!"

"She tried to warn us," Abby countered. "She told me not to trust the Council. Whatever else she may have done, she was right about that. She gave me her wand right before she died, Olivia, and afterward… I swear I could still feel something inside it. Some piece of her that was still there even after she was gone."

"Another reason not to use that wand," Olivia moaned. Her tart expression made it seem like the old Olivia might claw her way back to the surface at any minute. "Now I know why you didn't want anyone else to come with us. You knew they'd try and stop you."

"No," Abby said, stretching the syllable for an extra beat as she worked out how to explain it. "It may be my idea—"

"Bad idea," Olivia repeated.

"—but it needs your powers to succeed. The others can't stop me. Only you can do that. If that's what you decide to do."

"You need me," she said.

"I do."

"I do enjoy hearing you say it," Olivia said with a sigh, starting up the hill again.

At the top, tall brown grass poked through the snow where the windswept drifts were shallow. Abby thought back to all the times she'd visited this spot since the day they'd carried the willow sapling to the top of the hill and buried Miss Winters's wand beneath it. The past had rarely felt as present as it did at this moment. With the cold wind and the salty air blowing in from the coast, she could almost see Miss Winters again as she'd been on that first day when she'd presented herself as their new history teacher—could almost hear her voice again over the breeze. *Do you girls believe in witchcraft?*

What children they'd been. What naïve young girls.

Yet here she was putting her faith in Miss Winters for a second time. Trusting that the look in her teacher's eyes at the end had been real. Believing that when it came right down to it, she really had cared about Abby and her friends.

Abby cleared snow beneath the willow's spindly branches until her fingers brushed the frozen dirt beneath. She scooched aside and gave her friend—and what a strange thing *that* was, to think of Olivia Edwards as an actual friend—the space she needed to thaw the ground around the tree.

Olivia took a deep breath as if steeling herself to action. "Even supposing I can use another witch's wand," she said as the air and soil grew warm all around them, "we're still no closer to solving the other half of the problem. No time machine."

"The wand is the time machine," Abby said.

Olivia gave her a sharp look. "Explain."

"A wand remembers every spell it ever casts," Abby told her. "Tina told me that."

The frown lines on Olivia's face deepened. "I don't think I like where this is going."

The ground was soft as potting soil now. Abby scooped handfuls into piles beside the small willow tree until her fingers closed over something long and nubbly beneath the surface. Miss Winters's wand. She raised her eyes to Olivia's. "This is the wand that opened the portal to the Shadow Lady in the first place."

"You're not suggesting—"

"It's the only way."

Color drained from Olivia's face. She dropped her hands to her hips. "Absolutely not."

"Twice Miss Winters cast that spell," Abby said, "and twice the Shadow Lady clawed her way through to Willow Cove afterward. Who says it can't work the other way around? This time, we'll be the ones to go through. We'll take the fight to her."

"Have you considered that we might accidentally switch places with a half dozen doomed Puritan girls instead?" asked Olivia. "Because that was not my favorite part of seventh grade."

"I think we can skip that part, Liv."

"I knew I'd regret telling you to call me that."

"Too late. No backsies." Abby clasped the wand between her fingers. The last time she'd touched it, the whole thing had thrummed like an actual heartbeat in her hands. Today she felt nothing—no life, no pulse. There wouldn't be, would there? Abby no longer had the spark herself. In her hands, Miss Winters's wand was just another stick.

But in Olivia's…?

She held it between them like an offering. "It's our only chance now."

"The others won't go for it, you know," Olivia replied as the wand passed between them. "I don't care how much they still believe in you. None of them will agree to it."

"Maybe not if it's only me saying it. I think they will if it comes from both of us."

Abby stood and dusted herself off. Scowling, Olivia did the same. "I know I said we're friends now, but sometimes I really do still hate you."

"But you'll do it?"

Olivia pressed her lips together, staring off for what seemed like an eternity. Then she closed her eyes and nodded. "What other choice do we have?"

# 37

## Return to Whispering Hill

Voices. There were voices in Robby's head. He didn't know whose voices, not at first, only that some were sharp and angry, while another one—the voice beneath the others, intermingled with them—was softer, more alluring. More hypnotic.

"No, no, no," Amethyst was saying from somewhere far away.

*Come to us*, said the voice below the surface.

"Absolutely not!" Amethyst's voice was louder now. "Not today, not ever."

*Complete our circle of blood*, said the hypnotic voice. Becca's voice. It wasn't near him, it was inside him, as much a part of him as the blood in his veins. *She will have her revenge*, Becca told him. *You will help her get it!*

Robby sat up fast, too fast, and Becca's voice vanished like a quick-draining whirlpool until he was left with nothing but the memory of it. That and a headache, a throbbing pain at the base of his skull, maybe the worst of his life.

"They're arguing again," said someone not far from him. He couldn't place the voice until he opened his eyes and blinked in his surroundings. Sarika leaned over him, an uncharacteristic look of concern on her face. "That's what you're hearing. They only stopped long enough to sleep last night. Now they're at it again."

Spooks and Einstein lay dozing at his feet. Flapper nipped disappointedly at an empty bag of chips. The scattered sleeping bags and cloaks were lit by the glow of a half dozen artificial Christmas trees. Robby's head felt cobwebby and clouded. Becca's words had faded, but already he missed her voice. Already he wanted to hear it again.

"Who's arguing?" he managed.

Sarika jutted a thumb in the direction of the open crypt door. Sunlight spilled in around the edges, but no heat came with it. "All of them, I think."

Outside, Amethyst yelled, "If you think any of us are going to go along with this—"

"—you've completely lost your mind," finished one of the others. Piper, maybe, though he wasn't sure he'd ever heard her so sure of herself, so angry.

Sarika gave Robby her arm and helped him stand. "Olivia keeps threatening to wipe my memory when this is all over," she said as they lumbered toward the crypt door. "I hope she does. I hate this."

Robby emerged shivering from the crypt to find the coven arguing in the graveyard. Olivia was leaning against Zeus, her arms crossed; Abby's face was a determined mask. Clouds were gathering overhead, and fresh snow was falling in thick, flaky chunks. Robby's attention went to Amethyst, who was wagging a finger at Olivia. The rest of the group and Briony stood with them under a shadowy oak.

"We won't go along with it," Amethyst shouted. "Abby, tell her."

"It was my idea," Abby said.

The arguing made Robby's head hurt even more. "What idea?" he croaked.

"She tried to kill us with that wand," Piper said.

Abby flashed a tight smile. "I know that."

"What wand?" Robby asked, but his voice was weak.

"She wanted to steal our souls—"

"I know," Abby repeated, "but Miss Winters is gone, Piper. The Winslow sisters are gone. They never wanted to come back. A wand is just a tool, anyway."

Delphi eyed the snowy sky, nodding. "The Pleiades culminated weeks ago. The veil between life and death is closed. Perhaps it *would* be safe…"

"No," Amethyst said again, elbowing out from the others to stand face to face with Abby. "You have a soft spot for Miss Winters that I'll never understand, and that was fine, honestly, that was your business, but this—this is—" She shook her head, unable to even articulate what *this* was.

"That soft spot saved our lives last year," Olivia pointed out.

"Miss Winters saved my life as well," Briony said. "She saved this whole town."

"Let's just throw her a parade then!" Amethyst rolled her eyes. "I can't believe any of you think this is a good idea."

"I didn't at first," said Olivia. "I had the same reaction as you. Abby convinced me."

"How?"

"Because it might actually work."

"*What* might actually work?" Robby tried again, louder now.

Finally the others seemed to notice him. Olivia reached into her jacket and produced a knobby wand. A collective gasp reverberated over the wind, so powerful Robby could feel it. "This," she said, waving it around. "Miss Winters's wand."

Robby took an involuntary step back at the sight of it.

"You already dug it up?" Amethyst shouted, throwing her hands in the air.

Abby nodded in Robby's direction. "Olivia can use it to repeat the spell that Miss Winters cast last year. Only this time we'll be the ones to go through the portal."

Amethyst crossed her arms. "It won't work."

"It will!" Abby shouted.

"You're positive?"

"Definitely," Abby said. "Probably."

Piper's eyes narrowed. "Those words don't mean the same thing."

"I just don't know," said Daisy, rubbing her neck.

Robby felt the tide turning against the idea. The coven's uncertainty hovered over it like a storm cloud. "I don't understand how it would work," he said, "but if Abby thinks it will, that's enough for me. I have faith in her. I have faith in all of you."

"I know we can do this," Abby said.

"Only if it's all six of us," said Olivia, taking in the other witches one by one, "doing exactly what Miss Winters did. The same spell. The same blood magic."

"None of us knows what will happen," Abby admitted, "but it's better than doing nothing. And like Liv said, if it's going to work, it has to be all of us." Her eyes lingered on each of her friends before landing on Amethyst. "Trusting each other. Believing in each other. Doing whatever it takes for each other."

Amethyst let out a deep sigh. "I suppose that has gotten us this far."

"Sometimes I can still feel the noose around my neck," said Daisy with a shudder. "I don't know if I can go through anything like that again."

"There won't be any nooses this time," Olivia said gently.

Flapper waddled up the crypt steps toward the group. Piper looked from her seagull to Daisy as if something had only just occurred to her. "'Hope is the thing with feathers,'" she said with a shaky breath. "Isn't that Shakespeare?"

Daisy's lips parted. "Emily Dickinson," she corrected.

"Well, maybe she was right. Maybe other people's thoughts are worth adding to the conversation now and then," Piper said with a contrite tremble. "Maybe you're right to quote them. If all we have left is hope, maybe we should lean into it?"

A hesitant smile. "Maybe."

Amethyst eyed the assembled group. "Olivia is still the only one of us with powers. How exactly are we going to slay the mother of all vampires?"

"I've never had any powers," said Robby. "That's not going to stop me."

"Me either," said Zeus, nodding at him.

"As for the vampire slaying," said Briony, twirling a wooden stake between her fingers, "you can leave that part to me."

They marched through the cemetery gates in a long winding line, single file except for Olivia and Zeus, who went side by side with their heads ducked together against the cold. Briony, Piper, and the twins followed close behind, shivering inside their cloaks and looking miserable as snow collected on their shoulders. Robby hung back with Abby and Amethyst, who seemed to take turns fussing over him rather than talk to each other. Only Sarika stayed behind, having hastily volunteered to remain safely in the crypt and care for the animals.

A blustery breeze reddened Robby's cheeks and the wind-stirred branches whistled overhead, whipping more snow onto the trail before him. His head still felt thick with cotton, but somewhere just below the surface Becca's voice was beginning to wake again. His bite wound didn't hurt so much as itch this morning, and when he pressed a finger to his neck the two welts felt warm. It was the only part of him that did feel warm.

*Come to me, Robby.*

He stopped in his tracks. "Did—did you hear that?"

"Hear what?" Abby asked, glancing ahead at the others.

Robby listened again.    "Nothing," he finally said. Maybe it really was nothing, because even as Abby and Amethyst stood waiting for him, the only sound now was the wind whispering through the branches. "I think I've been imagining Becca's voice."

"We're all a little spooked right now," Abby agreed.

"Considering where we're going, we have every right to be." Amethyst ducked to be heard over the breeze. "I can almost understand the logic of casting Miss Winters's spell again, but why are we doing it in the same place as last time? Talk about returning to the scene of the crime."

"Delphi says it's a sort of liminal space. A weak spot in spacetime or something," Abby said, "but even if she's wrong, we know the ritual worked at Whispering Hill. We don't know if it will work anywhere else." Abby's gaze flicked toward her coven, growing smaller in the distance. She hurried to keep pace. None of them, Robby thought, really wanted to be separated from the larger group, not even in daylight.

*Come to me, Robby.*

Becca's voice was so clear it made him stumble this time. Only Amethyst's quick reflexes stopped him from falling. The skin around Becca's bite was suddenly throbbing.

*Yes, come closer!*

Abby and Amethyst called his name, too. They sounded miles away. Only Becca's voice was clear and close. Even closer than before. He tried saying her name but found he could only listen as her voice was joined by the others. Lucinda and T-Rex, Margery and Joey, a symphony of haunting tones. "I—I hear the music," he whispered.

Abby's face was practically pressed to his. "There's no music, Robby."

*You will complete our circle of blood,* the voices sang.

*The Shadow Lady will have her revenge.*

*Come closer, Robby!*

"They—they're saying—" he stammered, blinking as the voices faded again. The whole group was hovering over him now, concern stitched across their faces. "They're saying I'm coming closer to them. I think they know where we're going. I think they're waiting for us."

"Still think this is a good idea?" Amethyst said to no one in particular.

"I'm a liability," Robby realized. "This bite, this… psychic connection… they know exactly where I am."

"Then we'd better hurry," Abby told him.

"I shouldn't come with you."

Abby's eyes shot to the midmorning sky. The sun was low beneath a wintery sheet of falling snow. "It's daytime. The grove where we'll do the spell is outside. Once we get through the old hospital buildings, we'll be in the open. Even if they're hiding in the tunnels—"

"What tunnels?" demanded Briony.

"—even *if* that's where they are, we're going straight through the front door. We'll be done with this spell and well on our way to ending this before they even come out of hiding."

"You're sure about that?" asked Amethyst.

"Definitely," said Abby. "Probably."

"Those words still don't mean the same thing," Piper said miserably.

To Robby's surprise, the voices did not return as the group made its way again through the snow, not even when they passed Lucinda's farmhouse, which now stood empty and abandoned like so many others in Willow Cove. Even so, the memory of Becca's voice in his head left him feeling on edge.

*You're coming closer, Robby.*

By the time they reached the abandoned state hospital atop Whispering Hill, the sky was a white sheet, and a low rumble of thunder echoed through the halting snow. Amethyst muttered something about bad omens, then clamped her mouth shut at the gloomy look on Delphi's face. Robby caught Delphi's expression, too, before looking quickly away. After her premonition about them at the Midnight Castle, he still couldn't quite bring himself to make eye contact with her.

They shed snow in the foyer before Abby led them through the winding corridors to the open grove at the center of the complex. Last year, Robby had raced through these same halls to try to stop Miss Winters's spell. Now here they all were again, this time hoping to repeat it.

Olivia wore an expression of stony determination as the group took cover under the branches of an ancient oak weighted with snow. Robby couldn't help his gaze from roaming the shadowy edges of the grove. There were so many secret tunnels that might lead to this spot. Who knew if Becca and the other vampires were in one of them right now, waiting to come out when Olivia's spell darkened the sky? With so many dark corners, they probably could have come for him already. Could they be intentionally holding back?

The thought bothered him enough that he tried to catch Abby's attention, but her gaze was firmly on Olivia, who was handing out wooden stakes. Robby hated the feel of his between his fingers, hated the idea of using it on anyone other than the Shadow Lady. He shook his head to chase the thought away. It wouldn't come to that.

Under the tree, Olivia pulled Miss Winters's wand from her jacket pocket. She didn't make a show of it, didn't say anything inspiring or amusing before she began the ritual. Instead, she simply traced the tip of Miss Winters's wand across her own palm exactly as she'd done for the transmogrification spell. When a bright streak of blood pooled there, she approached Abby and repeated the cutting motion. The girls pressed their hands together, and then Abby stepped aside for Piper. Daisy's fingers trembled, but she held her chin high when it was her turn. After the whole coven had finished the mingling of blood, they formed a circle around the tree trunk. Olivia raised the wand again, her lips moving in silent susurration.

How much of the ritual she remembered from last year and how much was the work of the wand, Robby didn't know. But above them, the air was already turning a hazy shade of scarlet, a shimmering dome of red light. Another thunderclap shook the grove, and when Robby looked again at Olivia, her eyes were an eerie crimson that made him take an involuntary step back. Zeus was staring with concern. The seasons flickered like shaky stop-motion animation, with leaves sprouting and reddening and falling from the great tree in shuddering succession. Everything everywhere glowed with the reddish sheen of blood.

"Olivia, you're doing it!" Abby shouted.

Gauzy shadows and lightning-bright bursts of color fractured within the dome. The hairs on Robby's arms stood on end as the air crackled with chaotic energy. Time was bending around him, blurring at the edges. Inside the grove, he was at the very center of it.

"What now?" shouted Amethyst, her voice distant, diaphanous.

"Now Olivia needs to open the doorway!" Abby said. "Liv?"

"Give me—*unhhhh*—a second." A web of tiny blue veins made crisscross patterns beneath Olivia's fair skin. Snow melted and sizzled around the wand, and as she lowered the tip Robby first thought Olivia had given up. Then a crimson seam zippered in the air before her, widening bit by bit as she completed the spell. "Who wants to go first?" she croaked.

Zeus's mouth fell open. "You—you actually made a portal to the seventeenth century?"

"The portal was already there. I just—*unhhhh*—found the same weak spot as the Shadow Lady. Her spellwork was all over it."

"But it's hurting you!"

"Nothing I can't handle," she told him.

"I have so many great memories of almost dying here," Amethyst said as she approached the seam. "What's one more for old time's sake?"

One by one the girls passed through the portal after her. When it was Briony's turn, she crossed the threshold with a grim smile. Zeus squeezed Olivia's shoulder and whispered something only she could hear. Her lips crinkled and he let go and joined the coven on the other side.

"We'll be back as soon as we can," Abby told Olivia when only she and Robby remained.

Olivia grimaced, then tried to hide it behind a smile. "I'm not getting left behind again. You losers need me."

Robby's gaze darted to the darkened corners of the grove. To the tunnels where their vampire classmates might already be hiding. "We'd be leaving the portal wide open," he told her.

Olivia took each of them by the hand and marched toward the wavering seam. "Then I guess we'd better be really quick about it this time."

# 38

## All the Devils

Something exploded behind Abby's eyes as she passed through the portal, a single pop of color, and she let go of her friends' hands all at once. Robby crumpled to the ground. Beside him, Olivia wheezed and collapsed. Abby didn't feel herself fall, but a heartbeat later she was on the ground too. Rolling onto her back, she wiped sweat from her forehead and opened her eyes. The back of her hand came away muddy and red.

They were on some kind of rutted mountain road. The sky was a deep dark crimson, and all around her, the air hissed like boiling water, hot and thick. A giant bloody eye peered out between low clouds—the moon, it was only the moon—soaking everything with its scarlet light. "The Night of Blood and Shadows," Abby breathed.

Amethyst helped her to her feet while Briony gave Robby a hand and Olivia leaned unsteadily into Zeus. The twins clutched their stakes to their chests like life vests. Scattered tufts of grass grew to one side of the road, weedy and neglected. On the other, a sheer cliff dropped sharply into the reddish mist. Several open-topped carriages lay abandoned near the edge, their tall wheels sunk deep in the muck, their high backs jutting up like teeth. A few others had been flipped over as if by a careless giant.

There were hints of a distant village in the valley below, but the only other sign of life nearby was Piper, just a dark shape in the mist poking and prodding at one of the overturned carriages. Abby shuddered to think how it had ended up that way. She let her gaze drift up the curve of the road, where it disappeared for long stretches behind craggy limestone cliffs only to reappear higher up among the snow-capped peaks of the Carpathian Mountains. The crenellated walls of an ancient castle met it in the distance. Even squinting through her fogged glasses, Abby recognized it from memory. "That's—that's the Midnight Castle."

"This does not look like midnight," said Briony, her words raspy and shallow.

Robby's breathing was shallow too, but his voice was laced with something almost like awe. "It's just like Bree said. We're in the Shadow Lady's prison now, the exact moment the Council banished her in 1614."

"'The past is a foreign country; they do things differently there,'" Daisy murmured under her breath. "L.P. Hartley, *The Go-Between*."

"But why is everything so… red?" Piper asked.

Robby gestured at the scarlet sky. "It's called a Super Blood Moon."

"With a name like that, you know it's going to be fun," Amethyst said.

"It happens when the moon is entirely in the Earth's shadow and the sun is closely aligned with them both," Robby explained. "A lunar eclipse and a Super Moon rolled into one."

"Always with the science," said Olivia, shaking her head.

Delphi sank back on her heels. "In astrology, Blood Moons are usually associated with the apocalypse."

"I prefer Robby's explanation," Zeus told her.

Amethyst shot a nervous glance at Abby. "I remember saying the Midnight Castle looked like Dracula's lair back when we first met the Council. Nobody ever listens to me. People need to listen to me."

Daisy let out a slow breath. "In *Dracula*, they had to cut off his head and stuff garlic down his throat to defeat him. Did anyone pack garlic?"

"These stakes will do the trick. No need to complicate…" Briony's eyes widened as they focused on something in the distance, something behind Abby. Her voice trailed off and Abby followed her gaze back toward the shimmering portal home.

"Becca is calling me again," Robby said, though he still hadn't turned to look. "She's coming, she's—"

"She's here," whispered Abby, pointing.

The others spun to find their friend prying through the jagged seam of the portal. The remaining vampires spilled onto the road behind her, T-Rex and Lucinda and their other classmates, all of them with fangs bared in the reddish moonlight. Amethyst grabbed Abby's hand and took off up the slippery path.

"Run!"

Abby's foot caught on a rock and her ankle buckled. Before she knew it, she was down on the ground again, and she'd pulled Amethyst down with her. Her ankle screamed in protest when she scrabbled back to her feet. She knew immediately it was bad. Twisted, maybe broken. "My ankle," she gasped, "it hurts so much, I can't—"

"You have to!" yelled Amethyst, yanking her up.

Zeus and Olivia had already surged ahead, but they came back to help her up the steep slope. Robby, Amethyst, and the twins kicked up mud as they scrambled a few paces farther ahead. Where they planned to go was anyone's guess. They'd never be able to outrun the vampires. Abby tried again to put weight on her ankle. Her leg buckled with the sudden, shocking agony of it. "I'm sorry, I just can't—"

"Quick, this way!" yelled Piper.

Before Abby could see where they were going, Zeus had half-dragged, half-carried her under one of the overturned carriages. A door slammed shut behind her and the crimson sky went suddenly black. Then Olivia's wand flashed to life and spilled blue light across their panicked faces. Robby, Olivia, and Zeus were crowded close together across from her. Abby heard another door slam further up the slope and hoped it meant the rest of her friends had taken cover, too.

They only had a second to catch their breath before the first of the vampires thumped onto the carriage. Everything rocked as T-Rex's face appeared in a crack in the wood, then he was back to pushing and clawing at the carriage. The door wobbled and creaked as someone else—Joey Swett, Abby guessed—pried at it with long sharp fingers.

"This isn't much better!" cried Amethyst from under the other carriage.

Daisy's voice rose in panic. "'My kingdom for a horse!'"

"A horse." Olivia's blue-green eyes gleamed teal in the wandlight. "Daze, you're brilliant!" she shouted.

"I am?"

Olivia made a quick pattern with Miss Winters's wand in the small, enclosed space. Smoke seemed to rise from her fingertips, then all at once the upturned carriage lurched forward. Abby lurched with it. Piper screamed loudly from beneath the other carriage, and Abby grimaced just to look at Olivia's face—the effort, the determination.

"Tell them—*unhhhh*—tell them to—" Olivia began.

"Hold on tight," Abby finished for her, suddenly understanding. She wrapped her arms around the underside of the seat, squeezing so hard it even took her mind off her ankle. The carriage rocked again, its thick wooden paneling creaking against the muddy road. This time Abby yelled at the top of her lungs, "Everyone, hold on!"

"What's happening?"

"Who's doing that?"

"ARE YOU OUT OF YOUR MIND?!" called the muffled voices of her friends.

The carriage was moving again, shuddering harder, faster. It twisted at a half angle, then flipped all the way over, suddenly right-side up. For an infinite heartbeat, Abby floated above it before slamming hard against the seat again. Zeus and Robby crashed into her. Olivia collapsed, too, wheezing but grinning.

"Animation… spell…" she panted. "Even better than… real horsepower."

Abby could only stare. "You did it. Liv, you actually—"

*THUMP.*

The vampires! Now T-Rex and Joey were under the carriage as it barreled up the mountain road, apparently unshaken by the sudden reversal. Inch by inch they climbed the side of the carriage by sinking their fingers into the splintering wood. The other carriage raced alongside them up the mountain, and two more vampires were emerging like rats from beneath it, too. Lucinda and Margery.

"They're still after us!" Piper yelled.

The door to Abby's left flew off its hinges, and T-Rex appeared like a nightmare where it had been. Abby was barely able to shove Olivia to safety as the vampire lunged. His fangs missed her by a breath as she ducked low, then kicked him with her good leg. T-Rex flew onto the steep slope and vanished when the carriages disappeared around a bend.

Abby collapsed back onto the seat, her ankle throbbing, and scanned the opposite carriage for her friends. They'd managed to shake Margery free, but Lucinda was still dragging behind by one hand. Worse, T-Rex and Margery were both charging back up the slope after them, gaining with every heartbeat. Becca loped between them, her eyes burning a hateful scarlet.

"'Hell is empty, and all the devils are here,'" Daisy moaned.

"Do you hear the music?" Robby's face was close to Abby's, but his voice sounded distant. "Becca is leading them all to me."

Abby risked another look behind the carriage. Becca was like a phantom in the mist. Her clothes were ragged, her hair slick and wet. There was nothing of her friend's former self left in that face. "There's no music," Abby told Robby as the approaching castle darkened her vision, "and they're coming for all of us, not just you."

"No, I believe he's right," Briony said quietly.

The carriage jerked. Abby strained to keep upright. "You can't possibly know that!"

"I'm a vampire slayer," Briony called back. "I'm the only one who *can* know it."

"I will complete their circle of blood," Robby said, trancelike.

Briony shot Abby a look. "Vampires hunt as a pack. Becca wants Robby, and they will hunt with her until she is sated."

"Every time someone's bitten," said Olivia, "they all gather for the second bite."

"They're programmed for it," agreed Briony.

*CRACK.*

While they'd been watching the trailing vampires, Joey Swett had crawled from the undercarriage. He tore at the remaining door until its hinges shrieked from resistance.

"We are in big trouble!" yelled Zeus.

Robby locked eyes with Abby. "You need to jump."

"I'm not leaving you."

"I'll lead them away. You go find the Shadow Lady."

Abby let out a ragged breath. "Not a chance, Robby."

*CRUNCH.*

Joey's fingers were all the way around the door now. Olivia swatted at him, but her blows were weak and ineffectual. The door splintered and she stumbled back into Abby, who only just caught her in time.

"It's the only way!" Robby shouted, at least sounding more like himself now, more clearheaded than a moment ago. Their other undead classmates were still gaining. Another heartbeat or two and they'd be hurling themselves at the carriage again. "Abby, it was always going to be the six of you against the Shadow Lady. She's said it from the beginning, she wants revenge for—for who-knows-what. It was never about the rest of us."

*It was never about us.*

Something about those words tugged at Abby's thoughts. It was the same thing Zeus had said to her, too—a different conversation, a different context entirely… but her mind had snagged on them just the same. Why? She didn't know. She couldn't, not now. There was no time to dwell on it. "You're sure they won't follow us?" she called to Briony.

"Not so long as Robby remains here."

"We have to do something soon!" yelled Piper from the other carriage.

Zeus sent Joey flying with a thump, but the vampire only skidded once before he was back on his feet and racing after them again. Abby blew out a halting breath and met the gazes of her friends across both carriages. The girls nodded, scared but willing. "Buy as much time as you can," she told Robby. "Every second counts. We'll get to the Shadow Lady and we'll—"

"You'll fix it. I know you will," he cut in.

"Liv?" Abby asked.

"The animation spell will keep running," Olivia confirmed between exhausted breaths. "For a while, at least."

Abby pulled Robby close. Her ribs screamed from the pressure of her body against his, but she wasn't about to let go until she was sure he understood everything she needed him to know, even if she didn't have time to say it. "You're my best friend, Robby. My best friend in the whole world. Promise me you won't do anything stupid."

"I'll buy you as much time as I can."

"You be safe!" she said, holding back tears.

The carriage rounded another bend and she hoisted herself to the gaping door. The other girls moved into position too. Clutching their stakes, they leapt as one to the muddy road below.

# 39

## Blood and Shadows

Robby's whole world was a wobbly red blur. The vampires ignored the girls when they hit the ground, and now the two carriages thundered up the mountain with only Robby and Zeus between them. The wheels groaned over rocks and roots. Axles clanked. Wood creaked. The hood of Zeus's sweatshirt whipped like a banner of war behind him.

The hazy glow of Olivia's wandlight vanished around a bend. The carriages swayed closer together and then apart, again and again. The vampires ran in a pack after them, drawing closer with every breath. Brambles scraped at them and mud squelched beneath their feet, but nothing seemed to slow them down.

"You don't need to stay with me!" Robby yelled to Zeus over the rushing wind.

"I think I do! You're outnumbered and—look out!"

A flash of movement, and then Zeus was knocked onto the other carriage. Something threw itself on top of Robby, something wiry but strong. His face was pressed to the floorboards, but in a blur of movement he saw Margery's lips curled back in a snarl.

She clutched at his collar. The axles ground beneath him, clanking and rattling.

*Surrender to her, Robby!*

Margery hadn't spoken aloud, but he still heard her voice inside his head.

*Be one with her!*

"Get! Off!"

Robby pushed up on all fours just as Zeus leapt back and wrenched Margery away. Spinning free, Robby found his footing in time to see the carriages careening toward a tunnel carved into the mountainside. The trees on either side were twisted red shadows, and then the moonlight was swallowed by darkness. The carriage rattled so loudly Robby could almost imagine phantom horses huffing with every step. When they raced back into the light, Margery was gone and Zeus was dragging behind the carriage, clutching a splintered piece of it with both hands. Robby reached for him, then pulled back as Joey Swett climbed over his friend and up the back of the carriage.

"Jump!" yelled Zeus.

The two carriages pulled close, and Robby leapt to the other one, swaying to keep his balance when they separated once more. Joey coiled to leap after him, but somehow Zeus pulled himself back into the carriage and leapt over Joey faster than Robby could blink. With a swift kick, he sent Joey back to the road like a tumbling rock. Still in pursuit, Becca and Lucinda dodged and continued after them.

"Go, Zeus! I can take care of myself!"

"It doesn't seem that way!"

The coach swayed. Robby slipped, steadied himself. "I have a plan!"

"What plan?"

Robby's neck throbbed. He brought a hand to it and said, "Buying as much time as I can for Abby!"

"That's not a plan!"

"Just go! Help the others! And tell Abby I'm—"

*CRACK.*

The carriage lilted to one side. An axle had broken, and the coach clanked louder as it slowed and wobbled on two wheels. Robby fell forward and clung hard to the outer railing. His body felt stretched to the breaking point, but somehow Olivia's animation spell kept the carriage speeding up the mountain like a roller coaster. His vision blurred and he could only make out dark shapes as Lucinda and Becca caught up with the carriage at last. His strength was no match for theirs, and they yanked him up and pinned him between them.

*At last we will be together!*

Inches from his face, Becca's familiar features were twisted with hunger. She peeled away his collar, then shrieked at the sight of her own Star of David pendant jangling around his neck. Taking advantage of the distraction, Robby had just enough strength to shove Lucinda out of the carriage. The road curved like a horseshoe and she rolled to a stop in the distance, her scarlet eyes raging through the mist. The carriage dipped again, and the silver pendant clattered to the floor. Zeus pulled Robby into the other coach just as Becca lunged.

Skeletal branches grasped like clawed fingers. Becca panted on the opposite carriage, the distance between them stretching too far to jump, but not for long. Zeus pulled his wooden stake from his belt and stared at Becca like he might be sick.

"Put it down!" Robby shouted.

"I'm not going to let her change you!"

"And I'm not going to let you stake her," Robby yelled back over the rumble of wheels. "No matter what happens!"

"You know it's the only way."

The two coaches pulled closer. Becca crouched, the moment of truth almost upon them. Robby closed his eyes. "I'm sorry, Zeus."

"For what?"

Robby shoved Zeus as hard as he could. The surprise did the rest. His friend flew behind the coach and was gone a heartbeat later. Then the coaches pulled together again, and Becca landed beside Robby. *Every second counts*, he reminded himself.

Even if it seemed like his time was almost up.

# 40

## Certain Doom

"You don't have to carry me," Abby said.

They'd found a footpath up the mountain, narrower and more direct than the muddy road, but far too steep for Abby to manage without help. Her ankle still screamed whenever she put the slightest pressure on it. After a few minutes of jostling on Briony's back, though, Abby's cheeks were flushed with embarrassment and the only sound she could hear was the vampire slayer's labored breathing. Abby could also feel the altitude, and she wasn't doing any of the work.

"You're hurt," Briony said, swaying a little between steps.

"I'm too heavy."

The clouds parted overhead, and a shaft of red moonlight revealed patches of snow on the ground. In the valley far below, dark farmland and an unmoving river were postage-stamp small, tiny reminders of a time and place long gone in the world. Abby imagined the two coaches still racing up the carriage road, Robby and Zeus doing their best to buy time for the coven to end this once and for all. Ahead, Piper and Amethyst supported Olivia, whose wand glow lit the way. The twins huddled to either side, their wooden stakes clutched in their hands.

"You forget," Briony said between rasps, "I have superhuman strength."

"Please put me down. I can walk now."

"You can't."

"I can limp, at least."

Even the thought of putting weight on her ankle made Abby wince, but she hated being carried around like a child. She wished she still had her powers. She wished she could heal her ankle with a thought like she'd once taken for granted. Perhaps sensing this, Briony slowed enough for Abby to slide down to the path. Still offering her arm for support, she kept a watchful eye on Abby as they stumbled up the steep slope together.

The way the girl looked, so thin and young, Abby could almost believe Briony was still the teenager she seemed to be on the outside. But Briony had the experiences of a lifetime behind her, a hardness Abby had never really understood until now. Thinking of everything the Council had taken, it was easier to see where that kind of steeliness might come from. More than anything, Abby wished she could make them pay for what they'd done.

Maybe that was why she now noticed an unexpected softening of Briony's features. She did look young, but she'd looked that way the entire time Abby had known her. No, something else had changed, and it took Abby another moment to think what it was. Briony hadn't slain a single vampire on the chase up the mountain. She hadn't even tried to.

"You're different than you were before I left," Abby said, turning her gaze back to Briony. Her ankle still pulsed with pain, but the girl's support made it bearable as long as she watched her step. "More restrained, I mean."

"Perhaps the apocalypse changes people."

"I think you're starting to realize the vampires are victims, too," Abby suggested.

"I would have gone to any length to spare my sister. Maybe I owe it to her to spare your classmates, if I can." As Briony considered her words, her expression hardened. "Olivia told me what happened with Miss Winters last year. How it was your empathy toward her that saved your coven, not the strength of your powers."

"Good thing, since we're pretty short on powers now," Abby said lightly.

Briony's expression remained hard. "That won't work with the Shadow Lady," she warned. "There's only one way to end this."

Abby's gaze flicked to the long wooden stake in her free hand. She nodded. She *did* understand. "I'm fresh out of empathy for ancient vampire serial killers."

"Then we are agreed," she said, letting Abby lean into her as they completed the final switchback. A drawbridge slick with dew stretched across the gulch just ahead, and on the other side the twisted battlements of the castle rose like petrified giants through the mist. The heavy portcullis was locked in place, but eerie lights gleamed from the other side of the grate like a beacon drawing them nearer.

"Here we are," said Daisy as Abby and Briony caught up, "like moths to a flame."

"More like flies to a bug zapper," said Amethyst.

"Do we just… knock?" asked Piper.

"Yes, by all means, let's tell the evil vampire queen we're here," Amethyst replied.

Abby pursed her lips. "I think she probably already knows."

Crossing the drawbridge, Briony put her shoulder into the portcullis, but it was too heavy even for her.

"My turn," said Olivia, raising Miss Winters's wand. With her brow stitched in concentration, she whispered a spell. Her hand shook with each movement, but the portcullis groaned and lifted, slow and wobbly. "I think that's… that's all I've… got."

The wand dropped from Olivia's hand and Abby, quick-reflexed, snatched it before it fell to the depths below. Something prickled her fingertips as she took it, some kind of shock or cut, but when she checked her hands there was nothing. She pressed the wand back between Olivia's fingers, an easy smile on her lips, but Liv could only shake her head.

"Too heavy," she said, her voice thin and high. "I can't… can't anymore."

"I'll carry it for you," Abby told her. "You rest for now."

The others were already pushing through the gate, so Abby wrapped an arm through Olivia's—Briony took the other—and together the trio limped into the courtyard beyond the outer walls.

Amethyst stood with her hands on her hips. "The Shadow Lady could be anywhere."

"She waits like a spider in her lair," said Delphi, trancelike. Her gaze swept toward the central tower, the one called the High Tower back at the Midnight Castle. "Gossamer tendrils in the air. Blood like fire to each of the heirs—"

"Delphi, stop it, you lost your powers just like the rest of us," snapped Amethyst. "You're not fooling anyone."

Delphi blinked. "I—I know that," she replied distractedly. "But don't you feel… something?"

"Impending doom? Certain death? I can't *not* feel it."

Abby shook her head. "No, I think Delphi's right. The High Tower is where the Council would have imprisoned the Shadow Lady."

"How can you be sure?" asked Piper.

"It's where they imprisoned *us*." With that, she started toward the tower, limping but under her own power. This close to the finish line, her ankle wasn't hurting as much. It was strange, actually—the ankle felt better, *itchy*, almost like it was already healing. Another win for adrenaline.

There was no witch's seal barring the entrance, which was just as well because Olivia didn't look as if she had the strength for even that. Instead Briony was able to force the way open with a heavy shove. On the other side, flickering torches climbed up and down the circular stairs just as Abby remembered from the Midnight Castle.

"Which way?" asked Olivia, hunched over, breathing hard.

Abby studied the steps. The dust of ages covered them, but a faint impression of footprints led toward the subterranean dungeon.

"She's down there," agreed Delphi, following Abby's gaze. "I can feel it."

Abby gripped her stake in one hand. In the other, she squeezed Miss Winters's wand tight. "Then let's go find her."

The coach jerked side to side, slowing as Olivia's animation spell neared its end. Robby squeezed the stake between his fingers. Becca balanced across from him, teeth bared. They were alone in the reddish mist. The length of the stake was all that separated them.

*I'll buy you as much time as I can*, he'd promised Abby.

*Every second counts*, she'd said to him.

The cliff dropped steeply to one side of the road; trees crowded close by on the other. The stake brushed Becca's chest as the cart jerked and swayed, and Robby pulled it back, hand shaking. His mind raced. Becca's gaze never left him, but there was only malice in her expression now—no familiar smile, no kind eyes. She was thin as a rail, and all that remained was her hunger.

"Don't come any closer!" Robby yelled. "Not another inch."

*You cannot fight this,* Becca replied, a whisper in his mind.

The carriage was buckling on every root and rock now, swaying in the death throes of Olivia's spell. When it jerked sharply to the forested side of the road, Robby saw his chance and grabbed at a low branch. Something exploded in his shoulder, but he held on long enough to clear the carriage. He dropped to the ground, panting.

The carriage careened onward.

Gripping his shoulder, he sprinted into the woods as far from Becca as he could. His legs trembled and soon he was stumbling on his hands and knees, scraping and clawing along the rough ground—too slow, too late to get away. Then Becca was beside him, flipping him onto his back, leering like a wild animal. Miraculously, he still had the stake pressed between them. One push was all it would take to stop her. One bite was all it would take for her to change him. The night was silent and still between them.

"We just need more time," he rasped. "Abby can fix this."

Their faces were inches apart.

Her expression flickered.

Her eyes flashed.

She didn't bite, not yet.

"I know you're still in there," he pleaded. "You need to hold on a little longer."

The tip of the stake shifted against her.

She stared at him with those awful red eyes.

"You're the best person I know," he told her. "You can still fight this."

A noise rose in her throat, a hoarse whisper, low and weak. "I was… so… alone…" she said. Their bodies shifted. She rolled onto the ground beside him, her chest rising and falling, her face smooth again. "Before I met you… so alone."

He said her name again, a question between them. *Is it really you?*

Her eyes were clearer now. "You… made me… happy."

"Becca!" He pressed into her. "You're back?"

Already her crimson eyes were darkening again. Already the angles of her face were sharpening. Her lips parted and the tips of her fangs glistened in the bloody moonlight. "I think… one last moment… of myself," she said. "Thank you for that."

"Becca, no! Just hold on—"

"Can't… much longer…" She clutched at his hand, wrenching the wooden stake toward her. For just a moment the look on her face was hers again, entirely hers, as soft and kind as it had ever been. She leaned into the pointed tip of the stake. "It's okay now, Robby. I know what you need to do."

"No!" he cried. "The coven can save you. They just need more time."

"There is no more time." Her eyes were growing hungry again, her voice desperate and greedy. "It's now or never."

"Then I choose never."

He hurled the stake away even as Becca's mouth closed around his neck. Her fangs were like hot irons and suddenly a whole universe of stars seared across his vision. She pressed her lips to his throat and drank. His body went limp. His strength failed him. There were colors all around, but all he could feel was her bite, painful as a knife, soft as a kiss. When she'd had her fill, Becca lifted him into her arms like a child. Everything Robby O'Reilly had ever been was gone, and a new thing—a dangerous, *hungry* thing—took his place.

# 41

## The Spider and the Fly

"It's really bloody warm in here," said Daisy, crowding in close behind Abby as they inched carefully downward. The others followed a few paces back on the stairs, silent as the dead.

It *was* warm, Abby thought, warmer than it should have been so far below the surface, even with all the torches. Her glasses were clouded and her hair clung to her forehead like damp curtains. At least the pain in her ankle had faded to an irritating itch.

"Everyone, watch your step," she whispered, touching a hand to the wall for balance. Delicate cobwebs tickled her fingers, and she pulled back, surprised. The soft orange glow of torchlight revealed a torrent of shimmering strands all the way down. "Watch the cobwebs, too."

"I don't see any cobwebs," said Briony, a few steps behind.

"I see them," said Delphi airily. "I see them all."

"Me too," whispered Daisy, so soft that maybe only Abby could hear. "'Will you walk into my parlor?' said a spider to a fly."

"What?" Abby asked.

Daisy's breath steamed in the air between them. "I'm just thinking about a poem I know. The spider is luring the fly into a trap by making it seem warm and inviting."

"A trap," Abby repeated. Was that what was happening here? She eyed the flickering torches, the way down clearly illuminated for them. Had they snuck into the Shadow Lady's lair… or had she lured them here on purpose?

The orange glow grew brighter the farther Abby descended. She felt a shiver down her back, the same feeling she'd had the night she'd encountered Lucinda on the dark lonely road in Willow Cove. The feeling that the world was shifting again under her feet, that everything was about to change in ways she didn't fully understand.

*You are the witches of Willow Cove,* Lucinda had told her.

*You are the ones the Shadow Lady spoke of.*

*She will have her revenge!*

Even all this time later, Abby couldn't make sense of it. Revenge for what? None of them had ever done anything to the Shadow Lady. Did she want revenge on Miss Winters's bloodline for things that had happened a hundred years ago? But if so, why would she have fled back to her prison, willingly this time, hiding away when she already had the upper hand? No, there was something Abby was still missing, something right there in front of her if she could only grasp it.

*It was never about us.*

The idea came to her, sudden and surprising. Those words meant something, she realized. Zeus had said them. Robby had said them, too. But she wasn't thinking about Zeus or Robby anymore—she was thinking about the Shadow Lady, about all the things she'd said, all the years she'd waited to plot her revenge. Her anger was real… but what if her words were a misdirection?

"I—I think I know what she wants," Abby whispered, thrilled and horrified all at once. "The Shadow Lady is the spider. We're walking right into her web."

Daisy ran her hands along the wall, fluttering the cobwebs like strings. "You think she wanted us to come?"

Abby's gaze drifted to Miss Winters's wand. "I think we're doing *exactly* what she wanted."

"Then we should turn around," said Daisy, glancing back the way they'd come.

Abby shook her head and continued down the stairs. No matter what, there was no turning back now. She was forming a new plan—a bad one, if it could even be called that—but they were out of time, and it was the only chance they had left. They would all have to think on their feet if they hoped to come out of this alive.

At the bottom of the stairs, she found a stone sarcophagus waiting for them, and her mouth went dry at the sight of it. They were near the end now, one way or another. Filmy cobwebs spread out from beneath the lid, swaying in some unseen breeze, glimmering in the orange-red torchlight. Abby tucked Miss Winters's wand into her back pocket and approached the dais with only her stake in hand. Her friends gathered behind her.

"'Herein all breathless lies the mightiest of thy greatest enemies,'" breathed Daisy.

"We're back to Shakespeare now?" muttered Amethyst.

Daisy pursed her lips. "I find it soothing."

"I find *this* soothing." Briony clutched her stake. "I've waited my whole life for this moment."

"Wait a little longer." Abby caught the slayer's eye, then raised her gaze to her gathered friends. "Do you all still trust me?"

"None of us would be here if we didn't," said Olivia, pale and exhausted. Piper started for her inhaler, then dropped her hand without taking a drag. She nodded at Abby. The others murmured their agreement.

"Then no matter what happens, follow my lead," Abby told them.

One by one, the coven lifted their stakes while Abby and Briony pried at the lid, grunting under its weight. The air seemed to groan as it scraped free, then all it once the lid crashed to the floor with a thud and dust erupted like a cloud. Abby coughed while her friends leapt forward. Then they gasped. The sarcophagus was empty.

"She's not in there," said Amethyst.

"She's got to be somewhere," said Briony.

Abby trailed the thin cobwebs out of the sarcophagus. At the end of the filmy threads, the Shadow Lady clung to the wall above them, watching and waiting. "Follow the cobwebs," she breathed, her gaze locked in place.

"I told you," said Briony, "I don't see any cobwebs!"

Olivia raised a shaky finger, pointing. Briony followed her gaze. "Her I can see."

Maybe it was a trick of the light, maybe it was Abby's imagination, but the Shadow Lady's arms and legs seemed almost too long, too thin—too much like a spider in her web. Her lips were upturned, her expression greedy and impatient. "So nice of you all to come," she said in a soft hiss-purr that made Abby's skin prickle.

Piper's inhaler clattered to the floor. Amethyst reached for Abby's hand, her whole body crackling with terror. Abby stood her ground. "You want revenge? Come and get it," she called to the Shadow Lady, knowing with certainty now that the vampire queen had never wanted *them* at all. Knowing that their only hope was to keep that knowledge secret as long as possible.

The vampire dropped to the floor like a wraith. Briony darted toward her, but the Shadow Lady swatted her aside without even a glance. It happened so fast that Abby took an involuntary step back, a warning still on her lips. The twins retreated, too, but when they reached the stairs the Shadow Lady shook her head, her expression almost playful. "You brought a friend," she said, sweeping a hand toward Briony's motionless form. "I brought friends, too."

Abby spun around at the sound of footsteps. Lucinda was the first to emerge around the bend of the stairs, then Margery and Joey and T-Rex, all of them darting like shadows through the dim light. Then another pair emerged onto the bottom steps. Becca's fingers were twined with Robby's, and when his gaze fell on Abby, his fangs glistened in the orange torchlight.

Abby's knees buckled.

"No," she whispered.

The group spread like whispers across the chamber. Margery and Joey grabbed the twins. Lucinda ripped Amethyst from Abby's grip, while T-Rex and Becca moved to Olivia and Piper, lightning fast. Then Robby was at Abby's side and she dropped her stake as he pulled her into his embrace. "My circle of blood is complete," said the Shadow Lady. "A whole new coven to command at last."

Abby kicked hard at Robby's shins and slipped free for just a second. Her hand went to Miss Winters's wand, squeezing so tight her fingers tingled. "Let them go!" she commanded, leveling it shakily at the Shadow Lady.

The vampire only laughed. "You bluff, child. I know what the Council does to witches like you. Like *us*."

Abby gripped the knobby wood of Miss Winters's wand hard between her fingers. "You don't have to do this," she rasped. "I know why you want revenge."

"You know nothing."

"I know what the Council did to you. I know it's not us you want, it's them—it's always been them. You want revenge on the Council and they deserve it. Let my friends go and I'll help you get it."

"Abby, no!" shouted Amethyst.

The Shadow Lady's gaze flicked to Lucinda, holding Amethyst firm. "Bleed her."

"No!" Abby repeated. She held Miss Winters's wand between them, the moment of truth almost at hand. "You've orchestrated everything to get *this* wand, isn't that right? The one Miss Winters used to break into the Midnight Castle. A wand remembers every spell, and hers is the only one to ever do it. You saw us with it the night you returned. You knew we had it this whole time."

The Shadow Lady slinked forward, a flutter of threads trailing her like kite strings. "I knew you would never give it to me."

"So, you left us clues," Abby said. "Breadcrumbs. We had no choice but to use the wand if we ever wanted to find you again, isn't that right?"

The Shadow Lady was just footsteps away now. Every muscle in Abby's body tensed. She took a step back, squeezing the wand harder. The wand pulsed in her hand, warm and alive.

Abby's heart froze.

The wand was alive.

It was *alive*. But how…?

Her hand prickled with pins and needles. She stared at the faces of her coven, all of them spattered with mud that gleamed like blood. The shimmering strands still trailed the Shadow Lady like livewires crackling with energy… like cobwebs that only Briony couldn't see.

*Gossamer tendrils in the air.*

*Blood like fire to each of the heirs.*

Delphi's words rattled inside Abby's head. Others joined them. Delphi's premonition at the Midnight Castle. Prena's startled whisper. *You can light a fire with a single spark*, she'd said, because she'd understood what the rest of them had not. They were a blood coven. Olivia still had the spark of magic in her blood. She could rekindle the magic in their veins when she mingled her blood with theirs.

*Our blood is like fire.*

*We are reborn in flame.*

"Where one ember still glows," Abby breathed aloud, "an inferno may follow."

All at once she understood why Amethyst's terror had crackled like waves of heat between them. Why she could feel Miss Winters's wand pulsing with life again. Why her ankle no longer hurt, and why only Briony couldn't see the delicate strands shimmering behind Ereshkigal. Because they weren't cobwebs at all—they were the gauzy threads of the vampire witch's magic. Abby could see them because she was connected to her own magic again.

They all were.

"Your every step has led you here," the Shadow Lady was saying.

If Abby couldn't quite touch her yet, it was only a matter of time. "We both want an end to the Council's tyranny," Abby told her.

"No, Abby, don't do it!" cried Piper.

*Follow my lead,* Abby reminded her with a look. Piper quieted and Abby turned back to the Shadow Lady, her breath hitching in her throat. Her friends were still struggling, but even they felt distant now, muted. She squeezed her hand and felt the wand pulse between her fingers. She had her magic back, but could she count on it? Seeing magic, feeling magic—it wasn't the same as using magic.

"Reverse what you've done in Willow Cove," Abby suggested. "Make everyone whole again. I know you can."

"Why would I do that?" the Shadow Lady asked with cruel curiosity.

Something caught in the corner of Abby's vision just then. A shifting of shadows, a subtle movement in the darkness. Zeus? He was creeping down the stairs, his back pressed to the wall. A long wooden stake hung at his side.

"Because if you do," Abby said, sidestepping to shift the Shadow Lady's focus, "you won't have to take this wand from me. I'll give it to you willingly. I'll help you make the Council pay for what they did to both of us."

Behind the vampire queen, Briony was stirring again in the shadow of the sarcophagus. Abby's pulse quickened. She didn't dare whisper to her. She could only hope that when the moment came, the slayer would be ready. With the tip of her sneaker, Abby nudged the stake she'd dropped. The Shadow Lady's gaze trailed after it, then back to Abby.

*That's right, eyes on me.*

Abby kicked the stake hard to Briony. Her gaze met Zeus's and he lunged at the Shadow Lady from the other side, his own stake raised. The vampire leapt back a step and sent spellwork shooting toward them, Briony on one side, Zeus on the other— which left Abby a clear path straight ahead. Squeezing her hands into fists, she felt the power flowing again through her fingers. It was weak, barely there at all, but it *was* there.

"You want this wand?" she cried.

The Shadow Lady's head swiveled back toward Abby, her gaze greedy and triumphant. Abby opened her hand, held it out.

"You can have it!"

The wand shot from her fingertips like an arrow at the vampire's heart. When it pierced her chest, the whole world seemed to rock. The Shadow Lady's eyes went wide and her jaw opened in a silent scream. Her entire being seemed to fold inward like a shrinking shadow, the shimmering threads all around her blistering and bursting. One moment she was there, the next… *gone.*

Abby's weight gave out and she collapsed to the floor. Zeus reached her first, then Briony. A moment later Robby was there, too, and it was actually him now, not the red-eyed thing he'd become. His face was pale and confused, like he'd woken from a nightmare. Becca was also waking, her gaze puzzled. Lucinda and Margery and their other classmates were blinking, too, and then everyone, the whole coven, tottered toward the void where the Shadow Lady had been.

Breathing hard, Abby found her way back to Zeus, her muscles trembling to keep her upright. "You—you found us," she said.

"It was easy. I followed all the yelling."

She leaned into him. "You didn't want your friends to have all the fun?"

"Is that what we are now? Friends again?"

Abby squeezed his hand and grinned. "I'll think about it."

# EPILOGUE

"It all started with a spooky local legend," said the television news reporter, "and an unusual idea from the mind of local middle school podcaster Sarika Swann, who convinced her friends, classmates, and even some respected adults to pretend vampires were slowly taking over the small New England town of Willow Cove."

Crowded around his laptop with Zeus, Olivia, Sarika, Piper, and the twins, Robby strained to hear the report above their disbelieving huffs. The reporter's voice came out tinny and distant through the computer speakers, but with a made-for-television smile he explained that the disappearing kids, the shuttered businesses and homes, and even the rumors of vampires prowling the empty streets by moonlight were all part of a viral stunt coordinated by Sarika and the local tourism department. The people who'd fled Willow Cove were slowly returning. Those who'd never left seemed to be in no hurry to admit they believed they'd become vampires themselves.

"Everyone shush, here's my dad!" said Zeus, poking his finger at the screen.

"Willow Cove is just as spooky as Salem," Chief Madison was saying to another reporter on the front lawn of the police department. "That's the main thing we wanted everyone to know. The history of vampires in Willow Cove dates back more than a hundred years to the Great New England Vampire Panic of the nineteenth century."

Piper looked up from the corner of Robby's bed, where she was sharing a bag of cheese curls with Flapper and Einstein. "Do you think anyone will actually believe this?"

"Sarika is really selling it," said Olivia, elbowing her friend. "You're up to, what, a hundred thousand subscribers now?"

Sarika grinned. "Almost two hundred thousand. I'm famous!"

"And we even let you remember what happened this time," said Olivia.

"I know, thank you—wait, what do you mean *this* time?"

"'All's well that ends well,'" said Daisy brightly.

But was it? Robby couldn't help wondering. Tina was still trapped at the Midnight Castle. Abby and Amethyst were still moving. And Becca was… well, he didn't know *what* Becca was doing other than avoiding him. His hand went to the side of his neck. The pinprick scars still ached. He thought he'd made the right choice, really the only choice he could have lived with, but the longer Becca went without talking to him, the more he wondered if she felt the same way. All he could learn from texting with her was that she was living out of a hotel with her mother until her father arrived to take custody.

Gloomily, he snuck a gaze toward Abby's empty house. Poppy Delacroix had sheltered both Mrs. Shepherd and his own father during the vampire takeover, but she'd also told them all about Abby's powers and her coven—which only seemed to cement Mrs. Shepherd's desire to move. The shades were drawn and the SOLD sign still hung slightly askew, half in and half out of a snow drift. The new owners didn't seem to be in any hurry to move in, but that didn't change the fact that Abby and Amethyst weren't coming back.

A knock at the door drew Robby's attention away from the window. Delphi, who'd been gazing at the coiling plasma ball on his desk as if it were a crystal ball, was on her feet before him. "Finally!" she said, opening the door.

Mr. O'Reilly stood in the frame with his knuckles raised in a half-knock. Bundled against the cold, Becca appeared beside him. Her nose and cheeks were promisingly pink. She gave a shy little wave to the group. Robby's heart ached at the sight of her.

"My dad's parked in the driveway. We leave for the airport in five minutes, but I wanted to… I mean, I wondered if we could…" She gave Robby a closed little smile. "Talk, maybe?"

"I could go for a hot cocoa," said Olivia, springing up and dragging Zeus halfway to the door with her. "Anyone else want to walk to Hex-Mex?" One by one Piper, Sarika, and Daisy stood, stretched, and said goodbye. All except Delphi, who rolled back onto Robby's bed and propped herself up with one elbow.

"I'll stay for a few more minutes," she said cheerily.

"Um, sure," said Robby, only half listening.

Mr. O'Reilly closed the door. Robby opened his mouth to say something, but Becca raised a finger to his lips and shushed him. "Let me go first. Please." Her fingertips traced the contours of his face until they reached the small, raised scars on his neck. Robby flinched despite himself, and she pulled back. "Sorry."

"Don't be sorry."

"But I am, Robby. I really am."

"It wasn't *you*, Becca."

"I remember it, though. I remember every single minute of it. I don't know if I'll ever forget the things I did… what I did to *you*… and now I have to leave anyway. So, maybe it's better to end it this way. A clean break—"

"I don't want to break up."

"Even if it hadn't happened," she said, waving her hands vaguely, "the distance—"

"I don't care about the distance."

"Be realistic." She let out a long, tortured breath. "We'll still be friends. Great friends, even." Outside, a car horn beeped. Becca pursed her lips, then leaned into him and kissed him on the forehead. "I'll text you when I get settled at Dad's house, okay?"

She was already at the door when Delphi spoke up. "You didn't say it."

"Didn't say what?" Becca asked.

"You said maybe it's better this way. You said the distance will be hard. But you didn't say you want to break up with him."

One hand on the door, Becca said, "Of course I don't want to."

"Then it's settled."

Becca stared at Delphi for a long moment. "We'll be thousands of miles apart."

"He'll visit you. You'll visit him. You don't have to just give up."

Robby gaped at her. "But you said—your premonition—"

Delphi raised an eyebrow. "Mmm?"

"All that stuff about you and me at the winter dance?"

"Oh, we *are* going to the dance together," she said. "Becca's flight to Willow Cove is going to be cancelled due to weather. We'll go as friends—with your blessing, obviously," she added, raising her gaze to Becca.

Becca blinked and said nothing.

Robby blew out a deep breath. "You let me think—"

"I let you think about how much you care for Becca and how far you'd go to save her. You should be thanking me. As for the rest of it, some of what I saw only makes sense to me now. You two should stay together. I know you can make it work because I've already seen you do it"—she tapped her forehead—"in here."

Robby turned back to Becca hopefully. "We can talk every day."

Her cheeks warmed and for an instant her eyes gleamed. But then she shook her head again. "No, Robby."

"Becca!" he pleaded.

Her lips curled into a tentative smile. "It would have to be *twice* a day."

"Three times," he said, barely daring to hope.

The car horn beeped again, louder and longer. She ignored it. "You'll visit?"

"Every chance I get."

"I'll hold you to that."

"Took you both long enough!" said Delphi, clapping as she sat up. "But you got there in the end. Good work!"

"What about all the rest of it?" Robby asked after Becca dashed downstairs. "The stuff about us in high school…?"

Delphi shrugged. "It's a bit fuzzier the further out we go. I guess we'll just have to find out together when the time comes. Well, except for one thing I already know for sure."

"What's that?"

"You and me," she said with a grin, "really are super cute together."

The minivan groaned to a stop somewhere near the end of a bumpy dirt road. In the back seat, Abby tugged at the makeshift blindfold pressing into her temples. Her mother tsked and swatted at her from the driver's seat. "Don't look just yet, sweetheart."

"Mom, we've only been driving five minutes."

"I want this to be a surprise. No magical peeking, either." She killed the engine and whispered something inaudible to the two other backseat passengers. A door swung open, and Abby felt Amethyst and Briony slipping out onto the snowy road. Then Abby's door was pulled open from the outside and a familiar jangling of metal bracelets greeted her as Poppy Delacroix helped her out of the car as well.

"What's going on?" Abby asked.

Amethyst slipped a warm hand into Abby's and pulled her a few steps from the car. "Can I show her now?"

"I suppose that's only fair," said Mrs. Shepherd, "considering it all belongs to you."

Amethyst lifted the blindfold. Abby blinked as a stretch of snow-covered farmland came into focus. A very familiar stretch of farmland. "It belongs to all of us now," said Amethyst, grinning from ear to ear as Abby took it all in.

"Abby, welcome home," said her mother.

Abby was still blinking. "Amethyst, this is your grandfather's farm."

"It's ours now," Amethyst repeated, draping an arm around Abby's shoulder. "I mean obviously we still have to build the new house—"

Poppy waved a roll of architectural drawings in front of Abby's face. "It'll be just marvelous!" she trilled. "An exact reproduction of the original."

"The corner of the foundation will be right there," Amethyst said, pointing to a spot in the middle distance with her free hand. Then she raised her finger fractionally. "Dibs on the bedroom with the roof deck for me and Spooks."

"Who is Spooks?" asked Mrs. Shepherd.

Amethyst ignored her. "We can share the room if you want, though," she said to Abby. "Actually, I kind of hope we will."

Abby's mother tried again. "You're positive this is what you want to use the insurance money on, Amethyst?"

"That's what it's for, Mrs. Shepherd. Besides, we really need the extra room now. You seem to be acquiring a new kid every year."

"I'm more than a hundred years old," said Briony. "I'm hardly a child."

"You are in the eyes of the state," said Mrs. Shepherd.

Amethyst pulled Briony into the hug with Abby, an arm around each of them. "You do seem to be aging now that your slaying days are over. I saw you trying to hide a pimple this morning," said Amethyst, whose simmering crush seemed to have melted into something closer to mere admiration.

Mrs. Shepherd's expression was hopeful as she turned to Abby. "What about you, sweetheart? Are you happy now?"

Abby was so happy she could hardly speak. "We're really staying in Willow Cove?"

Her mom nodded. "I know it's not the same as being neighbors, but we'll only be a twenty-minute walk from Robby's house. And, of course, the rest of your—your coven—they're all here too."

"Two minutes from Robby's by broom," said Amethyst.

"No brooms," said Mrs. Shepherd pointedly. "No magic of any sort outside the bounds of this property. *That's* non-negotiable. Though you both may feel entirely free to use it for house chores once there's a new roof over our heads."

Poppy bobbed her chin. "I've explained to her how the ley lines work. You'll be protected here. The Council thinks you've all lost your magic and it's best you let them continue to think that, don't you agree?"

Abby said nothing for a long moment. It was going to take some getting used to, her mom knowing about her coven, her powers. Longer still to decide what to do about the Council. But somehow, for now, it all felt very right. She was glad her mom knew. Glad to have one fewer secret to keep. Things were changing, but not *too* much, and what was changing seemed okay to her.

The dynamic with her mom was different now, but it was a better one. A more honest one.

Amethyst's body went suddenly tense, and as Abby followed her gaze over the horizon, her own body tensed, too. "Um, Poppy, are you sure the Council doesn't know about this place?" Amethyst asked. Two figures were emerging through the woods, one tall and thin, the other short and squat.

It only took Abby a moment to make sense of the shapes. "Prena."

"And that's Bree with her in the wheelchair," echoed Amethyst.

Mrs. Shepherd's smile showed a few cracks. "Are they friends or…?"

"Or," said Amethyst. "Definitely *or*."

Prena smiled kindly at Briony, Poppy, and Mrs. Shepherd when she reached the car, but soon turned her attention to Abby and Amethyst. "Girls," she said, nodding her head. She looked the pair up and down. "You're both looking… well."

"'You can light a fire with a single spark,'" Abby said. "Did you know all along?"

Prena shook her head. "Only at the very end, and even then, only that it was a possibility. I am pleased with how it worked out for you, though. I wasn't exaggerating when I said you girls have great potential. It seems you've even solved your vampire crisis. How did you do it?"

"No thanks to you," muttered Amethyst.

"That's a matter of debate. Now is not the time for it."

"Actually, we did sort of follow your advice." Abby's expression was still guarded, but she tried to soften it with a gracious shrug. "We were patient. We were clever. And in the end, we waited for the right moment to strike."

Prena's expression relaxed. "I'm glad to hear that. And as long as you're still open to advice now and then…"

"Just tell us why you came," Amethyst cut in, "and then leave."

"I carry a message for you from Tina. Or perhaps I should say Bree does."

The girl in the wheelchair looked up at them from her seat, wide-eyed and wistful. "Never did imagine I'd see the twenty-first century," she said.

Prena placed a hand on Bree's shoulder. "The message, Bree?"

"Right, sorry." Bree unfolded a bundle on her lap and handed a small letter-sized envelope to Abby. "This is for Robby and his father. Don't ask me, I haven't read it, don't know what's in it." She blew out a breath. "As for the message to you, it's simple. Tina's a Fatekeeper now, same as me. She wants you to know she's safe and well. We're a sisterhood, all of us, and we look out for each other. You need not fear for her safety."

"She's not coming back," Abby said, feeling a cold shiver down her back.

Prena's expression grew serious. "Not until things change at the Midnight Castle. The moment is coming soon. I can sense it. I meant what I said before, Abby. I could use your help. You did promise to give it."

"That was before you helped the Council strip us of our powers," Amethyst said. "I'm pretty sure that voids the agreement even if you *suspected* it might all work out in the end."

Prena looked from Amethyst to Abby with a raised eyebrow. "Is that your position as well?"

"We're staying put in Willow Cove," Abby told her. "We're going to keep our town safe. That's my promise, for now at least."

Prena considered her for a moment. Their eyes met. Abby held her gaze until finally Prena's expression softened again. "Then your secret is safe with me. But you must know if the others on the Council learn you have your powers back, they *will* come for you."

Abby let out a slow breath. Her jaw clenched. Her hand closed into a tight fist. The magic was there, coursing through her veins, crackling at the tips of her fingers. Stronger today than it had been yesterday. Stronger every day now.

"Let them come," she said. "We'll be ready."

# ACKNOWLEDGMENTS

I'd like to thank my wife, Penelope, and children, Madeleine and Ethan. We made it through Covid, a move to a new house, layoffs, more layoffs, layoffs *again*, and (most terrifying of all) middle school during the drafting of this novel. I couldn't have done it without you.

Rebecca Moody and Dana Nuenighoff helped shape many of the most important scenes in this story with their insightful suggestions. J.L. Bell, Margo Lemieux, Ben Miller, Ed Loechler, and MaryKay Mahoney also offered heaps of helpful advice along the way.

I'm eternally grateful to the team at Owl Hollow Press, especially Emma Nelson, Hannah Smith, and Olivia Swenson, for believing in this book and waiting patiently while I finished it. I promise the next one will come quicker. Probably.

My agent, Becky LeJeune, has shaped this series from the very start, dating back to her helpful response to my query many years ago. And my fellow authors in the Spooky Middle Grade group have supported me throughout this journey as well. It's an honor to be part of our spooky little crew.

**JOSH ROBERTS** has written for publications as varied as *USA Today*, *The Boston Globe*, and *Business Insider* over a 20-year career as an award-winning editor and travel journalist. These days, he writes the kind of middle-grade and young adult novels he always wanted to read when he was a kid growing up in a spooky Victorian funeral home.

find Josh Roberts online at

#WillowCove
#TheWitchesofWillowCove
#TheCurseofWillowCove

www.ingramcontent.com/pod-product-compliance
Lightning Source LLC
Chambersburg PA
CBHW051438190726
48289CB00001B/240